W9-AYS-084

Critical acclaim for the novels of James P. Hogan

THE PROTEUS OPERATION

"A first-class thriller . . . his best book to date."
—*Chicago Sun-Times*

"An ambitious, expertly handled yarn."—*Kirkus Reviews*

"A very entertaining and engrossing novel."
—*Star Tribune*, Minneapolis

ENDGAME ENIGMA

"Tautly constructed, well-plotted, and well-written."
—United Press International

"A complex tale of suspense . . . holds your interest
all the way."—*The Charlotte Observer*

"Solidly based in current world tensions . . . a
fascinating glimpse into the future."—*Rave Reviews*

THE MULTIPLEX MAN

"Keeps the reader guessing . . . deftly developed."
—*The Washington Post Book World*

"Enough surprises and twists to please even the most
jaded reader."—*Science Fiction Chronicle*

REALTIME INTERRUPT

James P. Hogan

BANTAM BOOKS
NEW YORK   TORONTO   LONDON   AUCKLAND

*This edition contains the complete text
of the original trade edition.*
NOT ONE WORD HAS BEEN OMITTED.

REALTIME INTERRUPT
A Bantam Spectra Book

PUBLISHING HISTORY
Bantam trade edition published March 1995
Bantam paperback edition / January 1996

SPECTRA *and the portrayal of a boxed "s" are trademarks of*
Bantam Books, a division of Bantam Doubleday Dell
Publishing Group, Inc.

All rights reserved.
Copyright © 1995 by James P. Hogan.
Cover art copyright © 1995 by Peter Gudynas.
Book design by Mierre.
Library of Congress Catalog Card Number: 94-22710.
*No part of this book may be reproduced or transmitted in any
form or by any means, electronic or mechanical, including
photocopying, recording, or by any information storage and
retrieval system, without permission in writing from
the publisher.*
For information address: Bantam Books.

*If you purchased this book without a cover you should be aware
that this book is stolen property. It was reported as "unsold and
destroyed" to the publisher and neither the author nor the publisher has received any payment for this "stripped book."*

ISBN 0-553-57445-0

Published simultaneously in the United States and Canada

*Bantam Books are published by Bantam Books, a division of
Bantam Doubleday Dell Publishing Group, Inc. Its trademark,
consisting of the words "Bantam Books" and the portrayal of a
rooster, is Registered in U.S. Patent and Trademark Office and
in other countries. Marca Registrada. Bantam Books, 1540
Broadway, New York, New York 10036.*

PRINTED IN THE UNITED STATES OF AMERICA

OPM   0 9 8 7 6 5 4 3 2 1

To Maurine Dorris

Acknowledgments

The help and advice of the following is greatly appreciated:

Joseph Bates and Mark Kantrowitz, School of Computer Science, Carnegie Mellon University, Pittsburgh
Liam Cullinane, First National Building Society, Ireland
Beverly Freed, for background on real reality
Brenda Laurel, for background on virtual reality
Marvin Minsky, Artificial Intelligence Laboratory, MIT, and Thinking Machines Corporation
John Moody and the staff of Holland's Lounge, Bray, Co., Wicklow, Ireland
Brent Warner, NASA, Goddard Spaceflight Center, Maryland
Patricia Warwick, University of Wisconsin

REALTIME INTERRUPT

Prologue

Faces, places, formless spaces. Blurred thoughts, smeared thoughts. Images dissolving away under swirling water. Words tumbling in dislocated time. Then, clearness emerging suddenly, like a momentary calming of the wind in a storm.

There was a small, plain room with a bed, a closet, and a window with closed slats. He was sitting on the edge of the bed, wearing a heavy plaid robe. Where this was or how he came to be there, he didn't know. It could have been a hospital. He had a strange feeling of unreality about everything, as if the walls around him were all there was: stage props brought together in a void, with nothing behind.

He rose and moved to the window. The motion felt remote and disconnected, as if he were watching it from a vantage point that was distant yet still strangely within. Beyond the glass was a city with tall buildings and a river spanned by steel bridges. It felt familiar, but he was unable to name it. He searched his memories but found only faded and scattered fragments from long ago. Of his recent past—anything that might have some connection with where he was and why—there was nothing.

He turned as he heard the door behind him open. A man entered, dressed in a physician's smock. "Good morning, Joe. How are you feeling today?" the man said.

So his name was Joe? He made no answer.

The physician closed the door behind him and crossed the room. He had a square jaw and brow, smooth, pink features, wavy blond hair, and heavy-rimmed spectacles: a

1

physician caricature, the generic of a type, giving the fleeting feeling of possessing no more substance than the room.

"Do you know who I am?" he asked. Joe shook his head. "I'm Dr. Arnold. We've known each other for quite some time now."

"Oh," Joe said.

Arnold peered at him closely. "Do you know who you are?"

"I'm Joe," Joe told him.

The physician frowned and seemed momentarily perplexed. "Well, of course you'd know that. I just told you," he said.

"It was a joke," Joe explained.

"That was funny?"

Joe shrugged. "Not in a way that you'd split your sides over. But kind of, I guess."

"Why was it funny?"

Joe was beginning to find this a strange conversation. "Well, if you don't know, I don't know how to tell you," he replied.

"Then tell me why *you* think it's funny," Arnold said.

"Look, you don't need to lose any sleep over it. It's not that big a thing. Why are we making such a deal out of this?"

Arnold stared at him intently. "But I *need* to know. It's important that I know everything that goes on inside your head. It's been pretty messed up, I'm afraid. You've been a very sick man, Joe."

Joe didn't feel as if he had been sick. Not just at that moment, anyway. He did feel that Arnold was a strange kind of person to be telling him that he had been. But then the coherence that had momentarily given clarity to his thoughts fell apart again, and what happened next dissolved back into confusion.

"It's great that you're up and about, Joe. We can show you the place, and you can start meeting some of the other patients. That will do you a lot of good."

The nurse's name was Katie. They walked slowly along a wide corridor with windows on one side, looking out at the river and the bridges. Moving felt more natural, but he still had occasional attacks of giddiness—especially when he changed his direction of vision too suddenly. Sometimes everything would go completely blank for a moment. Arnold said it was because different parts of his nervous system were out of synchronization and needed time to accommodate to sudden changes of input.

"What city is this?" Joe asked.

"That's good: you're getting curious about things. This is Pittsburgh," Katie said.

Somehow it did not come as a complete surprise. He had a vague recollection of coming to work here. But the clearer details of his still-blurred memories were from another city of high buildings with a river.

"How long ago did I come to Pittsburgh?" he asked.

"The second-largest city in Pennsylvania, with a population of over two million, once known as the Gateway to the West," Katie recited, ignoring his question. She went on, sounding like a talking commentary at a museum exhibit whose button had been pushed. "In the eighteenth century it was a scene of intense rivalry between the British and the French, which caused five forts to be built here. It was a major producer of armaments for the Union during the Civil War, and subsequently grew to become the center of the steel industry through the 1960s."

Joe shook his head. "No, I was asking about me. How long have I been here? What did I come here for?"

"I think you'd better talk to Dr. Arnold about that," Katie replied.

Joe sighed. In his scattered moments of clearer perception, he was getting used to this kind of thing. Arnold said it was because his mind wandered off into its own internalizations and lost logical continuity. "Are you a history major or something?" he asked as they resumed walking.

"No. I'm a nurse. Why?"

"Do all nurses talk like that?"

"Why shouldn't they? Don't most people take an interest in such things?"

"Hardly."

"What kind of things would you expect me to be interested in?"

It was such a peculiar question that Joe didn't know how to answer. When he looked at her, her eyes, although fixed on him, seemed to have an emptiness that gave him the feeling of talking to a shell.

"What do you think when you look at me like that?" she asked.

"That everyone I meet here is strange."

But it could be because of the way he was seeing things, he told himself. Maybe people never had been the way he thought he remembered.

He remembered being with a group of young people, laughing and teasing each other as they walked along a road by a shore, where waves broke over rocks below. It was an old town somewhere, of imposing, high-fronted houses built in terraces around squares with green lawns. Ships sailed out of a harbor, past a lighthouse at the end of a long stone pier.

"You were involved in some unconventional experiments involving processes deep in the brain, which have affected your mind and altered the way you see the world," Dr. Arnold told him.

"I seem to remember I worked with computers. I came to this country to work with them from somewhere else."

"Ah, excellent! You're getting better every day. Now I want you to meet Simon, who's going to be your regular counselor. Simon, this is the man we want you to help. His name is Joe. Do you remember your full name, Joe?"

"Corrigan. . . . Joe Corrigan. Pleased to meet you, Simon."

One Saturday night there was a dance for the patients to get to know each other and begin rediscovering long-unused social skills. Corrigan felt as if he had been caught up in a charade of walking character clichés.

"How are you finding it, Joe?" Dr. Arnold inquired, rubbing his hands together like an anxious headmaster showing his face at the annual high-school ball.

"Tell me these people aren't real," Corrigan answered.

Arnold seemed unsurprised but interested. "Why? What's wrong with them?"

"I feel as if I'm in an old, corny movie."

"The parts of your memory are starting to come together again. Not as much of what you think you see is really out there. Your mind is filling the gaps by projecting its own, stored stereotypes from long ago. Don't worry. It's a healthy sign."

There came a day when Corrigan grew tired of being restricted. He wanted to get out in the air and work with his hands. In a shed in the rear grounds of the hospital he found some garden tools, and decided on impulse that he would plant a vegetable patch. There was no need to seek approval —one of the advantages of being deemed unstable was that nobody was surprised at anything one did. In any case, asking would simply be an invitation to be told no. A phrase came to mind from somewhere in his past and made him smile: "Contrition is easier than permission."

The world was coming more together now, and although he hadn't said so, inwardly he considered himself to be virtually back to normal. But when he turned over the first fork of soil, there was nothing underneath—just blackness. He stared, confused, then closed his eyes and shook his head. When he opened them again, nothing was amiss: he saw earth, roots, a shard of pottery, and a few rocks.

"You see, you're not as well as you imagine yet," Arnold told him when Corrigan described the experience. "Your perceptions can still be disrupted by sudden changes of mood or intent. That is why it is important for you to get into the habit of thinking smoothly. Avoid discontinuities. . . . But wanting to get out and about again, I can understand. It's perfectly natural."

"Maybe I could visit my old company?" Corrigan suggested. He could remember a little now about the organization that he used to be with, and his work there. It had involved supercomputers and other advanced hardware.

"That project was abandoned a long time ago now, Joe," Arnold replied. "And I'm not sure that digging up those ghosts would really be for the best. But I agree that we should begin broadening your experiences as a start to getting you on the road back to a normal life."

"How long have I been here?" Corrigan asked.

"It's getting close to three years now," Arnold said.

"Don't I have any family? Why does nobody come and visit?"

"They did, in the early days. Don't you remember?"

"No."

"You didn't respond well. It set off a regression that threw us back months."

"I'm better now. Can't we try again?"

"Sure. But it would be best if not for a while just yet. All in good time, Joe. All in good time. . . ."

He remembered courts of cobblestones and lawns, closed in by tall buildings with frontages of old stone. An archway led through to a busy street with green, double-decked buses. There was a pub by a river, filled with talkative youths in heavy-knit sweaters and pretty girls who wore black stockings. They danced and sang to music in the back room.

"You have to get rid of Simon," Corrigan said. "I can't get along with him. It's not working."

"What's the problem?" Arnold asked.

"There isn't any communication. I feel like I'm talking to a sponge."

"Are you sure the problem is with him and not you?"

"I didn't say it was him."

"What's the biggest problem area?"

"He doesn't understand jokes."

"Is that so terrible?"

"It means he isn't human. To be effective, a counselor really ought to come from one's own species."

Arnold considered the statement. "I'm not so sure of your conclusion," he replied finally. "I believe there are traits among certain animals that some researchers have tentatively identified as indicative of humor." To Corrigan's amazement, Arnold showed every appearance of being perfectly serious.

"That was a joke," Corrigan said wearily.

*   *   *

They gave him an apartment of his own—still under supervision, but at least it was a start toward regaining independence.

"I had a wife," he said to Arnold one day.

"Things weren't so good between you, though, were they?" That was true. Corrigan could recall more now of the conflicts of those final months—both professional and domestic.

"What happened to her?" Corrigan asked.

"She got a divorce on the grounds of your incapacitation," Arnold said. "I think she's abroad somewhere now."

"Now that I'm out again, maybe we could track down some of the people I used to work with. There must be some of them still around. Maybe I could even get some kind of a job there again."

Arnold didn't seem overenthusiastic. "Maybe, in time. But we feel that reviving those associations too soon could trigger another relapse. Let's see how well you rehabilitate in the short term first."

"Joe, this is Sarah Bewley. She's going to be your new counselor. We've been talking about you to a company that does a lot of work in your field, and they're willing to give you a try at a job. Isn't that great? It will also be farewell from me pretty soon. I'm moving on."

Sarah elaborated. "It's a Japanese corporation called Himomatsu, who are concentrating on virtual, self-modifying environments. That is the kind of thing that you used to do, isn't it? Naturally, it won't be as senior a position as you had before, but we have to start somewhere. I've arranged an interview for you with their local general manager on Monday—his name is Rawlings. If they do decide to take you on, you'll be going on a familiarization trip to Tokyo."

"You've been busy," Corrigan complimented.

"We just want to see you functioning again, Joe."

"Sarah," Joe said, "is the world going crazy, or am I not as well as I feel?"

"Didn't you like Japan?"

"It was all the bad tour guides you've ever seen, come

to life. They do everything in regiments over there. Some-body's churning them out of a clone factory."

"It's a different culture. You have to make allowances," Sarah said.

"They drill their employees on parade grounds. I thought I was joining a company, not the Marine Corps," Corrigan protested.

Sarah smiled patronizingly. "That's just a new idea that they're trying out. Employee motivation is important. You can't learn if you don't experiment."

"They've got dude-ranch-style fantasy farms, where you can act out daydreams. Later, the scripts get incorporated into VR scenarios. Unreality is getting more real than reality."

"People probably felt the same way about movies once."

"They've got education being dispensed by actors posing as media characters, actresses endorsing scientific theories, and ads in everything you look at—even grade-school political messages on cereal boxes. And it's getting more like that here every day. If this is where it leads, I'm not sure I want the job anymore."

"Give it a try," Sarah urged. "It will get you out again, and among people. Think of it as purely therapeutic."

Graham Rawlings didn't look happy as he perused the annual review from Corrigan's file. "It says that you haven't enrolled in the golfing tuition program," he observed.

"That's right," Corrigan agreed.

"Why not?"

"I don't want to play golf." (Wasn't it obvious?)

"But all our executives play golf," Rawlings said. "It's part of the accepted corporate image. Don't you want to share in the feeling of strength and security that comes from uniformity of outlook, shared ideals, and a common purpose?"

"No."

Rawlings seemed taken aback. "Surely you seek promotion and reward, recognition and success? Everybody needs to proclaim to the world what he is."

"But you're trying to make me exactly what I'm not."

Rawlings looked worried. "Maybe you're more ill than we realize. Possibly you should see a counselor."

"I've already got one."

"The corporation can provide a comprehensive package of counseling, regular physical checks, drugs as required, and remedial therapy."

"No, thanks."

"At the company's expense."

"But I feel just fine."

Rawlings sat back, shaking his head, as if that one remark revealed all. "That proves you're sick," he said gravely.

Sarah was prim about it when Corrigan stopped by her office to announce that he was quitting. "Well, I'm sorry it didn't work out, but I tried my best," she said. "So what *do* you want to do?"

"I'm not sure. Just be myself, I suppose."

"And what, exactly, is that?"

"Ask the people who are always telling me. They seem to know. I'm still trying to find out."

"Have you talked it over with Muriel?"

"She thinks I should do my own thing in my own way—try to find myself again."

"She sounds very supportive," Sarah conceded.

"If that's the right word. Lately she's been dropping hints about as subtle as a tax demand that we ought to get married."

Sarah sat back at her desk and regarded him thoughtfully, as if the world had just shifted on its axis and presented itself in a new perspective. "You know, Joe, that mightn't be such a bad idea," she said at last. "You've been on the program for nine years now. That kind of stabilizing influence could be just what you need. Then we could let the two of you find a place of your own independently. I can't think of a better road back to complete normality than that."

Muriel and Joe married early the following year. However, when they had talked about individualism and being himself, Muriel thought he was describing his determination to pursue a career vigorously within the corporation. When he quit, explaining that what he'd meant was that he was going to chuck all of it, and announced that he'd taken a job as a checkout clerk at a discount store, it put a different complexion on things.

And, predictably, life continued on a downhill course from there. . . .

Chapter One

Few things, Corrigan thought irritably as he lay washed up on the pebbly shore of wakefulness from the warm, care-free ocean of sleep, could be more maddening first thing in the morning than a chatty house-computer—especially one afflicted with the kind of advanced neurosis that he usually associated with swooning aunts or psychiatric rehabilitation counselors.

"It's almost nine o'clock, Joe," it babbled again in the fussing English accent that projected Muriel's conception of professional conscientiousness with a touch of social style. "As a rule, this is your absolute *latest* for getting up on a Saturday."

Corrigan thought that it sounded gay. He pictured it as lean and limp-wristed, with a receding hairline, mincing about the room and throwing its hands up in agitation.

"Oh. . . . Hmm." Corrigan yawned, stretched, and opened his eyes to the homey disarray of the apartment's bedroom. "Is it Saturday?"

"Well, of course it is, Joe. Why would I have said so if it weren't?"

Horace. What kind of a woman gave the computer a name like Horace? Corrigan allowed wakefulness to perco-late through his body gradually. She had gotten the name, and its emulated persona, from Horace Greal, the equally insufferable confidant and financial adviser to the playgirl-adventuress star of the series *Fast-Lane Lady*, which depicted high society, fast sex, and mega-money in a bright-lights, big-city setting. Muriel, apparently like most people these days, was able to relate to such roles totally, elevating experience by dissolving the barriers between fantasy and actuality, and letting "is" merge effortlessly into "could be." Corrigan couldn't. The two categories remained obstinately unfused in his mind. That, he was told, constituted the principal cause of the inner alienation, insecurity, and resentments that the experts assured him he felt. The only thing wrong was, he didn't.

Saturday. That meant that he wasn't due at work until the evening. He rolled over and contemplated the ceiling. As he began thinking what needed doing today, a disharmony of clashing chords tied together by an ungainly, clickety-clack rhythm started up from the apartment's sound system. Muriel's kind of music. He wondered if the choice presaged the role that she had decided to adopt for herself today. Would it be luminescent, green spiked hair, purple jumpsuit, and "Astra, Queen of the Mountains" (who also promoted Vaylon cosmetics and the Salon Faubert fashion styles), or imitation combat fatigues, calf boots, and . . . And then the last shreds of sleep fell away from his mind, and he remembered.

He rolled sideways and looked across the room. Muriel's bed was empty, unslept in. Yes, of course: she was away for the weekend, gone to see her crazy sister in Philadelphia. That brightened up the prospects for the day considerably. A feeling of relief softened the line of his mouth and caused him to exhale the unconsciously accumulated tension in the way he used to as a boy when he braced himself for the day ahead at school, then realized that it was Sunday.

A low whining sound came from the doorway as the twenty-inch display waddled through from the living room on its stumpy, rocker-footed legs. "There are a couple of news items that might interest you," Horace's voice announced. "A California court has ruled a firm guilty of discriminating against employees on the grounds of competence. Europe's prime minister is threatening to resign. Ireland's soccer team has qualified for the World Cup semifinals in St. Petersburg in August."

Corrigan got up, went through to the bathroom, and pointed at the shower. The water turned itself on. "No, save it, Horace. I'm not interested in the mad, mad world. Today is strictly vacation. And while you're at it, will you spare me from that row that you're playing. I thought that a decent house-manager was supposed to know its residents' tastes. That's herself's, and she isn't here this morning, as you well know."

"What would you prefer, then? Something with fiddles and whistles, jigs and reels?"

To give credit where due, the edge of sulky disapproval that Horace managed to inject into its voice was masterful. Although he would never have admitted it—least of all to Horace—Corrigan never ceased to be amazed. Interactive ability of such sophistication might have been conceivable from the batteries of supermachines that Corrigan had once worked with, but to find it in a house manager was something else. The same was true of consumer technology in general. Corrigan could only conclude that, in the twelve years since his incapacitation, the entire state of the art had advanced much faster than he would ever have dared predict. That was the kind of thing that made a man start to feel old.

"No, let's forget the old country for today," he said. "How about something light and classical? Try Vivaldi." He stepped into the spray, and the shower door closed behind him. From outside, Horace's voice came indistinctly through the noise of the water. "Sorry, Horace," Corrigan called as he began soaping himself. "I can't hear you."

It wasn't that life with Muriel had turned into misery or taken on any of the other afflictions that marriages were supposed to deteriorate under. But simply, looking back over the past two years and the time that they'd known each other before then, there had never really been anything substantial for it to have deteriorated from. They shared the same abode but existed in two different worlds. She—in tune with today's ever-changing whims, able to mold and respond, donning and shedding identities to best express her mood of the moment as easily as she did her clothes—was a creature of the times. He, it seemed, couldn't even fit into the undemanding role expected for a mundane, basic self.

At first, when he had believed that togetherness would eventually bring closeness, he had tried to communicate thoughts that to him seemed important. Now he knew better than to bother making even simple observations. His reality was one that the rest of the world evidently didn't share. So on any level that mattered, he no longer tried communicating very much to anyone. And that was why he found the prospect relieving of not having to accommodate or be accommodated for a whole weekend, but, instead, of just enjoying being himself.

"I said, maybe this nostalgia for five-hundred-year-old music is an unhealthy sign," Horace resumed when the hot-air drying cycle stopped and Corrigan stepped out. The strains of a vigorous string concerto were coming through the open doorway from the living room.

"Oh, is that a fact? And what led you to this momentous conclusion?" Corrigan inquired, reaching for a towel.

"The symptoms are on record from expert diagnosis. Item: Doctor Manning's caution to Mr. Felmer in the series *Fraternity*, where Tim's preoccupation with dated European architecture indicated a pathological condition of reality-rejection. Furthermore, as Fenwick Zellor observed in *The Mind Healer*, a morbid fixation on the past is, in effect, the same—"

Corrigan laughed as he turned to the mirror and began palming shaving lather onto his face. "Ah, come on, Horace. You don't call that kind of stuff reality, now, do you? It's a how-to manual for misfits. Attitude-programming for the intellectually bereft, artistically inane, and socially clueless. Wouldn't you agree?"

By now, Corrigan was cheerfully resigned to the thought of being a permanent misfit. But he enjoyed goading Horace by implying that he alone represented normality, while the norms that the computer reflected were distortions. Horace had never been able to grasp the subtleties of what Corrigan saw as humor, and would miss the point entirely. Muriel had the same problem. Perhaps, Corrigan thought to himself, what the world needed was Irish computers. Perhaps he should have married an Irish wife.

Sure enough:

"If you ask me—"

"I didn't."

"Well, I *did* make it a conditional." If Horace had feet, it would have stamped one. After years, it still couldn't understand when Corrigan was having fun—or why. Corrigan grinned at himself in the mirror. Intelligent machines would finally have arrived—almost—when their adaptive neural nets could handle things like this, he decided. Horace went on: "I don't think that those comments are appropriate, Joe. You seem to be forgetting that *you're* the one with residual psychiatric readjustment problems." (And demonstrate a dash more of the human art called "tact" while they were at it, Corrigan thought.) "But you're suggesting that the rest of the world ought to change to conform to your perceptions. Hardly a rational position to adopt, *I would have thought*." The machine stressed the implied conditional, giving a wonderful emulation of sarcasm. Corrigan was impressed.

"I can only go by the way things seem to me, Horace," he said. "If you can't call a pig a pig when you see one, what hope is there?"

"Please explain the connection with pigs."

Corrigan sighed. (And better comprehension of metaphor, along with tact and humor.) "Some other time. What I meant was, there's no point in pretending that something looks other than the way it does. I'm told that my powers of projective immersion are impaired. And maybe they are. But it doesn't seem to have occurred to anybody that I might actually be happy with things being this way."

Corrigan finished drying his face and went back into the bedroom to select some clothes for the day. Horace's voice pursued him relentlessly like an anxious butler.

"Are you really the one to be the judge of that, Joe?"

"The judge of what *I* like? Sure. Who better did you have in mind?" Maybe a regular, button-up, navy shirt and plain, old-fashioned, gray slacks, he thought—non-projectively, non-immersingly expressing what he thought of bright purple jumpsuits and plastic imitation combat garb.

"I meant, of whether it's healthy to feel happy about it," Horace said. "According to the testimony of Doctor Newcomb, who as you may recall was the expert witness called in the trial of Jenny Drew in the—"

"Horace," Corrigan interrupted. "I thought you were talking about reality. Those are fictional characters in contrived situations. Get it? They don't really exist."

"Not as such, possibly," Horace admitted stiffly. "Nevertheless, they are based on carefully researched studies, and may therefore be taken as realistic depictions of composite actuality."

"In that case, reality has got problems," Corrigan said.

"Not you, by any chance?"

"If I have, I can live with them. So where's the problem?"

"You're happy to be out on your own like that, to be different?" As if it weren't already obvious. An ability to accept the fact had evidently not connected in Horace's associative net.

"What's more important, would you say?" Corrigan replied. "Conformity or contentment?"

"Invalid comparison," Horace pronounced. "Your contentment is something that only you know about. What you *do* is different. It's external. It affects other people, and hence what they do." There was a short delay, giving an effective impression of Horace weighing its words. "Therefore, the answer to which is more important depends on how seriously you take the consequences."

Corrigan caught the pause and stopped halfway through buttoning his shirt. "Horace," he said, looking away from the mirror. "Something's happened. What is it?"

Horace's voice became formal, sounding like a lawyer serving notice of a suit. "I have to inform you that Mrs. Corrigan is not staying with her sister in Philadelphia for the weekend, as you were informed. She will not be returning, and has instructed that her whereabouts not be revealed. It is her intention to initiate proceedings, and you will be hearing from her attorney in due course." There was a pause, Corrigan saying nothing while he knotted his tie and digested what he had heard. Then, reverting to its normal self, Horace added, "She left this message."

Corrigan slowly finished buttoning his shirt cuffs as Muriel's twangy Tennessee voice filled the room. "Well, I guess by now you know the situation—not that I can see you taking it as any big deal. But then I don't think we ever had much of that deep kind of stuff that they talk about, either way. I never could figure out that world you live in, someplace inside your head. All I know is that I'm in this one out here, and you're never gonna be part of it. . . . But then, some of that has to be my fault too, for hitchin' up with somebody who I knew hadn't finished havin' his head an' all that straightened out in the first place. Sorry I couldna been more help in fixin' that like we hoped—but them shrinks did tell us up front that it was a long way from a sure thing.

"Hell, Joe, no, I'm not the one who should have to be sorry about anything. I tried hard, dammit, you know that? But do you know how hard it can be tryin' to make it with a guy who's—I gotta say this, you understand me, Joe—like, a failure. As in socially, for instance. There's things that people aim at in life, things they try to be that make everyone feel together, like they're part of the same planet. And then there's that job of yours, where you don't care about being a success or have any ambition to try something better. But none o' that ever meant anythin' to you, Joe. . . . Hell, you probably don't even know what I'm talkin' about."

There was a heavy sigh. "Well, this isn't really coming out the way I wanted it to, so I'll wrap it up. Don't try getting in touch or anythin' like that, because there really isn't any point. I talked to a lawyer, and he'll be in touch soon. . . . I guess that's it. This seemed the best way to break it—without too much talkin' an' stuff. We never did talk the same language, anyhow. So . . . 'bye. I hope things work out."

By this time Corrigan had finished dressing. He checked the other closet, then the vanity. There were odds and ends, cheaper jewelry, clothes that she had grown tired of. The things that she valued more were mostly gone—far more than she would have taken for a weekend in Philadelphia.

But he had never doubted what he would find. His movements were automatic, filling the void while the meaning sank in. His feelings about it had not yet emerged from beneath a curious detachment. Yes, there was the sudden surprise. But along with it . . . not bitterness, nor anger at rejection, but—even now, poking enticingly out of hiding like an ankle glimpsed below heavy Victorian folds—an intensified version of the relief that he had experienced on awakening.

"Well, I'll be damned," he said finally in a tone that could have meant anything.

Horace, after deciding that a short, respectful silence was appropriate, had evidently checked up on how humans were likely to react in situations like this. "Don't do anything rash, Joe," it cautioned. "I understand that these things can be a strain. Breaking the place up would only make everything worse in the long run."

"Thanks, but I have no intention of doing anything of the kind," Corrigan told it.

"Do you want to sit down for a minute?"

"What for?"

"There are tranquilizers in the cabinet. Or shall I mix you a drink, even if it is early? If you like, I could get Sarah Bewley on the line." Then, via its optical sensors around the room, the machine discerned that Corrigan wasn't behaving in any of the ways categorized in its data retrievals. "Don't you feel rage, remorse, guilt, confusion?" it inquired. "An impulse to get even, to have revenge? Compulsions to commit physical assault or battery? Homicide?"

"I feel fine."

But of course, Horace realized: it had been presuming in terms of *normal* humans. With a deviant like Corrigan, anything was possible. "What are you going to do?" it asked warily.

Corrigan moved back to his own closet and took out a pastel-blue wool-acrylic jacket. "I think I'll go for a walk and eat out," he replied. "So don't worry about breakfast."

"But . . . that's it?" Simulated or not, Horace sounded genuinely befuddled—even, perhaps, with a hint of mild disappointment.

"Reality rejection," Corrigan explained, slipping on the jacket as he went through the doorway to the hall. "Look it up with the experts, Horace. I'm sure they'll tell you all about it."

On the table by the front door was a figurine of a grinning Irish leprechaun in a battered hat, clutching a curly-stemmed pipe. It had been a wedding present from Corrigan's marriage to his first wife, Evelyn—long ago now, before his breakdown.

"And the top o' the mornin' to yourself, too, Mick," he said as he let himself out the door.

The figurine had been among the personal things kept for him after the house that he and Evelyn had shared was sold. Apart from being a reminder of home, it had always held a strange fascination that Corrigan had never really understood.

Chapter Two

For breakfast, Corrigan went to a place called The Bagatelle that he used occasionally, a short walk from the apartment, just off Forbes Avenue in the Oakland area of Pittsburgh's East End. It was close enough to the way that he thought restaurants ought to be to still have seats at a counter, and booths for customers to sit at, and to look as if it was staying in the same place. Some of the experiments in progressive marketing that he'd come across, which seemed to be affecting everything these days, included eating reclined on couches, Roman style; a steakhouse fitted out as a train, with graphics-generated moving landscapes outside the windows; and a seafood restaurant housed in a transparent dome on the bed of the Allegheny River.

One of the peculiarities of being crazy—or still recovering from being crazy, anyway—was that it made the rest of the world look odd instead. Corrigan's therapists told him that a side effect of his condition inhibited his ability to respond to the socializing influences that gave normal individuals their sense of identity, purpose, belonging, and direction.

YOU ARE WHAT YOU SAY YOU ARE, a flashing sign in the window of an outfitter's store a block from the restaurant proclaimed, with a display featuring a life-size Long John Silver, complete with parrot and chest overflowing with gleaming plastic florins. The city's chamber of commerce was sponsoring a promotional drive on the theme of the Pittsburgh Pirates, and most businesses were offering discounts to anyone sporting pirate garb. The stores had stocked up with imitation flintlocks and cutlasses. Video banks were downloading pirate movies for half price.

The Bagatelle's staff were turned out in an assortment of striped jerseys, braided coats, and three-corner hats when Corrigan arrived, and the customers included a complement of eye-patched ruffians and baggy-britched buccaneers. Also scattered around were a trio of cowboys in Western gear, a Beau Brummel in silks and wig, and two girls wearing silver pants with scarlet, metal-trimmed vests, recognizable as uniforms of female engineering crew in *Starship Command*. All of them were adorned with the panoply of hip purse, camera and accessories, walkaround music player, and medication pouch that the role models on TV had elevated practically to the level of mandatory for proper dress. They greeted Corrigan's jacket and tie with curious, suspicious looks of the kind he was used to, and he consigned himself to a booth in an empty corner. The screen at the end of the table showed a menu and voiced the morning's special, adding a commercial for an insurance agency along the street. Corrigan entered his order via the touchpad, then sat back and let his mind turn idly to the prospect of life without Muriel. Snatches of conversation reached him from the nearest occupied table about what the celebrities were doing in some popular drama or other. The cowboys were making sure that everyone could see their boots, which must have cost a hundred dollars a pair.

He still wasn't reacting fully to the situation, he knew. Things might take days to sink in. A potbellied autovendor stopped by the booth and began reciting a spiel on the magazines, candies, pills, and other wares that it was carrying. Corrigan told it to go away.

Then one of the waitresses came across with his coffee. She was about twenty, cute in the face, slightly chubby, with dark ringlets poking out from below a blue-spotted kerchief tied around her head.

"Hi, Mandy," Corrigan said, looking at her name tag. "You ordered eggs and corned-beef hash with fries?"

"Right."

"The special today is German pancakes and sausage."

"I know. I want eggs and the hash."

Mandy looked puzzled and glanced away at the other

customers, as if double-checking something. "But every-body's having the special," she said.

"Well, that's manifestly untrue, isn't it? If *everybody* were, then it would include me, wouldn't it?—by definition. And I'm not." He watched her patiently, waiting for the pieces to connect. Quite simple, he tried saying with a smile. Just think about it.

Her eyes met his with the vacancy that he saw every-where. He felt as if he were dealing with a shell whose occu-pant had departed—or maybe never existed. "Logically, that's correct, I guess," she replied. Corrigan was used to things sounding strangely inappropriate. Mandy's brow creased. She seemed to be having a problem knowing how to continue.

The receptionist at the desk by the door saved her by calling across, "Mandy, is that a Mr. Corrigan there at that booth?" She was holding a phone.

"Are you Mr. Corrigan?" Mandy repeated.

"Yes, I am."

"Yes, he is."

"Call for you, Mr. Corrigan," the receptionist an-nounced.

A beep sounded from the table unit, and the menu van-ished to be replaced by a callscreen format. Corrigan tapped the pad to accept and pivoted the unit toward him. The features of Sarah Bewley appeared, looking concerned. Mandy made the best of her opportunity to escape.

"Joe, thank goodness I've found you!" Sarah was still the rehabilitation counselor assigned to Corrigan's case by the psychiatric care section of the city health department. She looked and sounded anxious. "Are you all right?"

Corrigan made a pretense of thinking the question over; then, knowing that she would miss the point, pro-nounced, "Probably more what you'd call mostly liberal." He played the same games with Sarah as he did with Hor-ace. For a psychiatrist, Sarah could be amazingly unperspi-cacious at times—or so it seemed to Corrigan. Years previously, Dr. Arnold had told him that his condition caused him to see things in peculiar ways and form linkages in his head that made no sense to anyone else.

"I was worried about you," Sarah said.

"Is that a fact?"

"Horace called and told me the news about Muriel. You know, if you'd only carry a compad like everyone else, it would be a lot easier for people to contact you."

"I know," Corrigan agreed. "That's why I don't. If I did, I'd have Horace checking up on me all the time. It's bad enough having to live with a neurotic computer, never mind being hounded all over town by it as well."

Sarah came back to her reason for calling. "You're sure you're all right? You're not thinking of doing anything silly, are you?"

"I was about to have breakfast, if that's what you mean."

"Joe, I'm so sorry! You must be going out of your mind. I know how something like this can affect people, especially somebody in your situation. Now, you're not to worry, understand? I can probably arrange through the department to have her traced. Then we'll get her back, and all sit down together and work out what the problem is. In the meantime I want you to carry on just as if nothing happened. Can you manage that for me, Joe?"

Corrigan blinked. What was this? First Horace; now his counselor verging on hysteria. "I'm all right," he said when he could get a word in. Sarah stopped, seemingly taken by surprise just as he thought she was about to launch off again. "It's probably for the best," Corrigan explained. "I don't think there ever was anything deep between us either way. It was all done for the wrong reasons. To be honest, I feel relieved now that it's sorted itself out at last."

"Relieved?" Sarah repeated. It was as if she needed to test the word, to make sure she'd heard it right.

Corrigan shrugged lightly. "Sure. You know: not being shut up in a box anymore with somebody that I really don't have that much to say to; able to be me without having to try and explain it, knowing that I wouldn't be understood anyway. Life could be worse."

Sarah stared out of the screen at him, suddenly calmer now, "Diminished emotional sensitivity index," she murmured knowingly. "That is one of the symptoms we should expect."

Corrigan felt himself getting irritated. If he didn't fit with what their textbooks and case histories said was to be expected, then that was just too bad. He felt fine. "Look," he said, "if you're trying to—"

"Careful, Joe," Sarah cautioned. "Hostility's natural— you've had a big loss. But you have to try to control it."

Corrigan closed his eyes and forced himself to be patient. "Sarah, really, I'm all right. I don't especially want to trace her. It wouldn't work, and anyway, I'm not interested."

Sarah looked unconvinced but seemed willing to let it go for now. "You and I should still talk about it," she replied. "I'm at my office this morning. Can you get over here? It would be a good time for us to get together anyway. Dr. Zehl will be stopping by in about an hour. He'd like to see how you're getting on." Zehl was Sarah's clinical supervisor from somewhere in Washington. He had a tendency to show up at irregular intervals, always with little or no warning.

"Is it all right if I have my breakfast first?" Corrigan asked.

"Of course." Sarah nodded in all seriousness, missing the sarcasm. "I'll send a cab to pick you up. Make sure you're ready by, say, ten-fifteen."

"Thanks. I'll bring some champagne."

"What for?" A blank look. She genuinely couldn't see it. Presumably Corrigan had made another of his erratic connections.

"Never mind," he said.

Mandy came back to the booth with his order just as Sarah cleared down. She looked pleased with herself. The food looked good, but Corrigan's breakdown had left him with a disorder of the olfactory system, so that for years nothing had tasted right.

"I get it," Mandy told him. "I was using 'everybody' the way people talk. But you pretended it was an overgeneralization. It was a play on double meanings, right?"

Corrigan had to think for a few seconds before he realized what she was talking about. "Oh, yes . . . right." He marshaled a smile and winked at her conspiratorially. "But I shouldn't let on about it if I were you, Mandy," he whispered. "People might think you're crazy."

Chapter Three

Sarah Bewley was short and plump, with a heavyset face cast in a frown that took the world too seriously. She had wispy brown hair and changed its style to reflect how she felt on any given day. When Corrigan arrived at her office, it was tied back in the flare of mane that was the nearest it could be coaxed toward a ponytail, which he knew meant she was logical and analytic today. (Loose and straggly meant speculative/exploratory; high and tied tight, businesslike/clinical.) He also noted that she was wearing a pastel olive-green skirt and matching top. A couple of weeks previously he had remarked that he thought a regular two-piece would be more appropriate for a professional woman than the mauve cat-suit with boots that she had been squeezed into at the time. Strange. He'd always thought that the therapist was supposed to alter the behavior of the patient, not the other way around.

Dr. Zehl, in tie and light-gray suit, was more what Corrigan would have considered conventional. He was tall, probably in his sixties, with a fresh complexion and high brow that encroached on a head of white, crinkly hair. What always struck Corrigan about Zehl was his eyes. Framed in rimless bifocals, they were constantly alert, shifting, silently interrogating, with a depth that Corrigan didn't find very often. Sarah, by contrast, although technically Corrigan's mentor, inspired no feeling of real contact in the sense of true, two-way communication of thoughts that mattered; so he amused himself by playing semantic games with her in the same way that he did with Horace.

Since it was Saturday, the receptionist and secretarial staff were out. Sarah let Corrigan in and showed him through to her office, where Zehl was studying the figures on one of the terminal screens. Corrigan sat in an empty chair by the machine opposite. Sarah seemed to get a kick out of showing off her computers. Compared to the kind of machines that he'd used over twelve years before, Corrigan found them quaint.

Unlike Sarah, Zehl didn't presume that all marriage breakups had to produce feelings of resentment, rejection, and traumatic distress. He understood Corrigan's position and agreed that if the experiment hadn't worked out, then it was probably as well to call it a day. Very simple, really. Yet Sarah absorbed the message as if she were witnessing a revelation. If feeling this way instead of turning into what sounded to him like a deranged lunatic was abnormal, then he could live with it, Corrigan decided.

Sarah was unwilling to leave it at that, however, but seemed intrigued by what she saw as his refusal to conform. "Is it simply an inability due to some kind of defect?" she asked him. "Or is it the result of a deliberate process: something you just *won't* do? Can you tell us?"

"I thought you were supposed to tell me," Corrigan answered.

"It doesn't seem to trouble you at all. You really don't have any qualms about it? Deep down inside, I mean. You don't feel out of things, insecure?"

"Yes, I feel out of things. No, I don't feel insecure. Whether that's deep down or not, I have no idea."

"You don't have a desire to be more a part of the world around you?" Sarah persisted. "To feel integrated, accepted by others?"

"Why should I?"

Sarah flashed Zehl a worried look. "At one time you were a professional, one of the best in your field," she said to Corrigan. "Don't you have any of that ambition anymore? Are you happy at the thought of being a bartender indefinitely?" It was like listening to a replay of Muriel and Horace, Corrigan thought.

"Look where the other kind got me," he said.

Zehl was staring at Corrigan with a different light in his eye: brooding, more reflective. For a moment Corrigan had the odd feeling that it was he and Zehl who shared some common insight that the circumstances precluded discussing openly, and not the two specialists.

"Getting back to the immediate future, Joe, what do you think you might do?" Zehl asked, moving them off the subject. "Any possible plans yet?"

"Yes, as a matter of fact," Corrigan answered. "Just a thought that crossed my mind while I was having breakfast. Maybe I could use a change of scene and start getting in touch with the rest of the wide world again. We've talked about it before, but with Muriel out of the way this might be the right time. I was thinking I could take a vacation back to Ireland."

Zehl frowned. Clearly he was far from instantly enamored at the idea.

"Ireland?" Sarah repeated. Her voice was quavery. For some reason the suggestion seemed to bewilder her. "Why would you want to go to Ireland?"

"I'm Irish," Corrigan said. "Sometimes people like to go back and see the place they're from." Surely it was obvious.

Sarah was shaking her head, but she seemed to be having to search for a reason. "No, I don't think so, Joe," she said. "I don't think that would be possible at all."

The abruptness of her response set Corrigan at odds again. "Why not?" he objected. "It's been twelve years now since the Oz project screwed up. I'm in control of my life again. I'm holding down a job that's good enough to keep me independent." He drew a breath and looked at her pointedly. "And it wasn't *me* who gave up on the marriage this morning and quit."

Sarah shook her head again. "Your condition is still more delicate than you realize. The stresses of traveling abroad would just be inviting trouble. Yes, you're right— you have made a lot of progress. Let's not risk undoing it all now."

"I went to Japan four years ago," Corrigan pointed out. He knew as soon as he spoke that it was a weak argument.

"Exactly," Sarah said, not missing the point either. "And look what happened. It triggered a relapse that you took months to get over."

Corrigan turned toward Zehl for support, but this time Zehl was on Sarah's side. "Sorry, Joe, I have to veto it," he said. He brought a hand up to touch his temple with a finger in a flicking motion, vaguely suggestive of a salute—it was a peculiarity of his that Corrigan had noticed before. "It's a nice thought, but you're not ready. Staying within a familiar environment is an important part of your cure. Sure, take a break if you need to, but keep it in the city, eh?" Zehl shrugged and made a palm-up gesture. "Maybe a few walks by the river. Go see a game, the zoo, maybe try a concert. How many of the museums have you visited? Get the idea? Easy, relaxing, familiar. You'd be surprised at the supportive effects of being in places you know."

"I know Ireland pretty well, too," Corrigan pointed out, although by now it was mainly through obstinacy. He had not been officially discharged from medical care, and Zehl had the authority certainly to overrule any long-distance travel plans, and probably to have Corrigan put back under institutional care if he judged it to be in the patient's welfare to do so—Corrigan didn't want to put that to the test.

Zehl raised a hand firmly. "No, and that's final. Next year, maybe, but not now. I'll pull rank if I have to."

Corrigan stretched out an arm and tapped idly at the keyboard beside him while he considered how to respond. "So, do you know what you want, Joe?" Sarah asked him again.

Corrigan scratched the side of his nose. "Not a lot," he replied finally. "The first thing is to do a lot of thinking. And I can do that anywhere. So for the time being it will be a case of simply carrying on as usual. If that changes, I'll let you know."

Chapter Four

Pittsburgh had seen a surprising amount of demolition and rebuilding in recent years.

The Camelot Hotel was located downtown on Fourth Avenue—a redevelopment of a site where an office building had stood previously. It was an experimental throwback from the glass-and-concrete architectural catastrophes that had been provoking mirth and outrage among everyone but the experts for decades. Standing out amid the gray slab canyons and arrays of faceless mirror rectangles, the Camelot presented a warm, defiant countenance of red bricks, arched windows, and a pseudo-Tudor foyer with wood-beamed ceilings—imitation wood, it was true, but visually pleasing nonetheless. A crenellated terrace reduced the severity of the vertical line, and, in keeping with the name, twin chateau-style turrets rounded off the design. Visitors and locals liked it, and a residential developer was putting up English Victorian-style row houses along several streets on the North Side. And Corrigan liked working there because it offered a respite from the various dementias of the age that he was supposed to want to normalize himself by imitating.

Plenty of people were out, healthily expressing themselves, when he arrived from the subway stop on Stanwix Street. Half a block before the hotel entrance, a couple were having a domestic tiff, screaming insults at each other in front of onlookers who yelled taunts or encouragement, depending on whose side they took. A street band was playing for nickels in front of a battery of equipment that must have cost several thousand dollars; a group of men wearing togas and holding staffs were sitting cross-legged on the sidewalk for reasons that were not obvious; some women were parading dogs glamorized with coiffures of various cuts and colors to reflect their mistresses' personas; and there were more pirates about.

Movement and bearing were important parts of the language by which people told the world who they were and what they owned. So business suits and hats strutted, blazers and sport coats strode, macho gear swaggered, uniforms of any kind marched, shapely skirts wiggled, and demure dresses minced. The modern world in miniature, the street was a stage of acted-out messages: the measured tread of confidence; paradings of success; hunched, defeated shoulders; a hanging head of shame. Nobody took any notice of Corrigan as he made his way uncommunicatively along the sidewalk to the Camelot's main doors. He was far from convinced that they took very much notice of each other.

A media celebrity called Merlyn Dree was staying at the Camelot, and Corrigan had to pick his way through a flock of garishly clad fans who were being held at bay outside the door by hotel security staff. Inside, at the front desk, a fat man in an overcoat was pointing at a sheet of paper and remonstrating loudly with a harassed-looking clerk.

"No, Crammerwitz booked the room, but it's under Mancini, okay? The basic goes to the company, and they pick up these calls, but not those calls. Dinner goes on the other company and not this one, because it's a different account. What's the problem?"

In a corner nearby, the latest experimental wonder in Artificial Intelligence that somebody had succeeded in selling to management stood ignominiously, dismantled and partly crated in preparation for being shipped back: automated, talking desk-clerks. They hadn't lasted a week. Whoever coded their database was probably very smart but had obviously never worked in hotels. Corrigan went on through the lobby, grateful that nobody had come up with any ideas for replacing human bartenders. That would need Artificial Wisdom, which was another matter entirely.

He went up the main stairway to the second-floor landing and through the staff door to the room behind the bar of the Galahad Lounge. The roster pinned to the message board told him that Sherri would be working the late shift with him. At least she was one that he found he could talk to. She listened, and seemed genuinely curious to understand what made him different. Sometimes he thought that Sherri would be better doing Sarah's job. But on the other hand, maybe that would mean he'd have to work with Sarah.

Maurice, who was in charge of the Camelot's three lounges, came in while Corrigan was changing into his work outfit of dress shirt with bow tie and maroon jacket. Small, dark, with the shaped mustachios that he considered went with the bar-manager image, Maurice was a Horace incarnate with a New York accent—meticulous about detail, and most of the time sounding like an animated company-procedure manual. Since his staff handled cash and dealt directly with the clientele, that wasn't all bad, Corrigan supposed. But Maurice confused all around him by being incapable of doing anything simply if a more complicated way could be contrived. On top of that, his particular brand of normality came in the form of a conviction that everyone in the trade was crooked, especially management, and customers worst of all. Corrigan stayed behind his shield of maladaptability and watched with baffled fascination.

"You were on yesterday afternoon before Jack, right, Joe?" Maurice was holding the notebook in which he entered the figures from the cash registers. Jack was another of the younger bar assistants. Maurice had confided that he knew Jack was on the take, because he styled his hair in the same way as Nelson Torrence of *Underside,* who conned wealthy widows and robbed banks.

"Yesterday? Yes, that's right," Corrigan replied. "Why?"

"Was everything okay when you cashed up? Last night, we were thirty bucks down."

Corrigan groaned inwardly. Jack had been delayed on his way in, making Corrigan late for a game that he'd wanted to catch at Three Rivers. By way of amends and to help out, Jack had offered to cash up Corrigan's shift for him so that he could be on his way. Although it was against the rules, just that one time Corrigan had let him—he had no qualms about Jack being honest. And just that one time, of course, something like this had to happen.

He sighed. "I didn't do it. I was late for something and got Jack to cover."

"*What!* You let him cash up your shift? You know better than that, Joe."

Yes, Corrigan knew. But it happened from time to time nevertheless, as Maurice knew perfectly well. The problem was that trust was a concept that lay beyond Maurice's powers of comprehension.

"My fault," Corrigan said. "I'm wide open. I'll eat the thirty, no problem."

But that wasn't what Maurice wanted. He moved a step closer and lowered his voice. "Come on, Joe, you know and I know that Jack's a snitch, don't we? He cooked your numbers and took a dip. But he doesn't have ta get away with it. All I need is a docket from you, and I'll countersign that you put it in yesterday."

In other words, a pure frame-up implicating Jack as trying to frame Corrigan. Corrigan couldn't see for the life of him why Maurice went about doing things this way. "Ah, no," he said, "that wouldn't be right at all. There's no knowing it was him. I might have made a mistake earlier, sure enough."

Maurice shook his head. "That's not the point. I don't care who goofed. I've been wanting to get rid of him anyhow. This is all I need."

"Of course it's the point," Corrigan retorted. "I'm not covered, and that's the fact of it. I'll not be a party to making up something that says otherwise."

"You're too careful to drop thirty," Maurice persisted. "I say he palmed it and tried to lay it on you."

"Maybe he did. I guess we'll never know."

Maurice shook his head disbelievingly. "Aren't you gonna fight that?"

"Maurice, there isn't anything to fight. I didn't cash up the shift, and that's all there is to it. For God's sake take it out of my check like I said, and let's be done with it."

Maurice seemed mystified. "I don't get it. You've got nothing to lose by doing it my way. This way you lose thirty bucks. Where's the logic?"

"You really can't see it?"

"I can't see it."

"I'd be losing my self-respect, and that's worth far more than what we're talking about."

"So if Jack's made thirty for nothing, that's okay by you?"

"Well, he's the only one who knows about that for sure, isn't he? If he did, then it wasn't for nothing. He made it at the price of becoming a thief." Corrigan shook his head. "In my opinion that wouldn't be a very good deal at all, at all."

Maurice seemed to freeze for an instant; then he looked at Corrigan with a different expression, as if a switch had clicked in his head somewhere, transforming him into a different personality. "Say, you know, that's an interesting way to look at it," he said. "I never thought about it before."

Try it sometime, Corrigan thought to himself.

Maurice went on. "How would you weight a payoff matrix to express the options? Logically it reduces to the same structure as Prisoner's Dilemma."

Corrigan stared at him in surprise. Years before, when he'd worked among engineers and programmers, intellectual topics figured naturally in conversation, and game theory was often one of them. But it was the last thing that he would have expected from Maurice.

Before Corrigan could reply, however, Sherri stuck her head in through the doorway from the bar. "Joe, great, you're here. We're filling up out front."

"Sorry, Maurice," Corrigan said, glad to get off the subject. "Duty's calling. We'll have to talk about it some other time." And with that, he straightened his jacket and went through to join Sherri in the bar.

In the far corner, a clique of Merlyn Dree fans had penetrated the defenses and were chanting some of his slogans and catchphrases around a table. Two macho-looking characters in sunglasses and pink fedoras were at the bar, waiting to be served. A bearded man in a pirate hat was prefacing every phrase with a loud, rolling "Arr!" to a group sitting near the door. A man in a yellow suit was loudly expounding that the art of selling lay in being a good listener, and a couple with their heads encased in audiovisual helmets were sitting as though in a trance by the far wall.

Normal, sane, ordinary people, Corrigan thought to himself as he checked the register and surveyed the scene. Nothing unusual. Yes, it was going to be another typical night.

Chapter Five

Jonathan Wilbur had had three scotches in the last half hour and was getting loquacious. He waved a hand expansively from the barstool where he was sitting. "New York, London, Tokyo. It moves around the world through computers all the time. Billions of dollars every day. I can buy a company in the morning, sell it at lunchtime, lose my ass in the afternoon."

"That's nice," Corrigan said, collecting empties off the bar.

Privately, he doubted if Wilbur had ever bought and sold more than the office furniture. He was young, dazzled by a world that was obviously new to him, and too anxious to make an impression where it didn't matter. Hotel bartenders saw it all the time.

"Ah, who gives a shit? . . . But I guess in your job you can't imagine money like that, eh, Joe?" With his double-breasted, charcoal suit, white silk shirt, and silver-gray tie with garnet clip, Wilbur at least looked the part. From past conversations, Corrigan knew that he kept up with the fashions that boosted the executive image: golf in summer, skiing in winter, woman's-magazine-cover home with gourmet kitchen, all the wines, European wardrobe, glitzmobile car. The only problem was, the bank owned all of it and he was perpetually one promotion away from being able to afford the repayments. If that was success, Corrigan preferred being a happy failure.

Sherri came back carrying a tray filled with more glasses from the tables. She was petite, blond, bouncy, looking trim in her bar outfit of blouse, maroon vest, and black skirt. "One Bud, one Red, vodka lime with lemon, margarita special, and a Greyhound," she said to Corrigan. He nodded and began pouring.

Wilbur had opened a briefcase on his knee, revealing it to be a portable office complete with laptop and screen, phone, fax/copier, and music player—presumably for necessary relaxation. While Corrigan was busy with the drinks, he lifted out the handset and tapped in a code. "Hi, A.J.? Jon here. Look, about that meeting, can we make it tomorrow? I have to see a guy about an offer, and it might take a while, okay?" He kept his voice raised to make sure that it carried. Sherri caught Corrigan's gaze, raised her eyes momentarily, and came around to pour the beers. "That'll do fine. I'll see you then. 'Bye." Wilbur closed the lid, glancing about quickly to see who was watching. Two girls at a table behind, whom he missed, seemed to be impressed.

"Actually it's a job offer," he confided in a low voice, in case Corrigan was itching to know.

"Is that so, now?" Corrigan said.

"Do you know Oliver, who comes in here sometimes?" Wilbur asked.

Corrigan did—and he wouldn't have trusted him as far as he could fly. "Big fella. Hearty kind—likes a joke. Not a lot of hair on the top of him," Corrigan said.

"That's the one."

"Ah, I do, sure. He was in yesterday for lunch."

Wilbur leaned forward and propped an elbow on the bar, covering the side of his mouth with two fingers. "Well, the job's with his operation, managing portfolios. And I'm telling you, it's not nickel-and-dime stuff with those guys. I mean, we're talking big-time here."

"Well, good luck with it," Corrigan said.

Wilbur scooped a handful of peanuts from a dish on the bar and studied Corrigan while he brought them up to his mouth. "You'd be about what, Joe, fortyish? A little less, maybe?" he asked.

"I'm forty-four." Corrigan transferred the cocktails to Sherri's tray. She picked it up and carried it away.

"Ever have any experience with big outfits, out of curiosity?" Wilbur went on. "Where the real wheels are, know what I mean?"

Corrigan could have said that he had once been the main instigator and joint director of a project whose backers could probably have bought Oliver's operation with the petty cash. Instead, he answered, "Oh, I'll leave that kind of thing to those who have a taste for it. I'm from a part of the world where people tend to take things a bit easier, you understand."

"Irish, right?"

"That's it."

"Yeah. Never got there." Wilbur's voice fell again. "But this thing I was telling you about with Oliver. He's gonna fix me up real good there, in exchange for"—Wilbur grinned slyly—"don't say anything to anyone, but you know how it is—a little harmless information about the place I'm at now. But anything's fair in love, war, and business, eh?" It was all straight out of a score of popular movie series. Corrigan found it hard not to smile.

"I wouldn't know about that," he said.

Oliver arrived a few minutes later, dressed showily in a suit of silver-dusted cobalt blue with a white leather topcoat thrown loosely across his shoulders. He stopped in the doorway to look around, saw Wilbur at the bar, and moved ponderously across to join him. With Oliver was a tall woman, mid-thirties to forty, with straight hair worn high, heavy on the makeup. She was wearing a long, low-cut dress, and glittered from throat to fingers with jewelry. Corrigan had seen her with Oliver a couple of times before. Delia, he thought her name was.

Oliver was all hale-and-heartiness. "Hey, Wilbur, old buddy. You're good on time, too, huh? That's great. Just what we need. Joe, how's it going? You remember Delia, right?"

"Hello again, Joe." Delia smiled, revealing teeth that had to have been surgically rebuilt, and displaying her purple eye shadow. She was an accessory to Oliver's image that went with the manner, the coat, and the suit.

"Let's see," Oliver said. "Gimme a screwdriver, gin with bitter lemon and a slice of lime here, and another of whatever that is for Wilbur."

Corrigan took three fresh glasses down from the overhead rack. Delia rested an elbow on the bar and watched him while Oliver started telling Wilbur about the volume of transactions that the firm had handled that day. A couple that Corrigan had been keeping an eye on by the far wall, arguing since they sat down, were losing their cool, the man getting angrier, the woman's voice rising, both gesticulating. Healthy expressiveness. The Merlyn Dree fans had started acting out some of his skits. The pink fedoras had latched on to the two girls who found Wilbur glamorous and exciting. Sherri came back with more empties and started loading the washer.

"I'm an associate with Oliver," Delia told Corrigan. "I don't know if he mentioned it. Foreign stocks and bonds department. That's the high-risk end, where you have to know your way around." She waited, inviting a response, then went on when Corrigan just nodded. "But the *money* you can make! I'm not even going to say what commission I grossed last quarter. But it bought me a Hampton Riviera with no payments. Getaway cabin in Vermont, Queensland beach scene in winter. . . ."

Corrigan looked at her with a neutral expression and said, "That's nice."

Delia's voice dropped to a more confidential note. "You get to meet all the right contacts, too. I pay less tax than I did five years ago. I practically bank my paycheck and live off the expenses."

"That's nice."

Oliver picked up his and Delia's drinks and looked around. "Let's move to a table. There's one over there. Come on, Jon, I'll give you some inside secrets about how to screw the most out of clients. If they've still got blood left, we're not doing our job, right?" He winked at Corrigan. "Talk to you later, Joe, okay?"

"Behave yourself, now."

"Why? Where's the fun in that?"

Wilbur took up his own glass and his briefcase, and followed the other two away. Sherri, who had been half listening, came up beside Corrigan to ring some cash into the till. Corrigan eyed Oliver and his two companions contemplatively while they seated themselves around the table, then said to Sherri, "Suppose you moved to a small town. And you found there were only two hairdressers: one whose hair was neat, the other a mess. You'd go to the one who looked a mess, wouldn't you? Because it would be she who did the hair of the other."

Sherri frowned for a moment, then smiled. "Yeah—true. What brought that on all of a sudden?"

"Oh, those three who were here just now. That fella Wilbur thinks Oliver is going to do him a good turn out of the kindness of his heart. He's expecting he'll be treated with fairness and honesty." Corrigan sighed and shook his head. "Why do people insist on looking for something where it clearly isn't? And then they blame the world when their hopes don't materialize."

"I don't know how you stand that woman the way you do," Sherri said. "She's so gross with her 'I've got this' and 'I've got that' all the time. But you can just stand there and say 'that's nice' like you do. You'll have to teach me how to do it."

Corrigan smiled wryly. "Oh, that's an old Irish story," he said. "You'd have no problem if you knew it."

"Well, tell me, then," Sherri invited.

Corrigan glanced around. There were no customers looking for attention just at the moment. As a rule he didn't bother telling jokes these days. People no longer understood them. Oh, what the hell, he told himself. Give it a try.

"It's like this," he said. "Two women are sharing a hospital room in Dublin, you see. One is from Foxrock. That's south of the city, where all the money is—she'd be one of your Delias. The other's the complete opposite: bottom end of the social spectrum—what we'd call a roight auld slag."

"You mean like parts of the South Bronx?"

"Maybe. Anyway, Delia wants to make sure there's no mistake about who she is, see. So she says to other . . ." Corrigan mimicked a prim tone: " 'Ah, I hope you don't imagine that I am accustomed to sharing like this. Usually, I go to the private wing.' "

He changed to a shrill, coarser accent. " 'Oh, yiss?' says the other, who we'll say was Mary. 'Dat's noice.'

" 'I'll have you know,' says Delia, 'that my husband is an extremely successful man and takes very good care of me. The last time I was a patient, he took me on a Caribbean cruise to recuperate.'

" 'Dat's noice.'

" 'And on the occasion before that, he bought me a diamond pendant to compensate for the discomfort.' . . ." Corrigan nodded an invitation at Sherri to supply the response.

"That's nice," she obliged.

"Ah, no," he said. "You have to do it with the proper accent. Come on, now: 'Dat's noice.' "

"Dat's noice."

"Perfect. And then your Delia says, 'Out of curiosity, does *your* husband show such consideration when you are confined?'

" 'Oh, yiss, o' course 'e does,' says Mary. 'When we 'ad our last one, 'e sent me fer elocution and etiquette lessons.' "

Sherri chuckled, and Corrigan continued, "Naturally, Delia's astounded. *'What!'* she exclaims. *'Elocution?* How would somebody like *you* even know what the word means?'

" ' 'E did, too,' Mary tells her. 'See, at one time, whenever oi 'eard people tellin' me a load o' bullshit, oi used to tell 'em ter fuck orf. Now oi just smiles at 'em all proper, like, and oi say . . .' " Corrigan paused expectantly. Anyone should see it now. But Sherri's eyes were still blank, waiting. He completed, " 'Dat's noice.' "

There was a barely perceptible delay, and then she laughed. But the laugh wasn't real. She had missed the point. Corrigan had seen the same thing too many times before. He turned to restocking the mixers shelf. What was it about the modern world that had changed people? he wondered. Sarah Bewley tried to tell him that nothing had changed, that it was his idea of humor that had been distorted. But the story he'd told Sherri was from his student days in Ireland, and everyone back then had found it funny. Or had nothing in those years happened the way he remembered it at all?

A knot of people appeared in the doorway, clustered about a squat, rotund figure whose name Corrigan couldn't bring to mind instantly—some kind of city official, who worried all the time about his public visibility. The last time they were in, the talk had been about sending political messages through the communications chips that some people were having put in their heads. One of the aides couldn't seem to comprehend why Corrigan was cool toward the idea. "Why would anyone choose to stay out of touch?" he had wanted to know.

Then a man with shoulders like a blockhouse came in and stopped, obviously checking the place. Moments later, a commotion of voices came from the hall outside the lounge. The Dree fans leaped to their feet with a clamor of squeals and shouts as the idol himself swept in ahead of an entourage of photographers and starlets, resplendent in a white glitter suit and red shirt, blond hair falling to his shoulders, arms held high to acknowledge the accolades.

The funny thing was that although Dree featured in commercials everywhere and appeared at all kinds of public events, he didn't sing, dance, play, act, tell stories, or entertain in any way that was traditionally recognizable. As far as Corrigan was aware, he didn't actually *do* anything. He was the ultimate celebrity: well known for no other reason than being well known.

Even Sherri was standing enraptured as the circus moved in and took over the bar. *"You call this having a good time?"* Dree yelled to the general delight: his standard catchphrase.

"You ain't seen nothing yet!" they chorused back. All the way from Jolson. Sherri joined in; so did Delia, Wilbur, and the girls talking to the pink fedoras. The party dispersed to a corner, and an aide came across to the bar to give their order. Corrigan turned to set out the glasses, and as he did so he noticed a woman looking in through the doorway. She was tall, with long dark hair, wearing a suede coat over a satiny black dress. The noise and antics inside made her start to turn away; but then she caught sight of Corrigan, seemed to change her mind, and came in.

She had been in about a week before, he recalled. They had talked on and off about nothing in particular through much of the evening, and she had left alone. She was from California, liked Gershwin, the theater, old movies, and dogs, had been curious about Ireland, and seemed to know something about computers. Her name, he remembered moments before she sat down on a barstool with a quick smile of recognition, was Lilly.

Chapter Six

Lilly made a living of sorts at a shoe-finishing shop—shoes were imported plain and unadorned from factories in Asia, then colored and trimmed locally to reflect the current buying patterns before tastes had time to change. That in itself seemed odd to Corrigan, for she displayed all the qualities that he would have thought equipped her for something more challenging and rewarding.

Her eyes, which were dark and depthless, studied the world with a reflective awareness that Corrigan hadn't seen in a half-dozen people during as many years. She had the kind of intelligence that was intelligent enough not to flaunt itself; the quiet self-assurance that doesn't mistake misapplied assertiveness for confidence. In short, she exuded style of a quality that was very rare; and that was also very puzzling, for it didn't add up to the kind of woman who would show any interest in bartenders. Yet for some reason, Lilly seemed to be very curious about Corrigan indeed.

"Do you live in the city, Joe?" She asked when the workload eased and he sauntered back to the end of the bar where she was sitting.

"In a flat in Oakland, the East End."

"Are you married, or what?"

"I was until this morning."

"What happened?"

"She left last night for the weekend. But then the house computer told me that it's for keeps and played a billet-doux."

Lilly's eyes searched his face for a moment. She had

shifted her stool so that her back was to the body of the room, where everybody else seemed determined to prove that they were potential celebrity material too. "What's called for, commiserations or congratulations?" she asked.

Most people would have spouted a set line from a soap—with no thought that it might or might not be appropriate, let alone the notion of trying to find out. But Lilly didn't. She thought; she asked; she listened. That was how she had struck Corrigan the last time she was here.

"I'm not breaking my heart over it," Corrigan replied. "Sometimes these things happen a long time before, and are just waiting to be acted out." She understood, nodded. There was no pointless interrogation. No more needed to be said. "How about yourself?" Corrigan asked.

Sherri deposited another tray of empty glasses and bottles on the bar before Lilly could answer. She was looking worn. "Another round of everything for Dree's people. Four beers for the tab on table three. One gin and tonic, one scotch on the rocks, two white coolers."

"They're working you hard tonight, Sherri," Lilly said.

Sherri exhaled a sigh. "You can say that again." She looked at Corrigan. "When the guy gave me the big order I told him, 'That's nice.' Did I get it right?"

Corrigan stared down at the glasses as he poured, not knowing what to say. How did you explain inappropriateness to somebody who just didn't have the wiring to feel it intuitively? This wanting to know why he thought something funny was another thing that he found all the time with people—and the main reason why he had stopped telling jokes. He was unable to understand why something that they obviously didn't share should be so important to them. He could see why Sarah Bewley would be interested: trying to understand him was her job. But why would anyone else care about his peculiarities when *he* was the odd person out?

"Hey, bar," the Merlyn Dree aide in charge of ordering called from across the room. "Back up on that order there. Make it another one for *everybody*!" He looked around. "When *we* drink, everyone drinks. Right, guys?" The room yelled its approval.

Then another group arrived, and things got hectic. Corrigan worked nonstop until they finally closed things down around 3:00 A.M., in all of which time Lilly never did get a chance to answer his question. In one brief lull, however, they did agree to going for a coffee somewhere, afterward.

"I pretty much keep myself to myself," Lilly said. They had come out into the night air and were turning off Fourth into a passage that connected through to the late-night lights around Market Place. There was a moment's hesitation, as if she were unsure about confiding something. "I guess I don't really relate much to most of the people you meet these days. Things seem to change faster and faster. Not a lot of it makes sense anymore."

Her words mirrored his own situation perfectly. Was that what she had somehow recognized, and why she was showing such interest in a bartender? "I know what you mean," he said.

"Yes, I think you do. I don't feel that with people very often." She glanced sideways at him as they walked. There was more than idle curiosity at work. "You must meet all kinds in a job like yours."

"You saw a few of them yourself tonight."

"But you don't just see them," Lilly said. "You seem to see into them, as well. I was watching."

"I know you were," Corrigan answered. "So that makes you a bit of the same yourself, doesn't it?" Lilly conceded with the quick smile of somebody being caught out, at the same time managing to convey that it was because she was not used to it. Compared to the empty stares and clumsy gropings to extract meaning that he saw every day, it felt like communication bordering on mind reading.

A promotional scouting robot spotted them as they came out into Market Place and rolled across to intercept them, flashing colored lights and logos of nearby places that were open late. "Hello, there! Enjoying the city late tonight?" it greeted jovially. "For your further entertainment we have Jermyn's cabaret bar less than half a block from here, still open for drinks, dancing, and shows until dawn. Getting hungry? The Lilac Slipper offers the best in contemporary and traditional Cantonese cuisine, ten-percent discount for Pirates. Or, for more erotic tastes, ho-ho . . ."

Lilly sighed. "Maybe I could pass on having that coffee out. I'll fix you one at home. How does that sound?"

"Sounds good," Corrigan said. "How far is it?"

"Over the river, north. We'll need a cab. Do you have a compad? I'm not carrying one."

"I hardly ever use them." Corrigan looked at the robot. "Can you call us a cab?"

"Sorry, I just make reservations. But why do you want to leave? It's Saturday night. You want to be part of the scene, right?"

"Wrong." Corrigan steered Lilly away to search for a pay booth. The robot pursued them, babbling tenaciously, until a mixed group of people appeared on the far side of the street, and one of them called it away.

"Aren't you into being part of the scene?" Lilly said it in a light, mocking tone that combined several wavelengths —phrasing it as a question, but simultaneously telling him that she already knew and understood his answer because they both recognized and laughed at the same absurdities.

"Guilty," Corrigan replied.

"You don't need to find yourself?"

"I wasn't aware that I ever lost myself."

"But that's *terrible*."

"Now you know the worst."

They both laughed. She slipped her arm loosely through his.

There was a gift store, with various curios and Pittsburgh mementos in the window. Suddenly Corrigan stopped and stared in at them. "What is it?" Lilly asked.

He pointed to a figure of an Irish leprechaun, identical, as far as he could judge, to the one in his hallway back at the flat. "That's Mick. He keeps popping up wherever I go. Do you know, I've one the same as that at home. It was a wedding present."

"Was that to the wife who left yesterday?"

"No, there was one other before—a while back, now."

"Maybe he's haunting you," Lilly said. "Can you have leprechaun ghosts?"

"Well, if it's a crock of gold that he's after, he's wasting his time haunting me," Corrigan said.

They resumed walking. "So, when you see into people,

what things do you see?" Lilly asked, getting serious again and picking up their earlier subject.

Corrigan thought back to Wilbur, Oliver, and Delia. "Oh, the strange ways they go about trying to get what they want," he replied.

"Such as?"

"Well, if you asked them, I suppose most of them would say that what they want is to be happy, wouldn't you think?"

"Uh-huh."

"A young fella was in earlier. He's pinned everything on a job that he's after, and if you want my opinion it's a scoundrel he'll be working for." Corrigan made a brief, empty-handed gesture. "You see these people chasing after money and success and the like, because those are the things that they think will make them happy. But they're making their happiness depend on what others have the power to give or take away. So don't they become slaves to the people who control those things? And can people who are not free be happy? They cannot. So have such people obtained what they set out for? They have not. They're looking in the wrong places."

They found a pay booth. Corrigan called a local cab company, giving his name and their location. "I see you're not listed with us," the synthesized voice commented. "We have an introductory discount for opening an account tonight."

"No, thanks."

"Can I register you for our bonus-mileage club?"

"No."

"How about the all-in-the-family group scheme? Brand new."

"We'd just like to go home. Is that all right?"

A baffled pause, then, "A cab will be there in five minutes." Corrigan shook his head as the call cleared.

"Are you free, then, Joe?" Lilly asked.

"I'd say so, yes," he replied.

"And why's that?"

He shrugged and gave her a quick, easy grin. "I'm what you might call a self-unmade man. I didn't always do what I do now, you know. It took a lot of effort to work my way down to it. But now I'm free to live according to the things I believe in, and nobody can compel me to think or believe anything I choose not to. So the things I do value, nobody can take away."

"Are all the Irish like that?" Lilly asked. She sounded fascinated.

"Oh, God, not at all. You've never met such a crowd of rogues and villains in your life."

"So how come you're different?"

"Ah, well, I went through some bad experiences a few years back. Maybe that changed some things, if you know what I mean."

Lilly hesitated, obviously wanting to be tactful. But for some reason it seemed important to her. "Things?" she repeated. "What kind of things? Do you mean psychologically?"

Corrigan spotted the cab approaching and stepped forward, raising an arm. "Exactly," he said over his shoulder. "The pieces are coming back together again, but they don't seem to function the way that most people's do."

They climbed in, and Lilly gave the address on North Side. As soon as the door closed, a screen in the rear compartment began running commercials. Corrigan paid an extra dollar to shut it off.

"Being different might not be such a bad thing," Lilly said. "You said you used to work in computers, but you sound more like a philosopher. What kind of a society lets its philosophers end up working in bars?"

"Believe me, there's no better place to learn the subject," Corrigan assured her as the cab pulled away.

Chapter Seven

Lilly lived in a two-bedroom unit in a complex north of the Allegheny Center. It was clean and comfortable, feminine but not cute and lacy, casual without being a mess: all about what Corrigan would have expected. She produced a liter of Californian Chablis to go with the steak sandwiches that they had stopped for on the way.

Now Corrigan was able to give her his full attention for the first time. She was attractive not just physically but in the rarer, more appealing way that comes with the feeling of two minds being in tune. He hoped that his coming back here with her wasn't going to be interpreted as going along with anything more intimate that she might have in mind. The day had been emotionally fatiguing, and he had worked a hectic shift through to the early hours. Enough was enough. If ever there had been a time when a rain check was in order, this was it.

But such fears proved groundless. Lilly was more interested in hearing about his years in computing and the "bad experiences" that he had mentioned which put an end to them. For anyone to ask was a novel experience in itself. So, although the hour had surpassed ungodliness, he refilled the glasses and settled himself back to regard her across the empty plates on the table.

"Is it stuffy in here after the food?" Lilly asked suddenly. "I can't tell. I've got a sinus problem that stops me smelling things."

"It's okay," Corrigan said. "I used to be with one of the big companies here: Cybernetic Logic Corporation—I worked at their corporate research center out at Blawnox. They were big in Artificial Intelligence–based systems. Still are, for that matter. The aim of the AI field had always been true, human-level intelligence, one day. But around the turn of the century, the technology was plateauing out. After some progress and mixed results, there didn't seem to be any obvious way to advance things further."

"Yes, I know CLC," Lilly said. "They've got a building downtown, near Westinghouse."

Corrigan nodded. "Well, about twelve years ago, CLC set up a big research project to try a new way of achieving AI. It might come as a surprise, but I practically invented it." He paused, but Lilly merely returned a stare that could have meant anything. Corrigan went on: "You see, traditionally there had been two approaches to AI: top-down and bottom-up. Top-down meant trying to understand all the complexity of this thing we call 'mind' in sufficient detail to code it into programs." He waved a hand in front of his face. "Forget it. The immensity of the task would make it intractable, even if we knew what to code."

A strange half-smile was playing on Lilly's lips, but in his soliloquizing Corrigan failed to notice. He continued: "The other way, bottom-up, meant trying to create simple neuronlike configurations that could be made to evolve, the same as we did. The problem you run into there is that you don't realize how efficient animal nervous systems are until you try imitating them. You can spend ten years, fifty million dollars, and the best brains in the business putting TV cameras and legs on a computer to make it walk, and the average twelve-month-old will run rings around it—literally. The simple fact is, computers don't interact very well with the real world outside. They haven't had a billion years of evolution optimizing them for it. They operate better on their own, internal worlds."

Lilly nodded, finally, and raised a hand. "It's okay, Joe. You don't have to go on. The project was called Oz—set up under a new CLC division called Xylog, across the river, along Carson Street—yes? The idea was to let an AI evolve by interacting with a virtual world."

Corrigan stared at her in astonishment. "Xylog! That's right. Some of the buildings are still there . . . I don't know what they're used for today. How in heaven would you know about that?"

Instead of answering immediately, Lilly continued, "But Oz was shut down in the preliminary test phase. Before that, were you working on the program that led up to it: a project called EVIE?"

Corrigan shook his head bemusedly. "How in God's name—"

"I've got one more," Lilly said. "Then you'll get your answers. What happened? Why was the Oz project abandoned, and what did it have to do with your winding up in a place like the Camelot?"

It wasn't something that Corrigan normally talked about, especially to people he hardly knew. But these were hardly normal circumstances. "How much do you know about how the interaction was going to be implemented?" he asked, to avoid launching off into needless explanation.

"Enough," Lilly answered. "The idea was that the system would learn by manipulating humanoid animations to emulate real-person surrogates projected in from the outside."

The AI would evolve by controlling artificial characters in a virtual world. As a substitute for the directional thrust of biological evolution, the system would endeavor to shape the behavior of its creations closer to that of surrogate representations of volunteer participants coupled in from the outside. Thus, the virtual world would contain two kinds of inhabitants: humanoid "animations," manipulated by the computer; and "surrogates," controlled by real people, represented as themselves. The test would be to see if the machine could make the behavior of the animations indistinguishable. From her reply, Lilly was aware of all this.

"And am I right in supposing that you know how the surrogates were coupled in?" Corrigan said. "VIV? DIVAC? You've heard of them?" He meant the latest developments at that time in direct-coupled neural I/O, which had appeared on the scene after the earlier VR paraphernalia of head-mounted displays, bodysuits, and so forth. It had come out of work going on at places like Carnegie Mellon and MIT, certain government departments, and Advanced Telecomms at Kyoto, that involved interaction directly with the neural structures of the brain.

"Yes." Lilly nodded.

Corrigan sighed. "But we didn't know as much as we thought we did, Lilly. We were going straight into people's heads—nothing like it had been tried before. And there was too much haste and competitive pressure. We didn't spend the time that we should have to get it right. People started coming unglued with mental disorientation and perceptual disturbances. I was one of them. I've been slowly getting my act back together ever since."

"So was that what ended your first marriage?" Lilly asked.

Corrigan nodded. "Evelyn was a neurophysiologist from Boston who joined the project back in the early days—what you'd call my kind, I suppose. But I was young and brash, too obsessed with my career. Things soured, and when I turned into a vegetable, she opted out. I don't blame her, really. She did well to put up with it as long as she did."

"And the second one—the one who left last night; it wasn't the same with her?" Lilly said.

Corrigan leaned forward to top up their glasses. "Oh, that was a joke from the beginning—not done for what you'd call exactly the most romantic of reasons. My rehabilitation counselor suggested it. She thought it would help to bring a better focus and some stability into my life." He drank from his glass and looked across at her. "Okay, enough of that. Now suppose you tell me how what you seem to know fits with working in a shoe-finishing shop."

Lilly shrugged lightly, as if to say it was all very simple, really. "I used to be with the Space Defense Command up to twelve years ago—OTSC at Inglewood. I was a scientific evaluator involved in the development of DIVAC."

"My God," Corrigan murmured.

SDC's Operational Training & Simulator Center in California was where the final component had come from to make a full-sensory direct-neural interface possible. Up until then, direct-neural I/O coupling had been at the lowermost level of the brain, and research had been confined to the body's motor system. DIVAC, standing for *D*irect *I*nput *Vi*sion & *AC*oustics, besides adding speech and auditory capability, succeeded in entering at a higher level to achieve the long-awaited goal of integrating vision as well.

Some of the surrogates who were to have been projected into the simulation from the real world outside had been supplied by the military. "Were you one of the Air Force volunteers who were brought in?" Corrigan asked. He had met some of them then, but not all.

"Yes," she replied. "I was part of a group from California. A guy called Tyron came out from Pittsburgh and interviewed the candidates. I was one of the ones selected. Later, we were flown to Pittsburgh, checked into a hotel there, and the next morning we were driven to Xylog to begin preliminary tests."

It didn't take too much guesswork to see what was coming. "And? . . ." Corrigan prompted.

"I'm not sure. That's where it all gets vague. The next recollections I have are of being in a world of jigsaw pieces in Mercy Hospital. The shrinks told me that there had been problems that nobody anticipated, and the project was shut down. I was a mental basket case for a long time afterward. . . . And I've just been muddling along and trying to get something of a life back together ever since." Lilly exhaled abruptly and looked at him in a way that asked what was the point of this. "But I don't have to tell you any of this," she said. "That's what happened to you too, isn't it?"

Suddenly, Corrigan sensed what had drawn somebody like this to a bartender. She had known this about him, somehow. That was why she had come back to the Camelot tonight. It was what this whole meeting had been leading up to.

"Can I ask you something?" Lilly said.

"Sure. I'm not promising to answer."

"What do you remember people being like before?"

"Before when?"

"Before Oz. Before you had the breakdown."

"Why?"

"I'd just like to know. It has to do with something I've been thinking about for a while now."

Corrigan considered the question. "It feels like a long time ago," he replied finally. "Like trying to think back over the top to the other side of a hill. . . . But what I *remember* is being more like most other people. You know . . ." he waved his hand to and fro over the tabletop between them, "the way it is with you and me now: being understood without having to spell everything out."

"You could talk about the things you think inside?" Lilly said.

"Exactly."

"Like you and I seem to be able to do. Why should that be so strange, Joe? Are you saying you don't feel that way with people anymore?"

Corrigan was unable to stifle a guffaw. "You've got to be joking! Come on, you've been telling me yourself how it is. You saw that bunch we were among all evening. What is this?"

Lilly didn't react to the frivolity but continued looking at him steadily. "The strange thing is, I remember it all the same way," she said. "Why should that be? How did you explain it to yourself?"

Corrigan did his best to draw together his scattered musings of many years into something coherent. "I suppose, as a process of projection: projecting back out of my head a picture of how I wanted things to be . . . probably subconsciously." That was how the specialists explained it. "By being projected into a past that was no longer accessible, what I wanted became unchallengeable. Hence the fragments of my identity that were coming back together had a basis that was secure. Psychological foundation-building. Does that make sense?"

"It makes too much sense, Joe. Way too much."

Corrigan frowned. "What's that supposed to mean?"

Lilly's face softened into a thin, vaguely despairing smile. It caught Corrigan the wrong way, striking him as condescending and mildly mocking. "Doesn't what you just said strike you—just a little bit, maybe—as incredibly insightful for someone who's supposed to be crazy?" she said.

Supposed to be? What was she saying? Well, true, he didn't believe himself to be crazy, exactly—not anymore; but for the disorientations that he had experienced in the not-so-distant past, it was probably as good a description as any. All the experts that he'd talked to had confirmed that he was a casualty of a massive assault on the neural system. Who was this person to be questioning it now?—even if she had been an Air Force computer scientist once.

"I don't relate to people anymore," he said. "My mind works along different paths, with a lot of short circuits. It makes connections that mean things to me, but which other people don't follow. My own internal virtual reality. That could be getting pretty close to most people's idea of crazy."

Lilly shook her head. "That won't wash, Joe. If those connections were the result of disruptions that *you* experienced, they'd be private and unique—purely subjective. But even if I had been affected similarly, how could it result in the *same* connections?" She gave him a few seconds to object. But he couldn't. What irked him was that she was right. She must have felt this affinity the first time they talked in the Camelot. While he had been camouflaging his abdication from life, she had remained the scientist.

She went on. "You want to know what I think? You've got it the wrong way around. The 'virtual' isn't any aberration that you and I have manufactured inside our heads." She waved an arm in a circular movement to indicate the room, the building outside of it, and everything beyond. "It's all of this." She waited, but Corrigan was still too preoccupied with his internal self-admonishments to register what she was saying. Finally she commented dryly, "You guys did a hell of a job."

Corrigan shook himself out of his fuming and downed a half-glass of wine in a gulp. "What are you talking about?"

"Oz was never abandoned," Lilly said. "It went ahead as scheduled. We're still in it. This whole world full of lunatics that we're in *is the simulation*! It has been for the last twelve years."

Corrigan stared at her with a mixture of dismay and annoyance. Just when he had started to believe that she really was different, and had confided in her things that he'd mentioned to nobody, not Muriel, nor Sarah Bewley . . . now this. It was like hearing a physics Nobel Laureate suddenly start prattling about ESP. He groaned and shook his head.

"Oh, for God's sake. . . . You're being ridiculous."

Lilly was unfazed. "Think about it," she urged. "A lot of things add up. Do you *remember* Oz actually being canceled?" She didn't wait for an answer. "Neither do I. You were *told* that it had been—just like I was. The memories from that period were suppressed and confused by some kind of electronic drugging, and those stories about being incapacitated were fabrications to paper over the join. You were never crazy, and neither was I. It was the *world* that was learning to get better, not us."

Corrigan was already shaking his head. "You don't know what you're talking about," he scoffed. "Memories of what? Oz never reached the full-system phase. All that ever happened was a series of preliminary tests that got abandoned."

Lilly stopped short of looking openly derisive. "How do you *know*?" she pressed.

"How do I know? Because *I* practically conceived the project, that's how." Corrigan pointed a finger. "Who were *you*? A volunteer helper. One of the techs." He knew the gibe was uncalled for, even as he said it. What she was saying ought to have been preposterous; not wanting to face the nagging thought—even now—that it might not be, was making him react unreasonably. "Do you really think that if we'd been in Oz all this time, *I* wouldn't have seen it?"

"Then I'll ask you something else: out of curiosity, how much traveling have you been able to do in the last twelve years? Let me guess: you've been confined to Pittsburgh and maybe one or two other places, right? And another thing: I'll bet that you have problems with smelling things, too. Am I right? The DIVAC interface couldn't handle the first cranial nerve. So couldn't it just—"

Corrigan rose to his feet unconsciously and cut her off with an impatient wave. He was tired and fatigued, and the alcohol wasn't helping. "I don't want to hear this," he groaned. "Will you stop trying to tell me what my own job was about? You don't know anything about it. All we'd designed was a series of tests. The full, integrated-system phase wasn't going to be until much later—if we ever got to it at all. I hadn't put specifications together for a full-world scenario."

"Well, maybe somebody else did," Lilly retorted.

"You're being ridiculous."

"Why? How did the world turn so weird suddenly? What happened to families, people we knew? If this is real, why isn't CLC papered with billion-dollar lawsuits?"

Corrigan scowled and shook his head. "I don't want to listen to any more of this. I think it's time to go."

Lilly sighed and conceded. "Perhaps it is," she agreed coldly. "We can talk about it another time."

"Good night, then."

"Right."

Lilly sat, staring ahead impassively while Corrigan showed himself to the door. He collected his coat and let himself out. The morning air outside was cold. He called a cab and departed back for Oakland without noting the address or the street he was on.

Chapter Eight

The employees at Cybernetic Logic Corporation called it their "museum." Officially it was known as the Interactive Technologies Collection. Housed on the ground floor of the Executive Building of the company's R & D facility at Blawnox, behind the reception area and conveniently close to the visitors' dining room, it formed a fossil record of the evolution of experimental people-to-computer communication through the second half of the twentieth century.

There was a working TX-2, the first transistor-based computer, used by Ivan Sutherland's group at the MIT Lincoln Laboratory in the early sixties to pioneer interactive graphics; "Alto," the first personal computer, which emerged from Xerox's Palo Alto Research Center in the seventies; head-mounted displays, from the early Air Force program at Wright-Patterson, to the flight simulators of the eighties and NASA's experiments at Ames into telerobotics; and a whole range of eye-tracking devices, gloves, bodysuits, and force-feedback hardware from university projects, industrial labs, and government research institutes. Prized most of all was SNARC, Marvin Minsky's original neural network machine from 1951. The "Stochastic Neural Analog Reinforcement Calculator" consisted of three antiquated nineteen-inch cabinets containing over 400 vacuum tubes, with learning capability instilled by means of forty industrial potentiometers driven by magnetic clutches via a pair of bicycle chains. The assembly was lost in the late fifties, only to reappear half a century later in a government surplus supply store in New Orleans. The proprietor said he had thought it was a gunlaying predictor from a World War II battleship.

The young woman standing in an open area of floor in front of a graphics screen was in her late twenties, with fine-boned features, silky, shoulder-length fair hair bordering on platinum, and clear blue eyes. She was a postgraduate in neurodynamic physiology from Harvard and had come to Pittsburgh for a job interview. Her name was Evelyn. Evelyn Vance.

Corrigan made some final adjustments to the collar that she was wearing above the neck of her blouse. It consisted of a lightweight aluminum frame entwined with electrical windings and pickup heads, rising high under the chin like a surgical brace and close-fitting at the base of the skull. The whole assembly rested on padded shoulder supports, and a cable connected it to an electronics cabinet alongside the display unit, where another man was watching the screen as he entered setup commands from a keyboard. He was older than Corrigan, graying, with a ragged mustache, and looking more Evelyn's idea of the old-time engineer, in a tweed jacket with open-neck plaid shirt, and cords. Corrigan had introduced him earlier as Eric Shipley, a senior scientist on the project.

"Did you ever hear of Tempest technology?" Corrigan asked Evelyn. "From the late seventies."

"I was just being born then," she replied.

Just turned thirty, smooth, confident, crisply dressed, Corrigan looked the part of the young, successful, upward-bound executive. The pretty young thing from Massachusetts, nervous, yet excited at the prospect of trading academia's security for the greater opportunities—and hopefully glamour—of the commercial world, was impressed. And he knew it.

"It was a technique that the security agencies developed for tapping in to a data-transmission cable by reading the magnetic field fluctuations around it." He nodded to indicate the collar. "This combines a much more sensitive pickup system with standard front-end neural decoding and a lot of the mathematics from various medical imaging systems. In fact, it was a joint venture between your place and here: Boston and Pittsburgh. MIT and Carnegie Mellon put it all together about three years ago. It's called MIMIC."

"That has to be an acronym for something."

"Miniaturized Motor Intercept Collar. You'll see why in a moment." Corrigan looked over at Shipley. "How are we doing, Eric?"

"Just about there. . . ." Shipley entered a final command, and the silhouette of a human female figure appeared, centered in the screen. "Okay," Shipley said. Evelyn looked at Corrigan questioningly—mainly by moving her eyes, since the collar impeded head movement.

"Move one of your arms," Corrigan directed.

Evelyn raised an arm, and the figure on the screen did the same thing. She raised both arms, then swung them in circles; the figure duplicated the motion. She smiled, enjoying the spectacle. "Hey, I'm impressed," she said, smiling and talking through her teeth.

"You can move about," Corrigan said. "Watch the cable, though."

Evelyn stepped forward, then a pace sideways, cautiously at first; then, getting really into the experience, she laughed and broke into a short routine of dance steps and gestures. The figure on the screen mimicked everything faithfully. "I had no idea it would be so smooth."

Her movements were not being interpreted from TV images, position-detectors in suits, body-mounted light-emitters, or by any of the other familiar methods for encrypting human physical motion directly into computers. Instead, the collar surrounding Evelyn's neck and lower brain stem was picking up the motor output signals on their way down to the spinal cord to direct her musculature system. The same signals were being fed to the programs controlling the figure dancing on the screen—which Shipley had adjusted to superficially resemble Evelyn in shape and body proportions.

Evelyn spent more time experimenting, showing a lot of interest, asking some good questions. The figure's head didn't move, she discovered, since the system only picked up signals on their way down from the brain. It didn't matter very much—she was hardly able to move her own head anyway. As an input interface it was ahead of anything that she had realized existed.

"I'm surprised that it's in your museum already," she

said as Shipley switched off the equipment and Corrigan
helped her remove the collar.

"It's been three years," Corrigan said.

"That still seems soon."

"The accelerating rate of progress. It got overtaken.
We're into a new version now."

"Do I get to see it?"

"Yes, but not here. We'll have to go over to the labs. It
gets better."

They went through an exit at the rear of the building
and followed a path by a lawn between the several other
buildings and parking lots forming the rest of the complex.
The architecture was a mixture of old brick-and-stone and
new concrete-and-glass, standing on the site of a former
steel plant. The ovens and furnaces had gone, but the
serviceable buildings had been restored and converted into
office and laboratory space, and a number of brand-new
facilities erected in the spaces created by the demolitions.

For the past several years, Evelyn had been working as
a researcher at Harvard on noninvasive stimulation of the
visual system. The field was a development from early experiments in the sixties by animal researchers seeking ways
of exciting selected brain centers without the need of surgically implanted electrodes, which tended to interfere with
the processes that they were supposed to measure. The result was a variety of techniques using additive external electric fields, summation of beams of certain electromagnetic
frequencies for which the skull and its underlying cerebral
tissues were found to be transparent, ultrasonic waves and
pulses, and other approaches, all focused upon the common
goal of controlling the firing of selected brain patterns pain-
lessly and without intrusion, from outside the skull.

Collectively the subject was known as "DINS" (DIrect
Neural Stimulation) technology. This was also Shipley's
area of expertise, and he needed another specialist. Hence,
Evelyn took it that, assuming that she was made an offer
and accepted it, she would be working primarily with him
rather than with Corrigan. Nevertheless, Corrigan seemed
to have taken charge of the interview process. Evelyn attributed it to his natural flamboyance and enthusiasm. Shipley
didn't seem to mind, and it added to the image of irrepress-

ible Irish roguishness that Evelyn had begun to form of Corrigan.

They entered one of the older buildings and went up a level and a short distance along a corridor, past a door marked J. M. CORRIGAN, to double doors inset with small glass panes. Inside was a large room cluttered with the paraphernalia of electronics R & D labs anywhere: cabinets and equipment racks draped with tangles of cable, making it difficult to tell which piece of hardware was associated with what; several office desks, littered with books and papers; a wall of metal shelving holding boxes, supplies, unidentifiable gadgets in various stages of assembly or dismemberment; a workbench along one wall, with tools on a pegboard above, soldering irons on stands, more shelves and drawers of electrical components, oscilloscopes and electronic test equipment. A couple of techs in shirts and jeans were working around a rig on the far side; another was wiring up a connector on some kind of assembly stripped down on the bench; a girl was operating a terminal at one of the desks.

Corrigan led the way over to a cluster of racks and cubicles on the far side. A tall, loose-limbed figure with a generous mane of neck-length yellow hair, clad in a loose sweater and tan denims, was sprawled in front of a console. It was a typical lab-lashup, makeshift affair, consisting of several monitor screens, some electronics, and a panel, all fitted in a framework bolted to the body of an old steel desk. He unfolded himself in a lazy, unhurried movement and sat up to greet the arrivals with a grin.

"How are we doing here, Tom?" Corrigan inquired.

"All set."

"This is the group's software supervisor, Tom Hatcher."

"Hi, Tom."

"Tom, this is Evelyn Vance, that I told you about. We've just been across in the museum and seen MIMIC." And to Evelyn: "Now we want to bring you up to date on what we're doing now."

"So you're the lady who's gonna be joining this crazy outfit, eh?" Hatcher had a slow, easy southwestern drawl that went with his manner.

"We'll see what happens, anyway," Evelyn said.

There was another chair, upholstered in black and built upon a tubular steel frame, positioned in front and to one side of the console, where it could be observed by the console operator. It had a collar structure built in front of the headrest, heavier and more intricate than the one that MIMIC used, and hinged into two halves to admit the wearer. Evelyn commented that it looked like a pilot's seat. Shipley confirmed that it was from an Air Force jet.

In front of the chair was a flat metal surface a foot or so square, bounded on the far side by vertical glass plates set at an angle like an opened book. Behind the plates was a collection of shiny tubes and mirrors that Evelyn recognized as the laser and optics of a hologram projector.

"That's your next ride," Corrigan said. "Take a seat."

"You mean I don't get to dance this time?"

"Oh, sure you will. I told you, it gets better."

Shipley held some of the trailing cables aside and beckoned Evelyn toward the chair. "It looks as if I'm going to be electrocuted," she said, stepping forward.

"Medium, rare, or well-done?" Hatcher asked from the console. They all laughed.

The headrest, Evelyn saw as she sat down, was in fact an integral part of the collar unit itself. Corrigan moved over to stand by Hatcher, and they went into a technical exchange about loop gains and parameter settings.

"Where did you get your background in DINS?" she asked Shipley as he closed the collar and began securing connections—partly from curiosity, partly to get him to talk more.

"Oh, I used to be with part of the SDI program—using active optics to precorrect laser beams for transmission distortion." He had a deep, gruff, but not unkindly voice. Corrigan could be fun to have around, but when it came to more serious business, she hoped that she would be working with Shipley. He went on. "That needed fast algorithms to compute complex signal patterns in real time, and the math turned out to be ideal for generating brain-stimulation sequences, too. . . . Now you'll need to hush up so I can position the lateral pads."

The front portion of the collar immobilized her jaw, making this a lot more constraining than MIMIC and fixing her gaze on the holo-projection space above the metal plate.

"Okay, Evelyn, relax," Corrigan said, turning to face her. "You might experience a few funny feelings at first, but don't worry about it. This time we'll also be injecting sensations *into* your neural centers. Your brain won't be able to tell that they're not coming in via the sensory system. But first we have to calibrate to your particular ranges of scale and sensitivity. It only takes a minute."

Suddenly, Evelyn's body went numb from the neck down, as if she had undergone an instant spinal block. Then she felt a pins-and-needles sensation in her arms and legs, especially in the fingertips. When she tried wriggling them, they wouldn't respond. After a few seconds this faded, and more normal feelings returned, but blurred somehow, as if she were suspended in molasses.

Tom Hatcher called across to her from the console. "Feel okay? Blink once for yes, twice for no, three times or make dentist noises in an emergency."

She blinked, and could see the word "Yes" appear in green in a corner of one of Hatcher's screens. Evidently there was an eye tracker operating somewhere. A trained user would be able to communicate a whole vocabulary through eye movements.

"Weird—kinda like an all-around water bed, but okay?" Hatcher asked, checking.

She blinked once.

"Any discomfort?"

She blinked twice. A red "No" on the screen confirmed it.

"Now I want you to close your eyes and imagine that you're standing normally on the ground. Open your eyes when you start to feel heavy, then blink once when it's about right."

Evelyn closed her eyes. An instant later, sensations came over her that were completely at odds with the situation she knew herself to be in. She could *feel* herself standing: feet pressing on the floor, back erect, arms hanging loosely. But too light. She felt precariously anchored, like a balloon just touching the ground, waiting for the first breath of wind to carry her away. But even as she thought it, her weight started to increase. Then she was twenty pounds too heavy, her spine sagging. She opened her eyes abruptly. The heaviness slackened off, reduced slowly . . . and she felt normal. She blinked.

"Close your eyes again," Hatcher called. "Now imagine that you're holding a grapefruit in each hand. Lift them sideways to shoulder height, keeping your arms straight. Open your eyes when they get heavy. Blink once when they feel about right."

The routine went the same as before.

"Now raise both arms straight up over your head—without the grapefruits. . . . Point them straight forward from the shoulders. That's great. . . . Now raise each leg in turn, knee bent, until the thigh is horizontal. Okay. . . . Now keep your eyes closed and try walking a few steps."

It was uncanny. Although Evelyn knew that she was sitting immobile with her head held in a restraint, she could feel herself walking across a floor. A bit lumpily and jerkily, it was true—but *walking*.

"Does it feel quite right?" Hatcher's voice asked. Evelyn opened her eyes and blinked twice. "Tell me which of these corrections feels more normal. This? . . ." The discontinuity got worse, as if her leg were actually coming apart at the knee with each step. "Or this?" The feelings became smoother, almost right now. "Which was better?" Hatcher asked. "The first one?" Two blinks. "The second one?" One blink. After a couple more trials they had it perfect.

"Okay." Corrigan pulled another chair close and sat down where Evelyn could see him. "MIMIC reads muscle-control information directly from the brain," he said. "DINS transmits information into the brain, bypassing the normal sensory apparatus. This is what happens when we combine the two together."

A solid figure appeared in the holo-space, again female, wearing a simple red, loose-fitting dress. Once again, Evelyn could feel herself standing—in the same attitude as the figure, she realized after a second or two. She moved her eyes to look at Corrigan inquiringly. He nodded. She looked back at the holo-figure and made to move her arms. From the corner of her eye she could see that they remained motionless on the armrests of the chair. Instead, the hologram figure moved its arms. But unlike the case with MIMIC, this time Evelyn could actually *feel* it: the weight shifting and pressures in her joints altering as the shoulder and elbow angles changed, the tensions in her muscles—even the light rubbing of the dress material against her skin. Yet she knew that all the time she was sitting unmoving in a chair. It was unbelievable.

"Still feel like a dance?" Corrigan asked, his eyes twinkling. "There's no cable to worry about this time. The motor outputs from your brain are being read as before with MIMIC, but a DINS signal is suppressing the onward transmission of them into the spine—like an externally induced anesthetic. At the same time, the computer is synthesizing the feedback signals that you ought to be experiencing, and injecting them back the other way."

She walked the figure forward, then back, sideways and in circles, finally pirouetting and launching it into a series of twirls and minor acrobatics. At first it was odd to feel the figure's internal dynamics, yet at the same time to be observing it from a viewpoint outside. Corrigan watched, letting her get the hang of it. And then something changed suddenly, like the image of a wire cube reversing: the two bodies of sensation fused, and she was able to project herself inside, compensating unconsciously for the discrepancy in visual space.

Corrigan sensed it. "Managed to make the flip?" he asked. She blinked at him once and forced a parody of a grin.

"Try these," Hatcher's voice said. A flight of steps appeared in the display. Evelyn walked the figure over to them and began climbing. The sensations of her legs lifting and pushing, foot tilting and shifting the weight onto the ball, felt completely real.

"The illusion is totally compelling if you close your eyes," Corrigan said.

She did, and there was no longer any doubt: she *was* climbing a staircase. Already her thighs were starting to ache; and—surely not—she could feel her heartbeat accelerate from the effort, even slight perspiration. She opened her eyes again. They must have looked alarmed.

"Don't worry," Corrigan said. "It's all simulated. You're bone dry and as relaxed as a sleeping baby. . . . So now you can see why MIMIC is in the museum already.

This is its successor. We call it 'Pinocchio.' What do you think?"

The three of them got down to specifics over lunch in the staff dining room at the top of the Executive Building, back at the front of the complex.

"We're looking for more help on the neurophysiology side to go into the next step," Shipley said to Evelyn. He had said little since his few words about his SDI background, over in the IE Block, which Evelyn now knew was dedicated to various aspects of Interactive Environments. Now that they were into Shipley's territory, Corrigan no longer played the lead but was happy to sit back and let him get on with it. Evelyn sensed an easy, informal working relationship between them. She was finding the prospect of becoming a part of it increasingly appealing.

"What is the next step?" she asked.

"Pinocchio Two," Shipley replied. "As things stand, we're limited to the medulla. The system can't handle the Trigeminal and the Abducens. To go further, we want to bring somebody into the team with the kind of background you've had at Harvard—experience of connecting at the pons."

Evelyn thought for a second. "That's why the face and eye movements didn't look right, isn't it?" she said. "I noticed when Tom went to close-up. I pulled a face deliberately, but the holo was still smiling."

Shipley raised an eyebrow at Corrigan. Corrigan nodded that he liked what he was hearing. "You're right," Shipley told Evelyn. "The face is dubbed, purely for effect. The computer fills in what it thinks is appropriate."

They were saying that Pinocchio's combined motor-intercept and DINS interface coupled in at the lowest region of the brain stem, the medulla oblongata, the main railroad of the nervous system, where the seventh through twelfth of the body's twelve cranial nerves terminated. These were the nerves serving the body's voluntary and involuntary motor systems, along with the sense of balance, which was what enabled body movements and sensations to be reproduced in the ways that Evelyn had experienced. (These nerves also handled speech, taste, and hearing, but those faculties were not subjects of the current research.) The remaining functions—jaw and upper-face movements, ocular motion, vision, and smell—were handled by the first to sixth cranial nerves, which synapsed in higher regions of the brain.

In particular, the fifth and sixth cranial nerves, known as the Trigeminal and the Abducens, both synapsed in the next region above the medulla oblongata: the pons. Shipley was saying that they now wanted to extend the coupling level up to the pons. Such a step could be in preparation for only one thing.

"So the eventual intention must be to add vision," Evelyn concluded. That would require going further, to the thalamus, the next region above the pons. "You've already got hearing and speech, potentially, at the medulla—via the Acoustic, Glossopharyngeal, and Vagus. Extend from the pons to the thalamus, and you'll have it all: full-sensory direct-neural."

"Except for olfactory," Shipley said, smiling faintly.

"Oh, yes, of course." Evelyn checked herself. Smell was handled by the first cranial nerve. The most primitive of the senses, it was the only one to enter the brain above the thalamus and go directly into the cerebrum.

"Well, now you know what we're up to here," Corrigan said, sitting back in his chair. He turned an inquiring eye to Shipley. Shipley returned a nod that he was satisfied. Corrigan looked back at Evelyn. "I think we've heard all we want to. To hell with the bureaucratic nonsense—that can catch up later. There's a place here for you if you want it. What do you say?"

After what she had seen, there wasn't a lot for her to think about. But she didn't want to appear too eager.

"What sort of longer-term prospects would we be talking about?" she asked.

Corrigan threw out a hand carelessly. "Unlimited. It could be the beginnings of a whole new research section dedicated to higher-level coupling. You could end up running it."

That seemed good enough. "Confirm the figures in writing," she said. "If there are no surprises . . . Well, yes. . . . I'll take it."

"Splendid." Corrigan looked at Shipley for an endorsement. "Come on, Eric. Congratulate the lady, at least."

"Pinder hasn't confirmed the appointment yet," Shipley reminded him.

"He's the VP of R and D," Corrigan explained to Evelyn. "He's away today. Don't worry about it. It's just a rubber-stamping thing."

Shipley gave her a reassuring nod. "Joe's right. You're just the person we need. I don't think there'll be any problem."

Over the remainder of lunch they talked about lighter things, asking Evelyn about her other interests and swapping personal anecdotes. Then they took her to meet Peter Quell, Pinder's deputy. Apparently, Pinder was with a group visiting the Air Force Space Defense Command in California. Quell stood in for him by delivering some routine corporate messages about CLC being a caring company, and the career opportunities being unlimited for somebody who could fit in, after which they went to Shipley's office and spent a half hour clearing up miscellaneous questions that Evelyn raised. That concluded the business for the moment. While Shipley stayed behind to catch up on what was happening in the lab, Corrigan had a cab called to take Evelyn back to her hotel and walked her back to main reception in the Executive Building. While they were waiting, he talked her into having dinner together that night, before she caught her flight back to Boston the next morning.

Chapter Nine

Corrigan and Evelyn met for dinner in the downtown Vista Hotel, where she was staying. The interview had told him much about her. Now the informal setting gave her an opportunity to satisfy more of her curiosity about him.

"Oh, I'm from a place that I'd be surprised if you've heard of," he told her as they sat in the lounge over drinks, waiting for a table. "On the coast a few miles south of Dublin." He wrote the words "Dun Laoghaire" on a coaster and asked her how she'd pronounce it.

Evelyn shrugged. "Dun Layo-ghe-air?" she tried, sounding it out phonetically.

"It's Dun Leery." Corrigan grinned. "You can always win a dollar bet in a bar with that. The piers there are famous. They enclose what used to be the biggest artificial harbor in the world at one time."

"When was that?"

"Back in the eighteen hundreds. The granite was brought down on a cable railway from a quarry a little farther down the coast. It was driven by gravity. The weight of the loaded cars going down hauled the empties back up."

"Neat."

Corrigan sipped his gin and tonic and nodded. "Great engineers, those Victorians. They made things to last. Big brass knobs on everything—not plastic ones that come off in your hand all the time."

"So how did you end up in computing and things like that?" Evelyn asked.

Corrigan pursed his lips and stroked the tip of his nose

with a knuckle. "Well, now, I was more of a mathematician to begin with—you know, in college. Then I got this, kind of, scholarship thing . . ."

"Never mind the false modesty."

"Good. It doesn't come naturally to an Irishman anyway. I got to Trinity—that's one of the Dublin universities. That got me in touch with the computer scene, and I came over to the States to do postgraduate work on AI."

"They do a lot of that at MIT, up in Boston," Evelyn commented.

"I was there for a while—at the AI lab that Minsky and John McCarthy started. Plus, I did a sabbatical with Thinking Machines there, too. You know them?"

"TMC at Cambridge?" Evelyn nodded. "Sure."

"Then I was at Stanford for some time, and after that Carnegie Mellon, which brought me to Pittsburgh. That was up to a couple of years ago, and then I joined CLC."

Evelyn regarded him for a moment. "Okay, I know you must get asked this a hundred times a week, but when are we actually going to see it—the real thing? Does anyone know?"

Corrigan snorted and made a face. "Ah, they've all got themselves bogged down on semantic issues, if you want my opinion—spending more time arguing over what intelligence is instead of actively doing anything to pursue it. We use the word to mean two different things: the 'survival' kind of intelligence that makes us different from animals, and the 'intellectual' kind that makes some people different from others—or think they are, anyway. The problem is that nobody can make their minds up which one they're talking about."

"Which kind do *you* mean?" Evelyn asked.

"Oh, I got out of the whole thing and left them to it."

"So is that why you're into virtual sensory worlds now, instead?"

"Exactly." Corrigan showed his hands in a gesture of candor. "I'm in a hurry. I plan on going places in this world. There isn't the time to wait for the likes of them to die off or get their act together." It was a calculated brashness, playing off the light in Evelyn's eye.

"Something tells me you'll get there, too," she said. "Is this the male competitive urge that I sense surfacing now?"

Corrigan smiled and shrugged in a way that said she could take it any way she liked. "Ah, well, now . . . Let's just say that Eric can run the caution-and-conservatism department."

"Eric Shipley, you mean? I thought he was a nice guy."

"Oh, don't get me wrong. He's a great guy to work with. Good scientist, knows his stuff. . . ." Corrigan sighed and showed a palm briefly. "But he has his own style, and it's got him where he is."

"He seemed content enough to me," Evelyn said, letting it sound as an objection. She still liked the thought of working with Shipley. Sharing a dig at his expense—even so slight a one as this—didn't feel comfortable.

"*He* is," Corrigan replied.

The hostess came over to tell them that their table was ready, and they went through into the restaurant. Corrigan had already ordered while they were in the lounge, and they began their soup course straight away. When the waiter had left, Evelyn returned to the subject of Shipley.

"Why did it bother him that Jason Pinder wasn't here himself today?" she asked.

Corrigan shrugged unconcernedly. "That's the way Eric is. He seems to think that if Pinder attached as much importance to this job as Eric thinks he should . . ."

"Which job? You mean *my* job?"

"Yes: the one we're talking about . . . then he would have made sure that the interview was fixed for a day when he was here, instead of leaving it to Quell."

All of a sudden Evelyn felt uneasy. "What do you think?" she asked.

Corrigan waved a hand unconcernedly. "Ah, Eric worries too much about underhanded corporate politics—especially where influences are involved that he believes science could do without, such as SDC or anything else connected with the military. He should have lived in the nineteenth century and been one of those gifted, all-around amateurs that you read about."

"It doesn't bother you?" Evelyn said.

"The thought of getting mixed up with the Space Defense people?" Corrigan shook his head. "Not really. Why should it? That's where the money is. It might add some excitement to life. It's like everything else: you deal with the complications as they come."

He grinned. She smiled back. It was what she wanted to hear, and she thought no more about it. Over dinner, Corrigan brought up the possibility of his coming up to Boston to visit her. It was about time he looked up some of his friends there, he said. At the same time, he could show Evelyn some of his old haunts. Evelyn thought it would be a great idea.

At the Space Defense Command's Simulator Center at Inglewood, California, the time was three hours earlier. Jason Pinder and a party of technical and management executives that included the CLC president, Ken Endelmyer, were finishing the VIP tour. They had seen the motion platforms mounting cockpit mockups that even experienced Air Force space pilots reported as being "better than the real thing"; they had played with the telemanipulator helmets and armgloves used to remote-direct spaceborne repair and construction robots from ground and orbital stations thousands of miles away. Now they were in a section of the Visual Environments labs for a demonstration of a device that had been undergoing development and improvement for some time: the Vision & Voice head assembly, known as "VIV." They had heard the presentations, watched the videos, and handled the equipment. Now it was time to lighten things up a little and conclude with some fun.

Don Falker, chief engineer of CLC's Artificial Vision division, stood a short distance apart from the group. He was wearing a lightweight plastic helmet fitting close, like a skullcap, that supported a set of miniaturized vision goggles in front of his eyes and padded earphones. A microchip package in the crown communicated via an IR frequency link to nearby processing equipment. In his hand, he was holding an imitation Ping-Pong paddle made of aluminum, covered front, back, and around the edge in tiny reflecting surfaces. Similarly equipped, standing a few feet away and smiling a little self-consciously, was Therese Loel, head of CLC's Engineering Systems Group.

The man in charge of the proceedings was around forty, lean and tanned, with thinning hair, graying at the temples, and silver-rimmed spectacles. He had a presentation style that was smooth and polished, dynamic in content but coming relaxed and easy, developed over years of dealing with high-level individuals. His name was Frank Tyron, SDC's civilian project manager of the VIV program.

"Hold your other hand horizontal, as if you were about to serve a ball," Tyron called to Falker.

The stereo image being presented inside Falker's goggles showed a nonexistent, computer-generated Ping-Pong table, with Therese Loel transposed so as to be facing him from the far end of it. To everyone watching, Falker simply extended an empty hand palm-up and looked at it. A program analyzing the output from a pair of cameras mounted on the walls tracked the movement, and another program added a Ping-Pong ball to the image that he could see of his hand. Therese Loel saw it appear too, but the view in her goggles showed Falker at the far end of the table.

"Go ahead," Tyron invited, speaking into a mike.

The onlookers watched as Falker tossed the invisible ball up and hit at it with the metal paddle. Sensors around the room tracked the paddle's motion from laser reflections, and the ball in the optical representation followed the computed path.

"Hey!" Therese cried involuntarily, and jumped sideways to play a return stroke.

"I can hear it hitting the bats and the table," Falker said, playing a backhand. "The synchronization is perfect. This is *good*!" Therese returned, but the ball went high.

As state of the art, simulating a Ping-Pong game wasn't especially a revolutionary, or even a new, concept. What was different about this demonstration was the quality. There was nothing crude or cartoonlike about the images that the two players were seeing. The table in front of them and the room around it (actually a stored representation, encoded from videotape, of the games room in the OTSC Recreational Gym in another part of the establishment) were *real*. The figures at far ends *were* Therese Loel and Don Falker, superposed into the scene without the helmets—the missing facial details were added from TV images captured beforehand. Even with a fast forehand smash shot, the images of ball and paddle stayed clean and true: no flicker, no blurring. This hardware was *fast*.

The others couldn't keep from laughing at the two goggled figures lunging and swiping over a table that nobody else could see. Even Ken Endelmyer was smiling between two of his cohorts. What made the spectacle even stranger was that the two players were facing roughly the same way. The images that the computer was creating in the two sets of goggles were correct for the perspectives that each was perceiving.

"It's okay, Don," Tyron called as Falker turned automatically to retrieve the ball from the floor. "You don't have to chase after it. Just serve another."

"Oh, really? Okay." Falker faced the virtual table, raised his left hand again, and—to him—a ball appeared in it. "Say, I've got another one." He played it. "What happens to the first?"

"It evaporates."

Falker and Loel continued their game for a few minutes more, then stopped to allow a couple of the other visitors to try. While the helmets were being taken off and donned, Tyron took a spare unit from a rack by the wall. He turned to address himself particularly to Endelmyer and Pinder.

"We can give you Pinocchio with voice and vision *now*." He made a dismissive gesture, conveying that there really oughtn't to be anything to think about. "The way you're planning to go at present, it will take years at least. Even if you do shift the interface boundary from the medulla to the pons, you're still as far away as ever because visual data enters farther still above that." He patted the helmet resting in his hand and said again, "We can give you it *now*, using technology that already exists, right here. No banking on uncertain future developments. No speculating with unnecessary risks. It doesn't mean that you have to abandon your plans for extending to the pons. But going this way could relieve the time pressure for getting results."

Endelmyer looked inquiringly at Pinder. His expression said that it sounded good to him and he was looking for endorsement. Pinder obliged. "I think it would be worth looking into, Ken. It would give us a mainstream hybrid thrust toward full-sensory now: tactile from Pinocchio, visual and speech/auditory via the regular sensory apparatus, using VIV. The pons research gets relegated to lower-priority status as a secondary approach. It may produce results sooner or later. Either way, we can afford to wait."

It was what Endelmyer wanted to hear. From the things that had been said earlier in the day, it was also clear that Tyron was dangling the prospect of not only a working technology that would advance the project immediately, but of high-level political backing and generous additional funding too. It was also a good psychological ploy aimed at Endelmyer, who, Tyron knew—having done his homework as any good salesman would have—had hankerings for rubbing shoulders on the Washington circuit.

The meeting broke up on a promising note, with individuals from both sides gravitating into chatty groups. Endelmyer drew Pinder and Tyron to one side, along with a man called Harry Morgen, Tyron's right-hand man. "Personally I'm satisfied," he told them. "You've done an impressive job today, Mr. Tyron. Although I cannot give you a definite response today, you may take it that I will be reporting back to the CLC Board in an extremely positive light. Thank everyone who has been involved, from all of us, for their efforts."

Chapter Ten

Dun Laoghaire, the town that Corrigan was originally from, means, in Irish, "Laoghaire's Fort." It is generally assumed by historians that a fort once existed there, belonging to King Laoghaire of the fifth century, whose principal abode was at Tara, about thirty-five miles away. In more recent times it grew in less than a century from an insignificant fishing village to a major port and Victorian resort town. Its lifestyle in that era characterized the Dublin professional class: merchants, bankers, ex–army and –navy officers and others of the well-to-do, who flocked to live in its handsome terraces by the sea, yet within easy rail distance of the city.

The more scholarly of the town's progeny went, traditionally, into the arts, humanities, and literature. It was not noted for its contributions to the sciences or cutting-edge technologies, and this made it all the more remarkable to Joe Corrigan's relatives and friends when he walked away with every honor in mathematical computing at Trinity and took off across the Atlantic to do the rounds of the AI labs at MIT, Stanford, Carnegie Mellon, and other unheard-of places.

He had taken to the U.S. scene as if it were his natural element. After a land less than half the size of Florida, the vastness of the country seemed to mirror the scale of everything he found around him. It wasn't just that the buildings were taller than the repatched and replastered Georgian frontages of Merrion Square and Leeson Street, the avenues wider, the stores grander than Dunnes or Clery's, the cars longer, and the hamburgers huger. It had to do with ambition and opportunity, also. After the venerable but crowded surroundings that he was used to working in, the promise and lavishness of scale of American research was breathtaking. Imagination raced unchecked. Funding was unlimited. In two years he had become highly visible in the part of the academic computer world associated with intelligence modeling, and those who were supposed to know about such things listed his name among the front-runners that they expected to see heading the field in ten years' time. Corrigan, however, still intoxicated by the combination of early, practically effortless, success and his newfound continental-size lifestyle, succumbed easily when the talent scouts from CLC made approaches to recruit him.

That had been two years ago, when he was still only twenty-eight. Since then, his project management and personal technical contribution had put the development of Pinocchio a year ahead of its original schedule, further strengthening his reputation, and with the way ahead open for his rise into senior management, his self-confidence was at its peak.

This was the moment that Evelyn had chosen to appear, combining all the attributes of physical attractiveness, intelligence, professional presence, and social acceptability that would be required of the one accessory still missing from his life. Maybe it was an unconscious recognition of this that led him to react to her with a seriousness that had been singularly absent from the various female encounters that had dotted his career path until then. Perhaps it was an echo of some primeval male impulse to stake out his territory before potential rivals had a chance to appear. Possibly it was the part of his nature that scoffed at caution and enjoyed the mild impropriety of the situation. More likely, a combination of all three. But four days after Evelyn's interview, he found himself deplaning from a Delta Airlines evening flight at Boston's Logan Airport, and took a cab to the Hyatt Hotel, where he had made a reservation for the night, overlooking the bank of the Charles River.

Evelyn had arranged to take the next day off, and she collected him after breakfast the next morning. She was pleased to see him, even if somewhat awed at his having made the time; she was nervous that she might be misreading more into things than reality warranted, then relieved when he seemed to show as much enthusiasm as she felt.

They went first to the AI Laboratory at MIT and visited some of Corrigan's former colleagues from his first years in the States. His postdoctoral work at that time had been on the emerging subject of "psychotectonics": unraveling the roles and dynamics of the sometimes competing, sometimes cooperating hierarchies of functional agencies that make up the phenomenon called "mind." Although it was Corrigan's work here on the simulation of evolving neural networks that had earned him his initial recognition, he had moved later, as he had told Evelyn when she was in Pittsburgh, to join Carnegie Mellon's group working on "Trunk Motor Intercept" technology, which eventually produced MIMIC.

The aim of one project that he showed her at MIT was to expand a machine intelligence's everyday world-knowledge by getting it to solve detective mysteries. In another, devoted to speech interpretation, they watched a computer creating a cartoon on the fly in response to a narrative being read by Evelyn. On the floor below, a supercomputer from Thinking Machines Corporation in nearby Cambridge was generating admittedly not very good critiques of literature texts. Finally, in yet another room filled with screens, racks, and tangles of cable, Corrigan introduced the department head, Jenny Leddel. She was graying, entering middle age, and wearing a woolen cardigan with a tweed skirt.

"This is Evelyn, from Harvard, who I told you about on the phone," he said. "She's going to be joining us down in Pittsburgh."

"Stealing our talent now, eh?" Jenny said, nodding knowingly. Her eyes sparkled with a mischievous light, young for her years. "It figures."

"It hasn't been confirmed yet, Joe," Evelyn reminded him.

"Ah, don't be worrying yourself about that at all."

"How are things going with Pinocchio down there?" Jenny asked Corrigan. "I've been following the reports. It sounds exciting."

"Going well. We'll have to get you down there sometime to see for yourself," he said.

"I'd like that."

"We're all set for P-Two: going up to the pons. That's what Evelyn will be working on."

"You achieved a full two-way integration, yes?"

"DINS with MIMIC. We've had it running for about three months now."

"Complete internal haptics?"

"Total. It works. Uncanny. Evelyn tried it a few days ago."

"What about the secondary instabilities that Goodman's people at Chapel Hill kept running into? You didn't have a problem with them?"

"Our DINS expert came up with a C-mode suppression filter that cured it. A character called Eric Shipley. Do you know him?"

"I'm afraid I don't."

"He's good—the old-school type. Infuriatingly plodding at times, but he gets it right in the end."

"We could use a few like that here," Jenny said. "Too many these days trying to fly before they've grown feathers." She gave Corrigan a pointed look as she said this, but he missed it. Jenny didn't make an issue of it, but turned to Evelyn. "Anyhow, enough of that. We're ignoring you. Joe says you want to talk to Perseus."

"Sure. If he wants to talk to me."

This was the latest to come out of the learning systems based on goal-directed, self-adaptive, neural-net analogs that Corrigan had worked on during his time with MIT: systems that experimented with problem-solving strategies. They devised new variations of what seemed to work best, and forgot about what didn't—the process known in nature as "evolution." An ideal strategy-testing environment—full of clearly defined challenges and yielding easily measured results—was the classical dragons-and-dungeons type of adventure world. Perseus, accordingly, was a computer-created character who explored such mythical realms, with similar goals to achieve and obstacles to be overcome. Half of AI research, it seemed, was wrestling with the problem of trying to impart world-knowledge.

Jenny tapped commands into a console to activate the system. A simplified image appeared on a screen of a typical D & D setting of a large room, assorted objects, with passages, stairways, and tunnels going off in various directions.

"What does Perseus stand for?" Evelyn asked.

Jenny shrugged. "Nothing. It's just the name of a guy from Greek mythology who killed monsters and solved problems. We thought it was appropriate."

Evelyn looked relieved. "I thought everything had to be an acronym."

"I guess we got tired of them." Jenny entered another code. "And here he is." A caricature figure had appeared in the room, lightly clad in ancient-hero style, carrying a sheathed sword and wearing a helmet.

Jenny tapped a key, and an icon showing an ear appeared at the top of the screen. "Hello, Perseus. How's it going?" she asked.

"I haven't found a way through the Misty Room," a voice replied from a speaker above the screen. It sounded quite human. This project evidently embodied some sophisticated language processing too. "It becomes pitch black, whichever way I go, and I lose direction. But the inscription on the wall in the cavern mentioned 'rays that cut through the mists.' It suggests that there might be a special kind of light, or lamp, somewhere."

"This has got better since the last time I saw it," Corrigan murmured.

The figure on the screen looked up and around. "Who else is speaking?" its voice asked.

Jenny touched a key and the icon vanished. "Watch for the ear," she said. "He can hear us while it's showing." She brought the icon back again. "Just some friends. They don't affect you. What's new?"

"After some reflection on the matter, it occurred to me that the implement I found in the Burial Chamber was of just the correct shape and size for making holes in the ground. So I decided to dig around where the earth appeared to have been disturbed. And I found this." Another screen showed a close-up of Perseus's schematicized hands, holding an oil lamp of old, Oriental design.

Any five-year-old would have known what to do instantly. Perseus, however, seemed mystified, turning the lamp over and contemplating it. "There are no obvious buttons or switches. It seems built to contain liquid, but it is empty. Its use escapes me."

Corrigan couldn't bear to look, but turned his head

away, muttering inaudibly, "Rub the lamp. Rub the lamp."
Jenny gave a thin smile and shrugged.

Evelyn motioned to herself, then at the screen, asking
through gestures if it would be all right for her to speak.
Jenny nodded and mouthed, "Sure."

Evelyn stared with a strange, not-wanting-to-believe-
this fascination for a few seconds at the figure on the screen,
now returned to fumbling with the lamp.

"Perseus," she said.

The figure stopped what it was doing. "Is this another
friend?"

"Yes. . . . Can I ask you a question?"

"I assume so, since you just did."

"I meant a different question."

"Why should you be unable to ask a different one?"

Evelyn frowned, then saw the problem. "No, I didn't
mean 'can' in the sense of 'able to.' I meant would you
mind?"

There was a pause, then, puzzled, "How should I
mind?"

Jenny flipped the ear icon off for a moment. "His con-
ceptual world is limited to exploring the physical environment. Implied permissions belong to a dimension of
relationships that he can't comprehend. Don't project too
much into the illusion."

But that was the trouble. For Evelyn, the illusion was
too convincing. She couldn't avoid the conviction that she
was listening to a real person speaking from a real place.
Somehow, the sight of the visually simple, cartoonlike form,
clashing as it did with the capacity for experience that she
found herself perceiving, produced uncomfortable feelings
that she didn't want to think about. Yet some macabre curiosity compelled her to probe deeper.

"When we talk to you, who do you think we are?" she
asked Perseus.

"Friends," he replied.

"Are we the same as you?"

"Obviously not."

"What makes you say that?"

"I can't see you. You don't appear, like all the other
beings that I meet."

"But we must exist somewhere. Isn't that true?"

"Jenny and others have asked me this before. I assume that you must exist outside somewhere."

Evelyn's discomfort increased. This was now positively disturbing. "Outside of what?" she persisted.

"Here. The caves." Perseus carried on into an explanation that must have gone back to some earlier occasion. "All things must end. Therefore, the place that I am in must end at a boundary. So beyond the boundary there must be an 'outside.' Perhaps my quest is to find the boundary and reach the outside. I do not know this for certain."

"Did *he* figure that out himself?" Evelyn whispered. Jenny looked across at her and read the expression on her face.

"It's getting to you, isn't it," she said understandingly. "It's okay. Don't worry. A lot of people are affected like that. Maybe that's enough for the first time." She killed the screen.

Evelyn was still not at ease. "Is he still active in there, while the screen's off? Or does he go into a suspended state until you switch it on again?" she asked.

"It's just an illusion," Jenny said. She looked at Corrigan. "Shouldn't you be getting along, anyhow? Didn't you say something about wanting to catch Marvin before he leaves?"

They met Minsky in a staff cafeteria on the second floor, where he was grabbing coffee and a sandwich before dashing off to keep an appointment elsewhere on the campus. Tall, smooth-domed, continually observing the world through thick-rimmed spectacles but never quite able to take it seriously in its entirety, he was one of the lab's original founders. Corrigan had known him sporadically in his time at MIT and was pleased that their schedules had enabled a meeting during this quick visit.

Minsky, it turned out, had returned from Ireland himself recently, where he had been partly vacationing and partly checking the state of contemporary computing developments at Trinity and University colleges. His experiences from a drive north to Ulster, where trouble was still going on with the British administration, had left him less than impressed, however.

"Why are they still fighting each other up there?" he grumbled to Corrigan. "Why don't they study mathematics, or something else that would give them better things to do?"

"Oh, that's nothing to do with us," Corrigan replied. "It's another country up there. I'm from the Republic, remember."

Minsky pulled a face. "I'm not sure I noticed much of a difference. Down there, if you're an American and don't know the price of anything, you're fair game."

"The lads have to make a living," Corrigan said unapologetically, refusing to be provoked.

"You mean it isn't true, what the song says?" Evelyn put in. " 'When Irish eyes are smiling . . .'?"

"You've probably been ripped off," Minsky completed with a snort. Corrigan laughed. Minsky glanced at his watch. "Anyway, I have to dash in a few minutes. So I gather you've been to see Jenny Leddel."

"Perseus is coming along nicely," Corrigan said. "Evelyn got a bit spooked, though."

"There was something eerie about it." She shivered and shook her head.

Minsky smiled. "Yes. It gets a lot of people like that. It makes them wonder if we're inside someone else's AI experiment in the same kind of way."

"That's exactly what I *was* thinking," Evelyn said, astonished. Minsky's smile widened.

"The approach seems to be working," Corrigan observed. He glanced at Evelyn. "Setting it up with the potential to learn, and then letting it interact with an environment."

"Jenny should have let Perseus start out as more of an infant," Minsky commented. "There are still too many defined attributes. Instead of telling him what a sword is for, let him wave one about and hit things with it, and find out for himself. That way, he might even discover things that programmers never think to include—such as, that they make good back-scratchers."

Corrigan related the episode of Perseus and the lamp. Minsky nodded emphatically.

"Which makes my point. He should have been allowed to read picture books and fairy tales. Then he would have been familiar with genies and known what to do."

Evelyn was about to ask if he meant literally exposing a computer to the processes that a child goes through, say, by equipping it with appendages of some kind to manipulate things, but Minsky preempted her. Corrigan was used to his sometimes disorienting habit of getting people out of step in a conversation by answering questions before they were asked.

"Computers aren't very good at interfacing with the real world and extracting the information they need. We have the advantage of this enormous knowledge-base that we call 'common sense,' which enables us to make subtle, context-based connections. That's what makes people so good at things like comprehending metaphors: we're wired to see quickly what matters and what doesn't. Recognizing faces is another good example." He waved a hand as he collected together the paper plate, coffee cup, and remains of his sandwich. "Computers are better at tasks that don't require any deep familiarity with what's out there—ones that can be dealt with in relative isolation, algorithmically."

"Computers interact better with other computers," Evelyn said.

"Yes. Quite." Minsky nodded. "So what you do is plug your infant into another computer that's pretending to be a world. But getting a virtual world to be real enough is another matter."

Corrigan clapped his hands as if that was a cue that he had been waiting for. "And *that's* why we're doing what we're doing at CLC in the meantime," he told Evelyn. "Learning how to make better virtual worlds. So now you can see where the work you'll be doing fits in. Believe me, it's going to be a lot of fun."

"Promise?" she said teasingly.

Corrigan spread his hands in appeal and turned toward Minsky. "Look. Aren't the Irish eyes smiling?"

"You're going to be ripped off," Minsky said to Evelyn, shrugging.

But Eric Shipley was in a far-from-fun mood when Corrigan got back to Pittsburgh the next day. "Pinder has been having visitors from California and D.C." he told Corrigan.

"Space Defense Command, and DOD. High-level stuff. Something's in the wind. I don't like the feel of it."

Corrigan remained unperturbed. "Politics and science are inseparable these days, Eric. You've got to move with the times. This could be an impending moment of opportunity."

"Well, we'll find out soon enough," Shipley replied. "Pinder has called a major meeting to review progress and plans for the whole Pinocchio program. Tomorrow morning in town, nine o'clock sharp."

Chapter Eleven

Jason Pinder opened the meeting, which was held in one of the conference rooms in the corporate headquarters building on First Avenue. He was slight and wiry in build, and with his short, straight, sandy hair, clipped mustache, and invariable habit of dressing in conventional suits of gray, tan, or brown, had always put Corrigan in mind of a retired British army officer or a schoolmaster. But the mild gray eyes turned out to be a deceptive front for a mind as compulsively restless as a computer's registers, ceaselessly analyzing, shuffling, and sorting in search of better options. Not that this came as any great surprise. Anyone who had made it to the upper ranks of a leading-edge company like CLC could be assumed to possess the requisite qualities.

Next to him, crisp and businesslike in a black suit and snowy shirt, was the swarthy, curly-haired figure of John Velucci, executive director of CLC's Legal Department. "Tell me why he's here," Shipley muttered to Corrigan as they sat down. "Want to know what I think? Whatever this is all about has already been decided. The meeting is to tell us the way it is."

"You're too suspicious, you know, Eric," Corrigan answered. But the words were automatic. For once, even Corrigan's manner was curious and restrained.

Also present from CLC were Pinder's deputy, Peter Quell; Tom Hatcher, Corrigan's software supervisor on the Pinocchio program; and a hardware wizard called Barry Neinst. Neinst was described on the organizational charts as responsible for "Advanced Processing," and appeared on the bar of loosely affiliated names, connecting vertically to Pinder's, that was tagged collectively "Direct Neural Coupling." What this really meant was obscure, and in practice he led a somewhat nomadic existence, wandering between Shipley's DINS section, the MIMIC/Pinocchio group headed by Corrigan, and a collection of graphics specialists known as "Interactive Imagery." This latter group was represented by Ivy Dupale, a short, bouncy, frizzy-haired brunette who had been put in charge as a temporary measure eighteen months previously, and the situation was never regularized or revised.

There were four people from the Space Defense Command's Operations Training & Simulator Center at Inglewood: Henry Wernheim, solid, craggy, with silver, wavy hair and steely eyes, the director; Frank Tyron, lean, tanned, and bespectacled, project manager of the VIV program *(VI*sion & *V*oice head-mounted assembly); and two of his technical support people: Joan Sutton and Harry Morgen.

After making the introductions, Pinder opened, addressing himself principally to the side of the table where the CLC people were sitting.

"I don't have to tell you that the field we're in is an exciting one, and one that is crucial to some of the most important developments going on in the world today. That includes the public and private space programs that are currently coming together here, across in Europe, and in Japan." He paused, allowing a suitably serious note to assert itself. "Hence, we can expect a lot of competition worldwide, both in terms of the funding being made available, and of the caliber of talent that we'll be up against. And, indeed, we see a lot of that happening already. What it means is that we're going to have to work extra hard and move fast just to stay in the same relative place. What it means even more is that we at CLC are going to need, and will appreciate, all the help we can get." He glanced along the other side of the table to indicate the visitors. "I am pleased to be able to inform you that, as a result of recent negotiations, we now have an opportunity to benefit from some very substantial help indeed, from a solid, trustworthy direction."

"Here it comes," Shipley murmured by Corrigan's side. "That was the sugarcoating."

"But he could be right."

On Corrigan's other side, Tom Hatcher and Ivy Dupale exchanged what-do-you-think looks. Just at that moment, neither of them seemed to be especially thinking anything. Beyond them Barry Neinst remained semi-oblivious in a world of his own, probably involving parallel arrays and pipeline architectures.

Pinder continued, "Over the last few weeks, Ken Endelmyer has had us going through some hard numbers, reviewing the progress and future prospects for Pinocchio. As you all know, the tentative plan has been to proceed to Pinocchio Two, or 'Son of Pinocchio,' as it has come to be known informally: extension of DNC into the pons, plus the addition of speech and acoustics." Shipley nudged Corrigan softly with his elbow. The word "tentative" had never been used previously. For the past year at least, Pinocchio Two had been firm.

Pinder glanced around briefly. "The problem with it, however, is the long lead time that we're talking about: two to three years by the best estimates, which puts us into 2009–2010. And vision would come even later, assuming further extension to the thalamus." He looked at Corrigan and raised a hand, lightening the moment by making as if he expected Corrigan to protest. "Okay, Joe, I know you worked a miracle in getting Pinocchio One up a year ahead of schedule. But that's not an experience the corporation can bet on happening every time."

His voice reverted to its more serious note. "So the company has decided to add a second string to our bow that will reduce the risk of being left with nothing on the international scene three years from now. What we're going to do, instead of relying on Pinocchio Two totally, is initiate a program to run in parallel that will add vision and acoustics now, as a hybrid system. That will give us experience of operating with vision sooner rather than later. Also, we're guaranteed something to show, farther down the line." He looked around to invite comments.

"How do you mean, hybrid?" Hatcher asked. There was only one plausible way. "With DNC tactile into the medulla, and using the regular sensory apparatus for vision and voice?"

Pinder nodded. "Just that. Combine the Pinocchio One

interface with the VIV system that SDC has produced. It's perfect for the job. Frank Tyron here is the project manager of the team that developed it. The Space Defense Command has a lot of interest in the outcome too, which means that the ground is all prepared for some good cooperation. They're eager to get started. So, I'm sure, are all of us. We've even got a project designation: EVIE. Extended Virtual Interactive Environment."

There was some shifting and shuffling on the CLC side of the table. The SDC people waited calmly, giving the impression that they had known more about all this to begin with.

"Where will this alternative line be located?" Corrigan asked finally. "Here? In California? A bit at each? What?"

"We've talked about that," Pinder replied. "It would fragment things too much to have it spread out. VIV development is complete, so there isn't much reason to have any of this in California. So it looks like it'll be right here, in Pittsburgh. Frank has agreed to relocate here for the duration, and will head up a liaison group from SDC to supervise VIV integration."

"It will stay under CLC's control, then?" Corrigan said.

"Oh, no question." Pinder nodded reassuringly.

Shipley, however, was less sanguine. "What about the plans for expanding neurophysiology?" he asked. "How will they be affected? Are we still going to hire Evelyn Vance from Harvard?"

"Of course," Pinder answered. "Nothing's changed. As I said, Pinocchio Two will carry on in parallel. The difference now is that it can be run without the pressure to produce results to order—the way research ought to be."

Shipley detected something devious nevertheless. "So where will she fit in?" he asked. The intention had been that Evelyn would join DINS initially, with the possibility of later moving to a yet-to-be-established autonomous neurophysiology section. That was the group that Corrigan had hinted she might end up heading.

Pinder showed his hands. "Well, naturally we've had to reexamine some things to accommodate the new opportunities." So something *had* changed. "EVIE will consist of wedding VIV to Pinocchio One, which will require Frank's people and Joe's. Pinocchio Two, which is what Evelyn Vance is being brought in for, will be an extension of it. Therefore, it seems to me, she ought to start out as part of that general group, rather than with DINS. You'll be busy enough dividing your time between both teams anyhow, Eric, without taking on more at this stage."

So there it was: Shipley would not be getting Evelyn as he had been led to believe. He didn't seem especially surprised. The rest of the meeting passed with a more detailed airing of goals, aims, and first guesses for completion dates.

When they talked it over in the lab afterward, Shipley was less stoic than he had appeared earlier. "I've felt this kind of atmosphere before," he told Corrigan. "It's the first step to politicizing the territory. This started out as a line of pure research. Now the science is going to take a back seat."

"Ah, come on, now, Eric, and admit that you're just sore about Evelyn being switched out of DINS," Corrigan said. "I think it was a bit mean too, if you want to know the truth, but I'm guessing that Jason had his orders."

"Hell, you know I'm not interested in those kinds of games," Shipley told him. "But I think you should watch out. Tyron has got 'political animal' stamped all over him. Didn't it strike you as significant that with all these changes, there still isn't a clearly defined slot heading up DNC? It's still as vague a mess as it was before."

Corrigan shook his head. "You've got it the wrong way around, Eric. Think about it. This will allow some sound consolidation on Pinocchio Two—the chance to do it right. You've got to agree that this hybrid idea is a bit of a mishmash. I mean, in the long term where can it lead? When P-Two expands to take in vision, what's left for the hybrid? Then, I'm a-thinking, it will be Frank-me-boy who'll be finding himself with nowhere to go."

Shipley remained unmoved by Corrigan's confident optimism. "We'll see," he replied neutrally.

Chapter Twelve

Evelyn's position was confirmed, and a month later she moved from Boston to a rented apartment that Ivy Dupale helped her find in Aspinall, on the north bank of the Allegheny River. One of the better-preserved older districts of quaint streets with traditional stores and houses, it suited Evelyn's taste and was conveniently close to Blawnox.

Evelyn soon became good friends with Ivy, and she and Corrigan continued seeing each other out of working hours. They were well matched to each other's needs. He, on his way up and all set to fly, had an appreciative and willing admirer; she, the emerged fledgling, found a guide and protector. They sampled the restaurants, from the best French at Cafe Allegro on the Southside heights overlooking the Monongahela River, to the traditionally romantic, old-stone-built Hyeholde, set in a wooded estate out near the old airport. They toured the bars, took in the zoo, the theaters, and did the round of Pittsburgh's museums. Some weekends they spent at his place, some at hers.

Tyron and his group from SDC installed themselves in space provided at Blawnox, and work commenced on the initial phases of EVIE. The new, more comprehensive interface warranted going for a greater degree of realism than had been justified with MIMIC. Accordingly, Ivy Dupale's graphics group were given the go-ahead to enhance Pinocchio with an upgrade that had been in abeyance for some time: the addition of "Personal Attribute Files."

The hologram figure generated by Pinocchio was not a representation of anyone in particular, but simply a generic human form with rudimentary features and attire. The PAFs were lists of data descriptors specifying the features and physical appearance, build, and dress of an actual person: Corrigan, say, or anyone else on the research team. An individual's PAF could be superposed on the generic Pinocchio form to create a lifelike miniature of whoever was coupled into the system at a given time—or, just for the fun of it, of anyone else whose file was in the system. Having one's PAF compiled and filed for Pinocchio became something of a fad around the company, and most of the senior executives managed to find some pretext for stopping by to see their analogs cavorting in various simulated environments.

Then, one day, Therese Loel of the Engineering Systems Group, who had been one of the party that visited SDC in California, approached Pinder with a request. ESG was the "specials" part of Pinder's domain: a facility within the R & D division for designing and building customer-specified systems to order. In this it came halfway between one of CLC's regular manufacturing divisions, who made and sold standard products, and R & D proper, which was funded either internally or under specific research agreements contracted outside. Therese had talked briefly about EVIE to some of her acquaintances at Feller & Faber, a major international client of ESG's based in New York and involved in prestige marketing. CLC had supplied a package of AI-based learning software to track and predict market trends, which had proved quite successful; now, some people at Feller & Faber wanted to learn more about this new development and where it might be pointing. Could Pinder arrange for someone who knew more about the subject than she did to accompany ESG's sales personnel on a visit to the customer and give them an overview?

Pinder was keen to spread the word about the new venture, and agreed. There were really only three people who knew enough about both the Pinocchio and VIV aspects that together composed EVIE: Corrigan, Eric Shipley, and Frank Tyron. However, Shipley's disinterest in anything connected with selling or publicity was notorious, which ruled him out. Tyron was fully committed, and in any case could hardly be used to promote CLC's private interests since he was not an employee. And that left only one. Accordingly, Pinder called Corrigan over to his office, filled him in on the situation, and told him to get in touch with the ESG sales executive assigned to the account, Henry Glinberg, who would make the arrangements.

They caught an early-morning flight up to La Guardia a week or so later. Having prepared himself for worse, Corrigan found Glinberg to be lively and alert, personable and appealing—the kind of salesman who made people feel important by listening, even when nothing they said was the slightest bit interesting. He didn't contradict, disagree, or antagonize with unasked-for opinions—preferring to win sales rather than arguments. And he dressed and groomed himself well but not flashily: enough to make a person feel respected by being worth the effort; not so much as to make them feel cheap. His company came as a stimulating change from the tech-intellectual surroundings that Corrigan had grown used to, and after an hour Corrigan could cheerfully have bought a lifetime's insurance, a new car, or anything else from him—and then done all his friends a favor by recommending their names too. It seemed to be generally considered a social virtue for somebody to be "easy to talk to"; "easy to be around"; "easy to get along with." Corrigan could recall countless occasions, from buying an airline ticket to making a hotel reservation, when he'd practically had to battle with a company's employees to be allowed to spend his money with them. Why, he wondered, was it so difficult to be "easy to buy from"?

From the airport they caught a cab to CLC's Manhattan branch office near Lincoln Center, where they met up with Mat Hamils, sales manager for the New York City area. Feller & Faber was his customer, and he would be taking them there—Glinberg was a Pittsburgh-based ESG specialist who supported customers throughout the Northeast. Before leaving to go crosstown, they reviewed the situation over coffee in a meeting room adjacent to Hamils's office.

"So in terms of spectaculars, you're saying that EVIE will bring everything together sooner—touch, vision, talk, the works," Hamils concluded. Clearly, he was thinking ahead and had customer demonstrations in mind.

"Yes," Corrigan said.

"But it's hybrid, not full direct-neural," Glinberg reminded Hamils. He looked back at Corrigan. "Pinocchio Two will be all-neural, though—right, Joe?"

"Sounds better," Hamils commented, nodding.

"But it just adds speech and hearing to the existing motor I/O," Corrigan said. "Vision won't be until later."

Glinberg frowned. "I thought you said something on the plane about a new section being organized to move the interfacing up from the medulla to the pons."

"Yes, but for vision you have to go in at the thalamus. That's another level higher yet."

"Oh." Hamils nodded that that was something they'd just have to accept. "Okay. So when will it happen?"

"It isn't scheduled at present," Corrigan replied, conscious as he said it of sounding negative. Hamils shot Glinberg a glance that said he couldn't see this as a star attraction for getting prospective customers excited.

There was a short silence. Then Glinberg clapped Corrigan lightly on the shoulder. "But doing it right takes time, eh, Joe? P-Two will be better in the end."

Corrigan acknowledged with a faint grin. "Right," he agreed.

Hamils looked at his watch. "We'd better be moving," he announced. They drank up, collected briefcases and things, and headed for the elevator.

"Do you get to see many customers, Joe?" Hamils inquired casually as they got in.

"Not really."

"The main person we're going to see today is a guy called Victor Borth. He's general manager of F and F's New York office, and a working director of the firm. A very influential person."

"I see."

"Sometimes there's politics involved in these situations," Hamils went on. "Just stick to answering questions, and keep it technical. We'll let you know when. Okay?"

"Sure," Corrigan said.

It was only when they were in the car and heading toward the East Side that it dawned on him that people who knew too much were considered a potential menace—he had been tactfully told where his place was.

*　　*　　*

The offices of Feller & Faber occupied four floors of a soaring face of copper-tinted glass in midtown. The visitors were conducted from the elevators through a reception lobby of rust-gold velour furnishings, ceramic and chrome, and art noveau prints, into corridors flanked by designer-decor office spaces and computer displays glowing in glass-partitioned rooms.

They had arrived early to let Hamils take care of some routine matters before the main meeting, and Corrigan found himself tagging along on a quick tour. Somebody from F & F was due to attend a trade exhibition in Russia, and there was talk about a joint promotional effort involving CLC marketing people from Pittsburgh. A man called Gary had a problem with a service invoice. Pat wanted advance information from CLC engineering on a new line of image analyzers not in production yet. Could Sandra in the Manhattan office get two more sets of manuals on the stock-forecasting package? The proposal to Mercantile Bankers in London was looking good, and there should be a decision next week.

After the racks and cubicles, scratched metal desks, and tiled vinyl floors of the environment that Corrigan was used to, it all seemed very glamorous and exciting—a glimpse of the real world, where the events that shaped the news were made to happen. In comparison, the world that he was from looked woefully pedestrian and academic—a behind-the-scenes support facility to serve this, the stage.

Finally, they came to a sumptuous corner office looking out over Manhattan in two directions. It had deep russet pile, integral mahogany shelves and fittings, and framed travelogue scenes looking down over a conference area set off around a circular, glass-topped table. From the immense desks with computer side-tables and recessed consoles, the office was evidently shared by two people. One of the desks was unoccupied. From the other, a man of about Corrigan's age rose to greet them, smiling genially. He had a trim, athletic build with collar-length yellow hair, and looked aristo-cratically debonair in a tan jacket and maroon cord shirt worn open with a silk cravat in place of necktie.

"Nigel, how are things?" Hamils pumped his hand. "Is the world still taking good care of you?"

"Never better."

"You know Henry Glinberg, up from Pittsburgh again to see us."

"Of course. Hello again, Henry. Did you fly up this morning?"

"Hi, Nigel. Yes. Can't afford the time to stay over every time. You customers keep us too busy."

Nigel's smile broadened, easily, unrepentantly. "How would you pay the rent without us?"

Hamils indicated Corrigan. "And this is Joe Corrigan, from the DNC group at Blawnox. He's the guy that Jason sent up after Therese Loel talked to Victor."

Nigel shook hands with Corrigan, languidly yet firmly, without undue assertiveness. "*Very* pleased to meet you, Joe," he said. Just a simple business introduction, and yet he conveyed the impression that he really meant it. Style, Corrigan thought to himself. The art of gentility and charm. Something that didn't come very easily from talking to machines all day.

"Me too," he responded.

"Nigel Korven," Hamils supplied. "He's one of the senior consultants who take care of F and F's key clients." Corrigan took that to mean what the sufficiently sophisticated were called, in place of "salesman."

"So you're the expert from afar, who's going to tell us about Direct Neural Coupling and where it's leading," Korven said. "It sounds absolutely fascinating. Some people here are extremely eager to meet you."

"As long as they understand that it's just for information," Corrigan said. He was about to explain that the research was still in an early stage, but caught a faint shake of the head from Hamils.

"Do I detect an Irishman?" Korven said, changing subjects smoothly. "Over here permanently, I hope?"

"As far as I know," Corrigan said.

"Good. That's something we could use more of." Korven turned to Hamils. "Well, I think the others are just about ready for us next door. We can go straight on in." He picked up a folder from his desk and selected a few other papers. "Did you get that house in the end, Mat—the one you wanted?"

"The one up near the bridge, right. Got it for eight grand off the asking, too."

"Splendid. Your wife must be very happy about it."

"She's delighted. First thing is a warming party. You'll have to come along."

"I'd love to, Mat. I'll have to see if I can find somebody pretty to bring along."

"Somehow I can't see you without a woman around, Nigel," Glinberg said as they moved out of the room.

"Oh, but I don't keep them," Korven answered. "It's better to have new ones frequently. They're so much more pleasant to be around when they're on their best behavior and trying to make an impression." He winked reassuringly at Corrigan. "Right, Joe?"

Hamils drew Corrigan aside as they were about to follow the other two out into the corridor. "Let CLC decide what its policy is," he murmured. "We want these people to feel that we can help them solve their problems. They won't connect if you make it sound too remote."

Corrigan nodded. "I'll remember."

They went into a room a few doors away, where two more people were waiting at a large central table. Korven introduced Walter Moleno, fortyish, dark-haired and tanned, with a thin mustache: "Our man in Southeast Asia, back on one of his rare visits home."

Moleno shook his head. "It's not a place, I keep telling you, Nigel. It's a computer. They don't need VR out there. They all live in computers already. I come back for the reality experience."

"In New York? My God! A bit like going to Kansas for the views, isn't it?"

The other person was a woman called Amanda Ramussienne: probably in her mid-thirties, with high, angular features, wavy ginger hair, and alluring, green, feline eyes that caught the light in a way that made it seem to be coming from inside. Her makeup was generous but professional, and the image completed by a beige dress and gold jewelry that blended impeccably and had not come from the neighborhood mall. She spoke animatedly, with lots of expression and gestures, and in some other setting Corrigan would have guessed her background to be theatrical. Korven introduced her vaguely as an "analyst"; from the preamble after they sat down, Corrigan gathered that her work involved contact with the media.

"I had lunch with that *awful* creature from Time-Life again yesterday," she told Korven. He smiled a mixture of amusement at her feigned indignation and despair that she should have known better.

"You mean the fat one who smokes buffalo shit?"

"Of *course* the one who smokes buffalo shit. He definitely wants me to go to bed with him. He even had the nerve to say so. . . ." She waved imploringly at the ceiling. "What is so special about this job that I should put up with this? I mean, when is the harassment thing going to be extended to apply to customers too?"

"Why not try seeing it not as harassment but as opportunity?" Korven suggested sagely. "Most *men* would."

"If it were the sexy, good-looking ones who came on, I might," Amanda agreed with a sigh. "But why does it *always* have to be exactly the opposite kind?"

"Who are we waiting for?" Hamils cut in. "Victor?"

"He'll be in when he's finished a call he's on," Moleno said, nodding. "We thought half an hour here to get to know each other. Then we'll collect a couple of others and go for lunch."

"Have we picked a place?" Korven asked.

"Just downstairs." Moleno looked at the three from CLC. "It's one of those weeks, I'm afraid. Everyone's flying with both feet off the ground."

Hamils nodded. "What kind of mood is Victor in today?" he asked.

Korven turned his head toward Amanda. "Oh, I don't know. What would you say? Is the beast human today?"

She nodded. "Yes, I'd say so. He wasn't devouring anyone the last time I saw him."

"We think he's human," Korven told Hamils.

Corrigan looked at Hamils inquiringly. "Victor's okay," Hamils said. "But at times he can be a bit . . ." He looked diplomatically to the three F & F people before choosing a word. "What would you call it? Temperamental? . . ."

"Obstinate. Opinionated. Bombastic," Korven supplied, with the candid air of somebody saying what everyone else knew perfectly well anyway. "But we all love him, just the same."

"Just don't argue with him," Hamils translated. "If he gets something wrong, let it keep and tell us afterward. We'll straighten it out later."

There were a few seconds of silence, seeming to say that nothing more could make things any clearer after that. Then Amanda treated Corrigan to one of the smiles that talk-show hostesses use to get the show going again after an awkward hiatus. "How much do you know about the kind of business we do here, Joe?" she inquired.

"Not a great deal, to be honest. Something to do with marketing and forecasting, isn't it?"

"Those terms are a little obsolete now," Korven said. "You can charge more for 'econodynamic trend analysis.'"

"Ah. Yes."

At that moment the door opened as if on a spring, and a short, stockily built figure marched in and stumped to the end of the table, where he deposited some sheets of printed figures and a notepad. He had a smooth, tanned head fringed by dark locks that reflected a sheen, heavy eyebrows, and a solid, rounded face with pugnacious jaw and chin. His fingers were thick and stubby, with tufts of hair on the backs between the joints, but the nails were well manicured. He was wearing a dark three-piece with hairline stripe and—a rare sight for the day and age—a white carnation pinned in his left lapel. Mat Hamils knew Borth, of course, but Glinberg apparently had not dealt with him directly in previous visits. Korven completed the introductions.

"So you work for Therese Loel," Borth said, taking in Glinberg with an unblinking stare that gave away nothing. His voice was blunt, direct, straight to the point.

"That's right," Glinberg confirmed.

"Harry's the ESG specialist, based out of Blawnox," Hamils filled in. "We call him in as needed."

Borth's gaze shifted to Corrigan. "But you're the guy Therese said they'd send up, who knows about the computers that let you play Ping-Pong in your head."

"Joe's from the main corporate R and D facility, also at Blawnox," Hamils supplied.

Corrigan frowned. There was some confusion already in what Borth had said. DNC coupled direct into the nervous system. The simulated Ping-Pong was something different: a demonstration that the SDC people used to show off their VIV helmet, which utilized the regular senses. But before Corrigan could frame a reply, Borth changed tack:

"Have they told you much about the kind of business we're in here?"

"We were just about to when you came in," Amanda said. Her manner had changed with Borth in the room. She was all seriousness and attention now—no longer a vivacious artiste, but suddenly the business professional.

Borth remained standing, and spoke moving back and forth at the end of the table. Presenting to a group seemed to be his natural style.

"We live in a complicated world. All the time, it gets more complicated. Everywhere you look, where people are dealing in long-term plans—in business, in industry, in technology, in politics—more money is having to be put down up-front, the lead times are stretching farther into the future, and what happens at the end of it is anybody's guess. Bigger stakes; less certain outcomes. In other words, it's all getting to be more of a gamble." He paused, looked from side to side, and showed his empty palms, as if inviting anyone who could to dispute that.

"Guess wrong, and you can be wiped out even though nothing was your fault: the bottom drops out of a market that everyone said couldn't fail; a trend turns around; the public loses interest in some fad that was going to be the rage for the rest of time . . . and nobody knows why." Borth held up a fan of stubby fingers and began ticking off examples. "How many of you remember the savings-and-loan mess years back, when they poured billions into stacking up downtowns with high-rise office space that nobody wanted? Before that there was the synthetic-fuel thing. Eight billion they blew on it—because the world was about to run out of oil. Then we're drowning in oil, and the whole thing's a fiasco. Screenpad Corporation spent eleven years making plans and tooling up, saying they were going to make paper obsolete. There's still plenty of paper around today, but they're not."

He raised an emphatic finger. "*But* . . . if you call the shots right, you can be made for life. Not that many years ago, all the pros laughed when a couple of guys in a garage said everyone could have a computer. Amspace in Texas came up with a cheap, clunky, surface-to-orbit pickup, instead of the Ferraris and mobile homes that the Air Force and NASA had been making, and they created a global space-trucking industry.

"Now look at the things that some people are telling us will be next." Borth looked around again, appealingly this time. "Nanomachines? Adaptive fiction? Bioregenerative materials? Talking houses? Where do I put my money for the big paybacks ten years down the line?" His gaze came back to rest on the three people from CLC. "You can see the problem—and believe me, it is a problem. That's where we make our business: helping people out there to make those decisions. And naturally there are other outfits who do the same thing. Sometimes we're right more often than they are. Sometimes they get the edge on us. Frankly, there isn't a lot of difference: we all hit at around the same percentage. But I can tell you this: there's *lots* of money out there, *big* money, just waiting for the first outfit that can come up with a way of doing it better. We happen to think that smarter computers is the way to go. That's why we're interested in anything new that CLC has got coming down the pike."

Borth sat down finally, indicating that he was through. He continued looking expectantly at Corrigan. Corrigan, however, having had his orders, left it to someone else to respond. Hamils launched off into a fairly standard line about Virtual Reality technologies offering new ways for users to interact with data: Through suitable presentation to the user's senses, information normally handled as abstract symbols could be transformed into the furnishings of a directly perceivable "world." Processing would then take the form of manipulating those objects via intuitively meaningful actions as used in the everyday world. Glinberg gave the commonly cited example of a bicycle. "To compute the correct angle to lean at for taking a corner at a particular speed requires solving a complicated equation of physics. But the five-year-old kid just *feels* the right thing to do, and does it. Well, the way you do forecasting at present is tackling the problem as numbers; what Joe's people are working on will give you a bike."

"So it's not one of these systems that thinks it knows

my job better than I do," Borth said, assuming the position of one of his clients. "I'm still the best judge of my own business. It simply gives me a better way of seeing the angles."

"Exactly," Hamils said.

Which gave a clear and concise picture, certainly. And it was obviously the kind of thing that the customer wanted to hear. The only problem was that it bore no resemblance to what was actually envisaged at CLC. Pinocchio Two was aimed at shifting the coupling level of the existing motor interface to a higher region of the brain stem and adding speech; EVIE was a short-term kluge to gain experience with vision before the whole thing was redesigned to DNC. The kind of thing that Hamils was talking about, if it ever materialized at all, was years away in the future, at least.

Corrigan tried to inject some measure of perspective but received a firm "not now" signal from Hamils. Borth gave no indication of wanting a detailed technical explanation of either project. It made Corrigan wonder what he was doing here at all. He suspected that the reason was primarily for effect: to maintain an image of CLC's corporate responsiveness. Therese Loel knew of the huge potential market within F & F's client base, and had mentioned the DNC program simply to be sure that nothing of possible relevance was missed. Borth had asked for a specialist; the company had obliged. Now everyone was reading too much into it.

"Have you seen our research organization down at Pittsburgh?" Hamils asked Borth.

"I've been to the head office in the city a couple of times, but never out at the labs, no," Borth replied.

Hamils inclined his head for a moment. "Maybe we could offer you a trip down there to see what goes on?" he suggested. "Then Joe's people could show you the whole state of the art. What do you think?"

"Sounds good," Borth replied. "I'd like that." He glanced at his colleagues. They seemed interested. "We'll all come," he announced.

Hamils looked pleased with the morning's work. "Joe will set it up when he gets back," he said. "Okay, Joe? Can you fix that for us?"

There it was at last: a direct question. What else was

Corrigan supposed to say? "Sure, I'd be happy to." He forced his expression to remain calm and composed. "That would be no problem at all. But we are in changeover mode to the new project just at this moment. . . . Could we schedule it for a little later in time?"

Chapter Thirteen

"You come home at some unearthly hour, and all you've done since is drink coffee. No sleep, nothing to eat. Why can't you admit that it's a textbook case of delayed shock response, following your recent emotional trauma?"

"Horace, shut up. You don't know what you're talking about. In fact, you don't know anything about what's going on at all."

"There's nothing to be ashamed of, Joe. It's perfectly normal. The symptoms were described exactly by Fenwick Zellor in—"

Corrigan flipped the manual override on the kitchen monitor panel to "off." Then he returned to his chair at the table, topped up his mug, and resumed contemplating the design of floral bunches and foliations on the wallpaper opposite.

Although he was looking away from it, he knew that above the work surface behind him was a spice rack fixed to the side of a cabinet—a flimsy, wooden affair of two shelves and supporting ends, holding an assortment of small glass jars. It was outside the range of his immediate attention—as far as could be ascertained from outward appearances, anyway—and the likelihood of anything else in the room affecting it in some way in the next few seconds was vanishingly small. That meant that it would rank low in the probability tables constantly being updated by the program that tried to guess which features of the surroundings were likely to be objects of action or change in the immediate future.

The number of discrete objects needed to make up a

simulated world that aspired to be in any way authentic was stupendous. Every one of those objects had, associated with it, a list of latent attributes that might require activating at any time, according to circumstances. A book taken randomly off a shelf and thumbed, for example; a rug kicked back across the floor; a candy bar broken—all would involve the sudden revealing of new information that had previously been hidden. The number of conceivable ways in which a given situation *might* develop in the next instant was so astronomic that no method of organizing the data could make all of the possible continuations equally available for processing in the time necessary to create smooth, realistic transitions: the computers couldn't generate dirt and worms under every square foot of grass in Pennsylvania all the time, just in case somebody were to decide on a whim to pick up a shovel and dig a hole somewhere.

So what the system did was identify the most likely continuations, based on its accumulating experience of how people tended to behave, and make sure that the pertinent descriptors would always be the fastest accessible. Thus, there was a small but not insignificant possibility that the mug in Corrigan's hand might slip and shatter—and the pointers to such details as the internal structure, texture, and fracture modes of the porcelain would therefore be high in the current access tree. There was a bowl containing two oranges an arm's reach away from him on the table, and the distinct possibility presented itself that he might decide to peel one of them; subfiles defining the properties and behavior of the pulp, fruit, juice, and pips would all have been shuffled up to ready-access status when he arrived in the vicinity and sat down. Similarly for the pages of the magazine lying underneath the fruit bowl, the contents of the pockets of his jacket, slung over the back of another chair, and the details of the palm of his hand, resting on the tabletop—in case he chose to turn his hand over and look at it. But for the spice rack behind him—out of sight, and not something that a person would normally pay attention to. . . .

In a slow, natural movement, consciously suppressing muscle tension and keeping his gaze on the far wall to avoid signaling any intentions to the eye-tracking software, he set the mug down and leaned back in his chair. Then, abruptly, he leaped up and whirled around, in the same movement shooting out a hand to smash one of the spice rack's ends outward.

If his attention hadn't been totally focused, alert for every detail of what happened, he might well have missed it, even then. But for someone who knew what to look for, everything was wrong. For a brief instant—barely perceptible, but definite—there was a break in the movement of his hand just as it touched. The sting and the sound came a fraction too late. And there was a fleeting moment of blankness in the break before the detail of splintered wood and the exposed grain added itself. He stared, oblivious to the clattering of spice jars falling on the countertop and rolling off to the floor. When he pried off one of the shelves hanging by an end and snapped it experimentally, the effect was perfect. He dropped the pieces onto the counter and sat down again at the table.

So it was true.

He snorted humorlessly to himself as Lilly's words came back: "It makes too much sense . . . Way too much." Wasn't he, she had said, being just a little too insightful for someone who was supposed to be crazy?

Of course, it was too much of a coincidence that both he and she, involved in the same project twelve years ago, should have undergone similar psychologically disrupting experiences, and afterward have perceived a world severely distorted to begin with but steadily improving with time.

And that both he and she should suffer from an impaired sense of smell. The first cranial nerve, the Olfactory, serving the most primitive of the senses, is the only one to synapse in the cerebrum. They had never been able to carry the DNC interfacing level beyond the thalamus.

And that in all this time their travel options should have been limited for "medical" reasons. The preparations for Oz had included a major program of systematically recording and encoding all the architectural, geographic, and other visual details of the city—a process known as "realscaping"—in order to re-create any scene realistically in a virtual presentation. But there had to be limits. The program had covered only Pittsburgh and the surrounding area—and the effort entailed by that had been massive enough. In addition, Xylog merged its database with others compiled by cooperating organizations that had carried out similar schemes elsewhere. One of those had been Himomatsu Inc. of Tokyo, which explained how Corrigan had been able to "visit" Japan four years previously.

Why hadn't he seen it sooner? Because he had been too busy proving to himself that if he didn't fit in with the world, then he didn't need the world anyway. Because he had been trying to pretend that he could bury the resentments that came with remembering a life of success and achievement all snatched away. Because he thought he deserved better. Yet the same could be said on every count about Lilly, but she had seen it. . . . And so had he, as soon as she started questioning things. It had been staring him in the face all the time, but she'd had to spell it out. That was what had galled him.

Presumably, then, Lilly must have been right in her guess as to why they had no clear recollections of what had taken place after commencement of the preliminary tests, when the project had supposedly run into problems and been canceled. Their memories had been suppressed and a cover story manufactured to camouflage the cruder, early phases of the simulation, when the system was in its infancy of learning. The disruption had been progressively reduced as the simulation got better, and the corresponding improvement in perceptions and thought coherence offered as evidence of "recovery." The possibility of suppressing the memories of the real-world surrogates in this way was something that had been talked about often enough, but in all of Corrigan's experience the decision had been not to use it. That was why his first reaction to Lilly had been to reject the suggestion as impossible. Evidently he had been wrong.

So exactly what was going on and why? He didn't know. He would need to start practicing some real philosophy for once, and get in touch with Lilly again. But that was going to have to wait for a while, he decided. Virtual or not, there were some aspects of this reality that were simply just too "real"—and which, for the moment at least, there was nothing he could do to change. Before any more consideration of what it all meant and what he was going to do next, he would have to get some sleep. He got up, shrugged at the mess of the broken spice rack and scattered containers, and made his way blearily through to the bedroom.

Chapter Fourteen

Corrigan stood with Mat Hamils, the New York City–area sales manager, outside the main entrance to the Executive Building of CLC's Blawnox R & D facility. With them were Victor Borth, Nigel Korven, and Amanda Ramussienne from Feller & Faber. Five months had passed since Corrigan's visit to New York. Pinder had decided to hold things until the first implementation of EVIE was operating, and then there had been a further delay while the PAF system was expanded to handle several operators simultaneously; but finally, the long-promised F & F trip to Pittsburgh for a demonstration had been arranged.

Borth raised a hand in front of his face and wiggled his fingers. He turned his head to his two companions watching him, pursed his mouth approvingly, and nodded. He looked across the parking lot toward the main gate, and beyond at the tree-clad hills dotted with houses in the distance. The day was sunny and bright. Intermittent traffic sounds came from an unseen highway. To one side, a lawn edged by flower beds bordered the paved area where they were standing. A bee buzzed around the gladioli. Farther away, a crow landed on the lawn and cried raucously.

"I'm impressed," Borth announced.

"I certainly prefer this improvement in the weather," Korven agreed. The drive from the airport had been filthy, through heavy traffic with rain falling continually from a leaden sky. Hamils glanced at Corrigan and looked pleased.

There were still some peculiarities about the scene, however. The flowers and the grass looked normal enough close up; but with increasing distance they lost detail too quickly and became smeary, as if viewed by somebody shortsighted. The distant scenery was too flat. And although there could be no denying that the colors were an improvement over even high-resolution conventional graphics, they lacked some subtle, indefinable quality of richness and depth out in the sunshine. In some areas of sharp contrast, such as shaded spots underneath trees, or the view back inside the lobby, which was illuminated by tinted light, they were simply . . . wrong. Some correction mechanism that the brain applied to create the hues that it "knew" to be true, regardless of the raw data that the optic nerves were reporting, was not being emulated.

"Let's go for a walk," Corrigan suggested.

They stepped off the paving in front of the entrance and began following the driveway in the direction of the gate. Although their movements seemed acceptably smooth and natural, they all felt a hint of a vaguely disconnected, floating sensation that Tom Hatcher had described as "walk by wire," which resulted from motor feedback not being perfectly synchronized with vision. Borth was relieved to note that a wrinkle in his sock that had been bothering him all morning was no longer there.

A car entered the gateway and approached, slowing as it got nearer, and drew up in front of them. Driving it was Joan Sutton, one of the SDC technical people assigned to support Frank Tyron on what was now officially designated the CLC/SDC EVIE project. Tyron himself was in the passenger seat. They got out, grinning unabashedly at the amazed expressions on the faces of the three visitors.

"Fantastic! I could almost believe you're really there," Borth exclaimed.

Corrigan was especially pleased with the results of the improved Personal Attribute Files that Ivy Dupale's graphics section had been working on. Not only were individuals interacting within the simulation; they were doing it with accurate eye and facial movements superposed onto the figures being generated from the PAFs. The incorporation of regular skin-potential sensors into the VIV helmet gave face-muscle movements, and eye-tracking came as standard.

Accepting the unvoiced invitation, Borth stepped forward to examine the car, a 2007 Dodge, which was obviously the star part of the demonstration. The detail was uncanny, with paint and chrome reflecting the surroundings convincingly. When he reached out and tested, the hood was warm to the touch. There was even some realistic ticking and creaking of metalwork cooling down.

Borth grunted and moved to the driver's-side door, which Joan Sutton had left open. She moved aside. Borth peered in, then began poking around curiously. He moved the panel, column, and foot controls with a hand, feeling them resisting and responding. "This is good," he told his colleagues. Amanda came to the other door and ran a hand over the upholstery and trim.

"Better than what I can afford to drive, Victor," she declared pointedly.

Borth sniffed. Then he frowned, turned and moved his head over the back of the seat, then sniffed again. "It's got no smell," he called to those outside. "This looks like a new car. It ought to have the new-car smell that you always get. It doesn't."

"We can't give you a sense of smell," Corrigan said. "It's handled at a different level of the brain."

"Oh, is that so?"

"It was described in the information that was sent," Amanda reminded him.

"Was it? Okay."

Amanda turned on the radio, and it played a local Pittsburgh channel—injected through the VIV audio system.

"What about the parts that you don't see?" Korven queried. It was the obvious next thing. Corrigan caught Hamils's eye and winked confidently.

Borth pulled the hood release and walked around to the front. Korven raised the hood. Engine, battery, generator, hydraulics, air conditioning—everything was there, with all the hoses and accessories. If they looked, they would find water in the radiator, fluids in the reservoirs, oil in the sump. The glove compartment had maps in it, and there was an inside to the trunk, complete with spare wheel and a jack. Within reasonable limits, the team had covered every base.

And then Joan Sutton inadvertently dropped the keys, which she had been toying with. They struck her thigh and glanced off to fall under the car, just behind the front wheel-arch.

"It's okay. I'll get 'em," Korven said, and squatted down to reach. Then he stopped, looked in farther, then pulled his head back and grinned up at Corrigan. "Gotcha!"

"What?" Borth inquired, coming around.

"This car doesn't have an underneath," Korven said, gesturing. "It's all just blank."

Corrigan sighed and showed his palms to acknowledge defeat. There was no way to anticipate everything.

To finish the demonstration they entered the Executive Building and went through the reception area, past CLC's "museum" and the visitors' dining room to a rear exit. From there they crossed a parking lot to the IE Building and went upstairs to the lab area that had been allocated to EVIE. Here they found seven chairs fitted with Pinocchio collars and VIV helmets, arranged in the same positions as the real chairs that they had sat down in at the commencement. Tyron ushered them in and invited them to take their places.

"I hope you're sure that we'll end up coming back out," Korven teased as he settled back. "I mean, I wouldn't want somebody to hit a switch the wrong way, or something, and send us into another simulation inside a simulation."

"What a fascinating thought," Amanda said. "Is it possible?"

Borth and Hamils were fiddling uncertainly with the collar attachments. There were no technicians to help this time. Since only seven working EVIE interfaces had so far been built, nobody else could be projected in from the outside.

"It's okay. You don't have to worry," Tyron said. "We cheat a little." As he spoke, the devices positioned of their own accord, and the participants found themselves in blackness, suddenly conscious once again of the helmets confining them.

Tyron's voice came again, now sounding muffled and remote from the outside. "You can take them off. That's it."

Borth and Hamils had a moment of confusion in unraveling what was real and what wasn't. One by one they all removed their headgear to find themselves in the same place, only this time there "really." The approximation had been good, but this had an entirely different feel about it. Jason Pinder was present also, along with Therese Loel from ESG, Tom Hatcher, Ivy Dupale, and a number of technicians who had been operating the equipment.

Borth was grinning like a kid stepping down from a funfair ride. A good sign. "This is it?" he quipped. "We're back now? You guys are sure?"

"You'd better be," Therese said. "It's almost time for lunch. The virtual variety isn't all that nutritious."

"Incredible!" Hamils declared. "Absolutely incredible." He directed the words at Pinder, but they were for the F & F people's benefit. "You know, you're really onto something here, Jason. There's no end to what can be done with this."

"I wonder how authentic it's possible to get?" Amanda Ramussienne said, staring thoughtfully back at the connecting gear as she stood up.

"My dear, what *do* you have in mind?" Korven asked her in a tone that required no answering.

The visitors were clearly impressed, and it seemed that the way was open for getting down to some solid business talk on the market area that all were agreed still held enormous potential. But things turned out to be less straightforward in the world of not-so-virtual reality. Borth put it bluntly from the end of the lunch table, back in the Executive Building a little under an hour later.

"It's nice," he told them. "And clever. Very clever. Don't get me wrong—I can see that some very smart people have put a lot of effort into this. I don't want to knock that. But when you get down to it, it's still a toy—the kind of thing that kids might get a kick out of playing more realistic games on. You guys get my meaning?" He looked around. Beside him, Pinder stared woodenly at the table. Korven continued to look smooth and imperturbable, as always. Amanda's face had taken on harder lines than her normal sultry image. Corrigan had noticed that she tended to mirror whatever mood of the moment she sensed in Borth. Conversely, she seemed the only one at F & F who could handle him. Korven and the others always went to Amanda first when there was a delicate issue to raise with him, or when he was having one of his grouchy days.

Borth went on. "What we're looking for is *real artificial intelligence*. We've explained it all before. Our clients want to predict the outcomes of complex situations. What you've shown us here is neat, but it only anticipates what the people who programmed it were able to tell it to anticipate. So it's no better than the people, and we can hire them already. See what I mean?"

It was exactly what Corrigan had tried to point out after his first meeting at F & F many months ago. But sales and management had been interested only in not cutting off options. If this was going to be a debacle, it wasn't of his making. He maintained a detached, inwardly self-vindicating silence.

Tyron shook his head. This was the first time that he had heard straight from the customer what was wanted, and it was nothing like what CLC or anyone else was in a position to supply. He was too astute a politician to get into an argument over it, but this thing had to be put to rest. "What you're asking is virtually impossible," he said, glancing from side to side for support from the CLC people. "The world of human affairs is an extreme example of complex, chaotic dynamics that are unpredictable by definition—far more so than the weather system, economy, or other things that you hear about. Even in simple models, the tiniest changes in starting conditions can produce wildly differing outcomes. Nothing known to science can make predictions about systems like that. One chance-in-a-million accident can ruin a company. A singer with a cute face can start a craze that alters the world. For most things that happen, nobody will ever know what the causes were. . . ." He looked at Pinder. Pinder nodded his endorsement. Tyron came back to Borth. "That's simply the way it is. We're up against laws of nature here. Nothing is going to change it."

Corrigan was intrigued to note that Borth didn't seem to be hearing anything especially unexpected, but doodled on a pad and nodded idly until Tyron had had his say. It was Amanda who came to the point of what this was all really about. And she did so with surprising candor.

"You're all thinking like scientists," she said, smiling in the manner of someone ending the joke they had all been playing, of pretending that they hadn't known all along. "Most of the people that we deal with are frauds, flakes, and phonies. I mean, who are we talking about? PR departments that think reality is what they say it is. Madison Avenue and political hygiene experts who make their own reality. Media crazies who never knew the difference in the first place. They all operate in worlds of manufactured images—images built on the public's credulity and wish-fulfillment fantasies, sustained by illusion and delusion. What matters is not what happens to be true, but what people *believe* is true, and what they *want* to be true."

She held up a hand to acknowledge what Tyron had just said. "Yes, sure, *we* know that most of what happens in the world happens for reasons that nobody understands. But there will always be somebody who gets the credit for having called it: the leader of whatever the current in-fad is; today's guru-of-the-moment . . . Anyone with the right *reputation*. Whether the reputation is based on fact or fantasy doesn't matter.

"Well, right now the trendy word in cocktail-party science is AI. If somebody like us can make it believable that they can bring real AI to bear on the complexity-prediction problem, it'll have the clients lining up all down the block."

"Even if it has known . . . limitations?" Therese Loel still hadn't fully gotten the message. She couldn't bring herself to say, "won't work."

"It doesn't matter," Korven interjected softly. "In this world, what you believe to be real *is* real. Amanda said it: *Reputation.*"

"The Rainmaker Syndrome," Amanda said. "If you dance long enough, eventually it'll rain. If lots of people make predictions, some will hit lucky, and that will be good enough for the rest. When enough people try a cure for something, some percentage of them is going to get better anyway. And there's your reputation. When it happens in the market we're talking about, somebody's going to collect a bonanza."

Borth closed his pad and looked up. "But EVIE and Pinocchio aren't it. They play at being what the world is right now. What I want to see is how the world is gonna be, say, five years from now. Show me *that*, and we can start talking deals."

Chapter Fifteen

In the middle of 2008, Frank Tyron left the Space Defense Command to take up a position with CLC's R & D division as "Development Manager, Simulation Graphics," reporting to Pinder. In this, he took charge of a new group that combined the people still on assignment from SDC, plus the loosely structured graphics and holo-imagery section that Ivy Dupale had been heading informally. The remaining parts of the DNC department outside Shipley's DINS lab were consolidated as EVIE and placed under Corrigan. The corporation assured all concerned that these moves represented an overdue streamlining and rationalization, needed to better serve a "fast-growing and exciting new area faced with increasingly severe competitive pressures from abroad."

There was disgruntlement within the DNC group over Ivy's being passed over in this way by an outsider. Evelyn was one of the most indignant, but being a comparative newcomer to the scene, she was hesitant about how much of a fuss it was her place to make over it. Privately, she made representations to Corrigan.

"I think it's scandalous, Joe—especially after the job she did getting the synchronization bugs out of the EVIE imaging system. Can't you talk to Pinder about it, or something?"

"My line is research," Corrigan told her. "Corporate politics isn't what I do." He also wondered if the change was entirely bad; it could represent a step toward the more cosmopolitan flavor that he felt the project could do with.

"So you won't do anything?"

"Eve, I *can't* do anything."

Corrigan was also preoccupied at this time with the problem of efficiently representing and storing the enormous amount of detail implicit in any realistic depiction of the world—which the F & F demonstration had highlighted. To represent everything absolutely faithfully was impracticable but also unnecessary, since a reality was real enough if it looked real enough. The problem, then, was to find good ways of being able to cheat and get away with it.

Fractal algorithms provided a method for generating a lot of material from minimal information—the way Nature compresses its assembly directions in DNA. The principal drawback was that to produce a convincingly realistic output, some kind of randomizing capability needed to be introduced, which meant no two results of applying the same input formula would, in general, be alike. Hence, two separate runs to generate a tree, say (or leaf, or rock, or mountain, or snowflake), from the same set of starting parameters would both look like a tree, but they wouldn't be the *same* tree. This would probably be all right for representing things like forests, skies, or general scenery where precise details didn't matter too much; but other situations demanded a different approach.

So in these latter cases there seemed to be no alternative to having to store all the detail that might be required. Even with the kinds of faster processing methods and special-purpose hardware that Barry Neinst had been exploring, this imposed severe limitations on how large a world they could hope to simulate accurately. For the world to be sufficiently varied and interesting, not all of it could be represented everywhere, all the time. Nor, of course, did it need to be. So the system was organized to concentrate on the parts making up the immediate experiences of the individuals experiencing the simulation. Thus, indeed, in these worlds the Moon was not there when nobody was looking at it; and the question of trees falling in deserted forests didn't arise, since with nobody around, forests ceased to exist.

For smoother continuity, and to reduce the occurrences of "black-hole glitches"—as when somebody opened a door to find themselves staring into a featureless void for a perplexing moment—various ways were tried for getting the system to anticipate and pre-access the branches that were most likely to be needed next. But none of them proved wholly satisfactory. Following chess-playing-machine parlance, this became known as the "look-ahead" problem. Solving it, along with "realscaping" more of the Pittsburgh area, was the main focus of the EVIE group's work through the second half of the year.

During that period, Ivy Dupale resigned from the company and got a job on the West Coast.

With Christmas approaching, Corrigan and Evelyn drove out one evening to Eric Shipley's house in Franklin, north of the city. Tom Hatcher and several others from the project were also due. It was a homey, unpretentious place, nestled in a fold of wooded hillside that provided seclusion, yet with the township center conveniently less than a mile away. It was the main house of what had once been a farm. The outbuildings were now converted or demolished, and most of the land sold off, except for a couple of acres forming a shady, somewhat overgrown garden bordered by a creek at the rear. Shipley lived there with his graying, genially disposed wife, Thelma. They had two sons and a daughter, all of them grown and gone in different directions. The children's rooms were always kept the way they had been for their frequent visits home.

Hatcher was already there when Corrigan and Evelyn arrived. With him were two of his programmers, Charlie Wade and Sue Lepez, and also Bryan Reed, one of the electronics technicians working on EVIE. There were sodas, coffee, and beer. Later on, a couple of pizzas arrived. By the middle of the evening the talk had ranged over shop topics and settled on the do's and don'ts for surviving in a popular VR game called "Sniper." Shipley drew Corrigan away to go and see an old nautical chronometer of polished teak and gleaming brass that Shipley had in his study. It was not long, however, before they were back to the subject of developments within CLC. Corrigan sensed that this was the real reason why Shipley had taken him aside.

Most people—including Corrigan himself—had seen the consolidation of EVIE under his direction as an effective promotion, and an indicator that he was solidly on his way upward to better things. Shipley, however, wasn't so sure.

"You said yourself, once, that in the long term EVIE doesn't lead anywhere," he reminded Corrigan. "You called it a short-term stunt, a hybrid mishmash. So what does that say about anyone doing you a favor by putting you in charge of it?"

But Corrigan was still riding the wave. "Ah, come on, Eric," he said lightly. "You wouldn't want me think that you're having an attack of sour grapes, now, would you? Don't you remember, too, that EVIE was to be the main-thrust program for two years? Whoever runs it now will automatically pick up whatever comes next."

"That could be changing, Joe. There's been a lot going on involving Tyron and Pinder at the division level that we're only getting parts of. My guess is that corporate thinking has been turning away from EVIE ever since that business with Feller and Faber. In other words, they're sad-dling you with a lame duck."

"What else would they have in its place, then?" Corri-gan challenged, his voice a touch sharper. They were still a year or more away from shifting up to the thalamus—and there was no guarantee that it would work even then.

Shipley shrugged and showed his hands. "You tell me."

"Why assume that they've got anything else at all?"

"Then look at it this way. If EVIE really is a sinking ship, whose name is being quietly dissociated from it and who'll be the skipper who goes down?" Shipley paused to let Corrigan think about that. "Then ask yourself what Tyron and his people were *really* brought in for. It certainly wasn't just to take over Ivy's section. That's a holding oper-ation."

This time Corrigan said nothing but stared hard at him for several seconds. Shipley waited, holding his eye ques-tioningly. Before they could resume, however, the long, loose-limbed figure of Tom Hatcher sauntered in from the living room, holding a can of beer in one hand and licking pizza grease off the fingers of the other. Evelyn was behind him, looking fresh and casually appealing with her long, fair hair, white top, and red, clinging slacks.

"Not interrupting anything, are we?" Hatcher drawled. " 'Cause if we are it's too bad. This is a party."

Corrigan hesitated, then grinned. "No, it's okay, Tom. Just shop as always." It was a good time to ease things up a little anyway. Evelyn squeezed past Hatcher to hand Corrigan a sausage on a cocktail stick, then snuggled close while he slipped an arm around her. Hatcher went over to look at the chronometer that Corrigan had been examining earlier.

"Say, that's some piece. They don't make 'em like that these days."

"Not a shred of plastic in it, and the knobs don't come off in your hand," Corrigan agreed.

"Can't say I'd want to carry it around on my wrist, though."

"You didn't have to. You had a ship to carry these around."

"Where do the batteries go?" Hatcher moved to admire a highly polished period revolver, mounted as a display on a board fixed to the wall nearby. "Looks like a .44 Dragoon Colt," he commented. "Probably from the Civil War."

"Right on," Shipley said, nodding.

"I didn't know you were into that kinda thing."

"I'm not. Thelma picked it up at a yard sale for five dollars."

"Does it work?"

"No—just an ornament."

"Too bad." Hatcher's interest in guns was well known.

Shipley nodded in the direction that Hatcher and Evelyn had come from. "What's going on back there?" he inquired.

"Shop," Evelyn said. "Is it ever different with this bunch?"

"Charlie's talking about his accelerator for the new look-ahead tree," Hatcher explained. "I had enough of it all day. I came here to get away."

They still hadn't found a reliable way of paralleling the human intuition for knowing what people were apt to do next. In a test the previous day, the system had properly anticipated all the things that one of the experimenters could reasonably have been expected to do with a magazine when he picked it up and rolled it—except use it to swat a simulated fly. Hence there was a hangup upon impact, in which time the velocity of the magazine fell to zero, and the fly was able to walk with impunity onto the object that was supposed to have flattened it.

Machines were good at organizing the world into neat hierarchies of computed probability. The real world, however—essentially because of the way that the people in it behaved—didn't work that way.

"Charlie's still an idealist," Hatcher said. "He just won't accept that the world isn't logical."

"Well, it doesn't work by formal, Aristotelian logic," Shipley agreed. "You see, that's purely deductive: you start with what's true, and from that the way the world has to be follows. That's what machines are good at. But in real life you start with experience of the way the world is, and then infer the reasons why and hope they come close to being true. Inductive: that's what people do—and even they aren't sure how. That's why textbook science and real science aren't the same thing."

"Is philosophy a hobby of yours, Eric?" Evelyn asked. She had been running her eyes over the shelves of books around the study.

"Oh, I dabble in a bit of everything," Shipley replied affably.

"So the universe is inductive," Corrigan concluded.

"Isn't it obvious?" Shipley said.

"I thought that philosophers have been having a problem with induction for centuries," Evelyn commented.

Shipley shrugged. "It's of their own making—as are most of humanity's problems. They started by assuming that the universe *couldn't* work inductively—because they couldn't reduce it to formal rules—when it obviously does."

"So we have to teach the simulator how to be inductive," Corrigan said. "How *does* real-world logic work, then, Eric?"

"Being ninety-percent right, ninety percent of the time," Shipley replied. "It's what science, business, war, and evolution are all about."

"What about sex?" Hatcher asked, looking away from the Colt and taking a swig from his can.

"Oh." Shipley smiled. "That's made up of all of the above."

A thoughtful expression came over Hatcher's face. "Maybe the way isn't to try and *teach* the system how to be inductive at all," he said. "I mean, if we're not really sure how we do it ourselves, we're hardly in a position to spell out the rules, are we?"

"What other way is there?" Corrigan asked.

"Maybe the thing to do is turn it the other way around."

There was silence for a couple of seconds while the others puzzled over this. "How do you mean?" Shipley asked finally.

"Let it learn in the same way as we do: by observing the behavior of real people in the environments that it creates. With EVIE, we've got all the technology you need." Hatcher paused, then went on, more excited visibly as he warmed to the idea, "Instead of the inhabitants of a world evolving in response to the environment, the environment learns to get better by watching the reactions of the inhabitants. See what I mean—it would be turning nature upside down."

"Hmm." Shipley drew back, frowning. "I'll have to give that some thought. . . . It's interesting, that, Tom. Very interesting."

Corrigan had taken down one of the books that Evelyn had noticed and was turning the pages idly. "Epictetus? I've heard of him."

"Greek slave, taken to Rome," Shipley said, moving over.

"Got freed and became a philosopher," Corrigan completed.

"He's the reason why I've never been interested in politics or prestige," Shipley told them.

"Really?" Evelyn said,

Shipley grinned. "Oh, I was kidding. But he does say some interesting things."

"Such as?" Corrigan asked curiously.

"That you shouldn't seek happiness through things that other people have control over," Shipley answered. "Otherwise you end up being enslaved to them."

That didn't seem to leave very much, as far as Corrigan could see. "What else is it that you should want, then?" he asked.

"Live for your own values and beliefs: things that nobody can take away," Shipley answered. "Then nobody can own you."

The veiled reference to their private conversation earlier would have been enough on its own to goad Corrigan into dissenting, even without his innate Irish argumentativeness. "It sounds like a pretty empty cop-out, if you ask me, Eric," he opined. "The kind of thinking of somebody who would never try going for anything for the fear of losing it. Where's the challenge and satisfaction in living a life like that?"

"It's being free, Joe. Fearing nobody. Look at the antics of some of the people we see every day and ask how many of them can say they have that."

Corrigan shook his head. "You live your way, I'll live mine. I couldn't accept a philosophy like that."

Shipley seemed unperturbed. "Maybe you should go back and get in touch with your roots again, sometime, Joe," he said. "To Ireland. There's a tradition there, too, that understands the kind of things I'm talking about."

"Oh, you don't buy that load of rot, too, do you, Eric?" Corrigan groaned. "Thieves, rogues, and scoundrels, the lot of 'em. They'd sell their grandmothers for the price of a pint—and then leave you stuck with the tab if you look the other way."

"I'd still like to go there," Evelyn said. It was something they had talked about a number of times.

Corrigan looked at her. "Well, maybe it is about time that you and I took a break somewhere." He raised his eyebrows. Her face split into a smile, and she nodded eagerly. "How about Florida, or maybe Mexico?" he suggested.

"Somewhere a bit sunnier than Pennsylvania in December, anyway," she said. "It's no better than Boston."

Corrigan thought for a few seconds longer. "Then let's make it California," he said. "There's a string of places dabbling in neural stuff on the West Coast that I've always been meaning to check out. And there's an old friend of mine from MIT called Hans Groener who's doing things at Stanford on sleep and dreams that sound interesting, but I've never had a chance to see it."

"Sure, California'll do. Why not?" Evelyn said. "I've never seen Yosemite."

"Do it," Shipley told them. "Everything's slowing down here for the holidays. And you've probably got some leave that you need to take before the year's out, Joe."

Why not? Corrigan thought. "I'll call Hans tomorrow and see what we can do," he promised.

Chapter Sixteen

Despite his fatigue and having been up all night, Corrigan did not sleep well. He awoke halfway through the afternoon, still feeling woolly headed and groggy. All he could remember from his disjointed recollections of the early-morning hours was that Lilly's place was north of the river, somewhere near the Allegheny Center. He cleaned up and put on some fresh clothes, then fixed himself a snack. Computer-injected hunger signals felt just the same, even if his real body was in repose, getting its nutrients from dermally transfused solutions. After that, he left without turning Horace on again, and caught a bus to the North Side.

But nothing that he saw jogged his memory as he wandered up and down the streets of the district contained in the crook of the I-279 Expressway, north of Three Rivers Stadium. Any of a score of apartment-block entrances that he passed could have been hers. Any of the streets that he walked along could have left the hazy image that was all he could piece together of unremarkable frontages glimpsed in predawn shadows.

It made sense to him now why recent years should have seen so much redevelopment around Pittsburgh. For every part of the old city that was "demolished," new, simulated scenery could be substituted that would not have to conform to anybody's real-world experiences. Nobody could walk around inside the Camelot, for example, and be puzzled by not finding things the way they used to be. The "realscaping" task was thus considerably eased.

He wanted to tell Lilly that she had been right, but

everything was okay—the experiment was going as it should. Yes, their memories of the actual commencement of Oz had been suppressed, and alternative stories given to mask the transition from the real world to the illusory. But it didn't follow that something sinister was going on. Some such provision would have been necessary to ensure that the responses of the surrogates—the real-world participants coupled into the simulation—would be natural and valid.

And boy, had that part of the scheme worked as planned! Until Lilly waved the facts in front of his nose, he himself—one of the principal creators of the simulation—had failed to realize that he was inside it. She had thought to question where he had not because she had known less. He had been involved in the planning of Oz. Hence, if any deception were intended, he would have known about it. Since he didn't, there couldn't be any; and once the impossibility was established in his mind, there was no place for the possibility to coexist. The irony was that it had been able to work in his case only because of his knowledge that it *couldn't* work.

The main cause of Lilly's distress and anger was not so much the deception—she was a military volunteer, and things like that happened and could be compensated for—but the twelve years that she saw as stolen from her life. And who could blame her for that? But what he knew, and she almost certainly would not, was that those twelve years were also an illusion. The system coupled directly into postsensory brain centers, which enabled data to be coded in a prereduced, highly compressed form that eliminated delays associated with preprocessing in the perceptual system. This meant that time inside the simulation ran about two hundred times faster than real time in the world outside. Hence, the actual time that they had spent hooked into the virtual world would be closer to three weeks than the twelve years that they remembered subjectively. Although even that was longer than the durations projected for the test runs that Corrigan had expected to be taking part in, it wasn't outrageous. They were all scientists and volunteers, after all. They would have had little problem agreeing to something like that.

He hoped that if he could find her and reassure her of at least that much, she would see things in a different light and be less likely to start doing anything rash that might disrupt the experiment. There was no reason for the test conditions to be affected by the mere fact of their knowing what they knew now, as long as they continued to act as if nothing had changed. The system could only monitor external behavior: what a surrogate did and said. Since nobody possessed the knowledge to tell it how, the system was not able to decode inner thought processes from deep inside the brain and read minds. If it could, there would have been no need for Project Oz in the first place.

The whole idea had been that the system would learn to make its animations more lifelike by imitating the behavior of real people injected as surrogate selves into the simulation. It had no way of knowing *why* the surrogates that it watched behaved in the ways they did—any more than they frequently did themselves. At the end of the experiment nobody would know, let alone have been able to specify beforehand, the precise structure of software structures and linkages that had self-organized to make such mimicking possible. The neural structures responsible for the complexity of human behavior in the real world had evolved by principles that were appropriate to carbon chemistry. Trying to duplicate them in code would have been as misguided as building airplanes that flapped feathers. Oz was designed to build, in ways appropriate to software, whatever structures it needed to achieve similar results. Nobody needed to know exactly what the final structures were, or how they worked. The aim was to achieve directed coevolution: the end-product, not the mechanism for attaining it, was the important thing.

That had been the theory, anyway. Whether it would work was what Oz had been set up to test. And from the bizarre goings-on going on in the world around him, Corrigan's first conclusion had to be that as far as its prime goal was concerned, the project had wandered somewhat off the rails. For, far from modeling themselves on the surrogates, the system animations seemed to be going off into self-reinforcing behavior patterns of their own, while—if his own and Lilly's cases were anything to go by—the surrogates had become misfits. That in itself didn't trouble him unduly. This was research, after all; perfection could hardly be expected from a first-time run—and especially in an undertaking as unprecedented and as ambitious as this.

Hence, it was no surprise that the animations fell short of true human emulation in some aspects. What was astounding was that they came so close. The empty stares and "flatness" were minor flaws compared to the extraordinary degree of realism—even if it did tend somewhat toward the eccentric—with which the personas that he encountered daily were able to act out their affairs and effect the continuity of leading consistent background existences offstage. So what if the system had overstepped the boundary of neurosis when it tried to make Jonathan Wilbur an embodiment of human criteria for personal success and failure; or if Maurice at the Camelot couldn't master a value system that didn't reduce to a simple profit-and-loss calculus? They had fooled Corrigan. It was sobering to realize just how effective the combined weight of suggestion and authority had been in persuading him that the defects he had perceived in the early stages were in himself and not in the world around him. Now so much seemed so obvious.

The universal ineptness at fathoming humor and metaphor that he had observed for years—processes that involved the associative genius of human intellect at its subtlest—should have given the game away. And if not that, then surely the curious and unnatural persistence of people like Sherri and Sarah Bewley when they pressed him for explanations of where they had missed the point. Of course. All the time it was the *system*—wanting to know how it could do better. Mind reading was not an option.

In the real world, when people acted strangely or unsociably, others tried to gain some insight to why by getting them to talk. In the same way, when the system sought deeper understandings of what motivated the surrogates, it put animations around them to ask its questions for it. And the closer the relationship, the more personal—and hence relevant to the purpose—their questions could naturally be. Maurice, his boss at work; Sarah, his rehabilitation counselor (and the earlier attempt in the form of Simon, which had failed)—both were examples of the computers trying to get close, wanting to discover what made him behave as he did. No wonder he sometimes found himself reflecting that Horace, Sarah, and Maurice sounded the same. They *were* the same. His house manager was the system in disguise, too.

And even his wife! For hadn't it been Sarah who first came up with the suggestion that marrying Muriel might be a good move—for "therapeutic" reasons? Weird but frighteningly effective, he had to concede. Acting through one manufactured personality, the system had insinuated itself into his personal world in the form of another. Corrigan could only marvel at the ingenuity of it. Already the project was surpassing anything he had imagined, even in his wildest moments of selling it to others.

And now there was the risk that just at this crucial stage when Oz was surpassing all expectations, Lilly, unless he could get to her, might jeopardize the whole thing. But he was not going to get to her this way, he admitted to himself finally. Until he figured out another way, or until she got to him again, the thing was to carry on acting normally. That meant going in to work today, just as if nothing had happened. He crossed back over the river to Downtown and decided that it wasn't worth going out to Oakland. On the other hand, it was too early to go straight to the Camelot just yet.

There was a bar not far from the Vista—the hotel where Evelyn had stayed when she came down from Boston for her job interview—that he used to frequent a lot during his time with CLC, but which he hadn't been in since his "breakdown." He knew every scratch on the countertop in that place, the prints and curios on the walls, all the scuff marks and stains in the pattern on the wallpaper. There was no way that the realscaping crews could have covered *every* place in town.

Out of curiosity, he made his way there. The street had acquired its share of changes over the years, but apart from a new door and a coat of paint, the bar still looked pretty much the same—outside. But that was the easy part. He went inside. . . .

And sure enough, it had all been remodeled. New counter, new walls, new everything. Corrigan sighed and ordered a Bushmills, straight up. It could have been his imagination, but he was sure he detected a hint of a knowing smirk on the face of the pudgy, balding bartender.

"Okay, you got me," Corrigan conceded, raising his glass.

"Ah . . . pardon, sir?"

"It doesn't matter."

There was a pay phone in an alcove by the cigarette machine. Corrigan changed a twenty into quarters and sauntered over. He set his drink on top of the phone and tapped in the number for Information International. The codes were all different from the ones used in the real world —the change had been explained as necessitated by changes in procedure by the phone companies. Corrigan couldn't remember offhand why the Oz designers had done that.

"How can I help you?" a voice inquired.

"I'd like a number in Ireland, please."

There was a confused pause. Corrigan smiled at the thought of the drastic axing and reassembly of a whole section of the system's pointer tree that those few simple words would have caused.

"Why do you want a number there?" the voice demanded, sounding belligerent. Oh, yes, Corrigan thought to himself, it all seemed so obvious now.

"What the hell does it matter why I want it?" he retorted. "Would you please just do your job."

Another pause, then a different voice, a woman's, with a believable brogue: "Directory, which town, please?"

"Dun Laoghaire."

"Yes. And who would you be wanting there?"

"There's a grocer's shop on the corner of Clarinda Park and Upper George's Street, called Ansell's, that stays open late. What's their number?" It would be approaching ten P.M. in Ireland—five hours ahead of Pittsburgh time.

A long pause. "Ah, I don't seem to have them listed anywhere. Are you sure it's still there? It might have changed."

"How about the New Delhi? It's an Indian restaurant along the street."

"No. I don't have that either."

Corrigan grinned. The system was throwing every obstacle at him that it could come up with. "Then tell me the number of the Kingston Hotel at the bottom of Adelaide Street."

"A hotel is it, you said?" The system was trapped. Corrigan could sense it, there in the voice.

"Yes, the Kingston, on Adelaide Street. If that's gone too, give me the number of the police station around the corner."

He got the number, and after parting with a fistful of coins was through. "Is this the Kingston?" he inquired.

"Yes, it is," a young woman's voice replied.

"And are you at the reception desk there?"

"I am. Who's this?"

"Just somebody who would appreciate it if you could help settle a small bet we're having here. I wonder, would you mind stepping across the hall for a moment and looking out the front door to your right, and then describe to me what you can see?"

"Oh, no, I couldn't be doing that."

"Why not?"

"It's, er . . . not company policy."

Corrigan had to stifle a laugh. His eyes were watering. "Then tell me what the large picture is above the main bar in the lounge."

"That was taken away, I'm afraid."

"I'd like to have seen them do it. It's painted on the ceiling."

A sudden shrill tone announced a disconnection. "There seems to be a technical fault," Corrigan was informed when he checked with the operator.

Still smiling, he went back to the bar with his drink. In a niche among the shelves of bottles, standing between a darts trophy and jar of ticket stubs, there was a figurine that he hadn't noticed before. It was of an Irish leprechaun, complete with hat and pipe. "So, you're still haunting me, eh, Mick?" he grunted as he sat down on the stool. It was uncannily like the one he had in his hallway at home.

Chapter Seventeen

The hills behind the Bay to the east looked invitingly sunbaked after the chill and wet of winter in Pennsylvania. Below, as the plane descended on its final approach into San Francisco International Airport, fingers of houses and marinas creeping outward along the water's edge formed complex, convoluted patterns like frost on a windowpane.

Corrigan, looking casual in an open-neck shirt, light windbreaker, dove-gray jeans, and sneakers, slipped a hand over Evelyn's and leaned closer. He had been more relaxed than she had ever known him, telling stories and cracking bad jokes all through the flight. "You know, Eric was right," he said. "We've been cooped up inside CLC for too long, worrying about its politics. It's not worth it. This is the kind of thing we should be making more time for. There might be something to be said for those old books of his after all. People need to get their values straight."

She smiled and treated him to a look of mock superciliousness. "Why go back two thousand years to find that out? I've been telling you the same thing for ages."

"Have you? I never noticed."

"My point exactly."

"Then you're right too. Let the world be advised that Joseph M. Corrigan is switching to a lower-wattage lifestyle. The high-power stuff, I'll leave to the Pinders and the Tyrons. And the blood pressure that goes with it."

"Half your time would be empty," Evelyn pointed out.

"No. On second thought, most of it."

"Great."

"What would you do with it?"

He kissed her on the cheek and pretended to think about it. "Oh, I'd find something."

They spent the next couple of days sight-seeing around the city. They went to the aquarium, planetarium, botanical gardens, and museums in Golden Gate Park, rode cable cars, and ate the best at Fisherman's Wharf, Japantown, and Broadway. They rented a car and drove north across the Golden Gate to the wine country, around the Bay to visit some of the researchers at Berkeley, and back across the Bay Bridge in the evening to see the SF Symphony, playing the winter season.

When they got back to the hotel, Corrigan called Hans Groener, his onetime colleague from MIT days, to confirm their visit to Stanford for the next day.

"Yes, that will be fine, Joe," Hans said over the phone. "Also, I have a surprise for you."

"Oh? What's that?"

"I talked to an old friend of yours who's out here now, and who would like to say hello again. So I invited her to join us for dinner tomorrow night and make it a foursome—Ivy Dupale."

"Hey, terrific!" Corrigan called across the room to Evelyn. "How about this. Hans knows Ivy. She's joining us for dinner tomorrow night."

"How wonderful!"

"Fine, Hans. That'll be just great."

The following morning they left San Francisco again and headed southward this time, to Stanford University. Hans was involved in sleep and dream research, which Corrigan looked on as something different and quite probably interesting, but not really relevant to his own line of work. It would be good to see Hans again anyway, even if the visit did turn out to be mainly social. But after he and Evelyn arrived at the sprawling campus with its Spanish-inspired facades of rounded arches and shady colonnades, and had talked with Hans in his laboratory for only half an hour, he realized that he had been mistaken. Hans's work could turn out to be very relevant indeed.

The DINS technology used by Pinocchio and EVIE used a configuration of electrodes inside the collar to create a dynamic pattern of ultra-high-frequency electric fields that penetrated the lower brain regions and brain stem. The fields superposed and were precisely shaped to add or cancel in different spots that could be very finely localized, which was how desired neural centers were activated selectively. However, attenuation and dispersion increased with penetration depth, reducing selectivity and hence the effectiveness of the technique. This was the main factor that had restricted direct coupling to the medulla.

For several years, papers had been appearing in the scientific literature, reporting on an alternative approach using intersecting photon beams tuned to several narrow-frequency windows at which body tissue was found to be surprisingly transparent. It was only in talking with Hans that Corrigan first came to realize how rapidly these investigations had consolidated and were advancing. The new, emerging field was known as "Deep Selective Activation."

"The window allows photons to penetrate coherently and maintain a tight focus, below disruptive ionization energies," Hans explained. "On top of that, frequency tuning to specific neural states provides an additional dimension for fine probing. There's no need for flooding the cells with huge numbers of photons." He was lean and narrow-framed, with straight blond hair and a pale, thin-lipped countenance. The movies would have cast him as an SS officer whose sadism was a compensation for a physique that fell short of the Wagnerian Nordic ideal. In reality, Hans played American folk guitar and bred parakeets. Most of his equipment was being rebuilt currently, and his staff hidden away in offices or at computer terminals: there wasn't a lot, really, to show that day.

"I knew you were dabbling in this, but I never realized it had come so far," Corrigan confessed.

"DSA has had a boost from a lot of government work that was declassified," Hans told him. "We've got quite a club springing up here on the West Coast. SRI are putting a team together. Todd's group up at Berkeley."

"We hoped to see him yesterday, but he's away this week."

"Hughes and Lockheed are in on it. Some department in the Air Force has been very active."

The significance of the remark didn't hit Corrigan just then. He was still telling himself inwardly that he would have to make a point of keeping more up to date with the literature in future. Get back to being a scientist again, and forget trying to turn into a corporate politician. Being back in academic surroundings was reawakening his appetite for intellectual excitement.

Evelyn was studying some charts of neural organization fixed to one of the walls. Corrigan's background was software rather than interfacing, and his personal expertise at the working level lay in the area of self-modifying associative nets. What Hans was describing came closer to the kind of work that Evelyn had had experience of at Harvard and was now doing with Shipley.

"Hans, what are these references to 'resonance modes' here?" she asked curiously. "I use this mapping system practically every day, but I've never come across those before."

Hans stepped across and looked pleased, rubbing the palms of his hands together and showing teeth with lots of metal. "Ah, yes, very good. You spotted it." He nodded approvingly at Corrigan. "You've found a smart lady here, Joe."

"And what else would you expect?"

Hans looked back and forth, taking in both of them. "This is something fairly recent that we've discovered through DSA. It's quite exciting—something that I think you will find particularly interesting, Joe. We call it associative neural resonances."

Corrigan's eyebrows rose. "Which are? . . ."

"Shortcuts to generating complex pictures inside the brain. We've found that triggering just a few, precisely selected, neuronal groups can activate entire chains of connected imagery."

"Wilder Penfield's experiments, back in the forties," Evelyn tossed in.

"Yes," Hans agreed. "Except we can do it from the outside." He glanced back at Corrigan. "You know how extraordinarily lucid dreams can be, yes? The images can be so rich in detail that it's often impossible to tell whether one is asleep or not."

"Sometimes I've been awake for five minutes before I realized I wasn't awake yet," Corrigan said.

"Exactly." Hans nodded and went on. "Obviously that information isn't coming from anywhere outside. It was already present there, in the mind. Random firings can set off whole trains of them that are linked together, which we experience as dreams—or it may be firings that are predisposed by recent repeated activity due to worry, intense emotional contexts, and that kind of thing."

"Like the way a bell rings," Evelyn said. "The complexity of the sound has nothing to do with how you hit it, or what with. It was already there implicitly, in the bell's structure."

"And with language," Hans said. "Words are just a code system to trigger associations already established in the listener's neural system from the experience of living. The information is in the listener, not the speaker. It seems to be a general characteristic of the neural system. And that is what we are learning to control. Activating just the right set of primitives can cause amazingly detail-rich images to be generated in the visual system. By 'playing' the input combinations like a keyboard, we can induce complete event-sequences to order, inside the subject's mind, without having to inject huge data streams to specify every detail. We simply reactivate what's already there. Much faster than conventional brute-force graphics. Much more efficient."

The significance was apparent immediately. Here, possibly, was a totally new way of approaching the problem that Corrigan's group had been grappling with of representing major portions of the real world. Instead of trying to supply every detail of an image, feed in just the right cues and let the subjects fill in the details themselves, from the inside.

But surely it couldn't be that simple. Hans watched the frown forming on Corrigan's face, knowing the objection that was coming.

Finally, Corrigan said, "These resonances. Are they unique—different for each individual? Or does everyone share the same ones? . . . I mean, if they're unique, they can't produce the same world for different people."

"Yes, I know what you're saying, Joe. But the fact is, there does seem to be a surprising degree of commonality. We are still very much in the fact-gathering stage, but the way it looks is that similar input code patterns do result in similar things being perceived by different people."

Corrigan was looking undisguisedly skeptical. "How could that be, now?" he demanded.

Hans refused to be put on the defensive. "How do we know that we all see the same world anyway?" he challenged. "Oh, sure, we agree on the same broad descriptions—I'm not disputing that. But how do we *know* . . ." he paused, looking first at one, then the other, to emphasize his point, "that what we're seeing is identical? We don't. You'd be surprised how much in ordinary day-to-day living, people habitually see what they expect to see, not what's there. Our tests show measures of agreement that are comparable. So the differences that we get are no worse than happen every day in the real world anyway." He shrugged and turned up his hands to make one final point. "And in any case, we all tend to dream about similar things. That says there's common circuitry at work somewhere."

"But surely the degree by which different people disagree can't be the same for all of them," Evelyn said.

"That's right—it varies as a Gaussian spectrum," Hans said. "Ninety percent more-or-less agree what it's like out there, and they define the 'norm.' But the fringe groups differ increasingly, until in the extreme cases they live in a different world entirely."

"And we call them insane," Corrigan said, getting the point.

Hans grinned at him jestingly. "Maybe you're tackling VR the wrong way, Joe. Instead of trying to shovel a whole world into people's heads, perhaps you should try inducing the right dreams, and let the machinery that's already there inside do the work. That is what it evolved for, after all. Just as the best cures use the body's own defenses."

Ivy arrived late in the afternoon. She was looking good, had found herself a place in San Jose, and was heading up a space-imaging program at NASA, Ames. She asked about Tom Hatcher, Eric, and the others back at CLC, but—not so surprisingly, Corrigan supposed—did not show a great deal of curiosity about the progress of the project itself. Corrigan took the hint and didn't push it on her. Evelyn got the same message.

From the university they went to eat at a place in Palo Alto that was a popular nightspot as well as a restaurant. Afterward, they stayed for a couple more drinks, and to dance. Late into the evening, while Evelyn was on the floor with Hans and the other two were taking a break, Ivy looked across at Corrigan over the rim of her glass and asked, "Are you going to marry her?"

Corrigan was used to Ivy's direct way of saying exactly what was on her mind. He had found it disconcerting at first; later it became refreshing. He grinned forbearingly. "Now, why would I want to go and be doing a thing like that?"

"You two go so well together."

"Exactly. Why go and spoil a good relationship?"

Ivy sipped her drink unblinkingly. "I think you should risk it. She wants to, you know. Women have this kind of radar. We can tell."

"There's an old Irish saying," Corrigan told her. "If you want praise, die; if you want blame, marry. People change when they feel owned. They start blaming each other for not coming up to expectations that were never realistic in the first place."

"If you're smart enough to think that, you can't be dumb enough to believe it, Joe," Ivy said.

Corrigan took a mouthful of drink, thought for a moment, and set his glass down. "Ah, enough of this heavy stuff," he said. "Have you got your breath back? This is a great one that they're starting now. Let's go back and show Hans and Evelyn a thing or two."

But Ivy's comment about he and Evelyn going so well together had struck a sympathetic chord in him somewhere. Some of the women back at CLC had said the same. For some reason, it was always the women who noticed such things—or at least, who mentioned them. And socially, it was one area where his life felt incomplete.

He was unusually quiet and thoughtful all the way through the drive back up to San Francisco.

Chapter Eighteen

It was too late in the season to visit Yosemite as Evelyn had wanted—reports were that the approaches were already treacherous due to snow. So, following a suggestion of some people that they talked to at breakfast the next morning, they postponed that for another occasion, and instead drove across the San Joaquin Valley and up into the Sierra foothills to the Mother Lode country of 1849 gold-rush fame.

They toured the old mining town of Columbia, preserved as a state monument, where the buildings remained inside and out just as they had been a century and a half before, and residents wearing traditional dress still worked the old crafts. The Wells Fargo Company office was still there, whose scales had weighed over one and a half billion dollars' worth of precious metals during the gold era.

Eight miles away they found California's largest public cave, Moaning Cavern, estimated to be a million years old and large enough to hold the Statue of Liberty upright and still leave room to spare. The bones of approximately a hundred people dating back to prehistoric times had been found at the bottom, 180 feet below the surface—probably the results of unfortunates accidentally falling into the cavern, since until its opening up in recent times the entrance had been just a small, vegetation-covered hole in the surface. The guide, who was also the owner, told them that from the positions that the bones were found in, some of the victims had apparently survived the fall and tried to climb out—a tough proposition, considering the overhangs. Traces of carbonized wood suggested that perhaps others at the surface had thrown down torches in an effort to help. "Of course, it's impossible to be sure," he told them, pinching his mustache and chuckling. "But we like to think that some of 'em made it."

They drove higher into the Sierra, the wild range separating California from Nevada. In every direction they looked they saw tree-covered hills, sweeping expanses of canyon and rock, unfolding vistas of lakes and mountains. Corrigan found himself intoxicated by the feelings of freedom and openness. They gazed down at foaming creeks far below them in sheer ravines, stared up in awe at sequoias with trunks more than twenty feet in diameter. From a crag high in the Sonora pass they clung close as they stared out over the vastness, and it seemed that all of it belonged just to them.

"This time you've got to admit it, Joe," Evelyn said. "Come on. There are some things that even Ireland doesn't have."

For once, Corrigan failed to rise to the provocation. The jocular side of him that would normally have responded reflexively was suppressed by a more serious mood. "You can judge for yourself when you see it," he said.

"When," Evelyn repeated bitingly. Corrigan had been promising for the best part of a year now that they would go there one day. She didn't take it seriously anymore.

"Sure." Corrigan kept his eyes fixed on the distant ridgeline and forced his voice to remain matter-of-fact. "We can go there for our honeymoon."

She drew her head back slowly, turning to look at him. "Are you serious?"

"Oh, I know I can be an ass about most things, but do you think I'd joke over something like that?" And then he relaxed and smiled, spreading his hands to indicate that was all he had to say.

"You mean it? . . . You really, really do mean it?"

"Of course I mean it, you silly cow of an American female. So do I get an answer, or are you going to stand there looking like that all day?"

She threw her arms around his neck. He pulled her close. They kissed and hugged, rubbed and nuzzled.

"So you will, then, eh?" he murmured.

"You know I will. Didn't you? . . . Couldn't you tell?"

"I wasn't sure."

"How could you not?" She drew back, shaking her head, laughing out loud, unable to contain herself. "So when? . . . Where? How are we going to do it?"

Corrigan shrugged, able to feign nonchalance again, now that he had gotten it out. "Whatever you like. Do you want to hire a cathedral, and maybe a symphony orchestra to go with it?"

She shook her head. "Nothing like that. Something small and informal."

"Short and quick?"

"Just that. I want it just to be us. It doesn't have anything to do with anybody else."

"I was hoping you'd say that," Corrigan said. "We can go straight on into Nevada and do it while we're here. How's that?"

Evelyn gaped at him. "While we're here? You mean now?"

"Why not? If you're going to live with Irish impulsiveness, you might as well get used to it. We could make Carson City or Reno tomorrow. A couple of days there. Then a flight to San Francisco or L.A., connecting to Dublin via London. You're always saying how much you like to support wild life. Okay, then, how about Christmas and New Year's in Ireland? Your life will never be the same again."

She shook her head disbelievingly. "But . . . what about work? We're expected back there. We can't just . . ." She left it unfinished, not quite sure what she had been about to say.

Corrigan made a dismissive wave in the air. "Ah, to hell with the lot of them. They can manage on their own for a while, this once. We've both got enough leave due to us. We've been saying ever since we got on the plane: it's about time we started living a little more for ourselves for a change. Well, I'm thinking, the time to begin that is right now."

"But shouldn't we at least call them and let them know what's happening?" Evelyn asked.

"Oh, not at all. We'll make it a surprise for them when we get back," Corrigan said.

"I don't think I've ever felt so happy."

They went back to the car. As they got in, Corrigan pressed the button to disable the phone from accepting incoming calls. "There," he said. "Peace guaranteed. Come on and get in. I wouldn't want you catching a cold. You're mine now, exclusively, for the rest of this year. CLC can start taking its share again when we're into the new one."

Eric Shipley had a feeling that something unusual was in the air when Pinder appeared in the DINS laboratory, being genial and showing an uncharacteristic concern about how things in general were going. As a rule he spent most of his time holed up in the Executive Building with the others of the managerial elite who had transcended the mortal plane of solder guns, screwdrivers, and rolled-up shirtsleeves. Shipley believed that a chief's place was where the troops were—in the trenches. When managers collected together in comfortable surroundings remote from where things were happening, it usually wasn't long before they started inventing realities of their own that were far more virtual than anything going on in the labs.

"It's come a long way since the days when it was you, some programmers, and a couple of techs," Pinder said, casting his gaze around. He was referring to the group that had first experimented with adding DINS feedback to the MIMIC prototype that Carnegie Mellon and MIT had developed jointly—the combination that became Pinocchio.

"It's going to go a lot farther, too, and get a lot bigger," Shipley replied, sensing the way the conversation was headed. He might as well give Pinder his opening now, he decided, and find out what this was about.

Pinder obliged. "And the organization has to adapt to anticipate that. It was fine for handling things the way they used to be. But that has all changed. We see things going toward a more comprehensive organizational structure that will combine all the interactive environment work under one reporting function. Bring all the decision-making together, eliminate the duplications."

By "we," Shipley presumed he meant the Olympians across the parking lot. Pinder refocused away from the distance, where he stared when he was being evasive, and back on Shipley, which meant that he was getting to the point. "Don't you think that the DINS group would function more smoothly all around as part of an integrated system like that?"

In other words, apart from possible semantic jugglings with job titles, Shipley couldn't expect any promotional prospects. Pinder was sounding out his reactions to merging DINS under a larger structure that would be headed by someone else. "Integrated" was always the managerese code word for "more controllable."

Shipley thought it was plain to everyone that his interests lay in science, not in whatever satisfaction came from exercising authority over people. He was not surprised, for he had never entertained the illusion that, by the generally accepted criteria, he was particularly promotable material. Neither was he concerned. The decision was one that he had made consciously, a long time ago. He replied, "I don't think that the neural work on P-Two and EVIE would be affected much, either way. If it fits in better with other plans, then fine."

"Such an arrangement would be acceptable?"

"I'm assuming that my present group remains intact."

"Oh, no question. You and your people simply transfer under the new system as is. It's really the other sections that get reorganized more, around you. You carry on as normal."

"Okay."

"We're responding to new opportunities in a changing world," Pinder said. "Naturally, the new organization that we're talking about would benefit from the direction of somebody whose background best qualifies them to exploit those opportunities. I'm sure you see my point—the contacts and resources that Tyron's government and industrial experience give him access to are something that the corporation can't afford to ignore."

"I see," Shipley said.

What he saw was Corrigan being shoved into a subordinate position incommensurate with his ambitions, tied to a project that Shipley was becoming increasingly certain was not going to be the corporation's mainline development thrust. But he had seen that much coming for some time anyway. More disturbing now was to see these overtures being made in this fashion, while Corrigan was away. It invited suspicions of more devious motives behind them. Shipley had no idea what these might be, but his instincts detected something underhanded.

Back in his office, he brooded for a while over the situation. Then he asked his secretary, Kathy Rentz, to find out Corrigan and Evelyn's planned schedule in California, and to try to get ahold of them. Kathy checked with Judy Klein in Corrigan's office and got back to Shipley half an hour later.

"They were due back in San Francisco today, but the hotel there says they called last night and canceled the reservation. Judy hasn't heard anything."

"Dammit. . . . What about their mobile number. Did you get that from the car-hire company?"

"Yes I did. I've tried it half a dozen times at least, but it's not accepting. Sorry, Eric. That's all I can tell you."

Chapter Nineteen

Corrigan didn't know Lilly well enough to have any real idea what she might do. She seemed sane and stable enough on the surface, but he had been confounded by human nature often enough to know not to trust first impressions. For his part, he had no difficulty accepting and adjusting to the situation—he knew the background to Oz and was committed to its success. But how might somebody else react in a world where no action could have "real" consequences, and who really believed that twelve years of a life had been stolen?

The trouble was, he still hadn't been able to trace her. He had gone to the North Side again, with no result, and got Horace to call companies listed under "Shoe Manufacture" in the city directory, to find out if any of them employed somebody called Lilly. This had produced four Lillys, none of them the right one. Either her firm was listed as something else, or she had told him a wrong story for some reason, or given him a false name for some reason, or she went by a different name at work for some reason . . . or any one of a thousand other possibilities that knowledge of human nature said happened every day. If this was the kind of thing that the machines were supposed to figure out, then good luck to them, Corrigan thought. Ten thousand years hadn't been enough for humans to even begin figuring out each other. Whether those twelve years had been real or not, he had to admit that they had certainly changed some of his attitudes.

What he needed to do, then, was talk to Dr. Zehl. It

was obvious now, of course, why Zehl seemed so different from most of the people that Corrigan met: he *was* different —not an internal animation created and manipulated by the system, but, like Lilly and himself, a real-person surrogate projected in from the outside. Corrigan realized now that he had met others, too, in the course of those years. If the original plan had been adhered to, there should be fifty or so of them mixed in among the regular population.

But Zehl was not one of the ordinary surrogates. Supposedly, he was Washington based, appearing and disappearing spasmodically, and often not seen again for long stretches of time. This, along with his position as Sarah's "supervisor," told Corrigan that he was really one of the controllers, entering the simulation from time to time in an effort to keep track of how things were going. In all likelihood he was somebody that Corrigan knew, but the physical appearance of injected surrogates could be changed at will. But whoever he really was, Zehl was Corrigan's only ready channel of communication to the powers outside who had the ability to determine Lilly's whereabouts, given the nature of the situation.

Corrigan called Sarah Bewley and told her it was important that he get in touch personally with Zehl immediately. Sarah, naturally, wanted to know what he proposed telling Zehl that he didn't feel he could tell her, his counselor, and the whole thing bogged down in a mire of pique and offended feelings that got him nowhere. In any case, Zehl was out of town and not contactable right now. Corrigan called Zehl's department in Washington direct, and after some bouncing around obtained a number that had Zehl's name listed. The voice that eventually answered, however, confirmed that Zehl was currently away and couldn't be easily reached. In fact, it would be the system covering for the fact that Zehl, or whoever, was not currently coupled into the system. The number Corrigan had called was a code to activate an external flag alerting an operator to page Zehl.

"This is the twenty-first century, isn't it?" Corrigan objected. "Are you telling me you can't get a message to him?"

"Well, maybe . . . if you leave it with me," the voice replied.

"Tell him it's from Joe Corrigan of Xylog. I want to

talk urgently about Oz. That should get him back to you minutes after he reads it."

But even a minute outside would still be something like four hours inside. The same speeding up of time that made more than a week of simulation time fly by while Zehl was absent for an hour also meant that Corrigan was going to have to wait for a response. A day for him equated to a little over seven minutes for Zehl, which meant there wasn't much time out there for anyone to hold lengthy conferences on what they were going to do. It also meant that Lilly would have free rein for a couple of days at least. But, unless he happened to run into her by chance or she decided to find him, there was nothing that Corrigan could do about that.

In the meantime, the best way to avoid having the time drag was to carry on as normal. But now that he knew the situation, he found himself in something of a quandary. Part of his nature—probably to do with his Irishness—rebelled from the prospect of obligingly continuing to act out his role as if nothing had happened, like a rat in a laboratory cage. The system had fooled him, and it couldn't be allowed to get away with it. On the other hand, he was a scientist involved with an experiment that was to a large degree of his own making, and his new awareness gave him a unique opportunity to function as a privileged observer on the inside. So he satisfied his instincts by teasing the system gently to its limits. This not only provided valuable practical data on where the limits were; but also, like playing word games with Horace and Sarah, he found it perversely and gratifyingly amusing.

"I've got a joke for you," he told Sherri. It was the middle of the afternoon, and the Galahad Lounge was quiet. "What do you call an insomniac, agnostic, dyslexic?"

"I don't know. What?"

"Somebody who lies awake all night, wondering 'Is there a dog?'"

She laughed obligingly, stared through him at the tariff list on the wall, and went away to clear some tables while she thought it over.

It was all so obvious, now that Lilly had forced him to recognize it. Strange, how the obvious was always the last thing you thought of. Or maybe not so strange, Corrigan reflected as he replaced glasses on the shelf below the bar. When you finally see the obvious, then obviously you stop wondering. It was the same as when people were always asking why everything they lost was always in the last place they looked: who was going to carry on looking after they'd found it?

Sherri came back to the bar and looked at him curiously. "So could an anemic, myopic, skeptic be somebody with a pale face who doesn't believe he's shortsighted?" she asked.

"Could be," Corrigan agreed nonchalantly.

"So is that funny too?"

"I'm supposed to be odd," he reminded her. "Why would you care how it strikes me?"

She corrected herself. "Would they have thought it was funny back in Ireland years ago? I'm just curious."

Corrigan made a show of subjecting the proposition to profound analysis. "Ingenious, yes. Funny, not really," he told her.

"Okay," she invited. "Now tell me why not."

Normally, Corrigan would have known better than to try, and hence wouldn't have raised the subject in the first place. This time, however, he was aware that he was really talking to a trio of TMC 11s and a SuperCray in Xylog's basement. It was about time, he decided, that they began really exercising their circuits to earn their keep.

"Imagine an insomniac, and imagine an anemic," he replied. "How do you picture them?"

Sherri frowned. "I guess one of them looks whiter."

Corrigan had to make an effort not to guffaw out loud. It was pure Horace and Sarah, leaping clear over the point. "Okay, that's the anemic," he agreed. "What does the other one look like?"

"How could I possibly know?"

"All right, let's try it another way. Why can't insomniacs sleep?"

That was easy. The system almost fell over, reciting from its lookup tables. "Well, it could be from any of a number of possible causes. Metabolic malfunction, hormonal imbalance, chemical stimulation by any of . . ."

Sherri broke off when she saw that Corrigan was shaking his head.

"They worry too much," he said.

"Maybe that too. But not all of them, necessarily," she answered.

"Never mind the others. The one we're talking about does."

"All right."

"Ah, now, you're accepting the fact, but you don't see the 'why.' What is it that he worries about?" Corrigan pressed. Sherri was looking bewildered. Never before had a simple question of hers led into anything like this. Corrigan made a tossing-away motion. "His boss is an arsehole, and his genius isn't being recognized at work; the car he just got fixed is making expensive noises again; his bank balance is printed in blood; and his wife, his girlfriend, and his mortgage are all a month overdue at the same time. His life is a mess. Subconsciously we feel fortunate and superior by comparison, and that makes us smile. So he's funny. The anemic isn't."

"Was I supposed to have thought all that?" Sherri asked, looking aghast.

"No. You're supposed to have *felt* it. It's the same someone-else-is-getting-it-and-I'm-not feeling that makes us laugh at banana peels and custard pies."

From the look on Sherri's face, Corrigan could have been revealing the secret of the philosopher's stone. At the same time, he might as well have been expressing it in Swahili.

"And that's it?" she said.

"Of course not. That's only the start. You want more?" Corrigan tossed out a hand. "Myopic means shortsighted, which in many contexts has connotations of stupidity and ineptness. Not funny, see? Being dyslexic might not be funny if you're dyslexic, but to the rest of us it conjures up pictures of getting everything the wrong way around: typical Irish."

"So we're superior again? Is that the idea?"

"Right. It reinforces the implication that we had before, and the way the two themes interweave is satisfying." Corrigan couldn't resist adding, "Of course, the unstated allusion to musical counterpoint is obvious, which makes the metaphor doubly satisfying."

"Yeah. . . . Right."

He went on. "Your making him a skeptic doesn't really work—skeptics are much too logical and sensible to be funny. The agnostic is funny because he doesn't know which way he thinks, which maintains the symmetry by casting him as a psychological dyslexic. And lastly, juxtaposing God with dog is delightfully irreverent, which a lot of people won't admit to being outwardly—but inside they find it hilarious. . . . So there you are. That's why it's funny. You did ask."

Sherri seemed to have so many questions jostling for attention at once that her eyes just glazed. Her eyebrows knitted, and her lips writhed. Finally she said, "I don't believe that you had to piece together all those connections. The number of permutations is too great. You'd never get through them." In its eagerness to know, the system was forgetting what was and was not an appropriate comment for a cocktail waitress.

"Not if you were a computer," Corrigan agreed. He winked. "But for people like you and me, it's easy. Right?"

"How do we know which connections to pick?"

"From the experience of life. When the person that you tell it to picks the same ones, and they don't know how either, you realize that despite your differences, there's something deep and mysterious that you both share in common."

Sherri was wearing the expression of a first-semester algebra student who had just glimpsed a textbook on tensor calculus. "You mean one joke says all that?" she managed in a strangled voice.

"Sure. In other words, you're not alone in the universe. It's a pretty good feeling to have, and you laugh. That's the other part of what makes funny things funny. Maybe it's the biggest part."

Chapter Twenty

It was Christmas week. The jostling crowds of returning migrants making their seasonal pilgrimage home, and foreign-born kin eager to explore their cultural roots, gave Dublin Airport the appearance and feel of a refugee transit camp.

The party started as soon as Corrigan and Evelyn came through the exit from customs into the arrivals hall, where they were immediately spotted by a boisterous trio of Corrigan's former student colleagues sent to intercept them.

"There's yer man!"

"Will ye look what he's brought back with him! Are there many more like that back there, Joe?"

"You're looking just great, Joe. It's good to have you back."

They were showered with rice, which they had avoided in Reno since the ceremony had been a simple, civic one, and draped with streamers. Corrigan was treated to a swig of Bushmills from a hip flask and presented with a wrapped bottle of something. Evelyn got a bouquet and was introduced to "Mick," "Dermot," and "Kathleen."

"Ah, Mick won't be so bad, once you get used to him," Dermot assured her.

"Dermot's all right, really. He doesn't say things like that when he's sober," Mick explained.

"Evelyn, ye can expect no sense at all out of any of them, now that the three are together again," Kathleen warned.

"She's probably right," Dermot agreed.

"And it'll get worse," Mick guessed.

The laughing, taunting, and backslapping continued as they trundled the baggage cart out of the terminal building and across to the parking levels. The air was chilly after California and Nevada, but Corrigan had had the foresight to invest in some warm clothes before they left.

"And what possessed you to end up with the likes of him?" Mick asked Evelyn. He was a hefty and solid six-footer, with the complexion of a radish and prizefighter features. "America must be getting hard-up for men these days, since the last I heard of it."

"Ah, it's his blarney," Dermot told them. "You didn't swallow the line about his uncle owning Aer Lingus, did you?" he said to Evelyn. "There's a long line of sorry women who are after hearing that one."

"Wasn't that how he got chased out of Ireland in the first place?"

"I thought that was to do with the wealthy widow-woman that he was sponging off."

"The one with the mustache and the warts on the nose, was it?"

"Not her at all, at all. Another one."

"Well, shame on the man."

"It'll do you no good. Sure, he never knew the meaning of the word."

"My friends," Corrigan sighed, grinning.

"Well, shame on the two of you," Kathleen declared. She slipped an arm through Evelyn's. "You just stick close to me, and I'll show you who the decent people are. We do have a few left over here, you know."

"And what would you know about them?" Mick challenged. "She's away over the water and gets herself a Brit for a boyfriend, and then comes back to preach at us about decent people! Did you ever hear the like of it?"

"Don't listen to them," Kathleen advised.

"Joe didn't listen to us either, and look what happened to him," Dermot said. "He's come back a Yank. It's the end of him."

"America's great," Corrigan told them. "A great place if you want to make some money."

"Maybe so," Mick agreed cheerfully. "But Ireland's the place to spend it."

*   *   *

They piled into Mick's Toyota wagon, and after negotiating the succession of traffic "roundabouts" to exit the airport, they were soon heading south on the main road into the city, still wet from rain earlier that morning, and congested by slow-moving crawls of traffic interspersed with Atha Cliath's bright-green, double-decker buses. Despite the gray sky, the chill and the damp in the air, and the sooty countenances of the old buildings—after Boston, Pittsburgh, and the West Coast, Corrigan found it exhilarating to be back among the narrow streets with their lines of shopfronts and busy sidewalks. There were trees and Christmas lights in the windows, pubs carrying signs for Guinness stout and Harp lager, local branches of the Bank of Ireland and Allied Irish Banks, and the "To Let" signs had names of auctioneers, not realtors.

"You know, this old city might be showing its age and crumbling in parts, but it's nice to be back in a place that was built for people to live in, not automobiles to flow through," he remarked fondly as he took it all in. "It's a good thing that they never let too many planners loose to improve it."

"The only way you could improve this mess would be by bombing it," Mick growled as the lights turned back to red a second time without the line moving.

Evelyn had wanted to see Trinity College, where Corrigan had earned his degree. He had warned that the wrong end of an eastbound trans-Atlantic red-eye flight would not be the best time for satisfying that kind of curiosity, and by this time she was in full agreement. So they postponed that item, and instead crossed the Liffey via the East Link toll bridge in the heart of Dublin's dockland to follow the coast road to Corrigan's hometown of Dun Laoghaire. Apparently, more people were gathering there to greet them.

"I didn't realize I was so popular," Corrigan said, permitting himself a small dash of self-flattery when he was told.

"And who said you were?" Mick challenged. "It's just a good excuse for a party. Sure, they don't even remember who you are."

Evelyn smiled to herself in the back with Kathleen. Evidently, immodesty did not sit well with the Irish.

Then came the cross-examination on Corrigan's work and what he had been doing—wearying after the journey, but to be expected. But behind the banter and lighthearted digs that never let up, Evelyn detected sincere curiosity and a genuine respect for his achievements overseas. Then it was Corrigan's turn to ask the questions, and the talk degenerated into a cataloging of names, and who was where and doing what these days, most of which meant nothing to her.

Mick, despite the wild-bachelor image that Evelyn had formed, was now married and working with the European Economic Community on economic modeling. Dermot said that the one thing he had in common with economists was that he didn't understand economics.

Kathleen was a systems analyst with British Aircraft Corporation, come back to Ireland for the holidays and the *"craic."* As far as Evelyn could make out, this was something of a catchall term for generally having a good time. Corrigan told her that along with reproduction and education, it made up most of the country's export industry.

Dermot seemed to have worked the most closely with Corrigan in former years. He was still with their former professor, Brendan Maguire, who had moved away from Dublin's urban environs to set up an EEC-funded research outpost of Trinity at what sounded like a remote spot, called Ballygarven, near Galway on the west coast.

"What's Brendan doing there?" Corrigan asked.

"What he's always been interested in: a bottom-up approach to AI," Dermot replied. "Your kind of thing, Joe. Now that he's got himself away from all the bureaucracy and the politics, he's able to do things his own way. Basically, he's defining clusters of agents as elementary software entities and letting them evolve. We call them his 'insects.' "

"A Minsky approach," Corrigan said.

"Exactly."

"I worked with Minsky for a bit while I was at MIT."

"I know. That's why I think you'd be interested. We'll have to try and get you over while you're here."

"I'll try and work it in," Corrigan promised.

"Brendan would never forgive you if he found out you were back and didn't go over there to say hello to him."

"How are you finding it over there yourself?" Corrigan asked.

"I like it."

"Isn't it a bit quiet after Dublin?"

"Ah, I've had me fill of this smelly city. Anyhow, there's good *craic* in Galway, which isn't too far. The scenery is grand, the women are fine . . . and the pints are as good as you'll find anywhere. That's the main thing."

"Now there speaks an Irishman," Corrigan pronounced.

"What's it like there?" Evelyn asked curiously.

"Ah, sure, there's nowhere to touch it," Dermot told her.

"Where is it?"

"Over on the west of Ireland," Corrigan said. "The Atlantic coast."

"The winds come in off the sea and over the cliffs as fresh as the day the world was created," Dermot went on, turning and extending an arm toward the window, as if it were all outside. "The mountains are wild and unspoiled, and the lakes as clear as pools of spring water."

"My God, he's getting lyrical," Kathleen muttered.

"Think of Yosemite—without California. And the people there, the friendliest you'll find anywhere in the world."

"Let's do go and see it," Evelyn said to Corrigan.

"We'll fit it in somehow," Corrigan promised Dermot.

"But it's so out-of-the-way," Mick said over his shoulder from the driver's seat. "What do you do when you want to go anywhere?"

"Why would I want to go anywhere?" Dermot asked him.

"You have to, sometimes. After all, you're here now, aren't you?"

"Well, I got here, didn't I? So it's obviously possible."

"I'll still take Dublin, meself," Mick declared. "Look at the bay out there, and Howth on the other side. You can't beat that."

"It's an open sewer," Dermot sneered. "Sure, you wouldn't have to be Jesus Christ to walk across to Howth. You couldn't sink through the pollution."

"Who has to walk, anyhow? We've got the DART."

"You need it. Walking would be quicker than this traffic."

"Do they argue all the time?" Evelyn asked Kathleen.

"Not all the time. When they do start really arguing, you'll know it."

In Dun Laoghaire, they followed the harborfront past stately Victorian terraces and arrived at the Royal Marine Hotel, where Corrigan and Evelyn would be staying. Immense in scale and magnificent in rendering, it was a fine example of the palatial resort hotels that had sprung up all over Europe around the middle of the nineteenth century— although since saddled with a modern extension in a clash of styles that reverberated all the way along the seafront.

They entered through an arched entrance lobby with marble columns and staircase, and went through to an enormous lounge, its walls adorned with huge, gilt-framed mirrors and paintings of sailing ships, and one side taken up by picture windows looking out over lawns with the harbor and its granite piers beyond. The place was packed with what looked like a dozen parties merging together and going on at once. People stood five deep around the paneled, L-shaped bar at the far end, and mixed groups, including children, filled the tables and milled about in the spaces between, while rosy-faced waitresses in maroon uniforms battled through it all carrying trays laden with bottles, glasses, and pints of black, creamy-headed stout. The hubbub of voices was overpowering. Through it the strains of a piano and accordion were coming from somewhere at the far end, and a circle off to one side were swaying and singing. Kathleen slipped an arm firmly through Evelyn's. "You'd better hang on to me in this," she said. "Ah yes, there's our crowd now, over that way. Let's see if we can fight our way through. . . . There's your ma, Joe—in the blue. Do you see her?"

"I do. She's looking well. Is Dad here too?"

"He should be around somewhere. Probably over at the bar."

And then it was all hugs, handshakes, and more back-slapping. Corrigan's mother, Helen, turned out to be a fine-looking woman, with rich black hair showing a few gray wisps, and high-boned, distinctly Irish features. She was groomed and dressed meticulously in a dark-blue two-piece, and carried herself well, with elegance. Her reception of Evelyn was not unwarm—curious and expressing a natural interest with dark, alert eyes that missed nothing; but at the same time she was clearly maintaining a measured reserve until she got to know this new addition to the family better. But the news that Evelyn, like Joseph, was a Ph.D impressed her. "Don't let him forget it," she advised Evelyn when they got a moment to talk between themselves. "He needs someone who's a match for him. These young flibbertigibbets that you see everywhere let the men turn them into replacements for their mothers, and it's the end of them."

Kevin, Corrigan's father, looked fit and hearty, with a square-jawed, pink-hued face, and wiry gray hair clipped straight and short. He was wearing a dark suit with vest, tie loosened and collar in disarray, liberally sated and jovial. "Well, he's taken his own sweet time about it, but he hasn't done badly," he pronounced, clamping an arm around Evelyn's waist. "What he did to deserve you is beyond me power to imagine, but there must be some sense left in him somewhere. Welcome to Ireland. And welcome to our house."

After that, Evelyn lost track of the introductions as they were shouted over the din or acknowledged with a wave from a table, over a frothing pint. There were Corrigan's two brothers and a sister, dozens—it seemed—of his old pals, friends of the family with names no sooner announced than forgotten, and innumerable cousins, uncles, in-laws, and aunts. And, of course, everyone was dying to meet the American wife.

"Carnegie Mellon, in Pittsburgh? Was Joe there? I didn't know that," a tall man in a tweed jacket said. "Did you know that Andrew Mellon was Irish-American?" Evelyn hadn't. "And so was William Penn, who founded Pennsylvania. In fact, he was native Irish—from Cork."

"The Irish seem very proud of their nationality," Evelyn remarked.

"Other people have nationalities," someone else chimed in. "The Irish and the Jews have a psychosis."

"The only thing you have to know about Irishmen is not to let them mix alcohol and politics," a chubby woman in a floral dress told Evelyn. "It's like driving. They can't handle both at the same time, you see."

"Where did ye say they're living now, over there? Pittsburgh, is it?"

"I thought a Pittsburgher was something you ate with chips at McDonald's."

Behind, Corrigan was unable to resist a little posturing as the worldly finder-of-fortune returned from afar. "Of course, I moved out of academics a while ago, now," he told a couple of men about his own age, both nursing pints of Guinness. "I'm managing a big AI project for one of the larger corporations—Pittsburgh based."

"That's nice," one of them said, staring woodenly.

"In fact, we're in the process of reorganizing for what everyone thinks will be a major breakthrough. Might well mean another promotion."

"That's nice."

Another woman said to Evelyn, "You should make money while you're young, and babies when you're older. People get themselves into such a mess trying to do it the other way round."

"I have relatives in Boston," her companion said. "We always try and get over there for Saint Patrick's Day. Americans do a much better job of organizing it. I think they understand it better than we do."

The drink and the talk flowed freely. As the mood grew mellower, Kevin Corrigan rose to propose the traditional Irish wedding toast: "May you have many children, and may they grow as mature in taste, and healthy in color, and as sought after . . ." he swayed unsteadily, almost spilling his drink, and Helen nudged him sternly, "as the contents of this glass."

"*Slainte!*" everyone chorused, and drank.

Then it was the turn of an uncle, also called Joe: "May the road rise to meet you, the wind be always at your back, the sun shine warm upon your face . . . Hell, there's more, but I forget what it is. Anyway, good luck to the pair of you. And let's be seeing more of you over here in future than you've managed so far. *Slainte.*"

"And may you be half an hour in heaven before the Devil knows you're dead," someone else threw in.

"*Slainte!*"

"May you live as long as you want," a woman sitting by Mrs. Corrigan followed, "and never want as long as you live."

And naturally, Mick couldn't be left out. "May you die in bed at the ripe old age of ninety-five," he said, raising his glass to Corrigan.

"Why, thank you, Mick."

". . . shot by a jealous husband."

By the middle of the afternoon, Evelyn could feel travel fatigue and jet lag catching up with her, on top of everything else. The room seemed to be rocking, and the faces and conversation were all smearing into a meaningless blur of sound and color. "I have to go up to the room and rest," she told Corrigan. "Can we make some excuse and get away?"

"Good idea," Corrigan mumbled—he wasn't looking especially bright-eyed and spiffy, just at that moment, himself. "There's going to be a party later, up at the house."

Evelyn shook her head dismally. "I'm not going to survive this."

"We're away," Corrigan announced to everyone. "Got to get a few hours' sleep. Have fun. We'll catch you later, okay?"

"Would you get that? He can't wait."

Ribald jeers and catcalls, mainly from the male company present.

"Tch, tch. What's the world coming to, at all?"

"Not an ounce of decency in the man."

"Will you give over?" Corrigan protested. "We've not even unpacked yet."

"Well, while you're at it you can unpack this as well." Jeff, one of the cousins, handed Corrigan a gift-wrapped box. Corrigan tore off the paper and added it to the pile of gifts and wrappings that had accumulated on the table, and opened the box. Inside was a figurine of a grinning Irish leprechaun, sporting a high hat and puffing a pipe. "To take back with ye's and remind you of us," the cousin said.

"It'll do that, all right, Jeff," Corrigan said. "Sure, it even looks like you."

"He needs a name," one of the women called out. "You have to give him a name, Joe."

Corrigan looked around him. "Ah, what else is he but a Mick, of course? We'll call him Mick."

Mick moved over and stared down approvingly at his namesake. "He looks happy enough to be a Mick," he agreed.

One of the men across the table started to sing, "When Irish eyes are smiling . . ." He looked at Corrigan and raised a hand invitingly for him to take it from there.

Corrigan couldn't. He was too exhausted, and the drink was hitting him the wrong way . . . and besides, he didn't remember the words. Then Marvin Minsky's line came to him, from the day when Corrigan and Evelyn had visited Boston. Grinning faces on every side waited for him to continue the song. He tossed up a hand, acknowledging defeat, and grinned.

"You've probably just been ripped off. . . ."

Chapter Twenty-one

Corrigan sometimes said that Europeans had exported Puritanism and the work ethic to America in order to be rid of both, and then get back to the business of enjoying life. The Christmas week that followed became one long round of eating, drinking, dancing, and more drinking, that persisted through into the New Year. By custom, annual holidays east of the Atlantic tended to be generous, and most people saved a healthy portion of them for the year's end. It seemed that nobody was at work who didn't have to be, and Evelyn lost track of the homes that were visited, and the pubs and hotel lounges sampled in the annual tribal loyalty-reaffirmation rites. Like many visitors to Ireland, she had a feeling of rediscovering the basics of simple warmth and spontaneous familiarity that can be too easily forgotten when pursuit of wealth and what passes for success becomes obsessive. Even allowing that she was being a bit romantic and impractical for the modern world, she suspended her disbelief willingly and delighted in fond reconstructions of bygone times, doubtless illusory, sparkling with wisdom and elegance that had probably never existed; but, after all, wasn't this supposed to be the most romantic time of her life?

What marred it a little was Corrigan saying scoffingly that she sounded like a tourist. For him this was just a break. He was becoming impatient to get back to the arena. Americans, it was often said—especially those with Irish roots that were imaginary—could be more Irish than the Irish. It was sometimes true the other way around, too.

Mick was not a lot of help in sustaining her romantic images of unsullied Irish charm and simplicity, either.

One evening in one of the seafront hotels, the customers sitting around the lounge began taking it in turns to sing solo. Every one of them seemed to have a party piece, which the rest would listen to appreciatively and applaud loudly— a far cry from dingy downtown bars where people went to get drunk, laid, or lost in anonymity. At one point, Evelyn felt her eyes misting as she listened to a wistful, soaring tenor voice evoking visions of homey farm cottages and green hillsides swept with rain.

"Can everyone over here sing?" she whispered, leaning across to Corrigan and Mick.

"Ah, it's the drink that does it. He'll be croaking like a rusty gate by morning," Mick told her, ruining the whole effect.

"Most of those songs were written by people who'd been away from Ireland so long that they forgot what it was like," Corrigan said.

"Or never been there, more like," Mick agreed.

"Six months over here, and you'd be writing the same about Pittsburgh," Corrigan told Evelyn.

They did visit Trinity College, finally, with its stiffly aristocratic frontages of gray, columned stone, staring down over an inner maze of interlocking lawns and cobbled courts. Evelyn was fascinated by the famous Long Room chamber of the Old Library, built in 1724, with its wood paneling, carvings, and gallery, containing hundreds of thousands of volumes going back to medieval times and before. Jonathan Swift, Oliver Goldsmith, George Berkeley, and Oscar Wilde had been students here, and again, walking among the ceiling-high shelves of cracked leather bindings and yellowing folios, Evelyn found herself reliving images of a time of tastes and sensitivities that had passed— even with the brash intrusion of a gaudily modern gift-and-souvenir shop, underneath on the ground floor.

They shopped in O'Connell Street, had lunch in the open, airy environment—with the sun actually putting in an appearance that day, reassuring the faithful of its existence —of the glass-enclosed mall by Stephen's Green. They saw Georgian squares and walked over the bridges along the

Liffey, jostled through street markets, and took the tour of the Guinness brewery.

And, partly as an aid to working off the effects of a week's overindulging, they joined the crowd of afternoon strollers walking the best part of a mile out to the lighthouse at the end of Dun Laoghaire pier. The weather that day— Mick said that four seasons a day was the norm in Ireland— was fine and dry, the wind brisk, the sea air bracing.

"I think it's wonderful," Evelyn said to Corrigan and Mick. "All these people out walking just for the pleasure of it. It's more the way things should be. Back home legs are getting to be for emergencies only."

"Have you seen what the price of gas is here?" Corrigan snorted.

Back at the house, Helen Corrigan showed her the traditional way of making tea, in a pot. "I don't care what those two say," Evelyn declared as they set out cups, saucers, sugar, and milk on a tray in the kitchen. "I think they do it to twig me. It's a side of the humor that I haven't really figured out yet. But people here still have a charm that you don't find in many places around the world these days."

"Ah yes, it's the charm of them that you have to watch," Helen replied, smiling faintly as she cut slices of still-unfinished Christmas cake.

"How's that?"

"People will behave as outrageously as the world will let them. And charm is how they extend the limits. Joe can be one of the worst. But it's not a lot of good telling you that now, I suppose."

Finally, Corrigan and Evelyn said their goodbyes and au revoirs to a final gathering of relatives and friends, and loaded their bags into Dermot's eighties-vintage Rover. Then they left Dun Laoghaire to drive across to Galway on the west coast of Ireland, where, as hoped, Dermot had arranged for them to visit Corrigan's former professor, Brendan Maguire, at Ballygarven before their return to the States.

Chapter Twenty-two

More rooms with fluorescent lights and pastel walls, racks of electronics, glowing computer screens. Not rooms formed of movable partition-walls and ceiling tiles, but solidly built from stone, with mullioned bay windows, modernized to a laboratory environment. Maguire had installed his research outpost of Trinity in a large old house a little above the town itself, known locally as "The Rectory."

Maguire himself was a short, rounding, Pickwickian figure with a crescent of ragged white hair fringing a balding head that had taken on the same, post-holidays, pinkish hue as his face. He had a pair of ferocious white eyebrows, and rimless spectacles that tended to sit halfway down a bulbous, purple-veined nose. He was wearing a crumpled tweed jacket of brown-and-tan check with a woven tie, plaid shirt, and baggy gray flannel trousers with turnups that hadn't been in style in fifteen years. From appearances, Evelyn would have dismissed him as a bumbling rural schoolteacher. Corrigan told her not to be deceived: it was Maguire's insistence on accurate thinking and old-fashioned rigor that Corrigan had to thank for his later successes in the States.

There was little here in the way of visually entertaining demonstrations. Maguire showed them screens of symbolic diagrams representing abstract software relationships, and charts that tracked growth and decay trends in mixed populations of numerically defined entities that he referred to as "species." The term was no misnomer. The aim of the research that Maguire and his team were engaged in was, in effect, to induce the emergence of intelligent behavior from neural-system analogs.

". . . assuming that anything that has appeared in the natural world so far can be called intelligent," Maguire said. "The notion shouldn't be so strange to you, Joe. We talked about it often enough."

"We did, that."

Dermot elaborated for Evelyn's benefit. "The idea, essentially, is to let a computer-intelligence follow the same route as we did and evolve from simple beginnings—instead of trying to reproduce in one step all the complexity that resulted from a billion years of selection and improvement."

"I've never believed that was practical, as I'm sure Joe will have told you," Maguire said to Evelyn.

She smiled. "At least a thousand times, at the last count. Top-down won't work, right?"

"That's right. We simply don't have the detailed knowledge to specify it," Maguire said. "Nobody has."

"So how far back did you go to begin?" Corrigan asked him, intrigued.

"The groupings that I showed you a few minutes ago approximate roughly to early molecular structures," Maguire replied. "We put a seed population into a simple world in large numbers and let them interact and compete. They've been running for the equivalent of several million years now, I'd say."

"And the species you have now are performing at about the level of insects?"

"Roughly, we think. The dynamics are completely different from biological competition. Making a direct comparison isn't easy."

"Pretty impressive, all the same," Corrigan commented.

"We do have the benefit of being able to guide things by conscious direction," Maguire pointed out. "We are able to introduce deliberately engineered genetic combinations when we see fit. That speeds up the process considerably. It's amazing the difference it makes when God goes into the stock-breeding business."

"It's fascinating, all right," Corrigan agreed. There was an odd light in his eyes. Listening to Maguire and Dermot had rekindled all kinds of enthusiasms from years that he had almost forgotten. He could feel the excitement of *real* science stirring again: knowledge pursued purely for the sake of knowledge.

"But we need a more realistic simulation of the physical environment if progress is to be sustained," Maguire went on. "One that will react back on the actions of the population more strongly and drive the selection mechanisms harder. It needs to close the overall organism-environment feedback loop more tightly."

"This is interesting. . . ." Corrigan's face took on a faraway look for a moment. "Kind of ironic."

Maguire looked at the others uncertainly. "What is he talking about?"

"The work that we're doing back at CLC right now," Evelyn answered. "On the face of it, it sounds as if it might be an answer to just the kind of problem you're talking about."

"Is that so?" Dermot said.

"In that case, you should stop messing around among those Americans, trying to act as if you were a millionaire or a celebrity or something, and get yourself back over here and help out," Maguire told Corrigan—but he wasn't being serious.

"No chance," Dermot declared. "He's been too seduced by now by thoughts of money and promotion in those big corporations over there."

Maguire snorted. "Well, don't let yourself be carried away by it all," he said to Corrigan. "Remember that the higher a monkey climbs, the more of an arse it looks."

Corrigan grinned. "Okay. But I will make sure you get all the information we can let you have that might help," he offered.

"That would be something we'd appreciate," Maguire said.

For lunch they drove down to the Cobh Hotel in the center of the town, which was where Corrigan and Evelyn were staying. Ballygarven was a small boating resort grown from a fishing village that stood at the head of an inlet where the sea twisted its way among rocky headlands and shingle beaches. Behind the town, heather-covered slopes and marshlands rose toward a ridge of granite-topped summits a mile or two away. Evelyn was doubly glad that she and Corrigan had decided to make this trip to the west of Ireland before they left. It was just as she had pictured, ever since Dermot began describing it soon after their arrival.

Food was served in the bar, which though modernized had not lost its old-world feel. Maguire steered Evelyn and Dermot to one side where there stood a table for hot food and another for salads, recommending the mussels and the lamb. Meanwhile, Corrigan went to the bar to take care of the drinks. He and Evelyn had checked in the evening before, and he already knew Rooney, the bartender. Several of the locals were in, taking a midday refreshment.

"Oh, the American's back, I see," Rooney said, taunting Corrigan good-humoredly. "Coca-Cola, is it? Or do I have to start mixin' some o' them fancy cocktails for ye?"

"Three pints, and enough of your lip, Rooney. And a glass of lager-and-lime for the lady, if you please."

"Are ye's back to see some decent scenery? Sure, don't the mountains way up above look green and fresh in the sunshine this mornin', after the rain?"

Corrigan looked pained. "What mountains are you talking about, Rooney? You don't call those humps out there mountains, do you? I'll tell you, we were in the Sierra Nevada in California just before the holidays, and there's real mountains for you. They've got one cliff called El Capitan, in the Yosemite Valley, that goes practically a mile straight up."

"Is that a fact?" Rooney said, putting a glass under one of the pumps. "And what would be the use of things as big as that to anyone at all? Our Irish mountains have got a top and a bottom to them, and that's all that matters. Why waste so much on all that useless middle? If you stand a little bit nearer they look the same anyway. But you don't have to spend half your life getting up, and then back down again." Rooney looked at the regulars in appeal. "Isn't that right, now?"

"It's fine by me," one of them agreed. "I'd never be seen dead on the top of either one of them anyway."

"You see, I was right. It's after turning into a Yank, you are. Everything has to be biggest, and that's all that matters. Never a thought for the quality of things."

"And when were you last there, Rooney?" Corrigan challenged.

"Oh, you'd be surprised if I told you, wouldn't you?"

"Go on, then. Surprise me."

Rooney set a foaming pint down on the countertop for the head to settle, and began pouring another. "Oh, I know all about the high life and such, as you might call it," he said airily. "I'm what you might call something of a self-unmade man."

"Oh? A self-*un*made man, is it?" one of the locals said.

"And what might that be?" another asked.

"I started out, long ago in me dim and distant youth, as the president of a big corporation, making half a million dollars a year," Rooney said. "But would you believe, I *needed* every blessed penny of it. There was the yacht to take care of, the private jet plane, and the mortgage on the mansion. All them social clubs and country clubs and golfing clubs, with their dues. . . . And you wouldn't want to hear about the kind of wife I had to put up with, and her tastes."

"Would ye listen to the man?"

"Okay. And? . . ." Corrigan said, smiling.

Rooney went on, "But I worked hard and assiduously, and by the time I was twenty-five I'd come down to regional manager. Got rid of the house for something smaller, the car for something slower, the wife for someone saner, and I found I could manage on two hundred thousand a year. So I paid off the debts, kept at it, and I was down to a branch manager by thirty, ordinary salesman by thirty-four, and I quit the salaried professions altogether before I was forty."

"Now there's a success story for you," one of the regulars murmured approvingly.

"It's different. I'll give you that," his companion agreed.

Rooney nodded. "By then I didn't need a salary anymore. Today, I don't owe anybody anything, and this job pays me all I need. It's only four shifts a week, and I get plenty of time to read the books I always wanted to, sit in the sun when it suits me, and go fishing with the kids." He thought for a moment, then shrugged. "To tell you the truth, I probably don't need the money that much at all, for we've a small farm that could get us by. But I keep it for the people that you meet."

Evelyn and the others had come over and were listening. "Another philosopher," she said to Corrigan. "You know, Joe, this is the kind of place that Eric should be in."

"Who's Eric?" Maguire asked.

"A scientist that we know back at CLC," Corrigan said.

"He'd fit in here," Evelyn said. "You're his kind of people. You talk his values. Corporate politics isn't his scene."

Maguire nodded and pulled a face. "Well, if he ever decides he's had enough, tell him to get in touch. We'll talk to him, sure enough. We've got some good people here, including some from Europe, but we could always use more. . . . And that applies to you, too, Joe, don't forget. If you get tired of being among those neurotics over there, we'll find room for you."

Corrigan laughed and raised his pint. "I think I can handle whatever comes up, Brendan. But thanks anyway."

The next day, Dermot drove Corrigan and Evelyn south to Shannon, where they boarded an Aer Lingus jet for New York. It had been fun, and it had been interesting—the kind of break they had intended. And in another way, a lot that they had not intended. But now it was time to get back to the real world. They had a big surprise to tell everybody.

Chapter Twenty-three

Jonathan Wilbur was in the Galahad Lounge again, sitting at the bar. It was early yet, with a few people at the other barstools and a group from a company marketing conference that was being held at the Camelot that week occupying some tables on the far side.

"How are things working out with Oliver?" Corrigan inquired casually.

"Oh, okay," Wilbur replied neutrally, and returned to playing with his portable electronic office. Corrigan sauntered back to the other end of the bar and checked the pressure in the dispenser. Wilbur looked up at him oddly from time to time but said nothing. Corrigan got the feeling that his behavior of late had been puzzling the system.

In the commercial showing on the TV, the couple who had arrived for dinner were healthily image-conscious, he in a satin-edged cloak and wearing a wig of constantly color-changing optical fibers, she in a *Psi-Woman* meditation jumpsuit, complete with requisite combination shoulder-purse and music/mantra player.

"Wasn't she the clairvoyant in that movie about the surgeon who put his wife's lover's brain inside the gorilla after they had the car crash?" a fat woman in a pink sombrero, sitting on another stool, asked the man with her while she stared absently at the screen and pushed pretzels into her mouth.

"Yeah. She showed the detective where the body was." The man was wearing a short, embroidered cloak and matador's black hat. It was South of the Border week. Anyone in Mexican garb got a ten-percent discount in most places.

On the screen, the two guests were sipping before-dinner cocktails. Suddenly the woman nudged her husband and pointed to a faint finger-smudge on her glass. *"Body grease!"* she whispered behind her hand. The husband hurriedly put down his own glass, at the same time glancing apprehensively from side to side at the cutlery and the china. Moments later, the scene ended with a shot of the couple departing on a pretext, and then the embarrassed host consoling his distraught wife.

"She can really do it," the woman in the sombrero said.

"Huh?" her companion said.

"In real life—she's really psychic."

"Oh."

"The police use her. A documentary last week had her in it, so it must be true." The woman looked at Corrigan for support. "She can find missing stuff by looking at pictures that they take from choppers over the city."

"That's nice," Corrigan said.

While on the TV, the hostess's wise and worldly mother was educating her daughter in the use of "Bodysafe." After spraying fingertips and palms, they embarked on a tour of the house together, rapturously drenching drawer handles, doorknobs, light switches, phone buttons, toilet seats, and anything else carrying the risk of indirect contact with another human being. The ad ended with the husband and wife again, this time waving goodbye to their guests after a brilliantly successful dinner party, and then flinging their arms around each other ecstatically— presumably after taking appropriate precautions with Bodysafe.

"You know, Joe, I think you've been holding out on me," Wilbur said at last.

Corrigan ambled back to that end of the bar. "Oh? Why would that be, now?"

"I think you saw some things coming that I didn't see, and you didn't tell me."

"Is that a fact?"

"About Oliver," Wilbur said. So, apparently, things weren't going so well. "What makes people so greedy? I mean, not only in business, but all these people that we read about. How do they get like it?"

"People will continue trying to get better at whatever others continue to admire," Corrigan answered.

"Aren't there any people of principle out there any-more?" Wilbur grumbled.

"Probably. But who's interested in principles? What gets you elected is where you stand on issues. And that's a shame, because issues change but principles don't. When you know a man's character, you know where he'll stand on any issue."

Already, as a now-cognizant observer inside the experiment, Corrigan was gaining some invaluable insights on how the system was evolving. This was the way they should have done it from the beginning—with the surrogates fully aware of what was going on. It was what he himself had always advocated in the endless debates on the subject. He didn't know how the decision had come about to go ahead with it—once it was decided upon, keeping the fact secret from the surrogates would be essential. The idea of it had been to guarantee that the surrogates' behavior would be as authentic as possible. But now he was surer than ever that it had been the wrong way to go. Knowing what was going on, he could steer the system into grappling with concepts of real substance for a change, and hence into showing the beginnings of emulating real, thinking beings—which had been the whole idea. Left to freewheel in its own direction for years, it had been industriously populating its world with morons.

Wilbur propped his chin on a hand and stared across the bar exasperatedly. "Joe, why are you a bartender?"

"To get the money to pay the rent."

"No, I mean why don't *you* run for office or some-thing?"

"I don't have the necessary lack of qualifications." Corrigan gestured to indicate the far side of the lounge. A manager from the Krunchy Kandy Corporation, which was the company staging its marketing conference at the hotel that week, was leading a mixed group of employees, all dressed similarly to himself in the pink-and-gold tunic and red frilled cap of the Krunchy Kitten, through a rendering in unison of the company's new TV jingle. "Anyway, who on earth would vote for me?"

The phone behind the bar rang. Corrigan picked it up. "Hello, Galahad Lounge. This is Joe."

"There's an outside call for you," the hotel operator's voice said.

"Thanks."

"Go ahead, caller."

"Joe Corrigan here."

"Ah, hello, Mr. Corrigan," a firm, genial voice—but at the same time, one carrying an unmistakable undertone of curiosity—replied. "This is Dr. Zehl speaking. I got a message saying that you wanted to get in touch with me."

The announcement came so unexpectedly that it took Corrigan several seconds to collect his thoughts. "Where are you calling from?" he asked.

"Does it make any difference?" Zehl—whoever he really was—had to be neurally coupled into the system again. If he were speaking via a direct channel from the outside, the mismatch in time rates would have made communication impossible.

The bar was an awkward place to have to take the call, but nobody was paying Corrigan any attention. He kept his voice low and faced away from the room, into a corner.

"Are we on monitor bypass?"

"Yes." The question would have confirmed what Zehl suspected—that Corrigan knew the situation. Zehl's reply meant that although the conversation was being handled by the system, its content was not being made available to the context analyzers. In other words, the line was not being tapped.

"So you know the score," Corrigan said. "Okay, I know what it's all about. Oz is running. We're still in it. You're one of the outside controllers."

"I see." Zehl's tone was wary, waiting to see what line Corrigan would take.

"Has anyone else in here figured it?" Corrigan asked.

"You're the first that we know of, so far."

"It's gone way past anything that was planned. I don't know how it got to be taken this far, but the results are amazing."

There was a pause, as if this was not the kind of reaction that Zehl had been expecting. "You're . . . satisfied, then?" he said finally.

"Yes, for the most part," Corrigan replied. "The memory-suppression took some figuring out at first, but I'm better off without it."

"How do you mean?"

"It works better this way. I can do a lot more on the inside, now that I know what's what. We should have set it up this way to begin with."

"Okay." There was an edge of relief in Zehl's voice. "So it seems to be working out."

"There might be a problem. One of the other surrogates has cottoned on to what's happening too. The trouble is, she doesn't know so much of the background, and she was pretty mad about the whole situation when I talked to her. I'm worried about what she might do."

"Why not talk to her? Tell her whatever she needs to know. It can't make a lot of difference now."

"That's what I want to do. The trouble is, I can't locate her. What I need you people out there to do for me is . . ." Corrigan's voice trailed off as he caught sight of the tall, dark-haired figure in a long coat, just coming into the lounge. He nodded a quick acknowledgement as he caught her eye, and turned his face back to the phone. "It's okay. You don't have to bother. I'll call you back later. Guess what. She just walked in the door."

Chapter Twenty-four

"I understand that congratulations are in order," Jason Pinder said from behind the desk in his office in the Executive Building. It was a meticulously neat office, with everything arranged logically and every need anticipated. "You never cease to surprise us, Joe. Well, give my best wishes to Ms. Vance. . . . No, that's wrong, isn't it. It's Ms. Corrigan now. Anyway, I hope you'll both have a fine future."

"Thanks," Corrigan said from the chair opposite. It was his first morning back. The summons to Pinder's office had come minutes after he appeared in the lab. Corrigan didn't believe it was just so that Pinder could be the first to offer his best wishes.

Pinder stroked his mustache with a knuckle and regarded Corrigan pensively for a moment before continuing. "I wouldn't want to spoil the romance at a time like this, but your going off without a word like that made it impossible for us to let you know what was happening. Nobody knew where you were."

Corrigan was far from sure that anyone from management had been trying to find out. Certainly, Corrigan's secretary, Judy Klein, had said nothing about being asked in the few minutes that Corrigan had had to talk with her before being called over to see Pinder. He knew that Shipley had been trying to get in touch with him before he and Evelyn left California for Ireland, but that was a different matter. Since Shipley was not expected in until the afternoon, Corrigan still didn't know what that had been about.

Pinder went on. "As you know, the whole DNC program has been the subject of top-level discussions in the company for some time now. While you were away, I was notified of certain decisions that have been made concerning revisions to our goals, and the organizational adjustments that will be needed to accomplish them."

Only then did the premonition hit Corrigan that a pie was about to hit him in the face. In the same instant, the certainty crystallized that this wasn't something that had suddenly happened in the last few weeks. He waited, saying nothing. Pinder continued:

"The change that will have the most impact as far as you're concerned, Joe, has to do with our reviews of the state of the art and the future developments that now seem likely in various fields. To put it bluntly, VIV technology is obsolete—or at least, on its way toward very soon becoming so. EVIE really can't be justified any longer as the company's main VR line. Going through the primary sensory system for vision and acoustics is a dead end. All the market indicators are for taking everything over to direct neural sooner rather than later." He showed his palms, then sat back, watching Corrigan with his marbly gray eyes to await his reaction.

It was one of the occasions when the normally smooth-working pieces of Corrigan's mind grated and jammed. First, after the success with Pinocchio One, Pinocchio Two had been enthusiastically pushed as the next logical step: extension of the existing system into the pons, in preparation for going further to the thalamus and hence being able to add DNC vision and acoustic. Then SDC had come along, offering a quicker fix through a hybrid approach using VIV technology, and that had become the mainline thrust in the form of EVIE, with P-Two relegated to longer-term, secondary status. But now, suddenly, EVIE was obsolete. What did it mean? Were the original priorities being reinstated?

"*Everything*, via direct neural?" Corrigan repeated. "That's what Evelyn's work is aimed at. So what are you saying? P-Two is on track again, after all?"

Pinder shook his head. "Fooling around at the pons—it's still years away from going to vision."

"What, then?"

"We can DNC to the thalamus right now. Scrub

P-Two. Forget messing around with hybrids. Full DNC with vision in under a year."

"How?" Corrigan asked, nonplussed. This was obviously the whole point that Pinder had been leading up to.

Pinder sat forward to rest his arms on the desk, fixing Corrigan with a direct stare. He held a breath for a second or two, then exhaled heavily. "Frank Tyron has drawn our attention to some recently declassified work that has been going on in SDC for some time, which changes the picture considerably. Basically, they already have a working method that couples to synapses in the thalamus. It's called DIVAC: *DI*rect Vision and *A*Coustics. He's put a proposal to the Board for going straight to a combined Pinocchio/DIVAC system now, rather than Pinocchio combined with VIV, and shooting for a full direct-neural system in half to a quarter of the time you're talking about. The Board's reaction is extremely favorable. Ken Endelmyer's with it all the way."

Pinder sighed and made an open-handed gesture that seemed meant to indicate that it was all as much a surprise to him as to Corrigan. But Corrigan didn't believe it. This kind of thing was not hatched overnight, without the involvement of somebody in Pinder's position. Shipley, he remembered, had seen something like this coming. At his house, Shipley had voiced his suspicion that EVIE was falling into disfavor, and putting Corrigan in charge of it was not necessarily to his advantage. Meanwhile, Tyron had been talking directly to the Board. The straws that Shipley had glimpsed had been in the wind for months.

Suddenly, a lot of things came back to Corrigan that he should have seen the significance of immediately, long ago. Hans Groener, in California, had talked about thalamus-level research going on there, and had mentioned the Air Force's involvement. But Corrigan had been so immersed in his own, self-centered universe that it had barely registered.

"So . . ." Corrigan waved a hand meaninglessly while he struggled to collect his thoughts. "What about Evelyn and the pons interface that she's working on? We brought her in with the aim of eventually setting up a neurophysiology group. What happens to that?"

Pinder nodded sympathetically. "I hear what you're saying, Joe. But the corporation has to take account of developments in other parts of the world. Not all of anyone's plans always work out as hoped. The decision is made: further major funding, either for EVIE or for further pons work, is out. But we would be prepared to keep it going in a low-key mode in case the DIVAC-based approach runs into snags—if that's something you'd be interested in doing." It didn't need Pinder's tone to convey that it equated to consignment to oblivion. Corrigan's expression said that he would not be interested. "Alternatively," Pinder said, coming to what was effectively the only option, "you could move into the mainline operation."

Just for a second, Corrigan had thought Pinder was about to offer him the job of heading it, but his use of the word "into" promptly scotched that.

"Naturally, positions will be available for you—yourself and Evelyn," Pinder said.

Corrigan swallowed dryly. His gut-feel already told him what the answer to the only outstanding question had to be, but there was no way around it.

"Who'll be running this operation?" he asked.

At least Pinder had the decency not to try to pretend that he hadn't been expecting it. It was, after all, as Corrigan could see by now, the whole point of the interview.

"Frank Tyron originated the proposal," he reminded Corrigan. "His contacts and experience are right for this kind of work. And the Board were very insistent that a program that will involve a lot of coordination outside of CLC, and especially liaison with government departments, requires someone with his kind of background. I'm sorry, Joe. I know you've done some good work, but that's the way it is." He placed his hands palms-down on the desk and concluded briskly, before Corrigan could react, "The project will be designated COmbined Sensory and MOtor Stimulation: COSMOS. We're at the beginning of a new year, and we want to get as much mileage out of that as possible. I'd like the current projects tidied up and loose ends cleared by the end of the week. There will be a meeting next Monday to brief everyone on the goals and tentative organizational structure for the new program."

Even with it spelled out like that, Corrigan couldn't bring himself to capitulating ignominiously to instant acceptance. "I'll have to think it over," he replied, too numbed for the moment to be capable of responding more effectively.

Pinder nodded. "I understand. Tomorrow morning will be fine."

Corrigan left in a daze shortly after. He didn't feel like a person at all, but more a financial statistic or a function in an organization chart, whose feelings and self-esteem faceless people in five-hundred-dollar suits and limousines could trample on at will. The indignation came later.

"Christ, Eric, they're just sweeping the two of us aside, putting us under this outsider that we don't even know." Corrigan turned and flung his hands out appealingly to Shipley, who was watching from a stool at a bench in the DINS lab. Evelyn sat listening from a paper-strewn desk to one side. "I mean, if we'd nothing of any note to show after these years, I could understand it. But there wouldn't be any plans for them to be making, without us. . . . You and I, we *made* this project. It's ours. They can't just hand it over like this."

"A lot of things have been going on that we don't know about," Shipley said. "Things that go back to before Tyron even joined the company."

"Oh? Like what?"

"I'd bet that Tyron had a lot to do with that information at SDC not being made public. He had some kind of deal worked out before he left the SDC—that he'd bring it with him into an area where it can be exploited commercially. Some people are going to make a lot of money out of this, Joe. But it won't be us."

It took a moment for Corrigan to see fully what Shipley was saying. "Surely not," he protested.

Shipley shrugged. "Why do you say that? It wouldn't exactly be the first time something like that has happened. As a matter of fact, I did some quiet checking on the side while you and Evelyn were away. There are no licenses payable for using the VIV technology that was pioneered at SDC, and I'm pretty sure the same is true for DIVAC. That means that the information can be used freely by anyone now, without restrictions. So Tyron can bring his know-how into CLC and earn himself a lot of gratitude. That's what it's all about."

Evelyn sat back in her chair. "What can you do?" she said. "I guess we're just a different kind of people. That's the way things have always been with half the world. Probably they always will."

Corrigan snorted. "Are you saying we should lie back and enjoy it? Well, you can if you want. But I'll be hanged if I will."

"What do you propose?" Shipley asked, not bothering to disguise his skepticism.

Corrigan turned away and banged the side of a steel electronics cubicle with the flat of his hand. "Right now, Eric, I don't know," he muttered. "But dammit, I'll think of something."

The den of Evelyn's apartment at Aspinall was darkened, lit only by the green-shaded lamp on the desk. Corrigan stood by the window, brooding to himself as he stared out at the lights of the city. So what, exactly, was Tyron proposing to deliver that was generating so much excitement and attention? he asked himself. Functionally it would still be EVIE. For anyone using the system, the fact that a different behind-the-scenes technology was supporting the vision and acoustics would make only a marginal difference. It was still what Victor Borth had called a "toy": something that played at imitating the world. That would be of interest to some enterprises, and no doubt Tyron and whoever he was in league with had identified some potential—possibly some quite substantial potential. But Corrigan knew that what the people with the *real* money wanted was something else. Okay, he thought to himself, so those were the rules, were they? . . .

"Joe, are you coming to bed?" Evelyn's voice said from the doorway behind him.

"Not really sleepy."

"It wasn't really sleep that I was thinking about."

He turned and smiled tiredly in the light at the window. "I have to say my prayers first. You know how the Irish are."

She came in and moved close to him. He slipped an arm around her. "Still letting it eat away at you?" she said.

"Oh . . . just thinking."

"You can't change anything. Start thinking about moving to another job if it'll help. We'll manage."

"Just walk away? Wouldn't some people like that!"

"I know that the Irish are fighters, too. But you can't fight this."

"Well, maybe you're being just a little bit too quick on handing down that verdict."

She turned her head and looked at him uncertainly. "Why? What have you got in mind?"

He thought for a second, then said, "Let me check on a few things first, before I start going into it. Okay?"

"If you say so."

He squeezed her waist and patted her behind through her robe. "Go and get warm, then. I'll be through in a minute."

"Hurry up," she whispered, kissing him on the cheek, and left the room.

It would still be before eleven in California. Corrigan went over to sit down at the desk and called Hans Groener's personal record onto the terminal's screen. He selected the phone number and pressed a key to initiate auto-call. Moments later, Hans's features greeted him. They talked for most of the next hour about thalamus-level interfacing. The next morning, Corrigan extended his leave by a few days and caught a noon flight to San Francisco. He and Hans spent the rest of the afternoon talking in Hans's lab at Stanford, and afterward into the early hours at Hans's apartment, going through research notes and generating reams of charts and diagrams.

On returning to Pittsburgh, Corrigan went straight over to see Jason Pinder.

Chapter Twenty-five

Corrigan's manner had changed since his last interview with Pinder. Although it had never come close to anything that could be called servile, common sense had always caused him to hold his opinions unless they were asked for, and then to couch them with a restraint appropriate to Pinder's position. Now, however, the words poured forth as from an inspired evangelist. Pinder, aware that Corrigan was neither naive nor new to the business, listened with intrigued curiosity.

"Before the company leaps into putting up a lot of money and committing itself for years ahead, it ought to ask one last time what it stands to get in return for the investment," Corrigan said. "When you sit down and analyze it, all that COSMOS is really promising is a more sophisticated version of what we've already got in the lab down there: a full-sensory interface. The only difference is that EVIE uses VIV for its vision and voice, whereas COSMOS will shift everything to the thalamus. But essentially it's still the same thing. And that same thing is what the people from Feller and Faber told us they didn't want—what Borth described as a 'toy.' What they do want, and what there's still a huge market for out there if someone can come up with a way to achieve it, the thing that the industry has been after for decades, is *true AI*." Corrigan drew a long breath as he came to the point that he was preparing to stake his future on. "Well, I think that I can deliver it."

They both knew enough of what Corrigan was talking

about to make questions unnecessary. All he needed was a cue. Pinder nodded. "Go on, Joe. How?"

Corrigan moistened his lips. "The top-down, analytical approach doesn't work. Everyone in the field agrees. The only way it's going to happen is by getting some kind of initially simple system to evolve."

"Which has been tried in enough places too," Pinder observed. "And the results have all been equally modest, to say the least."

"Agreed. But they've all been tries at equipping computers with sensory apparatuses like TV cameras, arms, legs, and wheels, and letting them loose to explore some kind of environment. But you don't realize how good biological nervous systems are until you try copying them. They were shaped by a billion years of evolution to interact with the real world. Computers weren't."

Which exhausted what everyone in the trade knew were the two acknowledged theoretical approaches. "So are you saying you know another way?" Pinder asked.

"Yes, I think so."

"What?"

"Computers do interact extremely well with their own, internal worlds. . . . So what you do is, invert the conventional approach." Corrigan spread his hands. "If training a machine intelligence in our world isn't effective, let's try doing it the other way around: by going into its world and doing it there."

Pinder frowned. "Sorry, I'm not quite with you, Joe. Doing what, exactly? Where?"

"People interfacing via EVIE interact with a machine-created version of the real world through the surrogates that they control. But the machine could also put pseudopeople of its own in there too—'animations.' You design the system to be goal-directed to make the behavior of its animations converge to that of the real-people surrogates."

Pinder sat back, seeing the implication at once and staring at Corrigan thoughtfully. "So its success would be measured through a kind of Turing test," he said.

"Yes, exactly."

"This is certainly a new one on me, Joe. I've never heard the like of it."

"What do you think?"

"It's intriguing."

Corrigan could see that he was making an impression and pursued his point further. "The system wouldn't need to know *why* the individuals that it was trying to imitate were doing whatever they did. Its brief would be simply to make its animations behave similarly, which it could accomplish from external observables. And that's what's different about this approach. In the past, we've always tried to press into service existing processing methods and associative structures—tools that were developed for other purposes. Well, very possibly they're inherently unsuitable for this kind of job and can never work. But the way I'm talking about, the system will be free to create its own organization of associations and linkages in a way that's appropriate to its goals."

"Information-processing architecture is appropriate to what information-processing systems do. Whatever it is that has evolved inside cerebral cortexes is appropriate to what cerebral cortexes do," Pinder summarized.

"That's it. And we don't need to know in advance what the final organization will be, any more than the first protoplasm needed to know the wiring for a mammalian brain. The system would learn the way children do: by trying to imitate 'adults' who already understand the way the world works, and making its own connections and associations accordingly.

"And we've got all the pieces needed to do it. Pinocchio provides the basics of a suitable vehicle for driving both the surrogates and the animations. EVIE, with the all-neural package that we're talking about for COSMOS, gives us a mechanism for coupling in the surrogates. A multitasking expansion of Jenny Leddell's Perseus system from MIT could drive the animations."

Corrigan judged this a good place to stop at for a response, and waited. Pinder stroked his chin and stared down at the desk. What Corrigan was proposing was clear enough. He was searching for the flaws. Finally he looked up.

"A world to support that kind of evolution needs to be context-rich," he said, meaning the degree of detail and its variability that the system would have to support. "The look-ahead for sudden context changes and recomputing

SDVs still hasn't been solved satisfactorily. And it would get a hell of a lot worse with this."

It was an objection that Corrigan had expected. Now he could offer a radical departure from anything that had been considered so far. "COSMOS only gives us a bit sooner what EVIE would have led to anyway, eventually," he said again. "But why get involved with the primary sensory system at all? If we are set on going straight to the thalamus, we can take advantage of new effects that operate beyond that level, that will crack that whole set of problems."

Pinder looked surprised. "Effects? What effects are you talking about?" he asked.

"When I was in California last month, it wasn't just for a romantic interlude and to get married," Corrigan replied. "I also wanted to update myself on some work going on out there that I'd been following." Not quite true, but it sounded better that way. "A group at Stanford is deep-coupling to the thalamus too. One of the people involved is called Hans Groener—I worked with him at MIT. His particular angle is dream research."

"So how does it affect us?"

"Input compression. One of the things they've learned to do is to use a high-level code to activate percepts already stored in the nervous system. I think it could solve the details problem."

"Dreams?" Pinder repeated. He thought about it and frowned. "But wouldn't that make it all subjective? Everyone would experience their own world."

"To some degree, maybe. But apparently there's a commonality to the coding that has surprised everyone. So, yes, in a sense the participants would be experiencing what's partly an induced dream; but—down to any level of detail likely to matter, anyway—the same dream. So the contextual environment would be much richer than anything we've ever contemplated before—and getting better all the time. The environment and the animations would stimulate each other into coevolving: one of the most powerful evolutionary mechanisms there is."

Pinder looked as if he wanted to believe it. But there was one more reality to be faced. "Children need years to grow up," he pointed out. "We don't have years. What prompted the decision to go for COSMOS was that it gives us something to go for now."

And that was that last thing that Corrigan had been waiting for. He nodded. "Yes, I know. And that's where the other interesting thing that Hans's people have stumbled on comes in. You know how it is when you dream—sometimes you find that what seemed to last hours all took place in a few seconds while you were waking up? Well, it seems that the effect can be achieved artificially when you go in above the primary sensory level."

"Artificially?" Pinder's eyebrows shot upward. "What are you saying? That it's possible to accelerate interaction rates?"

Corrigan nodded. "Exactly that. Time in the simulated world could run faster. So you wouldn't have to wait years for your child to grow up."

"What kind of an acceleration are we talking about?" Pinder asked, now definitely interested.

"Somewhere in the hundreds, probably. That means that the equivalent of years of growing up would take a few weeks of machine time." Corrigan sat back and extended a hand, palm upward, like someone offering the world. "There it is—all the ingredients for a true AI. And you could have it in as much time as we're talking about now for COSMOS—which the customer says is just a toy."

Pinder put the proposal to Ken Endelmyer, the CLC president, later that week, with the endorsement that in his opinion it was worth looking into seriously. Certainly, it was bold and vigorous in concept—maybe just what the whole field needed. A high risk, yes; but the potential rewards were huge, too, as they well knew. Endelmyer called in Therese Loel for an opinion. She was as intrigued as Pinder and agreed that there might be something in it. She also thought that the potential return from COSMOS was paltry compared to the market that this could open up. Endelmyer put the prospect, along with tentative estimates of what it would take to make the project fly, to the Board. Visions grew of this being pushed as the lead corporate research project, and it became a major funding issue. A month after Corrigan's talk with Pinder, orders came down from corporate headquarters to put the present plans for COSMOS on hold.

Corrigan and Evelyn had just moved to a house in Fox Chapel, a higher-income, professional residential area a few miles north of Blawnox. They threw a great housewarming party for their friends from CLC and elsewhere, and to add to the fun had one of the EVIE realscaping teams go through the house to capture the interior from all sides and angles for addition to the ever-growing database for the "simworld" of Pittsburgh and the surrounding area. So now, Corrigan explained to everybody, they would be able to relive the party all over again by coupling into EVIE when they got back to work tomorrow morning.

On the night of the announcement that COSMOS was on hold, Corrigan came home somewhat the worse after a celebratory drink or two in town. "Maybe Mister Tyron isn't so much of a big wheel after all," he said, sporting a cigar along with a satisfied smirk as he delivered the news. "It's like Vic Borth said: his field is just visual imagery. Toys. But this thing we're talking about now is going to need real know-how. It's getting out of his league."

Evelyn was less sure of that, but wrote Corrigan's brashness off to the effects of the drink and the strain that he had been under. Anyway, she didn't want to spoil the party. "Sit down and I'll get you a coffee," she said, forcing a smile. "Have you eaten yet?"

Corrigan stabbed his own chest with a thumb as he lowered himself heavily into an armchair. "If there's big money to be made out of all this, maybe I'll get to claim a share too now. Maybe we'll see who's who, eh?"

Evelyn's smile faded as she went through into the kitchen. She wasn't sure that she liked the side of Corrigan that was beginning to show itself. And she was nervous. She didn't think that somebody like Tyron would give up so easily—nor the kind of people that he had behind him.

Chapter Twenty-six

Maurice came into the still room as Corrigan was changing out of his work jacket and into his street clothes. "Where are you going?" Maurice demanded. "You've got another two hours left yet."

There were times when it was fitting for Corrigan to carry on taking orders from, and working for, a computer animation, but somehow he couldn't bring himself to ask permissions or have to make excuses. "Not tonight," he said, pulling on his topcoat. "There's too much to explain, and you probably wouldn't believe it anyway. It's quiet, and Sherri can handle it. I'll talk to you tomorrow."

Far from satisfied, Maurice followed Corrigan out into the corridor. "There is such a thing as proper procedures, Joe. You might show the courtesy of clearing it with me first." Lilly was waiting by the door from the Galahad Lounge, and moved across to join Corrigan as he appeared. "Oh, so it's like that, is it?" Maurice went on behind him. "You can't just walk off the job for a date, Joe. I mean, hey, what is this? This isn't gonna go away in the morning, you know. Just who in hell do you think you *are*?"

They came out onto the street, with its usual assortment of caricatures, crazies, and zombies. "I've been looking for you all over," Corrigan muttered as soon as they were away from the doors. "You've had me worried, I can tell you."

"You know where I am. What was so difficult?" Lilly's voice was clipped and bitter. Clearly, she was not over her indignation—at the deception, and him as the only accessible target representing those responsible. The latter was compounded by his defending the situation, which she interpreted as bland acceptance. He got the feeling that she had come to him only as a last resort.

"I tried to, a few times. But I couldn't find the place again. They've changed parts of the city that weren't scaped. I tried to get you at work, but I couldn't find it listed."

"Why all the trouble? What worried you so much?"

"I didn't know what might come into your head to try next."

"Did you think I might try suicide or something as a way out?"

As a matter of fact, Corrigan had. After all, no physical harm could come to an external operator from causing an internal surrogate to permanently deactivate itself. But for all anyone knew, the knowledge and the trauma of the event might leave some adverse psychological imprint. It was something that the system designers had talked about, but in the end been forced to leave as one of the many unknowns that the experiment would entail.

"Somehow it didn't seem like you," Corrigan replied. Lilly didn't respond. He went on. "I was concerned that you might try to disrupt the experiment. Oh, I don't know how, exactly. . . . Set fire to the city, start a riot, preach revolution from street corners—mess the whole thing up somehow. And that would have been a shame, because it's all doing so incredibly well—despite the flaws."

Lilly stopped in the middle of the sidewalk and stared at him incredulously. "I can't believe I'm hearing this." She shook her head. "I've heard of loyal servants of the System, but this is unreal. I mean, they've stolen twelve years of your life, and all you can do is stand there defending them like Horatius on his bridge and say—"

Corrigan raised his hands protestingly. "No. Look, it's not the way you think. We haven't really lost twelve years."

"Not lost? What would you call it, then?"

"I didn't mean like that. It hasn't—"

"Do you call being surrounded by this lunacy every day living a life?"

"Let me finish. . . ." Corrigan looked around. There was a small coffee shop, not too crowded, a short distance from where they were standing. He took Lilly's elbow and began steering her in that direction. "We can't talk like this. Come on, let's take the weight off our feet in there. A cup of something might calm you down before you break a spring or something, too."

". . . and we finally settled on a factor of 200. A day to us is only seven minutes outside. A whole week is less than an hour. So the twelve years that you're so hyped up about works out at about three weeks. . . . Hell, Lilly, you're a scientist. What we're going through is a unique experience. Three weeks isn't a lot to exchange for it."

Lilly, hunched over the opposite side of the small corner-table, sipped her coffee and sighed. Corrigan's words had had some effect. At least she was listening. She indicated their surroundings with a glance and a motion of her head. "So this is all an accelerated dream. We can afford to sit here and talk about it. It isn't losing us much."

"If we sat here for the next hour, it would be a whole eighteen seconds out of your life," Corrigan said.

Lilly fell quiet for a moment, reflecting on that. "You people might have told us," she said.

"Tyron didn't mention it when you were interviewed in California?"

Lilly shook her head. "They didn't tell us a great deal about it at all."

"Maybe they did tell you after you got to Pittsburgh," Corrigan said. "But then somebody sprung this memory suppression, and it got lost with the rest."

Corrigan felt more at ease for the first time in days. It seemed that he had saved the project and would have good news to report the next time Zehl contacted him. The thing now was to get Lilly back into playing her role normally. He made a conscious effort to discharge the atmosphere by being casual, resting an elbow on the edge of the table and draping his other arm along the back of an empty chair next to him.

"Out of curiosity, what gave it away?" he asked her.

"You mean how did I see through the simulation?"

"Yes."

"Oh, not because of any one thing that you could put a finger on. Lots of little things."

"But there must have been something that clinched it."

Lilly stared into the distance and tried to think back. "I think it was cracks in a sidewalk," she replied at last.

"You're joking."

"No. . . . I do remember a couple of days in Pittsburgh before it all goes blank—when the group from California that I was with first arrived. There was a briefing and some preliminary tests."

"Okay."

"Well, I spent some of my free time wandering around, taking in the sights. I like the older, East Coast cities—they're all so much alike in California. Anyway, I was standing watching something in one particular small street—it's not all that far from here—that had lots of old, cracked paving stones in the sidewalk, and I noticed that the pattern of the cracks near the base of a lamp outside an antiques store looked like the coastline of Labrador."

Corrigan shrugged. "What about it?"

Lilly drank from her mug, frowning with the effort of trying to keep clear what had happened around that time. "Soon after that it all gets lost. That was when the intensive tests began, and we were supposed to have had the breakdown and the rest of it. . . ."

"Yes. Go on."

"Much later, after all the therapy and rehabilitation, when I was out and about again, I ended up one day in that same street. The stones were still old and cracked, so they hadn't been replaced—but the pattern wasn't there." She raised her eyes and looked across at Corrigan. "And that was when a lot of other strange things that I'd been noticing started making more sense. It was a simulation. The system had the data to create realistic views of that street; it knew that the street had old paving stones, and that old paving stones would have cracks. So it put cracks in them. But it didn't put in the *right* cracks."

Corrigan looked at her, astonished. "And that was it?"

"That was it."

He sat back, nodding. All for the want of a nail . . . "I noticed similar things from time to time, too. I put it down to my own faulty memories." He shrugged, as if accepting the need for some kind of explanation. "That was what all the authority figures in my life had been telling me for years."

Lilly looked at him doubtfully over her mug. "You know, for someone who was involved from the start, there seems to be a hell of a lot that you don't know," she remarked.

"I'm not really in any better situation than you," Corrigan said. "We talked a lot about the pros and cons of suppressing the surrogates' memories, but as far as I was always aware, the decision was not to go with it. So what must have happened is that top management of the project set up another group to implement it secretly. . . ."

"But I thought *you* were project top management," Lilly interrupted.

Corrigan waved a hand. "Okay, maybe I should have said company top management. There were all kinds of people involved in Oz, both inside CLC and out—it was a hugely complicated undertaking. . . . Anyway, the idea was to make reactions to the simulation valid. But I always thought it was the wrong decision. Things work better if you know what's going on."

Lilly stopped him again. "Wait a minute. Are you saying that you didn't *know* about it—that there was going to be any memory suppression?"

Corrigan shook his head and showed his hands appealingly. "I couldn't be allowed to, could I? Think about it. If a surrogate knew in advance what the intention was, he'd see straight through any attempt at a cover story. If it was going to be done, that part *had* to be done by other people—without my knowing. Sneaky, yes. But what other way was there?"

Lilly tapped her spoon absently against the side of the mug, frowning to herself and watching it in a distracted kind of way. Corrigan realized that she was far from appeased. She had let herself be led into a diversion about the project's early days and cracks in paving stones to give herself time to mull over the things he had said earlier.

Finally she shook her head and said, "It still doesn't add up, Joe. You said you were one of the principal architects of this experiment, right? It practically grew from a proposal of yours in the first place."

Corrigan had a premonition then of where she was

leading. Suddenly he felt less comfortable. "Right," he agreed.

"And yet, twelve years into it, you could still be taken in?" Lilly stared at him disbelievingly. "If this was anything at all like the experiment you expected, you'd *have* to have recognized it. Even if your memories of actually commencing it were suppressed, you'd know enough to figure out what all that business early on had been about. The only explanation has to be that the possibility of a simulation that would keep running for years never entered your head. Therefore, it must have gone way past anything envisaged in the plans that you knew about. Maybe the reason I saw through it first was that I didn't know what the simulation was *supposed* to be."

Corrigan had to nod—he had said as much himself when they talked before at Lilly's place. The first phase was supposed to have consisted just of progressively more elaborate tests. A comprehensive, extended simulation of the kind they were in wouldn't follow until much later. "Nothing like this was even scheduled," he admitted.

"Well, it seems *somebody* scheduled it," Lilly said pointedly.

In short, had he ever been as in control of things as he imagined? And if he had not, then who had been in control?

And still was?

Chapter Twenty-seven

The CLC Board decided to go with the proposal to attempt evolving an Artificial Intelligence by means of machine-directed animations learning to mimic human surrogates in a virtual world. The project was designated "Oz," and to begin with, half a floor was allocated to accommodate it in the IE Block at Blawnox. This did not mean abandoning COSMOS, however, since an all-neural interface as envisaged from COSMOS would be essential for coupling in the human surrogates for Oz. Hence, COSMOS was recast as a subsidiary goal in the greater plan.

The COSMOS part of the program was left under Tyron's management, as had been the original intention, and the overall direction of Oz entrusted to Pinder, with Corrigan heading up the groups responsible for developing the animation-driver software. Peter Quell, Pinder's deputy, stood in as acting head of the rest of the R & D division. The most obvious aspect of this arrangement was the temporary nature of Pinder's overseeing role in getting Oz off the ground. When he returned to his regular job as R & D chief, an opening would be left for a permanent technical director for the Oz project. And just as clearly, the only two real candidates for the position would be Corrigan and Tyron.

Corrigan remained undaunted and cockily confident. "He's just an interface man," he said to Evelyn on one of the evenings that were becoming rarer when they both got away early enough to have dinner in. "We're into big systems now. Complex, adaptive systems. And that's *my* territory."

Evelyn was less sanguine. "Tyron's got people behind him, here and outside CLC, who've staked a lot on seeing their man in control," she reminded him. "They're not going to go away, Joe. I mean, who are we talking about that we know? Velucci was there at the first meeting with SDC, wasn't he?—he has to be involved. Probably others from corporate, above Pinder. Maybe even Endelmyer. Certainly Harry Morgen and the others who followed Tyron. And others outside CLC, who must have had a hand in keeping the work on DIVAC in the public domain and nonlicensable. They're not just interface people. And they're not people who are going to sit back and watch while somebody throws a wrench in."

Corrigan speared a piece of steak with his fork and held it in a so-what pose. "They need what I've got," he said. "I'm the only one who can deliver Oz in the time they're committed to, and they know it. So what can they do?"

"I don't know, Joe. But be careful," Evelyn said.

The months that followed saw a lot of activity to extend the funding and support for Oz onto a wider base beyond CLC. Corrigan was too preoccupied with technical issues to pay much attention to background politics, but one day the company announced that Feller & Faber were coming in as cosponsors of Oz, which would be set up and run under a new, jointly owned corporation, "Xylog," dedicated to the project. F & F in turn were able to channel further funding from their lucrative client base, and very soon the original scheme that was to have been housed on a half-floor at the existing Blawnox facility gave way to a greatly expanded vision using more, bigger, and better machines, many more people, and occupying a site of its own elsewhere. F & F and its associates would manage the financial side of the joint venture, with somebody from CLC—yet to be designated—directing the technical operations. So in essence nothing changed as far as Corrigan and Tyron were concerned; it had all just shifted to a higher level.

All kinds of visitors began appearing at Blawnox, eager to see the work. Some of them were very strange, but all commanded influence or were in positions to direct significant flows of money. Another thing they had in common was the perception that they brought of Oz. They did not seem to have been made to understand it merely as a means to achieving AI. Rather, they took the AI for granted and saw it in turn as the engine that would power a revolutionary method for testing new design concepts, product models and styles, marketing methods, political campaign strategies —anything at all—in an artificial world running hundreds of times faster than the real thing: a Reality Simulator.

The character that Pinder and Tyron had brought over from the Executive Building was as zany as any that Corrigan had met in the last few months. His name was Roderick Esmelius, and he was from Market Resource Researches Inc., one of Feller & Faber's clients. He was tall, lean, and eccentrically theatrical, with flowing, silver hair, a suit of maroon trimmed with pink, and sporting a cane. The assistant with him, whose name was Godfrey, had dark curls, heavy, black-rimmed spectacles, and a mauve suit. He referred to the project as the "Crystal Ball," and seemed to think that it could predict election results. MRR were contemplating buying into Oz to the tune of two million dollars to try out a brainchild of Esmelius's that he was sure would revolutionize advertising. He explained to Corrigan and Shipley, punctuating his words with flourishes and pauses for effect:

"It will have the greatest impact of anything since the advent of television. The problem is getting to people, you see. There are too many distractions and alternatives to pull audiences away." In other words, the program offerings were garbage. "People are busy and more mobile these days than they used to be. They don't have enough opportunity to be near their TV." Esmelius wagged a finger and swept his gaze over the whole group as he came to the crux. "So why not let it *accompany them* permanently, everywhere? We hear about putting chips in people's heads to link them to computers. So why not a TV in the head?" He paused expectantly. Pinder nodded an amen. Tyron smirked at Corrigan. Shipley, from his chair at a terminal where he had been working, tried to catch Corrigan's eye with a look that asked if they were hearing things right; but Corrigan was too busy keeping up an appearance of relaxed, can-do suavity. He had been getting more conscious about dress lately, and was turned out in a stylish jacket of gray and black fleck, with a pink shirt and red silk tie with matching handkerchief folded in his breast pocket. Gold had appeared on his fingers, cuffs, and in his tie clip, and he had upgraded his watch.

Esmelius went on. "Just imagine, watch anything you like, any time, anywhere you like. And what a medium for advertisers: a direct line straight into everyone's head! You can't beat it."

Godfrey carried on, pitching with the same enthusiasm. "We have a number of potential investors. But public acceptance would be the key factor in a venture like this. Now, if we could show them what the public's reaction would be, *before* anyone puts up the money to actually develop the technology . . ."

"You want to know if the Oz simulation could tell you," Shipley completed. Having listened to a dozen similar lines in the last two weeks, he knew what was coming.

"Yes, precisely," Godfrey said. "Can the Crystal Ball do it? It would pay for itself ten times over, just on that."

"You'd only need to give the inhabitants the *effect* of having such technology," Pinder put in.

"Quite so," Esmelius confirmed. "All we'd want to know is their reactions."

Shipley was looking dubious and about to say something, but before he could do so, Tyron came in, looking at Pinder. "The potential for this kind of thing must be enormous. Just think of all the applications that could be emulated in advance, without the need for detailed designs or even a working prototype. All you need is the concept."

Pinder was nodding like a pigeon pecking up seed. "I agree, Frank, I agree. It could begin a whole new science for allocating development funding and priorities."

Tyron answered Esmelius, but with his eyes on Corrigan. "Oh, I'm sure that our programming specialists won't find it a problem."

"It's a natural extension to the self-adapting routines that we've been developing, based on the MIT system," Corrigan said. "The channel simply becomes an additional subgroup integrated into the perceptual data stream routed to each animation designated as implanted with a chip. The evaluation and response matrixes would be generated by the modules we've already got."

"You're saying that your people could handle it, then, eh, Joe?" Pinder interpreted, just to make sure that Esmelius understood.

"Sure, no problem," Corrigan said.

"Splendid." Esmelius beamed. Godfrey made satisfied clucking noises. Pinder could have told them as much himself without bringing them over, Corrigan knew, but it was more reassuring to hear things like this direct from the source. Also, as Tyron had made sure would not be missed but which Corrigan was not too concerned over for now, if anything went wrong, it would have been Corrigan who had said before witnesses that everything would be fine.

The two visitors stayed a short while longer to raise some further points and view what there was to see in the labs, and then left with Pinder and Tyron to meet others for lunch.

As soon as the door had closed, Shipley swung around in his chair and shook his head at Corrigan exasperatedly. "Joe, will you tell me just what in hell you're playing at? This all started out as a serious attempt to achieve AI. Now it's turning into a circus. God, even in the last two weeks we've listened to one crazy from Madison Avenue talking about turning every home into a theatrical supply company; another who wants walking advertising machines pestering people everywhere; houses full of talking appliances—and now commercial TV in people's heads. The management here ought to know better, but they've all lost their heads over the prospect of unlimited funds. This is getting crazy, Joe."

Corrigan nodded. "Yes, you don't have to tell me that, Eric. I know."

"But *you're* going along with it, for Christ's sake."

"I'm not going to be made to back down in front of F and F clients." Corrigan leaned over a table to run an eye over the printout stacked on top. "That's exactly what Tyron is trying to do: get negative reports sent back to the financial people in charge of the operation, who haven't got a clue what's feasible and what isn't."

Shipley nodded emphatically, as if that made his point. "Sure, *I* can see it—only too well. But what good are you doing yourself if you're not going to be able to deliver? You'll look plain dumb. And Tyron sure as hell knows that too."

Corrigan turned, looking composed and self-assured. "Relax, Eric. None of this is going to be happening anytime soon. Only the first-phase objectives have been made firm, and they're realistic. This other stuff they're talking about hasn't even been scheduled tentatively yet. It's all politics. The important thing for now is to say what the people who write the checks want to hear, and not sound obstructive. Trust me. I'm beginning to see how this game works now."

Shipley looked back at the screen that he was working on and shook his head. "Lies and deception. Promises that can't be kept," he muttered. "It's not the world we used to know."

"Well, you know what they teach in law school: If you can't lie honestly, then fake it. Got to move with the times, Eric."

"And what became of science in all this?"

"Nothing worthwhile was ever gained without some calculated risk. That's true in science too."

Corrigan opened out the sheets and stared down at them. Maybe it was all changing too fast for Shipley to keep up with. He thought about the opposition he was up against, and wondered if he could afford to keep carrying a deadweight. Nothing worthwhile was ever achieved without having to make some sacrifices at times, either.

Financial notables, brokers, celebrities from the media, even a couple of senators—all became part of the regular scene as money flowed from bottomless expense accounts. Parties and nightlife became as much a part of the routine as progress meetings and system tests during the day. From the original concept, Oz grew to a mammoth scale requiring hundreds of new specialists and thousands of square feet just for the equipment. To accommodate the project, Xylog acquired a newly completed complex centered around an eight-story main building on Southside, where some warehouses had once stood just off Carson Street. So the day came when trucks and packers arrived at Blawnox to move the labs, offices, and hardware that would be absorbed into the Xylog operation.

Corrigan was at one end of what had been the main EVIE lab, supervising the crating of the CDC mainframe that Tom Hatcher's group used for associative array development, when Pinder appeared, ostensibly to ask how things were going.

"Fine," Corrigan told him. "The installation at Carson Street is ahead of schedule. I'll be going there first thing tomorrow to start getting it all on line, and we should have the section back in business by next week."

"Excellent." Pinder clasped his hands together behind his back and gazed around. Most of the lab area was bare, apart from discarded trash and wastepaper swept into piles. Lengths of disconnected cables protruded from underfloor distribution points and hung from overhead. A work crew was maneuvering the last of the large crates onto forklift palettes. "It's like moving out of a house, isn't it," Pinder commented. "Full of ghosts and memories. Funny how places always look so much bigger with the furniture gone."

"I thought this was the ultimate in modernism when I moved in," Corrigan said. "But compared to where we're going, it all seems quaint."

"Look at the kind of money that's going into Xylog," Pinder answered.

"I guess so." Corrigan had caught the quick, sideways looks that Pinder had been giving him as they spoke, and knew there was more to this than a casual visit. Such was usually the case when Pinder came over from the Executive Building.

Pinder glanced around. There was nobody in their immediate vicinity. He motioned with a nod of his head for Corrigan to follow, and walked slowly along by the outside wall until they came to a window overlooking the rear lawns and parking lots. "I'm a bit troubled by Shipley's ultracautiousness," he said, directing his gaze straight ahead. "I know it's good science and so on, but that belongs in the labs. What worries me is the negative impact that it's likely to have on the financial backers. At a time like this we can't afford that."

It was too close to the way Corrigan's own thoughts had been running for some time for him to be capable of making much of a show of surprise. Mainly out of curiosity to see where this was leading, he replied neutrally, "Has somebody been complaining?"

Pinder made a sucking noise through his teeth. "Not in so many words. But I've seen the looks and glances. And it's something that stands to affect you personally as well, Joe. I think you owe it to yourself to give some thought to a side of things that you might not have considered very closely."

"Oh?"

"Look at it this way. Eric has done some first-rate work in the past, I know—and I wouldn't want to belittle any of that. But I have to ask, is he really suited to a senior position in the new style of organization that's taking shape? You said it yourself—it's a streamlined product of the times. And running it is going to require a management team who all share a common level of enthusiasm, personal ambition, and a conviction that the job can be done. One dissenting note could create discord throughout. Your own future hinges on the success of this in a big way, as I'm sure I don't have to spell out. . . . So give me your opinion, straight. It's not a time to let notions of personal loyalty obscure sound judgment."

Corrigan stared fixedly out at the rear facade of the Executive Building opposite. Pinder had said it—all the things that had been swirling around in Corrigan's mind, but which he hadn't been able to bring himself to admit consciously. Even so, now that the opportunity was not only there but being pressed, a deeper-rooted reluctance to wield the knife prevented him from being blunt. "I don't know," was all he could muster. "As you said, it's something that I'd probably have to think over."

Pinder waited a few seconds longer, then sighed. "All right, I'll come out with it straight. Borth has seen it too, and he isn't happy. He's told Ken Endelmyer that he doesn't want Shipley in the venture. Management's view is that his former DINS work is part of the past now, and largely irrelevant, and they have concurred."

So there never had been anything for Corrigan to give

an opinion on. Pinder had simply been casting for a way to make him feel implicated. But if Corrigan had any protest to make, this was the moment to do it.

He turned and looked around the place where they had worked together, remembering feet propped on untidy desks; solder guns and birds'-nest tangles of makeshift racking; grubby diagrams tacked to pressboard; scratched keyboards and gray metal shelving. He thought of the future and Xylog: of glass-paneled corridors, deep-pile executive suites, and gleaming machine-halls. And he said nothing.

Pinder heard the silence and went on. "There is a core group from the DINS section that I'd like us to retain. Frank Tyron agrees that they're good and wants them transferred to COSMOS, but I think there's an equal case for integrating them into your side of the operation. I'm giving you first choice. What do you say?"

An offer of alliance, wrapped around the handle of the knife. He couldn't do anything to change the verdict now, Corrigan told himself. Only Tyron would benefit if he refused. It was a time for realism.

"Sure, I'll take them," he said.

Chapter Twenty-eight

The sign in gold indented lettering on a polished wood ground facing the elevators read:

Floor Six
OZ PROJECT SOFTWARE SYSTEMS DIVISION
ANIMATIONS ENGINEERING
ADAPTIVE ENVIRONMENTS GROUP
DATABASE MANAGEMENT
SUPPORT SERVICES

"Good morning, Mr. Corrigan," one of the two clerks waiting with bundles of files greeted as Corrigan emerged carrying a black Samsonite.

"Hello, girls," he returned, nodding, and headed toward the double doors leading through a glass divider to the sixth-floor reception foyer.

"Good morning, Mr. Corrigan," the receptionist said from her desk as he passed.

" 'Morning, Betty. You're looking very smart today."

"Why, thank you."

"We've got some important people coming today. Keep it up."

"Good morning, Mr. Corrigan," the young man in a charcoal suit going the other way said, halfway across the open-plan floor of work spaces and conference areas leading to Corrigan's office.

"Hello, Chris. Did we get those specs integrated for Bolger?"

"Completed yesterday. Run and checked out last night."

"Good lad."

Judy Klein was already at her desk in the partitioned outer area in front of his office. It looked like part of a set for the flight deck in a space-fiction movie, with its curvy furnishings and multiscreened computer side-table.

"Hi, Judy. 'Tis a grand day for living, to be sure, to be sure. What have we got?"

"Hello, Joe. Let's see. The arrangements for those people from Chase that Borth is bringing are confirmed. And there's a message from Amanda Ramussienne at F and F saying that she'll be coming too."

"Fine. And where have we fixed for lunch?"

"Delio's for twelve-thirty."

"That's great."

"Roger said to let you know we've signed off on the two new TMCs. There's a list of calls to be returned on your desk. And Pinder has put the meeting with Quell back to ten-thirty instead of ten. I said it would be fine. It doesn't clash with anything."

"Okay. Anything from Tom Hatcher yet on those referent transfer patches?"

"Yes. You're due to see him in half an hour with Charlie Wade and Jorrecks. He said he'll have the information then."

"Fine. I'll clear the calls first. If anything comes up while I'm down there, just put it through."

"Will do."

Corrigan went through to his own office and set the briefcase down on one corner of the broad sweep of curved, walnut-topped desk with its terminal, onyx pen-holders and neatly arranged piles of papers and reminders. The floor-to-ceiling windows formed a corner of the building, presenting fine views of the downtown Pittsburgh vista along the opposite shore on one side, and the meeting of the three rivers with the Ohio Valley beyond on the other.

The last few months had seen an intensification of the realscaping program for capturing every facet of visual imagery over the entire Pittsburgh area. Camera teams had been out every day, touring and recording all the streets, expressways, parks, and trails; from vehicles and on foot, from helicopters overflying the city, from boats out on the rivers. Back in Xylog the machines were running day and night, reducing and compiling the encoded scenes into cross-linked hierarchies of field definitions in the huge database that took up half a floor of high-density crystal-array recirculator memory cubicles. Hatcher had told Corrigan that they could reproduce any aspect of any scene out there, from any viewpoint, in any direction. Corrigan had studied the figures and experimented with some samples, and he believed it. The results of the similar but smaller-scale program that Himomatsu had carried out in Tokyo were now incorporated into the main Oz database, as was a part of the Inglewood area of California and a few other places, following experiments by SDC.

Having reviewed his priorities for the day and disposed of the calls, Corrigan went through the mail with Judy and gave her a list of follow-up actions for the morning. Then he went back out to the elevators and down past the Primary Operations Level, where the main banks of massively parallel processing lattices took up almost the entire floor, past the Interface Level with galleries of COSMOS coupling hardware for up to fifty real-world surrogates, past the Monitoring & Control Center, from where the whole operation was directed, and came out on the second floor. Finally he came to a door marked FINAL EVALUATION & TEST, which was where Tom Hatcher's group ran newly completed system modules prior to operational integration.

Hatcher's concessions to the new order of things amounted to switching to regular pants in place of jeans, acquiring a jacket, and, on special occasions, adding a necktie. But underneath, the old, easygoing casualness remained unaffected, and he was still more at home sprawled in front of a terminal with his coffee in a Styrofoam cup than listening to investment plans being expounded over pâté de foie gras. When Corrigan arrived, he was waiting with Charlie Wade, one of the old crew from Blawnox, and Des Jorrecks, the head of Xylog's applied psychology department. There were two broad areas to discuss:

First, results of tests to evaluate different strategies for creating animations that would best emulate people. Like people, the animations would shape their lives and personalities by pursuing goals. The intention was that these goals would arise internally, according to the animations' individual natures and experiences, rather than be imposed from without. But real people rarely formed distinct goals that they pursued consciously and deliberately all the time, such as to become a doctor, lawyer, physicist, or actor, or to head a country or win an Olympic gold medal; for the most part, they simply lived their day-to-day existences following unconscious drives and desires, and the bigger things just "happened." How, then, should such a nature best be simulated? What mix of drives, fears, ambitions, aversions was needed, with what kinds of relative weightings? How should such factors be represented as a statistical distribution across a whole population? Opinions on these questions changed constantly, and the short answer was that nobody really knew. A lot would be learned when the first runs were done in full-system mode, with the animation and environmental modules finally on-line and interacting together.

The other thing on the agenda was a subject that it seemed could never be laid to rest: the question of suppressing the surrogates' memories when they began the full-system tests. Those in favor argued that it would ensure greater authenticity of behavior. Those against, who included Corrigan, maintained that they were scientists running an experiment, and scientists needed to know what was going on. "All we have to do is play role models to a bunch of dumb machines. We're not trying to impress a panel of Shakespearean critics," Corrigan said after they had been through the technical arguments yet again. "And on top of all that, it will make it a more exciting experience for everyone: the thought of launching off into the unknown —a bit like going up on a space flight to another planet, or something."

"Aw, I don't know that it would get anybody that excited when you get down to it," Hatcher said. Hatcher was for suppression but resigned to a lost cause. Corrigan had vetoed the idea, there was not enough time left now to change the decision, and that seemed to be that. "These things tend to creep up on you so gradually, day by day, that you get used to it. I asked an astronaut the same question once. He said that they trained so hard for a mission that by the time it actually happened they couldn't tell the difference anymore. But then, that was the whole idea, I guess. Pretty much the same as what we're doing."

It wasn't just a matter of authenticity. There was the question of being better able to cope in an emergency, too. "What if something did screw up in there, Tom?" Corrigan said. "We're going straight into people's heads, interacting at deep perceptual levels that wire into emotional centers. And with the speedup, if anything unexpected did start happening, it would be hours out here before anyone knew about it."

Hatcher knew all that. He thought over it briefly, failed to come up with anything that hadn't been said a hundred times already, and shrugged. "Well, that's what the surrogates are being paid all that money for. We know there's a lot we don't know, and so do the volunteers who are coming in from outside. What else can anyone say, Joe?"

"I think Joe's got a point, all the same," Jorrecks put in. "Whoever's in there needs to be able to abort the run from the inside if it really goes off the rails somehow. But how could they do that if they didn't even know they were inside a simulation? I don't think I'd want to go in there under those conditions."

"You want an ejector seat," Charlie Wade said.

Jorrecks nodded. "Yes. But of course you couldn't have one if the memory was suppressed, since there would be no knowledge of the mechanism for using it. There's no way you could get around it. Any knowledge that an escape mechanism existed would also be knowledge that there was a simulation to be escaped from, which would defeat the whole purpose." Jorrecks looked at Corrigan for support. Corrigan nodded.

Charlie Wade looked at Hatcher questioningly. "Shall we tell them?" he asked.

"Why not?" Hatcher said.

Corrigan looked from one to the other. "Tell us what?"

"As a matter of fact, we think it is possible," Hatcher said.

Corrigan looked skeptical. "How?"

"But everyone would have to do it for themselves."

"What are you getting at, Tom?"

"Well, if it was me—if I was going in as a surrogate, and let's say that shortly before the full-system phase I was suddenly told that all memories of, say, the last couple of days were going to be suppressed."

Corrigan nodded. "Okay."

"What I'd do is this. I'd plant something inside the simworld that would be significant to me in some way, something that nobody else would know about. Later, after the run was started and I was in it, I wouldn't know I'd done it, because that memory would have been killed. But I'd still know the way I think, and I'd wonder what in hell this something—this whatever—was doing there. But if some kind of crisis developed to raise the stress level to the point where I had to get out, then I'd recognize it as a signal to myself. And from there it wouldn't take much fooling around with it to figure out what I'd set it up to do."

Jorrecks looked at Corrigan inquiringly. Corrigan thought about it for a few moments, and nodded. "That's clever."

"You think it could work?" Jorrecks said.

Corrigan smiled and had to nod. "It just might, at that, Des. It just might."

Hatcher clasped his hands behind his head and stretched his length out over the chair. "Does that mean you've changed your mind, Joe? Suppression's in, after all? We can go with it?"

"Not at all," Corrigan said, waving a hand dismissively. "It's dead and buried. Forget it. We've enough else to do as things are." Hatcher knew that and hadn't really been serious anyway. Just then, the phone on Hatcher's desk rang.

"I think we're done," Jorrecks said, seizing the opportunity and rising while Hatcher picked up the receiver. "We'll leave you to it, guys." Charlie Wade got up from his chair also and collected his notes together.

"Tom here. . . . Say, hi! Yes, he sure is." He held the phone out to Corrigan. "It's Eve, for you." Jorrecks and Wade left the room with a wave and a nod each.

"Hello?" Corrigan said.

"Joe, Judy said you were probably with Tom. Just checking to see if we're still having lunch."

Corrigan frowned. Oh, yes, that was right—she had suggested it that morning. He had mumbled that it would probably be okay, and then forgotten to get back to her when Borth's visit was confirmed. "Er, look, something's come up and I'm not going to be able to make it," he replied. "I should have got Judy to call you. I'm sorry about that."

Evelyn sighed. "Oh dear. And you were so late that I never got to see you last night."

"Everything's insane. It's all hectic now we're getting close."

"I know. Maybe dinner for a change?"

"I'll try." Corrigan looked across and caught Hatcher's eye. "Tell you what, why not have lunch with Tom instead? He's up to his neck too, but I'm sure he'd like the company." He held a hand over the mouthpiece. "Like to have lunch with Eve? I was supposed to, but I'm grabbed. I know you two always find plenty to talk about." Hatcher didn't seem overly happy, but nodded. Corrigan spoke back into the phone. "He says that's fine."

"Okay. Tell him I'll stop by there at, say, twelve. Okay?"

"She says how about twelve? She'll stop by here." Another nod. "That's fine. Look, I've got a ten-thirty, so I have to go. Talk to you later, then. 'Bye now."

"Goodbye, Joe."

"Thanks. You're a pal," Corrigan said to Hatcher as he put the phone down. "Borth's coming with some people from Chase. I'm tied up to do lunch there."

Hatcher shook his head in a way that said he didn't buy that. "So? You could have taken Evelyn there too. You're a head honcho and she's staff. Hell, this outfit can afford it."

Corrigan winked. "But the delectable Amanda will be there too. There are times and places for wives."

Hatcher couldn't contain his disapproval. "I'm sorry, Joe. Maybe I'm sticking my nose in, but I just don't like to see it. Everything used to be fine with you two. You've changed a lot, you know—especially since we moved to this place."

"Hey, give me a break, Tom. What's the harm in a change of pleasant company once in a while? I do plenty of good-husbanding out of hours, when it's the time for it."

"Ain't the way I've been hearing it."

"Look, I'm not asking you to get involved or make it your business, Tom. Just a small favor to cover when I'm double committed. I happen to think that taking wives along just for the ride isn't the proper thing to do. Whether the firm can afford it or not isn't the point. I also think that honchos should set examples, don't you?"

Hatcher turned back to his terminal. "This time, Joe," he growled. "Just don't do it to me again, that's all."

Chapter Twenty-nine

Today was the beginning of National Color Week, and Carson Street was filled with radiantly decked people marching to express themselves through visual combinations: yellow for happy, blue for somber, red for lively, green for simple, and other mixes and hues for other natures and dispositions—real, imagined, or self-fulfilling—in between. Self-playing instruments driven by microchips were all the rage, so nobody needed to be a musician to join in the festivities with a guitar, trumpet, accordion, or trombone, and "belong." The TV shows and movie ad inserts had been plugging fiber-optic augmentations to hairstyles and clothes, and half the costumes glittered and glowed like slow-motion Christmas trees.

Corrigan stood with Lilly on a rise above the main body of the crowd, staring at the site that had once held a modern, eight-story commercial structure of shiny white tiling and green-tinted glass, with separate buildings for offices and administration. All that was left now was one of them turned into an apartment block that looked like a psychedelic gift-wrap pack, another adopted as a "temple" by a cult who believed themselves to be reincarnated aliens from Sirius, and the main building demolished to make room for a hotel that never happened, now a campground for vagrants.

Even now, Corrigan found that it needed an effort to tell himself that what he was looking at had never happened. The conditioning processes of twelve years, everything he had seen, read, and been told through all that time added up to a powerful weight of persuasion that his instincts fought against simply dismissing. This had been Xylog. He could remember how it looked in those final weeks, the hectic days and bleary-eyed, all-night sessions to complete the preparations on time and straighten out the inevitable last-minute hitches. He had made some initial sorties into the final test simulations to check details from the inside. . . . And after that his recollections became confused and indistinct.

It was only long afterward, when he was well on the road to recovery, that he had learned how those final tests had damaged him, along with many others, with mental disruptions, hallucinations, breakdowns, periods of total blankness. The government intervened to halt the project. There had been hearings and investigations, and finally the project was abandoned and the site sold off. He had read the reports, watched the tapes. And here, in front of him, was what was supposed to be the incontrovertible evidence.

Except that none of that could have happened, for the simulation was still running.

"You weren't a permanent inhabitant like most of the other surrogates," Lilly said. "You were supposed to be one of the controllers—entering and leaving whenever you wanted."

"That's right." Corrigan had no explanation. He could only agree.

Lilly turned to him with an air of finality, as if that summed up everything that she had been saying since their first meeting in the Camelot. "So something that you weren't expecting must have happened during the last week or so."

"I don't know, I don't know," Corrigan groaned wearily. "It's all so confused from around that time. I can't remember."

"What happened, obviously, was that your memory was wiped too," Lilly said. "But according to you, it shouldn't have been. Which can only mean that somebody else set it up."

"You don't *know* that," Corrigan protested. "I could have agreed to something they sprung on me in the last few days. If that's the case, then of course I don't remember anything about it. That would have been the whole idea."

"You were one of the main designers," Lily pointed out. "Your place would have been supervising from the outside." She raised an arm to take in the locality of Southside around them, the river off to one side, and beyond it in the visible part of downtown Pittsburgh. "We're *twelve years* into this, and it's still running," she said. "Didn't you tell me before that this goes way past anything that had been planned? All that had been scheduled was a series of more extended testing. Nothing like this." She waited for a moment, saw that he had no immediate answer, and went on. "It's clear what must have happened. Somebody else had arranged a far more elaborate simulation than you were told about."

"That's impossible."

"Which meant that you weren't as in control as you thought. Your position wasn't so unassailable—that's what you won't admit. Sometime during the early phases you entered the simulation on a routine visit, and while you were inside they switched over to the extended version and wiped your memory to keep you here for the duration. Meanwhile, they're running things on the outside. . . . And you're telling me not to worry, everything's going just fine? That I should trust them?"

"Oh, for God's sake, you've been watching too many movies," Corrigan retorted irritably. He had a more than gnawing suspicion that she was right, but he needed time to think. "You don't have any evidence for all this. It's pure fabrication. These weren't the sinister people that you're trying to paint—just ordinarily ambitious people in a competitive environment. You're making it sound like intrigue inside the Kremlin."

"Oh, yes? Look what they did to you. You'd already stabbed your best friend in the back. And things with Evelyn were heading for the rocks. How soon afterward did that come apart? In circumstances like that, it would have been easy for them to convince anyone who asked that you'd elected to go in as a surrogate on your own initiative—to get away from it all for a while—wouldn't it?"

"Maybe I did," Corrigan retorted. "And that would put a hole through your whole paranoia theory right there, wouldn't it?"

And he had a point. Now it was Lilly's turn to feel less

sure of herself. "Why? . . . When did it finish with Evelyn?" she asked.

"Oh, it all came to a head about three weeks before Oz was due to go live. She split." Corrigan sighed. "She left me for being too pushy and ambitious. Muriel left me for being the opposite. It's true what they say about women, you know: there's no pleasing them."

"Tell me what happened," Lilly said.

Chapter Thirty

Evelyn stared across the living room at Corrigan, shaking her head disbelievingly. Her eyes were wide, her body taut like a threatened animal, her face a mask of someone he didn't know. All of the resentment and anger that had been pent up for months was pouring out with the adrenaline flush.

"How *could* you?" she shouted. "A man that you'd worked with for years . . . after the friend he's been to both of us. How could you let them just walk all over him like that? What did you do—just stand there? Didn't you say *anything* to stand up for him?"

Tom Hatcher had told her over lunch about Corrigan's part in the Shipley affair—but in a distorted way that made it sound as if Corrigan had asked Pinder to dump him. Apparently that was the version that Tyron had been spreading around the company. But Corrigan was in no mood to quibble over details or have to justify himself.

"What did you expect me to do?" he snapped back. "Their minds were already made up. . . . And anyway, they might have had a point. Eric would never have fitted in at Xylog. If the truth were known, he wanted out of it anyway." Shipley had been offered a mundane position in the general CLC research facility, but turned it down and quit the company.

Evelyn looked at Corrigan contemptuously. "Who are *you* to say what Eric wanted? At least he could have been given a chance to say so himself, instead of being discarded like worn-out shoes. Don't things like people's pride and dignity mean anything to you anymore? It's a shame, because they used to."

"Yes, they do," Corrigan answered, marching in front of her. He jabbed at his chest with a thumb. "And so do my own, for that matter. All I'd have succeeded in doing would be to make a sacrificial lamb of myself. And wouldn't Tyron have just loved that! Can't you see? It's exactly what he was hoping I'd do."

Evelyn hooked a wisp of her hair with her finger and whirled away savagely. "God, if you only knew how sick I am of hearing about Tyron, Tyron, Tyron . . . the whole pack of them."

"*One* of us is going to end up as the technical head of Xylog," Corrigan said. "It's down to that: either him or me. Doesn't that mean anything to you?"

"No, it doesn't. I told you, I'm sick of all of it. Maybe Eric knew exactly what he was doing. Perhaps you should have walked out too. At least you'd have stayed the person you were."

"And what, exactly, is that supposed to mean?" Corrigan demanded darkly.

Evelyn turned back with a pained, sarcastic face. "Oh, don't start acting as if you were stupid, Joe, on top of everything else," she implored. "When I fell in love with you, it was because I admired you for what you stood for: knowledge, honesty, the worth of people as people. But that's all changed. I loved you because you were what you seemed to be. You were genuine. Now you're turning into what I never thought you'd be: a phony."

"Grow up, little girlie," Corrigan said. "It's called getting on in the world. You don't expect people to stay as techs in labs all their lives, do you? Anyone who called herself a *wife* would be appreciative. Will you listen to yourself and hear what I get?"

Evelyn shook her head. "Getting on in the world? Is that what you call it? Getting on would be doing better what you do. Becoming a better person. But you're trying to ape these freaks that you idolize, who have taken over the project. You're trying to be one of *them*. That's what's so sickening."

It was her last plea for him to see things from where she stood, but Corrigan threw it back at her. "Well, at least they add a bit of fun to life for a change. Is that supposed to be bad or something? It might do you a bit of good to get out of that stuffy lab and away from your notes, and find out what life is all about for once."

Evelyn rounded on him like a goaded cat. "Yes, of course, there are plenty of more *glamorous* women out there, aren't there—with more tits than IQ points," she spat. "And pricey dresses bought on someone else's expense account. Is that the attraction in all these new playpens that you've been discovering?"

"Damn right!" Corrigan yelled.

Her eyes blazed at him for several seconds, inviting him to take it back. He glowered back defiantly. The hell he would. She turned away, tight-mouthed, and went over to the phone. "Well, enjoy," she told him. "And when you come to your senses, or your 'friends' decide to ditch you the same way they did Eric, don't bother looking. Have a nice life."

"What are you doing?"

Evelyn didn't answer him. "Hello? Yes, I'd like a cab, please. It's two twenty-three Elm, Fox Chapel. . . . Right away. I'll be waiting outside."

"Where do you think you're going?" Corrigan demanded.

"It's none of your business. Probably back to Boston." She disappeared along the hall leading to the bedroom, then came back a few moments later, clutching her purse and pulling on her coat.

"What about your things?" Corrigan said. "I hope you're not expecting me to send them."

"I wouldn't want anything that reminds me of this place. I'd rather start from scratch again."

"Well, isn't that typical," Corrigan sneered. "Have you ever seen anything through in your life? The project goes live in three weeks, and you won't even stick around to see the end of what you've been working for."

"I'm not interested in the stupid project. It's changed you and it's ruined us. You stay and watch your precious project. I wouldn't want any part of a world that your kind of friends created."

Anger surged up inside him suddenly then. His pride would not permit the affront of letting her walk out first to leave him standing there with the choice of either submitting passively or climbing down. He swept his jacket up from the chair where he had draped it and opened the door before she could reach it. "Suit yourself," he threw back over his shoulder. "It won't bother me. I'm going to get very, very drunk."

"Isn't that just—"

He slammed the door before she finished, and went out the front of the house. His car screeched out of the driveway moments later.

But he did not get all that drunk. After he'd had a couple in one of the bars downtown and calmed down a little, he went to the phone and called the Vista Hotel. A minute later he was through to Amanda Ramussienne.

"Why, Joe, how nice to hear from you," she purred. "I enjoyed talking to you at lunch *so* much. Where are you?"

"Just a few blocks away. It occurred to me that it wouldn't be very gentlemanly to let you go back tomorrow without so much as a goodbye. Have you eaten?"

"Not yet, after this afternoon."

"I haven't yet either. I thought you might like to join me. What do you think?"

"What a nice idea."

"How are you fixed?"

"Sure, I can make it. Give me forty minutes to spruce up."

"I'll be there at eight," Corrigan said.

"I look forward to it," she murmured. There was just the right hint of a double entendre in the way she said it.

Nothing had changed when Corrigan got back to the house in the early hours. Evelyn had gone. It gave him a feeling of unencumbrance and freedom, of decks cleared for what had become the only important thing in life. Oz was *his*. He had wrested it out of what had seemed a lost cause, when every sign had pointed to Tyron taking control via COSMOS. He felt like a grimly confident general on the eve of battle. Even if his closest ally had deserted him in the final hour, nothing could take away victory now.

Chapter Thirty-one

It was one of those awakenings that come suddenly, like a light being switched on, unlike other mornings when Corrigan could spend ages tugging himself free from the clutches of sleep. He felt unusually light and sprightly—more charged up than he could remember feeling in a long time. Maybe he would call Lilly and see about meeting somewhere for lunch.

After leaving the former Xylog site they had come back to Oakland, bought some wine and cooked themselves a dinner at his place, then talked on until the early hours. The suggestion of her staying over had permeated the mood of the evening unspoken. But few turnoffs could be more effective than an awareness of being in a simulation subject to monitoring and recording, and the understanding to wait for more conducive circumstances had been just as mutual, again with no need for anything to be said. The rapport they seemed to have was uncanny, he reflected as he stared up into the darkness. Or was that simply how any two real people would affect each other after twelve subjective years among animations?

Something was odd.

It could have been a difference in temperature or humidity, or perhaps a subtle change in the odor or acoustic properties. But something felt wrong about the room. And the pillow was silky. They didn't have silky pillows—Muriel thought they were too clinging.

"Lights, Horace," he called. Nothing happened.

He reached out and groped for the switch on the wall-mounted lamp above the bed. But his fingers found nothing, just a blank wall. And instead of the padded headboard below the lamp, he found what felt like a polished brass rail connected to a bedpost.

Bewildered, he pushed back the covers and sat up. The face of a clock was glowing at him from the bedside unit that the time was 6:30 A.M. There shouldn't have been a clock on the bedside unit, nor the lamp whose outline he could now make out in the light from the clock. He felt for the base of the lamp, found the switch, and turned it . . . to find that he was not in his apartment in Oakland at all.

But at the same time, the surroundings were familiar: the vanity with its mirror and lights, walk-in closet with louvered doors, satin drapes and shag carpet. . . . He was back in the house that he and Evelyn had lived in at Fox Chapel twelve years ago. The room was untidy, with the pants from one of his suits thrown over a chair along with a crumpled shirt and some socks, shoes tossed haphazardly by the closet, and clothes overflowing around the laundry basket.

He blinked, swung his legs out, and sat in confusion on the edge of the bed, trying to make sense of it. It made no sense. He got up, crossed over to the window, and peered through the drapes. The cluttered housefronts and cramped urban streets of Oakland were gone; instead, roomy, upmarket homes with wide driveways, standing comfortably secluded in wooded suburban surroundings. There was no doubt about it: this was Fox Chapel.

Numbly, he fumbled his way into a robe and went out into the hall and along to the living area. His briefcase was on the long coffee table in front of the couch, with papers and a notepad scattered in front of it, and pushed to one end were an empty coffee mug and a half-eaten sandwich on a plate. The side table with the computer monitor had been pulled forward for easy viewing from the couch, and the still-connected keyboard was resting on one of the arms. It looked as if he had been working late last night. He went over and shuffled through the papers. They were all to do with preliminary test schedules for the Oz project. He activated the terminal and checked the current date. It read Tuesday, October 12, 2010. Oz had been due to go on-line at around that time, late in 2010.

Still baffled, he went through to the kitchen. As he did so, he became aware of a different feeling in the way his body moved. He felt lighter on his feet, more lithe and supple than he was used to. The kitchen was messy, like the bedroom—dishes in the sink, more papers on the table, the things for preparing the sandwich in the other room not put away. He went over to the mirror by the shelf above the microwave and looked at himself. His jaw fell in astonishment. He was looking at himself twelve years younger and a good fifteen pounds leaner. He felt his face, ran the fingers of a hand through his hair. This was insane.

So what about the whole business of being a bartender and meeting Lilly? Had it all been a dream? No, he couldn't accept it. Dreams could be uncannily lucid, it was true, but never as real as those recollections—all the way through to seeing Lilly out to her cab and going to bed last night.

The only other explanation, then, was that he was in the middle of a lucid dream right now—dreaming that he was back in the days of the project. But surely no dream could be as real as this either. Or could it? The disconcerting realization came over him that he had no idea if he was asleep or awake, and he was far from sure how to find out.

Pain. The pain response didn't function in the dreaming state. That was why people always pinched themselves. He pinched the back of his hand. It hurt. He bit his tongue. It hurt more. He picked a pin out of an oddments bowl on a shelf by the refrigerator and jabbed his thumb with it, and it hurt like hell. Yet somehow he was still unconvinced. Perhaps it was possible to dream that you were feeling pain when you really weren't.

If he was not dreaming, and this was in fact 2010 with Oz about to go fully on-line, why was he unable to recollect anything that had happened at Xylog yesterday, or what he was supposed to be doing there today? His memories of such things were blurred and distant, as would be expected after the passage of twelve years. On the other hand, he could vividly remember going to the Southside with Lilly yesterday and seeing the site where Xylog used to be, going back to Oakland, and their cooking dinner together. If that had been a dream, why was yesterday so vague, now that he was awake again? If this was a dream, it was so real as to be scary—there didn't seem to be a way out of it.

He went into the den to check on the terminal there for any received E-mail that might give him a better perspective on what was going on. But when he activated the terminal he stopped, confused. He couldn't remember the procedure. This was silly. He stared at the screen, feeling stupid, but it was no good. He found the mnemonic for "Help," scrolled to the directions for accessing personal mail . . . and all of a sudden it came easily.

There were several items from various people, but they were too long-forgotten to mean anything. Nothing triggered any immediate associations. And then he came across a note from Judy Klein that read:

> Monday, October 11, 9:35 P.M.
> Joe:
>   Just a reminder to call Ed Meechum first thing regarding the interview scheduled for tomorrow (Tuesday). I do have the figures from F & F that Ed said he was interested in, so we should get you the slot.
>   Judy

He *remembered* reading that message before—years ago. It had been in the last few days before Oz went on-line, a few weeks after Evelyn walked out. That explained the state of the house. The project had been getting good media coverage, and Ed Meechum was the producer for an interview that NBC was due to shoot, describing the last-minute action. Exactly who would be interviewed had not been decided yet, and Corrigan and Tyron were both vying for the visibility. The figures mentioned in Judy's message were statistics from the tests run so far—hopelessly skewed, if the truth were known, but since when had the media worried unduly about minor things like that?—that F & F were banding around to impress their clients on the predictive power that would come out of Oz. In other words, pure hokum to reassure the investors.

But the point was, he *did* get the slot. He remembered being interviewed at Xylog late in the afternoon. It had been a circus of hyperbole and misrepresented facts, and thinking back to it now didn't make him feel especially proud of his performance at all, although F & F had been delighted. Afterward, he had gone out for dinner with Meechum and some other NBC people. Amanda Ramussienne had been there too, having come down that day from New York. They went to the Gaucho Restaurant in Station Square. Corrigan could remember it all. He stared at the words on the screen perplexedly. But how *could* he? How could he be remembering details—even if a bit vague—of events that weren't due to happen until later in the day? The whole situation was crazy.

He left the den in a daze and went to get a better look at himself in the bathroom mirror. Yesterday, there had been a nick on his thumb, where he had cut it cleaning up the pieces of a broken glass at the Camelot. It was quite pronounced, with a week or more of healing to go before the mark would fade. Yet today there was not a trace of it.

Something very strange had happened to him. He had definite recollections of having woken up like this, on this very day, but long ago. The recollections were indistinct and incomplete, as if being retrieved from long ago. What had happened after the dinner with the NBC people? He seemed to remember they had gone on to a club, and afterward he went back to the Vista with Amanda. And then, the next day, what? . . . He wasn't sure.

The first thing he could recall anything of after that was being in Mercy Hospital, slowly piecing himself together again. Dr. Arnold and the nurse . . . Katie, her name was; a strange Saturday-night dance, populated by caricatures representing the system's early attempts at constructing people; Simon, the counselor, and the time when Corrigan had dug a hole in the hospital lawn. . . . And after that a succession of memories over the years, becoming progressively clearer until the last few days, when he was forty-four, working as a bartender in the Camelot, and met Lilly.

But the person looking back at him out of the mirror was a young man of thirty-two. The computer said the date was Tuesday, October 12, 2010. There was a message in the system from Judy, put there last night, that corroborated it. Had that whole sequence of the last twelve years that he thought he remembered been nothing more than a creation of his mind? Was it possible for a mere dream to be so compelling?

He went back to the den and used the phone to call

Lilly's number. The call failed to connect, and he got a message asking if he needed information. That was right—the codes used in 2022 had embodied a new system of multifunction options that confused everybody. He was unable to recall any of the numbers that he had used in 2010, not even his own or Xylog's. Neither could he remember how to get a directory on the phone's miniscreen, so he had to go through the Operator.

"Information. What city, please?"

"Pittsburgh. Do you have a listing for Essell, please? Lillian Essell. The address is 7H Beech Ridge, on Boer Way."

"One moment. . . . I'm sorry sir, I don't have that name listed."

"It's on the North Side. I've been there."

"Well, it's not here. That's all I can tell you."

"How about the Camelot Hotel? Downtown on Fourth Avenue."

"Camelot, with a C, as in King Arthur?"

"That's it."

"No, I don't have that either. Downtown, you say? I've never heard of it."

"One more, then. Do you have the Xylog Corporation?"

"Xylog? You mean the place with the big computer project that's been in the news? I'm sure I have. Do you want the number?"

"Not right now. It's okay. I was just checking something. Thanks for you help."

"Thank you."

Corrigan hung up and stared at the phone. So nothing of the world that he remembered as of yesterday existed out there. Lilly, the Camelot, everything else . . . it had all been a fabrication? He walked slowly back to the kitchen and put on some coffee, forcing himself to try to think.

A dream so vivid that even now it eclipsed his recollections of the world that he found himself back in? The only explanation he could conceive was that in his sleeping fantasies, he had acted out how, unconsciously, he would have wished the project to evolve over years; and—as happens with dreams—his mind had created some bizarre images and interpretations.

Had the project become such an obsession with him as that? If so, then perhaps this was a warning sign, and this time he should take heed. Maybe what some people had been telling him was true, and he was letting himself get unhinged over the business with Tyron. Evelyn might have had a point, he reflected uncomfortably.

But if the whole business of being in the simulation had been a dream, how could it have included a distant memory of reading a message from Judy Klein that he had seen for the first time only a few minutes ago, after he got up? Obviously, the only answer could be that it hadn't been the first time. He must have got up sometime in the middle of the night, checked the mail at that time for whatever reason—and then gone back to bed and forgotten about it. Except that he hadn't quite forgotten it, and his mind had woven it into the dream. That was it. That was how it must have happened. He nodded to himself as he took his first swig of coffee, feeling relieved and unburdened inside now that he had straightened it out.

He washed, shaved, and dressed, and in the process decided that he would eat breakfast out, on the way to Xylog somewhere. It was a pity about Lilly, though. He could have gotten along well with Lilly, he told himself. It seemed that in the process of creating her, his subconscious had fashioned an ideal woman. He was going to miss having her around, even if they did argue a lot. It was funny how somebody could feel that way about a creation in a dream.

And then, as he fastened his tie and put on his jacket, he thought about Evelyn. Again, as if he were really reaching back over years, he remembered distantly how he had acted, and all of a sudden it made him feel shabby. He no longer felt any of the anger or resentment that had raged so violently in him only a week or two before. He could understand how she felt, see the bitterness he had caused, feel her hurt. And God, she had tried. . . . Why had he been so incapable of seeing all this before? Could a dream bring about such changes?

Before leaving, he went back to the den and retrieved Judy's message again in order to call Ed Meechum. But then he realized that he had no idea what the figures from F & F were all about. He would have to wait until he got to the office and reminded himself, he decided.

Chapter Thirty-two

For a dream, it was having the strangest effects. In it, he had not driven a car at all during his recovery and rehabilitation process, and later his therapists had discouraged him from acquiring one. By that time he had become used to not owning a vehicle, and living close to the city in Oakland had given no cause for change. But now, on the way in from Fox Chapel in his Mercedes, he felt as if he *really* hadn't driven for years. He was clumsy on lane changes, getting blared at a couple of times, and found himself uncertain about what should have been a familiar route that he had been taking every day since the move from Blawnox to Southside. Coming in on Route 28, he forgot that he had to exit onto East Ohio Street to get to 279 South, and instead carried on over the Veterans Bridge into the crosstown tangle, where he took a wrong ramp again and ended up in the early-morning downtown pileup, from which it took him fifteen minutes to extricate himself. The main problem was that the city he still remembered himself as living in for the past twelve years had changed more than he'd realized, and he had difficulty recalling the real one. However, he did remember his reserved parking slot at Xylog, found it, and after leaving his car, went up to the sixth floor.

"Good morning, Mr. Corrigan," the receptionist greeted, smiling, as he came through the glass divider from the elevator hall on the sixth floor.

"Good morning . . ." He couldn't remember her name. Nodding an awkward smile, he went on toward his office. Judy was at her post outside, looking relaxed but professional as usual.

"Good morning, Joe. I thought you said you'd be in first thing today. I was here extra early."

"Oh, yes. . . . Sorry about that. I got stuck in traffic."

"Did you get my message about the figures for Meechum?"

"Yes, thanks."

"Called him yet?"

"Not yet. I just wanted to check through them with you first. Remind me what they were about, would you?"

Judy looked at him strangely for an instant, but turned to her keyboard, tapped in a code, and brought a file up onto one of her screens. "It's the statistical correlations that Borth had done for the tests that we ran last week," she said.

Ah, yes, it came back to him now. To impress one of Feller & Faber's moneyed clients, Borth had commissioned a marketing analyst to massage the data from some test runs of "proto-animations" (i.e., primitive creations that had not evolved inside a full simulation yet) in such a way as to suggest that the buying patterns of real supermarket customers were already discernible. It was mainly fiction and wishful thinking, but the client was happy. Also, it would be good publicity material to slip into the interview with Meechum.

His memory refreshed, Corrigan asked Judy to get ahold of Meechum and went into his office. Inside, he stopped and looked around at the walnut-topped desk with its onyx pen-holders, shelves of reference books and reports that he liked to keep handy, diplomas and pictures framed on the wall. . . . Already, the sights of familiar things were triggering more memories and associations. The dream was beginning to fade at last; he could get back to being himself, and on with the important business at hand. There was a memo board with some cartoons and other clippings that, on the whole as he looked at them, struck him as somewhat immature and slightly silly for the office of a prospective technical director in this kind of operation. He made a mental note to get rid of them that morning. Also, on a shelf of a wall unit close by, was the figurine of an Irish leprechaun that cousin Jeff had given to Corrigan and Evelyn as a wedding gift during their honeymoon visit to Ireland. He frowned at it, puzzled. He was certain that Evelyn had put it on the window ledge in the den back at the house. What was it doing here?

Then the call tone sounded from the comm unit on one side of the desk. "I've got Ed Meechum," Judy's voice called through the open doorway.

"Okay." Corrigan activated the screen, then hesitated, confused by the display of icons and options that it presented. After a few seconds Judy turned and leaned across to peer in at him.

"Aren't you going to take it?"

"Er . . . I'm having a block today. What do I do?"

"Just hit Enter. It's on Auto Accept." She said it in the same tone that she might have used to tell him that turning the wheel steered the car.

"Oh, right. . . . Ed, hi."

Meechum's features appeared on the screen: lean, toothy, and with thinning hair, but at the same time healthy and vigorous, with a pink-skinned, open-air complexion. "How's it going, Joe? Got some news for me?"

"Yes. We've got the figures. Want me to copy them through?" The eerie thing was that he remembered saying something like this before. How could the "dream" explain that? . . . Unless he had somehow projected it into the dream in anticipation, because he knew he was due to call Meechum. How could one stupid dream have gotten him feeling as rattled and confused as this?

"Great," Meechum said. "How do they look?"

"Oh . . . I haven't really had a chance to go through them closely, Ed. But from what Borth says, they look like what you wanted."

"Me? Hell, it's you who's been pushing them on me, Joe."

"Oh, yes. Right."

"I've had Frank Tyron on me as well this morning, wanting to get a plug in about the new version of the interface hardware," Meechum went on. He winked conspiratorially. "But I remembered what we agreed yesterday." Corrigan had no idea who agreed what yesterday. "You're all set for filming at four o'clock. Is that okay?"

"How long are we talking about?" Corrigan asked.

"For the interview?"

"Yes."

"What I already told you: forty-five minutes, probably cut to around ten minutes' air time." Meechum looked pleased with himself, as if he were waiting for congratulations. He was saying that he was on Corrigan's side, and they both understood how everything stacked up.

Corrigan sighed inwardly. There was serious work to do and a major project with all kinds of unknowns confronting them. Getting the job done was going to need all the talent they could muster. Suddenly, the whole business with Tyron that had been dragging on and interfering with everything forever seemed so unimportant and idiotic. Why exacerbate it any further?

"Hell, there's time enough in that for both of us. Why don't we simply get Frank in on it too?" Corrigan said.

Meechum stared out of the screen incredulously. "Tyron? You mean you *want* to let him on the show? You don't mind? You're saying you'll hand him half the action?"

"Why not? He's done a good job on the COSMOS interface. It'll give you some good stuff."

"Well, sure . . . if you say so." Meechum shook his head as if this was all too much for him. "You want me to just go ahead and fix it with him, then?"

"Yes, do that."

Meechum nodded, shook his head again, then decided to drop it. "I was thinking, Joe, afterward, we could get a cocktail someplace and have dinner. Maybe that place in the mall along by the river, the Gaucho, was it?"

That was where they had gone in the dream, Corrigan remembered. Had it been somehow prophetic, in the paranormal kind of way that he'd heard tell about but never had any time for? Could there be something to it after all? He wondered if he was tied in some inexplicable way to acting out those things that he remembered, or was he free to alter them if he chose? Try it, he told himself.

"I've had enough of the Gaucho, Ed," he replied. "Let's make it somewhere different this time. How about the Sheraton? It's practically next door."

"Suits me."

Which seemed to answer that question.

"I'll get Judy to fix it," Corrigan said. "So we'll see you here later."

"Four o'clock."

The screen cleared, and Corrigan looked up to see that Judy was waiting just inside the doorway, holding a folder and some papers. He motioned her in. She approached and placed the wad on the desk. "Gary called through while you were on the line. He's on his way."

"Gary?"

"Gary Quinn."

Oh, yes. He had been one of Tom Hatcher's software engineers, Corrigan recalled. "What for?" he asked.

"What for? To talk about the spec you wanted to change. There's the file, with a fax that came through from Cindi in Blawnox." Judy watched uneasily as Corrigan sat down and turned the sheets. From his actions it was clear that he wasn't sure what he was supposed to be looking for. "Joe, you'd been here talking about it for an hour when I left last night. It's the spec for the second-level attribute cross-linkages. It has to be approved and sent through to Keith before lunch today."

"Oh, yes. . . . Right. I just need a minute to recap. It's okay, Judy. You can carry on."

But Judy stayed where she was, looking worried. "I have to ask, are you feeling all right today, Joe? You've been burning it at both ends for months. . . . And now this thing with Evelyn on top of it all. Let me slot you in sometime today for a check."

"No, it's all right. I guess I hit the bars a bit last night. Probably a reaction, eh? Everything's still hazy."

Judy shook her head. "What's happening to everybody this morning? Tom Hatcher was supposed to be here too, but his secretary says he hasn't showed up—not even a word. And the full simulation is scheduled to go live in three days' time. It's crazy."

"Maybe Tom's been feeling the strain and doing some unwinding too," Corrigan said, forcing a grin. "Be an angel for me, would you? Fetch me a strong, hot coffee, black with nothing, and I'll be fine."

Chapter Thirty-three

Somehow he muddled his way through until the late morning, when Amanda Ramussienne called. She was still in New York.

"Joe, hi darling." she crooned. "Look, I hate to do this, but I'm gonna have to break your heart. Something's come up that I can't do anything about, which means I'm stuck in town and can't make it down there today. Promise you won't hold it against me for the rest of time."

So it appeared that lots of things were free to change. Here was one less complication to deal with. Corrigan decided he could live with that. He forced a resigned grin. "Well, too bad. Life happens, I guess."

"And I was *so* looking forward to it! You still have that promise to keep."

"We'll get by." Corrigan had no idea what she meant. "I appreciate your letting me know."

"You're so understanding. I'll make it up with interest."

"I'll be here."

"Well, it's all a panic here. Have to go. You'll do great on the interview with Ed. I wanted to be there. So sorry again, Joe." She winked a promise, blew him a kiss, and vanished.

Corrigan sat, staring at the blank screen, wondering what had possessed him. Looking back from where he saw things now, the whole business with Amanda felt grubby and sordid. Had the phoniness and gaudiness always been that transparent? And then the full realization dawned on him that it hadn't all happened *then;* it was *now.* It was possible that he could straighten things out with Evelyn.

Then Judy came through to remind him that he was due to have lunch with somebody from another F & F client. The name meant nothing. "What's it about?" Corrigan asked.

"He's the one who thinks Oz could be used to try out an idea he's had for using media superheroes to promote products to adults the way they do already with juveniles," Judy said.

Corrigan remembered him. A complete flake. He had talked without stopping all through lunch, without telling Corrigan anything he didn't already know. Corrigan couldn't face the prospect of repeating it. "You know, maybe you're right," he told Judy. "Maybe I'm not feeling myself today. Can you fob him off for me? Tell him something vital has come up on the project—anything."

"Leave it to me," Judy said.

Corrigan went off to a coffee shop in Station Square to think and be alone.

For he was unable to avoid a conviction that had been steadily growing inside him all morning that the impressions that he had woken up with that morning of having lived years past today were *not* the result of some extraordinarily vivid dream or fabrication, but that it *had* happened, somehow, and now he was back at the age of thirty-two again and had lived this day before. But how could that be? Things like that simply didn't happen.

All he could think of was that the life he remembered living after having the breakdown and Oz being canceled had, in fact, been real, but distorted in the process of his gradual recovery—in other words, exactly what he had been told it was. In that case, everything he was experiencing now was an illusion, perhaps taking place in the course of some kind of catastrophic relapse manufactured out of his stored experiences from long ago. So was he really back in Mercy Hospital or somewhere in 2022, thinking that he was back in 2010, before he had the breakdown? But if everything he was experiencing was the product of a deranged mind, then anything was possible and his situation was a total solipsism, with no possibility of his being able to prove or disprove anything by any form of investigation or experiment, one way or the other.

But then, on the other hand, would a deranged mind be capable of thinking it through this logically? In which case it was real. But since time travel didn't happen, if it was true, it followed logically that it had to be a delusion. Unless, of course, he was only *thinking* that he was being logical. . . .

At that point he gave it up as hopeless and went back to the office.

One corner of the main reception lobby had been turned into a mini TV studio. Meechum was on a couch in the center behind a low, glass-topped table, with Corrigan sitting in an armchair on one side and Tyron on the other. The crew had set up lights and improvised a background from drapes, potted plants, and a sign bearing Xylog's corporate logo.

After a short introduction, Meechum turned to Corrigan and picked up his main theme. "Tell us, Joe, isn't it like being God, in a way? I'm told that Oz will be a world in itself, inhabited by computer creations that behave exactly as real people do. As the manager of Xylog's software division, you're the person largely responsible for those creations. How does it feel?"

Corrigan stared down at his hands for a moment, reflecting on all the hype and exaggeration and wishful thinking masquerading as fact that had been dispensed on the subject. A public circus was not the place where science should be conducted. It was time to make a start on setting the record straight right now.

He looked up. "Let's clear up a lot of wrong information that has been put out about this, that shouldn't have been," he said. "We are not about to create an artificial world that's going to model how people in the real world think and behave—the products they'd buy, how they'd vote on this issue or that issue, what they like, what they don't like, or anything else like that. Human behavior is one of the most complex phenomena ever studied. For forty years now, some of the most intensive research going on in the world has been aimed at trying to emulate the full versatility of what we call 'intelligence,' and for the most part it's got nowhere. All we're doing at Oz is exploring an alternative approach to achieving that: an Artificial Intelligence—a process that functions something like the way we do. That's all. Whether such an AI—assuming that we're successful—could form the basis of a lifelike simulation of the real world is a question that lies way in the future and is one that we're not even considering yet."

Meechum was looking a bit taken aback. He accepted as a matter of course that part of his job was to be a paid hack, and he had been ready to help plug the product in whatever direction his guests chose to steer things. But this sudden shrinking of a current sensation down to lifelike proportions was something that he had not been prepared for. "That's, er, something of a more cautious assessment than a lot of the things we've been hearing," he commented.

"My first role is as a scientist," Corrigan said. "I'm simply reporting the facts as to what the goals of the Oz project are, as currently formulated. I can also speculate on what it might lead to in times to come, if you like. But that wasn't your question."

On Meechum's other side, Tyron was following with a mixture four parts bewilderment to one of confusion. His first reaction on hearing of Corrigan's offer to share the show had been one of suspicion, and he had arrived ready to outdo anything Corrigan might try adding to what had already been said to please the ears of the project's financial backers. It did cross his mind as he heard this that Corrigan's intention might be to throw him off stride and steal all the thunder, but the fact remained that in the meantime, right off the top of his head, he didn't have a lot to say that was wildly inspirational to counter it. So when his turn came, he took up the theme that Corrigan had set and concentrated on the new interfaces and associated hardware that formed his main contribution to the project, the principles underlying its operation—which were fascinating—and what it could reasonably be expected to accomplish.

Meechum grew more relaxed as it became evident that the animosity that he had been waiting to see surfacing between them was not going to happen, and the rest of the interview went well. But it was Corrigan who set the tone, while the other two responded. Although he was physically the youngest, his unswerving dedication to principle and insistence on frankness inspired everyone watching. When they were getting up after the cameras stopped rolling, Meechum said, "Joe, that makes more sense than anything I've heard in ages. You carry a wise head on young shoulders."

Pinder, who had come down from the top floor to watch, walked over to Corrigan while the NBC people were packing away their equipment. He seemed intrigued in a guarded kind of way.

"You handled that . . . interestingly, Joe," he said. "Interestingly, but well. Very commanding and positive."

"Thanks."

"It was more down to earth than I expected. You, ah, seem to be taking a more sober view of things all of a sudden."

"I try to be realistic," Corrigan said. "Fooling yourself isn't going to help anyone in the long run."

"There could be some flak from Borth's people. It wasn't the crystal ball that they've been painting to their clients. This could burst a few balloons."

"Probably better now than later, then," Corrigan said. "Investors are the worst ones to fool."

Pinder looked at him curiously for a second. "Ed tells me that it was your suggestion to put Frank on the show as well."

"Sure, why not? Frank and his people have done some neat things. The idea was to make the show interesting, right?"

Pinder cast an eye around and lowered his voice reflexively. "What I'm saying is, it isn't exactly the best strategy for the longer term from your point of view—with things being the way they are." In other words, as they both knew, Pinder's term as acting technical chief of Xylog would end soon. Corrigan was not optimizing his chances of stepping into the slot by sharing the limelight.

"Let's get the ship launched first," Corrigan replied. "When we know it floats, then we can worry about who'll play captain." Which was what Pinder thought he had been hearing, but he had wanted to be sure.

"You've changed in a big way, Joe," Pinder told him.

Something about Pinder had changed too. He was too wary, feeling his way with probing questions that seemed somehow out of character. The assertiveness that Corrigan remembered was missing. It was almost as if Pinder hadn't known Corrigan as long as Corrigan had known him, and was unsure what kind of reactions to expect. But then, from Corrigan's distorted perspective of things, it had been a long time for *him*. Maybe he didn't remember Pinder as well as he thought.

And, indeed, Corrigan did seem to have undergone a change in his personality that appeared permanent. For by the time the party sat down to dinner in the Sheraton, the twelve years of pseudolife that he remembered himself as having lived were just as clear in his mind as when he had woken up that morning, while his recollections from yesterday and the days before, although jogged and reawakened to some degree by the events of the day, were for the most part just as remote.

However, as if to compensate for the loss of detail from his immediate past, he seemed to have retained the maturity that had developed in the course of living through years that were still ahead of him. This expressed itself as a charisma that affected everyone present at the table in the same way that it had enabled him to dominate—without domineering —the TV interview earlier.

Among those present was a Graham Sylvine, from a department in Washington that prepared appraisals for scientific-policy reviews. He had been following the Oz project for some time, and appeared in Pittsburgh without warning late that afternoon. He reminded Corrigan of somebody, but Corrigan was unable for the moment to put his finger on just who. "The next phase will be the first full-system run, is that correct?" he asked Corrigan.

"That's right," Corrigan confirmed.

"What does that imply, exactly?"

"So far we've only been testing parts of the simulation as separate pieces. Next we bring them all together as a full system. Also, we'll be introducing the first real-world surrogates: operators coupled into the simulation to act as models for the animations to learn to emulate."

"Did you hire actors?" a woman across the table asked. Corrigan smiled. There had in fact been some talk about doing just that. "We wondered about it," he replied. "The problem was that it might all work too well and we'd end up with a world full of actors. So we decided to stick with ordinary people just being themselves."

"I take it that you won't be one of these surrogates," Sylvine said.

Corrigan shook his head. "They're on a full-time commitment. I'll be going in and out of the simulation to keep an eye on how it's going, sure—but my place is really on the outside, watching the whole thing."

"What kind of risk is there in all this connecting into people's heads?" another woman asked. "It sounds horribly spooky to me."

"Naturally we wouldn't be proceeding without testing as thorough as it's possible to make it," Corrigan replied. "But I'd be less than frank if I told you that we know everything. Of course there are uncertainties. That's how you learn. Life and progress toward better things couldn't exist otherwise."

"Well, what we've been hearing today sure makes a change from all the PR bull," Meechum said. "Now I'll be frank with you, Joe. Listening to you talking today has been the first stuff about this whole project that I've really believed for months."

"It's about time, then," Corrigan said.

Sylvine was vague about when he would be returning to Washington. He asked Corrigan a series of technical questions about the basis of Oz and what it might lead to. The surrogates seemed of particular interest to him. He wanted to know what kind of world they would perceive from the inside. Also, he raised the possibility of memory suppression and was intrigued by Corrigan's account of how the possibility had been considered and rejected by the Oz designers. It occurred to Corrigan that perhaps this constantly recurring issue was of more concern to him unconsciously than he realized, and maybe that was what had caused him to cast himself as a subject of it in the dream.

The person that Sylvine reminded him of, Corrigan realized as he watched him, was Dr. Zehl—Sarah Bewley's supervisor in the dreamed simworld. He wasn't quite sure why, although it certainly had nothing to do with physical similarity. Perhaps it was that Zehl, too, had been from

Washington; or maybe his tendency to appear suddenly, without warning.

The woman who had inquired about risk was still watching Corrigan and thinking to herself. When a lull presented itself, she asked him, "Do you really think that we do progress toward better things, Mr. Corrigan?"

Corrigan wiped his mouth with a napkin. "Certainly we do," he answered. "Evolution is a self-improving process. Hence change is for the better, by definition."

"I'd have to think about that," the woman said dubiously.

"I never realized before that you were so much of a philosopher," Pinder said to Corrigan. He had been watching Corrigan and saying little throughout, still showing much of the interest and curiosity that had been evident earlier.

"That was one of the things I learned as a bartender," Corrigan replied unthinkingly.

Pinder looked surprised. "Really? I never knew you had been a bartender. When was that?"

For a second or two Corrigan was flummoxed. "Oh . . . that was way back, when I was earning my way as a student in Ireland," he said finally.

He looked around, grinning. Everyone smiled back. He could become anything he wanted, he realized. He was a young man again, free to relive a crucial part of his life— and as far as he could see, with the benefit of all the accumulated experience of having lived the next twelve years before.

Maybe this was a dream, and maybe it wasn't; he had all but given up trying to tell. But either way, it seemed he had no way of breaking out of it if it was, or of changing the situation if it wasn't. So he might as well make the best of it. This time around, then, he decided, it would be a great ride.

He tried calling around to locate Evelyn when he got back later that night, but nobody he talked to could give him a lead. It seemed that everybody he'd known in Boston had either moved or was out of town. None of the few that he did manage to get through to had heard from her.

Chapter Thirty-four

"I just thought you'd like to know, Borth called Ken Endelmyer at home last night," Pinder said from the screen of the comm unit on Corrigan's desk. The NBC interview had been aired as part of a current-affairs documentary following the six-o'clock news the previous evening. "I'm assuming that he wasn't very happy."

"Which was pretty much to be expected," Corrigan answered. His tone was matter-of-fact, with no second thoughts or regrets. "I still think it will do more good this way in the long run, after the dust settles."

Pinder rubbed his chin as if still pondering something that he had spent a lot of time on, and nodded. "I've been thinking about it since yesterday, and I have to agree. The air needed clearing. Things have been getting out of control for a long time. So the other thing I wanted you to know is that if things do get rough, you can count on my support. As you say, it will do everyone more good in the long run."

"Well, thanks. I appreciate it," Corrigan said.

"I'll keep you posted if I hear anything more," Pinder promised, and hung up.

Like the others at the TV interview the day before, and at dinner in the evening, Pinder too had succumbed to following Corrigan's lead, almost as if their roles of senior and junior in the line of command had been reversed. And it had happened so naturally and easily, Corrigan realized, that he didn't even think about it.

There had still been no sign or word of Tom Hatcher since yesterday, which was odd, considering that they were in the last days of preparation before Oz. Already some critical decisions had had to be delayed, and the software section-heads were getting anxious. Corrigan was wondering whether he ought to have somebody check with the police, when his desk unit buzzed again and Judy came through on voice.

"Ken Endelmyer's secretary at Head Office is holding. Also, I've got another reporter on the line, wanting to talk to you: a Lola Ellis from *Futures* magazine in L.A., but she's here in Pittsburgh right now."

Corrigan sighed. "Let's see what himself wants and get it over with. Slot the reporter in when you can for later." The Meechum interview had apparently made an impression—this was the third journalist this morning asking for more information.

"She's being very insistent," Judy said. "She seemed to think you'd recognize the name."

Corrigan grinned as he signed some letters that he had been checking when Pinder called. "A good try, but I've never heard of her. Fix an appointment, will you, and put Celia through. Oh, and could you try calling Tom's place one more time, Judy?"

"Will do. You're through," Judy's voice said. At the same time Corrigan's schedule for the day appeared on the screen, with Celia's face framed in a window in one corner.

"Top o' the mornin'," Corrigan said, accentuating his brogue.

"Hello, Mr. Corrigan. I'm sorry to drop this on you at such short notice, but Mr. Endelmyer would like to meet with you rather urgently. Could you get over here for, say, eleven o'clock this morning?" Coming from such heights, it was an order couched as a request merely for form. God, Corrigan thought to himself, he must really have stirred things up. He saw on his schedule that he had a couple of things fixed for around then, but they would just have to be shifted.

"Yes, that will be fine," he replied.

"We'll see you at eleven, then."

The window with the face vanished, and Corrigan called up a color bar to indicate to Judy the appointments that would have to be changed. Her voice came through again a moment later.

"Still nothing from Tom. I've put Lola Ellis in to see you here at four-thirty this afternoon. Uh-oh . . ." Judy had just seen Corrigan's changes flagged on her monitor outside. "What's this? Has something come up for this morning?"

"I have to report to the general," Corrigan said.

"What's up?"

"Celia didn't say. Firing squad, probably."

Judy paused just long enough to be discreet. "I thought you were very good. But you did rock the party boat a bit."

Corrigan snorted. "Well, maybe this is where I get told that I'm not going to get my captain's hat."

"That would be a shame," Judy said.

"Ah, not a bit of it," Corrigan told her. "We can always go and work in a bar."

But to Corrigan's surprise, the summons was not for him to be shot. He arrived to find that Victor Borth had come down unexpectedly that morning from New York. Pinder was there also, along with a couple of the other CLC vice presidents. It turned out that Borth had not contacted Endelmyer the night before to vent fury about Corrigan's performance, but to commend it.

"I was gonna get him fired," Borth admitted candidly. "I was as mad as hell." He made a short, stabbing gesture toward where Corrigan was sitting. "This turkey had loused everything up. It was going to be panic out there—backers running in a stampede to get out after some of the things he said." Corrigan caught Pinder's eye across the table. They shrugged at each other, both equally at a loss to guess what might have changed things. Borth went on. "Then I get a call from Milton Perl." Perl was Chief Executive Officer of Berrenhauser Trusts, one of the major backers, who had marshaled a consortium of commercial banks and investment houses behind the project. "And what do you know—Milt loved it! You see, they *had* been getting bad vibes for some time over the whole project, and they *were* talking about pulling out—the whole shooting match, the consortium, the works. Those guys aren't so stupid. . . . I mean, you don't get to be worth that much if you don't know your head from your ass, right? They knew it wasn't going to happen the way they'd been hearing it. 'Vic,' Milt says to me, 'I've been worried.' See, his people *knew* that nothing even close to this has ever been tried before in history, and that there are all kinds of questions nobody has answers to. But they also know that you never get anywhere if you won't take risks. 'We were willing to take a risk, Vic,' he says to me. 'But in return we expected honesty. All we wanted to hear was somebody tell us to our faces that there could be no guarantees. Then we'd know we were all on the same side and working to solve the same problem, right? But that wasn't what we got. Instead, all we got was bull-shit.' "

Borth pointed at Corrigan again. "Until *he* said it! And now Milt and his friends are happy people." Borth spread his hands and treated everyone to an uncharacteristically appeasing smile. "Okay, I admit that I laid it on a bit, too, at times. But I'm not one of these tech-whiz geniuses. I guess a lot of people got carried away in the excitement, eh? But now everybody's feet are on the ground again, and this is a good time to reappraise things."

Endelmyer looked startled. "Reappraise things? What are you saying, exactly?"

Borth raised a restraining hand. "Oh, it's okay, Ken. Don't get me wrong. I used the wrong word. 'Consolidate' might be better. The project stays, no question. But Milt does want to go over the goals and purpose again, now that people are making sense, so we're probably talking about putting back the start date."

"I hope he's not asking for a redesign," Pinder said apprehensively.

"Nothing like that," Borth assured everyone. "Like I said, Milt is a happy man today. But he does want to be clear on what the limits are and what can realistically be expected. As far as Oz goes, the technical design, organization, and operations stays with CLC, the way we've always agreed. The only thing that Milt *did* insist on in that area . . ." Borth leveled a finger at Corrigan again, "is that he wants *him* in charge of it."

They stayed for the remainder of the morning discussing details, and then went to lunch, which Borth insisted on standing. And so there it was. After months of rivalry, back-biting, and infighting that had produced nothing but tension and bad feelings all around, Corrigan accepted, as the talk flowed around him, that in under a day he had attained everything he'd wanted. And it had not had to be fought for or conceded grudgingly, at that, but was being thrust upon him eagerly. Just a little integrity had worked wonders when the compounded results of suspicion and fear of failure had been about to bring disaster.

And it was all due to this extraordinary situation that he found himself in, whereby he was able to apply an older man's experience to a young man's circumstances. If it had proved this effective in the course of one day, he wondered if there was any end to where it might lead in the years still ahead of him.

Back in his own office that afternoon, he found himself wondering if this might explain the phenomenon of genius, that the world had been baffled by for as long as people had been around to think about it. He had convinced himself by this time that his experiences of the day before had been nothing more than a peculiar form of déjà vu, brought on by the sudden activation of a heightened level of consciousness at which he was now functioning. Events since yesterday were diverging so rapidly from anything in the "dream" that any feeling of having lived this time before had for the most part already left him.

But the altered perspective and perspicacity of vision that had accompanied that strange sensation of regression—the calm, inner confidence that he knew where he wanted to go and why, knew how to get there, and that it would not be the end of everything if he messed it up anyway—remained. He felt like a mouse that had been raised to some privileged vantage point from where he could watch the others still scurrying about in the maze. He could see where all the courses led, what lay at the end of every decision path, and in which direction changes would alter them.

Perhaps, far from being unique, this altered state of perception that seemed, as yet, beyond the ability of physics and psychology to explain, was something that had happened to many individuals of exceptional achievement and ability throughout the past. If so, it was little wonder why so few of those affected had cared to speak out. Far better to be an Einstein or a Da Vinci without the complications of trying to explain what would probably never be believed anyway, than risk being locked up as insane. And then again, maybe many of those who did try to convey their experiences had been put away, excommunicated, burned, banished, or whatever for just that. It was often said that the borderline between genius and madness was very thin. And as he got to thinking more, it struck him as significant how much of the world's religious teachings could be interpreted as coded references to undergoing a mystical rebeginning of life: "born again"; "life after life"; "inner enlightenments" that can only be experienced, not described. Suddenly, it all took on a new meaning.

Through the afternoon, he went mechanically through the routine of taking calls, seeing visitors, checking on the project, and dealing with queries from Judy. There was still no word from Hatcher, and he told Judy to check with the police to see if there was any record of an accident. Pinder called to let him know that the rumor was already going around the top floor of Corporate HQ that Corrigan was tipped to be the technical director of Xylog. The news must have got back to New York ahead of Borth, too, for Amanda Ramussienne was on the line a half hour later.

"I see Pittsburgh is in the news," she crooned from the screen, giving him one of her special sultry looks through half-closed lids.

"Why? What's happened?" Corrigan asked.

"You don't watch it?"

"No time for trivia. Anyhow, I only believe the advertising. What's happened?"

"Oh, I assumed you'd know about it. There was a shoot-out at the airport there—less than an hour ago. A maniac went wild and shot some police officers. Anyhow . . ." She smiled a seduction. "But, as a matter of fact, if the rumors I hear are anything to go by, you are getting famous down there too. There's a whisper that you're going to get the tech-chief slot at Xylog."

"Who whispered that, now?"

"Oh, a little bird."

Corrigan shook his head despairingly. "Nothing's confirmed. We'll see how it goes."

Amanda became more serious. "So there is something to it, then?"

"It's looking promising," was all Corrigan would say.

She brightened up. "So when are you coming up to New York again? We need to celebrate."

"I told you, nothing's definite."

She pouted. "Well, what's wrong with *practicing* celebrating? I need your kind of company."

An icon indicated another call waiting, with a message caption superposed from Judy that read: MILTON PERL, BERRENHAUSER. "Amanda, sorry, but I have to go," Corrigan said. "Something's waiting."

"Let me know soon, then?"

"Sure. 'Bye."

Perl was calling to suggest that he and Corrigan ought to meet sometime and get to know each other better. Corrigan agreed, and they fixed a dinner spot for the end of the week. Then Endelmyer's secretary came through again to advise that a meeting was being scheduled for the following week to reappraise Oz, and the Board would like Corrigan to present his assessment and proposals.

But commercial and material success were by now beginning to look mundane to Corrigan. Carried away in his inner speculations, he found himself wondering about the possibility of devoting himself to more profound callings. He experienced a conviction of being destined for greater things: things that would shake the world, rewrite a chapter of science, shape history. . . . And then Judy buzzed through to say that Lola Ellis from California had arrived and was waiting outside.

As soon as Judy showed her in, Lola wearing a blue coat and carrying a white purse, Corrigan knew that they had met before, but something looked wrong. And she obviously knew him, for instead of acting like somebody being shown into the office of a stranger, she stood waiting expectantly . . . yet at the same time showing apprehensiveness, as if unsure whether he would know her.

Ellis, Essell. Lola. . . . *Of course!* He should have gotten it from the name alone. She was twelve years younger too, of course, but he should have known the features well enough.

It was Lilly, from his dream life. A twelve-year-younger version of Lilly.

But that made nonsense out of everything that he'd come to terms with over the last two days. For she didn't belong here. How could somebody from a dream fabrication suddenly walk into *this* life?

He nodded to Judy, and she left, closing the door. Corrigan and Lilly stood, staring at each other.

He shook his head, nonplussed. Lilly watched his face, giving him that same uncanny feeling that she had always been able to that she was reading the thoughts going on behind. Then she nodded, and he realized in the same moment what she had been looking for and had seen there.

"It's happened to you too, hasn't it?" Lilly said.

Chapter Thirty-five

Idiotic fantasies! Megalomaniac delusions!

Corrigan asked himself yet again how he could have allowed himself to be so carried away by it all. All he had needed to do was check the list of Air Force volunteers who were coming to Pittsburgh to see if it included a Lillian Essell from California. If it did, then she had not been a fabrication concocted in his head. Neither, then, had the rest of the simworld existence that he remembered.

They walked slowly along the embankment by the river between the Gateway Clipper Landing, where the tourist riverboats berthed, and the Smithfield Street Bridge. The day was dull and overcast with a hint of rain on the way, the river gray and sluggish. On the far side, the evening traffic was building up on the Penn Lincoln Parkway at the foot of the vertical, rectangular foothills of downtown Pittsburgh. They had got out of Xylog to be on their own and try to think through what it meant. Corrigan had been silent for a long time. Lilly stared ahead, her hands thrust deep in her coat pockets, leaving him all the time he needed.

Yesterday she had woken up to find herself twelve years younger, back in the hotel where the Air Force volunteers for Oz had been lodged that long ago, the day after her arrival from California. She remembered going to Xylog with the others, but her recollections of exactly what took place were vague, since, like Corrigan, she was recalling them from a perspective of many years later; soon after that they ceased completely, and the next thing she knew was being confused and slowly coming together again in the same kind of way as he had experienced.

And then she found herself suddenly about to relive that day again. As before, she had come to Xylog yesterday —and might even have bumped into him if he had happened to go across to the DNC Training Lab in one of the other buildings, where the new arrivals were being briefed and introduced to Oz. Like him, as she grappled with the weirdness of the situation and began experimenting, she discovered that she was not bound to relive what she remembered but could change things. Unlike him, she had thought to seek him out as part of what she, too, had been tempted to rationalize as a "dreamworld," and find out if he existed in this one. In a group from outside the company confined to a different building, she hadn't been able to get near him in the day yesterday, and he disappeared for the evening after the TV interview. So this morning she invented Lola Ellis.

There was no question that they had met in the simworld. When they compared experiences, they found that they remembered the same places, the same people, the same events, the same conversations together. The simulation had happened. There could be no doubt about that. But if that was the case, how could the simulation have not yet started?

One explanation, of course, was that the whole thing *had* been an internal creation in Corrigan's mind, and still was: that what he thought he was hearing and thinking now was just as much a part of it as everything else. In that case he was totally insane, there didn't seem to be much he could do about it, and the only choice open was to go with the ride and wait to see where it took him. But he had been around that same weary, frustrating loop enough times, and since no logical process could help if he accepted that as the answer, he rejected it through pure Irish obstinacy if nothing else. In any case, he told himself, if he were going to go to the trouble of going insane to invent an alternate reality to escape into, surely he would have made it a more entertaining and hedonistic affair than this.

A chill breeze was starting to lift off the water, the kind that nipped the ears and found chinks in clothes. Corrigan directed their steps across the court by the riverside parking lot, toward the Freight House—a onetime railroad terminal building, now converted into a complex of shops and restaurants. "Let's head inside and get a coffee or something," he muttered. "Maybe a bite to eat."

"Did you have lunch?" Lilly asked.

"No chance of missing it in this job."

He went over the facts in his head one more time. The simulation had been real—the way they both remembered. It had been taken to a degree of realism that went beyond anything he had known was planned. Their memories of going into it had been suppressed and a cover story manufactured to disguise the cruder early phases, which again, as far as he had ever been aware, had not been the intention. He was supposed to have been one of the controllers, able to enter and leave intermittently at will, fully aware of what was going on. The only explanation there could be to that much was that another design group that he didn't know about had been organized somewhere, who had vastly extended the scale and concept of the operation, added the memory-suppression option that he had declined, and then sprung it on the surrogates unannounced—as they would have to if the memory suppression was to serve any purpose.

Fine, so far. That much was what Lilly had already tried to tell him. But it still failed to explain how he and Lilly could be carrying recollections of their experiences inside a simulation that had not yet begun. The only answer to that was, they could not.

They came to the entrance into the mall. Corrigan stopped to gaze at the gaily stocked shops and booths, the decorations and colored lights, the crowds of evening shoppers; he went back in his mind over the events of the last two days. It was uncanny, but there was only one explanation left.

"When you woke up yesterday, you were back in a hotel, right?" he said.

"Yes."

"Not at Xylog. But if we were back in 2010 after coming out of the simulation, why didn't you find yourself in a lab somewhere, where you must have been to take part in Oz in the first place? And how was it that I found myself back at home in Fox Chapel?"

Lilly shook her head. She had been going through the

same convolutions as he in her own head, and had tied herself in similar knots. "Everything was so confused from
around this time. I've just about given up trying to make
sense of it," she replied.

Corrigan began moving again, leading them over to an
open-fronted store with counters displaying ladies' jewelry,
perfumes, and cosmetics. "It needed to be confusing," he
said, not looking at her but studying the items arrayed on
the shelves. "To disguise the crossover while the system was
still learning. We thought we were recovering from perceptual dislocations. But all the time it was the world that was
getting better, not us." He smiled in a peculiar, crooked
kind of way. "It's got a lot better since then, hasn't it, don't
you think?"

"What are you talking about?"

"It needed those cover stories so that the surrogates
wouldn't cotton on—the *first* time around."

Lilly caught the emphasis. "I'm not sure I follow. . . ."
But her voice was little more than a whisper, her eyes suddenly fearful. A part of her, at least, followed him, all right.

Corrigan picked up one of the sample bottles of per-
fume from the counter and dabbed it on the back of his
hand. He sniffed, then extended his arm toward Lilly. "Like
it?" he asked her.

She started to shake her head and say something, then
checked herself and lowered her face. There was no smell at
all. Nothing. She straightened up slowly, shaking her head,
refusing for a moment longer to face what it meant.

Corrigan nodded. "I can't smell it either. The first cranial nerve, the Olfactory, synapses directly in the cerebrum.
We never could get the sense of smell right, could we?"

For what it meant was, they had never come out of the
simulation at all. It was still running.

And not only that. Somebody on the outside was *rerunning* it from the beginning.

In a small room off the Monitor & Control Center on
the third floor of the main Xylog building, a small group of
people listened tensely to Tyron's aide, Harry Morgen, just
up from the gallery of interface cubicles on the level below.
Tyron was there, so was Borth, John Velucci from CLC Le-

gal, and also Joan Sutton, the other technical specialist who had first followed Tyron from SDC. A technician standing beside Morgen had brought a hardcopy of the trace report that he had asked for on returning from the simulation. Things were not going according to plan.

"She tried to contact him in Xylog," Morgen informed the others. "Now she's due to see him, posing as a journalist."

Tyron was peering at a screen showing a status update on Corrigan, revised in the last few seconds. "His behavior is way outside his computed assigned norms. The system can't make sense out of it. His SDV index is down to fifteen percent."

"What does all that mean?" Borth asked.

"That something unexpected is motivating them," Tyron said.

Joan Sutton was shaking her head in a way that said this confirmed all she had been fearing. She was the one who had urged more caution all along, and opposed the latest extension of the original plan, which had thrown everything into a new dimension of risk and uncertainty.

"The forced reset was too soon," she told the others. "It should never have been attempted at this stage. The erasure function was too much of an improvisation, to say the least. With the time-rate differential there was no chance for a rational evaluation."

"The opportunity was too much to let slip by," Tyron insisted, defending the decision that had been at his urging, and also for Borth's benefit. "We had to go with it."

As the representative from the top floor of Corporate HQ, Velucci was the de facto chairman of the proceedings. "That's all history now. Time's running. What's the recommendation?" he asked them. This kind of briskness had become routine. In the five minutes that they had been debating, the simulation had already moved into a new day.

"Too many uncertainties. Shut it down now," Joan Sutton said without hesitation.

"I disagree," Tyron said. "I say, send Harry back inside, maybe with you, Joan, to give a second opinion. We can still get a lot of mileage out of this."

Morgen nodded. "I support Frank."

"We can't quit now," Borth pleaded. "This is where all

the backers get their payoff. It's worth hundreds of millions."

"What about the people in there who are being rerun?" Sutton demanded. "They'll sue for every cent in the company."

"We've got enough money to keep them sweet. We've got lawyers. We can handle that when the time comes," Borth said.

Impasse. Everyone looked toward Velucci. He got a connection to Endelmyer at CLC's Head Office on one of the conference screens, summarized the situation, and requested a ruling.

"Are they in any immediate risk?" Endelmyer queried.

"No," Tyron answered firmly.

"We don't know," Sutton said.

"That's pure speculation," Morgen said.

"Any risk that we can positively identify," Endelmyer corrected.

"No," Tyron said again. This time Sutton remained silent.

"Is there evidence that they suspect?" Endelmyer asked.

"Nothing that Harry actually saw—only the SDV index," Tyron replied. "But that was yesterday their time. That's why I want to send him back in. Joan can go with him."

"As ourselves," Morgen interjected. "There isn't time for messing around through personas." Tyron nodded that he agreed. All heads turned back toward the screen.

"They knew what they were getting into. As Victor says, any objections can be straightened out afterward," was Endelmyer's decision. "Send Morgen and Sutton in. We keep it going."

Corrigan and Lilly came out of the west end of the commercial court on Station Square and began walking quickly back along Carson Street toward Xylog. All thoughts of coffee and sandwiches were forgotten. Of course Sylvine reminded him of Zehl, Corrigan told himself. It was more than simply that they were both from Washington, appeared at short notice, and asked lots of questions. Corrigan had already tagged Zehl as an external controller coming into the simulation, and something in Corrigan's subconscious had identified the same habits of speech, posture, and mannerisms in Sylvine. Sylvine *was* Zehl! It was the same person from outside, cloaked in two different identities. The difference was that this time, Sylvine hadn't instantly come across as being somehow more "real" than the others around him. The animations were getting good. Stunningly good!

There was an anger in the forced pace of Corrigan's tread on the sidewalk stones and the taut set of his face that Lilly had not seen before. It was an anger of the worst kind —the kind directed at one's own foolishness. While he had been fondly living fantasies of glory and success, believing himself to be in control of his imaginary project in its imaginary world, somebody else, outside, was very much in control of the real one.

"They must have been setting it up since before Xylog was formed," Corrigan muttered darkly. "Nothing like the scale of this was expected until way in the future. That was why I had such a hard time accepting it. Now I can see what's been going on."

"What? Tell me how you read it," Lilly said.

"This is what Borth's clients wanted all along—a simulated world that they could test marketing ideas in. And somebody told them they could have it. That was why the backers poured all that money in."

"You mean Tyron and company?"

"It has to be. Borth's no doubt in on it, Velucci certainly, maybe Endelmyer himself. I don't know. . . . But they've got friends in SDC. There could have been a whole department working on this behind a security screen. They must have done it the way you said once: waited until I went into the simulation on a routine inspection, then invoked the memory suppression to make it permanent and concocted some story to say it was my own decision. That gave them total control. And they've been in control of everything out there for the last three weeks."

They crossed the exit from a parking lot without slowing down, forcing a car that had just begun moving out to stop abruptly with a squeal of tires.

"Hey, asshole! You try'na get yusself killed or

sump'n?" Nothing abstract or unreal about this world. It was eerie.

"That much I follow," Lilly said. "But how do we suddenly find ourselves back here again—before the project has even started?"

"The backers didn't get what they had been expecting," Corrigan replied. "They got the crazy place that you and I remember." He tossed a hand up as they walked. "No good for their purpose at all, not even close—*to begin with.*"

Lilly walked a couple more paces, then came to a dead halt when what he was saying finally hit her.

"Ohmygod!" she gasped. Corrigan stopped and looked back. "But it was getting better, wasn't it," she said.

He nodded. "Faster than anybody ever dreamed it could—certainly much faster than anything I'd ever have dared bet was possible. We did a better job than we realized. Finally, after about three weeks of run time—twelve years in the simulation—it had got itself almost right. Not completely. There were still some flaws. In particular, the animations weren't copying the surrogates but had gone off on a zany tangent of their own instead; but for the most part, the realism that it achieved was incredible. And then somebody out there said, if it can get this close in three weeks, starting from scratch . . ."

Corrigan saw from the look on Lilly's face that she had already completed the rest for herself. What somebody had said was that they could do so much better still if they could start all over again, only this time with the benefit of everything that the system had learned the first time.

"They've reset everything back to the beginning," Lilly said. Corrigan nodded. But it still didn't add up. Lilly's face creased in puzzlement. "But how could they hope to run it again with us knowing what we know now?" she said.

Corrigan shook his head. "We weren't supposed to. They've got memory suppression. All that was supposed to have been erased, so that we'd start out again yesterday with clean slates, really believing that it was the real world, just before Oz was due to start. But they screwed up somewhere. That suppression didn't work. And now they're all set to run the whole thing through again—only this time from more realistic beginnings."

Lilly stared at him aghast. "The whole thing? You mean . . ."

"Sure. Why not? It's only a few more weeks. But the returns they stand to collect are enormous."

"That's out there!" Lilly choked. "It might only be a few weeks to them. But in here . . ."

Corrigan nodded curtly and took her arm to resume walking. "Exactly. If we don't find a way out of this, it's going to be another twelve years!"

Chapter Thirty-six

Lilly was still struggling to come to grips with it when they arrived back at the main entrance to Xylog. "They can't," she protested as they ascended the front steps. "No way. Not another twelve years. There's got to be some way of telling the outside that they've screwed up."

Corrigan nodded curtly. "Graham Sylvine."

"Who's he?"

They went through the glass double doors into Reception.

"One of the people that I had dinner with last night— supposedly an observer from Washington. But he's really that Dr. Zehl from before that I told you about—the same person. One of the outside controllers."

The receptionist at the desk smiled inquiringly. "Mr. Corrigan, right?"

For the first time in two days, Corrigan registered that her face was new. The plaque on her desk gave her name as Chris Iyles. "No Nancy?" Corrigan said.

"She left, I guess. I'm her new replacement."

"Hi." Newer than you know, Corrigan thought to himself. Every synthetic personality was one less real one to get right. The system didn't have attribute files on everyone. He gestured at the screen to one side. "A Graham Sylvine from Washington was here yesterday. Can you find out if he's still around?"

"Do you know who he's with, Mr. Corrigan?" the receptionist asked, turning to call up a schedule of visitors.

"He's been all over—here and at Head Office. That's all I can tell you."

"One moment."

Lilly flashed Corrigan a questioning look. He explained, murmuring, "Twenty-four hours to us is only seven minutes out there. It's not practicable to give advance notice' when you're coming in, which is why they're always showing up unexpectedly. But once you are in, there isn't any great haste about having to get out. So he could still be around somewhere."

But no. "I'm sorry, Mr. Corrigan, but it looks as if Mr. Sylvine left yesterday," the receptionist announced.

"Damn! . . ." Corrigan drummed his fingertips on the desktop. "Is Jason Pinder's secretary still here? She should have his Washington number." With the imminence of the project, practically everyone was working late.

"I don't understand," Lilly murmured. "He's not going to be there, is he? . . . Is there even a Washington here?"

"It'll activate a code to have him called on the outside," Corrigan said. "I used it with Zehl."

"She's not at her desk right now, Mr. Corrigan."

"Here, let me." Corrigan swiveled the unit and entered his own ID, which gave him access to Pinder's files up to "Restricted" level. He keyed through several layers of indexes, found the database for personal contacts, and located the record for Graham Sylvine. It gave a Washington number. Corrigan selected it and initiated the call.

Lilly looked away and watched the receptionist with a fascination that she tried not to show. Even now she was unable to detect any hint that it was an animation. Surely this wasn't possible.

A legend appeared on the screen to say that all personnel had left for the day, which was confirmed by a voiceover. Callers were invited to leave a message. Corrigan snorted softly, but he had expected something like this. "Joe Corrigan from Xylog, Pittsburgh, for Graham Sylvine," he said. "Tell him . . ." He paused. "Tell him that it won't wash this time either. He'll understand. The memories from last time have not been erased. Repeat: have *not* been erased. We need to talk. Get in touch ASAP." Corrigan hung up and stood staring at the screen. He was clearly dissatisfied, but just for the moment no immediate continuation suggested itself.

"That's it?" Lilly said, echoing what he felt. "That's all we can do?"

"The time differential," Corrigan muttered. "If it takes him five minutes to respond and connect back in, that'll still be tomorrow morning for us."

"There aren't any others?" Lilly said.

"Maybe Pinder," Corrigan said, half to himself. He found it difficult to believe that somebody of Pinder's seniority would have been misled into becoming a memory-suppressed surrogate. Therefore, Pinder would be participating in a fully aware state, probably having decided out of sheer curiosity as much as anything to see the launching of the rerun for himself, from the inside.

Corrigan's eyes, shifting around restlessly, came back to the terminal. He reached toward the keypad, then hesitated and shook his head. "No, let's do it from my office upstairs." He glanced at the receptionist. "Thanks, Chris."

"You're welcome." Lilly still had her visitor's badge from earlier. The animation nodded a smile as they went on through toward the elevators.

Upstairs, Judy was still at her desk and had a sheaf of messages. "Joe, where on earth did you go? The whole world's been calling. There are a couple of urgent—"

"Later. Can you get Jason for me right away? Whatever he's doing, it's more urgent."

"Tom called in at last, but he wouldn't leave a number. He said he'd call back."

Corrigan stopped. It was the first time he'd thought about Hatcher since he and Lilly figured out the situation. And suddenly he knew why Hatcher hadn't shown up for two days. Hatcher had been scheduled to enter the simulation as an observer periodically, just as Corrigan had. And the same thing had happened to him. Tom had been there, somewhere in the simworld, all those "years." And yesterday he had found himself back at the start of it, just like Corrigan and Lilly.

"How is he?" Corrigan asked.

"Acting weird. He didn't say why."

"If he calls, put him straight through."

Corrigan went through into his office with Lilly and

closed the door. "Let's assume I'm right and we weren't supposed to remember anything about having gone through this once before, but something's gone wrong. Pinder will be able to decouple straight away and let them know. That way we don't have to wait for Sylvine to get back to us."

Lilly sank down into a visitor's chair, but Corrigan carried on prowling about the room. "No, that isn't it," she said, watching him. "You're just mad as hell at what's been going on. You can't wait to get at them."

Corrigan stopped pacing and looked at her, then emitted a loud sigh. "Hell, what else do you expect?" He folded his arms and propped himself back against the desk. "They've been working some secret deal with Borth and his backers all along, and taken control when they got me inside the simulation. They've stolen the damn project. *My* project! . . ."

The call tone sounded from the desk unit. He straightened up and turned to accept. Judy's voice came through. "Jason for you. He's across the river at Head Office."

"Thanks. . . ." Pinder's face materialized. "Hello, Jason."

"Yes, Joe? I've ducked out of a meeting, so this had better be good."

Corrigan was still in two minds as to whether Pinder had been a party to the conspiracy. If he had, then much of what Corrigan thought he remembered didn't add up. But those memories were from what had been twelve years ago to Corrigan, and it was impossible to be sure. Giving the benefit of the doubt where due, he decided to play things low-key.

"It's no good, Jason," he said, shaking his head. "We know. You'd better tell the others. There isn't anything wrong with the set, as you've seen for yourself. In fact, it's way ahead of anything that I'd have bet on. But we know it's being rerun. The memory tape from last time didn't get wiped. It's still there."

"Joe, what are you talking about?"

Now Corrigan was irritated. He'd played it straight with Pinder, and he would have expected at least the same in reciprocation. "Look," he said tiredly, "acting dumb is unbecoming, as well as being insulting to the intelligence. We know what's going on, and we want out. I'm not saying you were involved personally, Jason, but some people out there are going to have to do a lot of explaining. I've had twelve years of this shit, and I'm not in a very patient mood for talking. So get yourself out of that cubicle and go and tell whoever's running things to shut it down—*now!*"

But Pinder, far from conceding anything, glared back with a look of outrage. His jaw clamped tight, his mustache quivered, and even on the screen his face turned visibly a shade redder. "Who in God's name do you think you are, and who do you think you're talking to like that?" he spluttered. "Allow me to remind you that you are not a director *yet*. And if this is a foretaste of how it's likely to go to your head, I have a strong mind to recommend to the Board that they reconsider."

For a terrible moment, Corrigan did wonder if he had made one almighty, god-awful mistake. But no, there could be no doubt. The memories of the simulation were clear in his head. Lilly was there, right behind him. There was no flaw in the argument. They had to be in a rerun, for all the reasons they had figured.

Conscious of Lilly watching him, Corrigan's mind wallowed as if in a gel. This sudden change in demeanor of Pinder's had thrown him completely. Earlier today and the day before, Pinder's disposition had been almost deferential, acquiescing to Corrigan on just about every point that had been raised. Corrigan remembered thinking to himself how their roles seemed almost to have reversed themselves, and in his headiness he had attributed it to the transformation that he then believed himself to have undergone. But now . . .

Then Corrigan realized what was happening. He swallowed hard and blinked. Pinder was being belligerent, yes; but at a deeper level nothing had changed. Corrigan had come on the line spoiling for a fight, and Pinder was simply responding in kind. He was still taking his lead from Corrigan. Corrigan stared disbelievingly. No wonder there had been something naggingly but undefinably different about Pinder, which he hadn't been able to put his finger on in two days. Pinder wasn't going to be of any help. Pinder really didn't have any idea what he was talking about. Not *this* Pinder.

"I'm . . . I'm sorry," Corrigan mumbled. "It's a misunderstanding on my part. I guess all this last-minute stress has been getting to me. I'll explain tomorrow."

Pinder's face relaxed immediately. Unnaturally so. Real feelings didn't just evaporate that quickly. Here was further proof if Corrigan needed any. He wondered how many other clues he'd been surrounded by for two days without noticing. "Very well, Joe," Pinder said. "I'll get back to my meeting. I hope you feel better tomorrow." The screen blanked out.

Corrigan sat down shakily on one of the other chairs. *"Jesus!"* he breathed, shaking his head.

"What is it?" Lilly asked.

He waved vaguely at the screen. "That wasn't Pinder. He isn't coupled in as a surrogate at all. That was a system animation."

"Never!"

Corrigan nodded. "He's been acting out of character since yesterday—only marginally, but it's there. You'd have to have worked with him to spot it. It even took me until just now."

"But how? . . ." This time Lilly was incredulous. "How could the system possibly learn to mimic somebody that accurately who wasn't in the first run? He wasn't there. He was never a surrogate."

"The system had a Personal Attribute File on him that it had been building up before then—from early experiments and calibration runs that he took part in. Practically everyone in the company tried it. It got to be a fad." He shook his head again, still having trouble accepting it himself. "God, they're getting close! . . . The whole idea of Oz was that the animations would improve by modeling their behavior on that of the surrogates. Something wasn't right the first time around, and they went off in their own direction instead. But near the end, some of them were getting amazingly good—remember Sherri at the Camelot?" Corrigan stared at Lilly wonderingly.

"People like Zehl were reporting back, and it amazed everyone else too. Then somebody got the idea of rerunning the whole thing—going back and *starting out* with everything that the system had learned. Think what *that* could produce. They'd stand a strong chance of actually being able to deliver what the backers had been expecting—but which nobody who understood the technicalities had taken seriously. So they gain control and collect all the accolades from the people with the money, while I'm stuck here on the inside. Neat."

"But you have to come out sometime," Lilly pointed out.

Corrigan shrugged. "Then what? What do I do, cry foul? File a lawsuit? With the money they've got behind them now, they can ride all of it. . . . At least, that's the way they'd figure it."

Lilly looked at him for a few moments longer, as if waiting for something. "Well?" she said finally.

"Well what?"

Suddenly, everything that she had been fighting to control since waking up the previous morning came boiling out. She had sought out the one person she knew who offered a hope of making sense of anything, and he was acting as if the situation were no more serious than missing their stop on the subway and having to ride it out to the next. In reality, the sheer enormity of it had numbed him past the point of being able to react.

"For Christ's sake, Joe!" she exploded, rising up from the chair and coming nearer. "These people have as good as abducted you and taken control of the project. We're just about to start all over again from the beginning. And you're just sitting there like . . ." She turned away to get a grip on herself. Corrigan heard her draw in a long breath. She turned back again, her hands turned upward and extended. "Surely you're not saying that all we can do is wait like a pair of dummies until someone outside decides it's gone far enough? There must be some way of getting out of here. There has to be a way we can *do something*!"

"Pinder can't help us. All we can do is wait for Sylvine to get the message," Corrigan said.

"Sylvine won't do any good either," Lilly answered.

"Oh? And what makes you say that?"

Lilly looked at the desk, then at the wall. Finally she brought her gaze back to meet Corrigan's and shook her head as if it should have been obvious. "There isn't any reason for them to be in a hurry, is there, Joe?" she said. "As far as they're concerned, the longer we're in here, the better. So why should they rush to shut everything down when the results are way past all expectations? Just because Sylvine comes out and tells them we've sussed it? Come on."

Corrigan looked back at her long and hard. It *was* obvious. "No reason at all," was all he could say.

He slumped back in his chair and spread his hands, indicating that he had nothing more to say. Then the desk unit buzzed. Corrigan accepted, and Judy's voice came through. "It's Tom." At once, Hatcher's face appeared on the screen. He was unshaven and looked haggard.

"Tom! Where are you?" Corrigan exclaimed.

"It doesn't matter. Look, I'm gonna have to make this quick, Joe, but it's important, so listen. First, let me see if I'm right about something. Did a very peculiar thing happen to you yesterday—yesterday in the morning? Like, I've seen all this before?"

Corrigan nodded curtly. "Yes. . . . Yes, it did."

"Okay. We're talking the same language." Hatcher saw Corrigan's mouth starting to open and cut him off with a wave of his hand. "Not now. I need to get together with you. I'll see you at your house—say, half an hour from now. You know and I know that nothing else in this place we're in matters, right? So is that okay?"

Corrigan nodded. "Half an hour."

"I just want to tell you one more thing in case I don't make it. Do you remember that talk we had, way back, with Charlie Wade and Des Jorrecks about ejector seats? Well, you went into the sim a day before I did, so you won't remember. But I do. You and I talked about it again after the phase-two tests were started. There were some funny things going on then that you'll have forgotten about, that we didn't like. We agreed that some insurance would be good to have. Do you hear what I'm saying, Joe? *The ejector buttons exist.* We planted one each, the way we'd talked about before."

Corrigan stared incredulously. "You mean—"

Hatcher looked around warily, as if worried about being watched. "Gotta go, Joe. Your place, half an hour. See ya." The screen blanked.

Lilly looked at him, not bothering to ask the obvious. He rose and ushered her to the door. "I'll tell you on the way," he said.

Judy swiveled in her chair as they came out. "Do you want to see any of—" But Corrigan declined with a wave.

"Sorry, Judy. We have to leave right away. Thanks for holding the fort. Talk to you tomorrow."

Judy eyed Lilly suspiciously. Corrigan paused, staring at her. Her eyes shifted from Lilly to him, her brows rising inquiringly. He peered, trying to pierce the veils to penetrate to the person inside. Was she? Wasn't she? . . . But it was no good. For the life of him, he couldn't tell.

Chapter Thirty-seven

They drove northward in Corrigan's simulated Mercedes, along simulated Route 28 by the simulated Allegheny River toward the simulation of Fox Chapel. Had the sign indicating the Blue Belt exit at Millvale really leaned over to one side as he was seeing it? Were the cracks and faces of the rock outcrop to their left exactly like that, or was the computer adding in its own details? Because his subjective recollections stretched back over twelve years, he couldn't know from memory how much of what he was seeing was authentic. Lilly was evidently pondering the same issues.

"This is your car," she said after a period of silence that had lasted since the Fort Duquesne Bridge. "I mean, not just the same model and color and everything that you drove now"—she was still seeing events from a viewpoint projected twelve years forward—"but *your* car, the one that you'd owned and gotten to know."

"Yes," Corrigan said. He could see where her thinking was heading, but it was easiest to just let her follow it through.

She motioned with a hand. "So what should there be inside that glove compartment in front of me?"

"I honestly can't remember. Have a look and see."

Lilly reached out and opened the compartment door. "Map of the city, another of Pennsylvania, black flashlight, insurance certificate, pen, wiping cloth . . . another pen, empty envelope, and an owner's manual," she recited, taking out the items and showing them briefly.

"Sounds about right," Corrigan said, glancing at her and nodding.

Lilly shook her head. "But this is what I don't get. How does the machine that's managing this simulation *know* what was in *your* car? When we were at my place, you talked about how a lot of detail can get filled in by a person's subconscious—like in a dream. But that isn't happening here. I'm seeing the same things as you, but the information can't be coming from my subconscious, can it? I never knew what was in your glove compartment."

Corrigan shrugged. "No big deal, really. Think about it. I'm comatose inside a COSMOS cubicle at Xylog, and my car is right outside in the parking lot. It wouldn't take somebody very long to inventory everything with a camera and input the images to the system." He paused to let her take that in, then added casually, "When you woke up this morning, where was it, exactly? Tell me again."

"A hotel that the Air Force put us in."

"After you arrived from California to take part in the project."

"Yes."

"And I assume that you put on some regular clothes out of your wardrobe, and picked up the purse and that blue coat when you were leaving. Right?"

Lilly glanced down at herself. "Well, sure. Of course I did. What else?"

Corrigan gave her a sideways grin. "Then how come I see a blue coat and all the right things? *I* don't know what was in your closet, do I?"

It took Lilly a few seconds to see what he was driving at. "The bags, all my things? . . . You're kidding!" she said disbelievingly.

Corrigan nodded. "Same thing. A crew goes out to the hotel, scans the rooms and itemizes the contents. Do the lot in under an hour. If the truth were known, that's probably why they put you in a hotel in the first place. Don't make any mistake, Lilly. There's heaps of money riding on this. These people are doing it right."

Lilly still couldn't buy it completely. "But you didn't wake up in a hotel room with just a few things," she said. "You were at home. There's no way they could have captured the whole of something like that. Every piece of junk in a desk drawer? The contents of a file cabinet? It's simply not feasible."

"It wouldn't be as hard as you think. Practically all of us who were on the project got our homes realscaped just for the hell of it, to make realistic test environments. So a lot of what would be needed is in the databank already. But you're right—it couldn't be perfect. I want to find out what differences you and I see when we get there. There could be something in that house that can get us out of this, regardless of what anyone outside decides. That's what Tom Hatcher was telling me back at the office."

"Okay. Then now suppose you tell me what that was all about," Lilly suggested. "Hatcher was the one who ran a lot of the software development at Xylog, right?"

"That's him. Well, there was something that he and me and a couple of others talked about once when we were arguing about memory suppression." Corrigan grunted as he braked to avoid a Buick making a sudden lane-switch without signaling—probably under the influence of a random number.

"Okay. And? . . ."

"One of the things that came up was how to get yourself out of the simulation—say, in some kind of emergency—if we had gone with suppression; in other words, if you didn't even know you were in a simulation. We called it the ejector seat. But can you see the problem? If your knowledge that it exists gets erased as part of the suppression, it's no use to you. But if you know about it from before the period that was suppressed, then you must know also that you're in a simulation, which defeats the whole object of having any suppression in the first place."

"How do you use a button that you know you're going to forget about?" Lilly summarized.

"Exactly."

She sat back in her seat, thought about it, and then looked across at him. "There's no way you can do it."

"Tom came up with a way whereby maybe you can. His idea was to plant something of personal significance in the simworld environment that would take on a new meaning when you know that you're looking for it. In other words *you* know the way you think, and when the need became strong enough, you'd realize that you would have put something close by somewhere—something that you'd recognize when the time came. So for as long as the simulation was running normally, it would effectively be invisible. Get the idea?"

Lilly did, but its relevance was less clear. From what Corrigan had just said, the notion had been purely hypothetical—something to think about *if* the decision had been to use suppression in the project. But—as far as Corrigan had been aware, anyway—the decision had been not to use suppression. So why would he have implemented an ejection button? She tried to think back to what she had overheard Hatcher say from the screen.

"Back in your office just now, he said something about you and he talking late into the project. You went into the simulation a day before he did."

Corrigan nodded that she had got it. "So my memory erasure went back a day earlier than his did. Something was going on that aroused our suspicions enough for us to decide that maybe an 'out' button would be a good insurance. And what he's telling me is that we went ahead and put them in somewhere. It means that there *is* a way out, Lilly, whether Sylvine and the rest of them out there feel like cooperating or not. All we have to do is find it."

They drove along a road of comfortably aloof homes lying in upper-middle-class seclusion among shrubbery and pines, and turned off into the driveway of a low-set, contemporary composition of lacquered timbers and stone chimney breasts, with brown shingles, a screened porch, and large expanses of glass.

Corrigan parked without saying anything, got out, and walked around to open the passenger door. Outside a house a short distance farther along, a man who looked like the occupant was standing with a woman by the mailbox at the end of a driveway. They looked across while pretending not to as Lilly climbed out of the car—unwilling to permit anything approaching eye contact, even at that distance, but too intrigued to miss anything. Then the gazes averted, and the chins began to wag.

"I think I'm the sensation of the street already," Lilly

said as they began walking up toward the house. "How long is it since Evelyn left?"

Corrigan snorted. "Three weeks. You know, it's funny. I can remember how smug and self-satisfied I felt when we picked this place. Now I think I'd prefer that flat in Oakland. Better neighborhood. Less insufferable people."

"Drunks, deadbeats, students, dancers? Even bartenders."

"Exactly."

The dog from next door was out front, secured by a sliding chain to a line that gave it the run of the lawn on the far side of the scattering bay laurel and flowering dogwoods separating the two properties. It was a shaggy gray mass of indeterminate origins, and had paused to watch them hesitantly, as if unsure what it was supposed to do. Corrigan stopped and looked at it strangely for a couple of seconds. Then he held out a hand and called jovially, "Hey, Bruce, old fella. How's it going today, eh?" The dog scampered as close as its chain would permit, tongue lolling from jaws panting wide in delight and tail wagging. Corrigan grunted to himself, followed Lilly up to the door, and let them in.

"I never knew you were a dog person," she said as he closed the door.

"I'm not. That was an experiment. Checking out the system."

"What do you mean?"

Corrigan cocked his head and pointed back over his shoulder with a thumb. "Its name isn't Bruce—I don't know what its name is. And it never acts like that. It hates me." Lilly frowned uncomprehendingly. Corrigan moved to the hallway window beside the door and looked out. The dog had gone back to investigate something under a shrub by the lawns; the two people across the street were still talking.

"The system is operating right on its edge," Corrigan murmured. "You see, it *didn't know* what to make the dog do. Somebody must have got a shot of the next-door dog when they were here realscaping the house, but they didn't know what name it answered to, or how it behaves. So the system took its cue from me. That's what it was designed to do." He inclined his head, still gazing out across the road. "Are those animations of real neighbors that somebody got views of, or are they characters that the system invented? I don't know, because I've never talked to anyone around here. But the system couldn't be aware of that. If I did know what the guy who lives there looks like, I'd be in a position to catch it out. If I walked across and went into his house, do I know what I ought to find there, or could the system get away with making up an interior of its own? It can't tell. You see, again, we've got it right on the edge."

Lilly looked out of the window, and then uncomfortably back at Corrigan. "This is getting weird."

"Hell, it's been weird for a long time, Lilly."

He helped Lilly out of her coat and hung it, along with his own, on the rack by the door. "That's interesting, Joe," she agreed after she had absorbed what he was getting at. "But how is it supposed to help?"

"I'm not exactly sure yet. But when something's stretched to its limits, that's when you find where its weaknesses are." He led the way into the kitchen and tipped the old filter and grounds from the coffeemaker into the trash bin. "Anyhow, simulation or not, it activates the same taste centers. Let's get the pot on."

"I could use one." Lilly looked around at the mess he had left that morning—the sinkful of dishes; papers from work spread over the table; bread, cheese, pickles, and mayonnaise for his sandwich still not put away. "Boy, you sure have been on your own for three weeks," she commented.

"Ah, don't start giving me any of that old bilge," he warned. "It's been hectic at Xylog. And since I woke up yesterday I've had other things on my mind than housekeeping."

Lilly opened the dishwasher and shook her head despairingly at the pile of crockery and kitchenware inside. "Where's the detergent?" she sighed.

"I can't remember. It's been twelve years since I saw it. Try the cupboard under the sink."

Lilly opened the door and squatted down to look. "The stupid thing is that there's really no need for any of this. Why go to the trouble of creating a simulated world and build in all the limitations of the real one? You could just have a code word or something that gets this done in an instant." She found the detergent, stood up, and poured detergent into the dishwasher while Corrigan loaded items from the sink. "You could make life really comfortable, when you think about it."

"Magic words, eh? You're right. That's exactly the kind of world we could create. We haven't scratched the surface of this business yet, Lilly."

She switched on the machine and began collecting assorted jars and dishes together to either throw out or put in the refrigerator. "You see what I mean," she said. "Look at all this. Why is it necessary to have stuff dry up and go bad? Couldn't we have a simulation without mimicking the effects of microbes?"

"Why stop at that?" he asked her. "Maybe you'd never get too hot or too cold, cut your finger, get a bruise, or catch flu, either. Talk to anyone anytime, and be anywhere in an instant."

"Well, why not?"

"People might never want to come out of it." Corrigan shook his head and set down two mugs that he had found for the coffees. "There's all kinds of things to find out. The whole thing's being rushed too fast, and for all the wrong reasons. That's how we come to be stuck in here." Which brought them back to the immediate issue at hand.

"You said we were here to look for the clue to a way out that Tom says you planted somewhere," she said.

"Mmm."

"What kind of thing are we looking for?"

"I don't know."

"That helps."

"The clue to the magic word." Corrigan poured the coffees and handed her one. "It was twelve years ago, Lilly. I hadn't planned on it happening this way. It was supposed to have been just a few days."

"What did you mean in the car when you talked about us seeing different things when we got here?" Lilly swept her free hand in a circle. "I see a sink, refrigerator, table with things on, a window over there, and the door we came in there. Isn't that what you see?"

"Oh, sure. But you'd expect that. Everything superficial would have been captured when the guys were here realscaping the house. Possibly Tyron's people came to get additional detail, too, at the same time that they did the car—after I was inside the simulation. So for stuff like that, the system has objective data that it can feed in the data streams to both of us. But at a more subtle level there are things that exist in my memories that it doesn't know about. Will my mind fill in the details subconsciously so that I see them and you don't? Or will I not see them, although I know I ought to? How will the system handle it when it's driven to the limit?" He sipped from his mug and looked around the kitchen casually.

"For instance . . ." Corrigan moved over to the microwave and took down one of the recipe books from the shelf just above. It was called *Cooking the Good Old American Way,* and showed big, elegant houses and a riverboat scene. "They did a thorough job," he commented. "This book of Evelyn's did have that picture on the front. But they had to stop somewhere. He opened the cover and showed Lilly the endpaper and flyleaf inside. "What do you see there?" he asked her curiously.

She looked, then raised her eyes to meet his uncertainly as if suspecting a trick and shrugged. "Nothing. It's blank."

He nodded. "That's what I see too. But what I know, and what you and the system don't, is that it was a gift from an aunt of Evelyn's, and it had an inscription inside. . . . You see—we've carried out one experiment already."

Lilly gaped. In two days, nothing had brought home to her the reality of the situation that they were in more effectively than that one, simple demonstration. Corrigan was straining the system's rules, watching for where the cracks would appear. Lilly realized then that he had a twofold strategy: either he would find the "magic word" and get them out; or failing that, he would find a way to crash everything from the inside.

She watched, still struggling to overcome the eerie feeling of it all as Corrigan replaced the cookbook. He opened one of the kitchen drawers and rummaged idly among the contents, but nothing caught his eye as the kind of thing that he had vaguely in mind. It was the usual assortment of utensils and implements that could have been imaged and recorded straightforwardly. He needed something that would let his mind work spontaneously, without prior expectations. He wandered around, taking pictures off the walls, lifting ornaments from their niches, trying to create opportunities for stumbling on details that a realscaping crew with finite time to contend with would have missed. The watercolor of a schooner that he took down from above the breakfast bar was just blank pasteboard on the reverse side. Was anything supposed to be written there—a date, a caption, an inscription? He couldn't remember. Was the maker's mark that he found on the underside of the vase from the ledge by the pantry the authentic one that had always been there, or had the system improvised it? He had no idea. He lifted a wooden-handled carving knife from its fixture on the wall—a relic from his student days that had followed him over the years through all his digs and apartments from Dublin to Pittsburgh. The handle had a deep, L-shaped gouge in it, dating from a time long forgotten, which had been hidden facing the wall. He held it out to let Lilly look at it.

"Tell me what you see," he said.

"An old knife. It's got a worn blade, a polished wooden handle held by brass rivets."

Corrigan turned the knife over in his hands. "Anything different this way?" He turned it again, showing her the first side once more, then the other.

"No. Should there be?"

"To me, there's a deep gouge in the handle. You don't see one at all?" He had found something.

"No. Nothing." Lilly looked up at him disbelievingly. "My God!" she whispered.

Corrigan had forgotten that gouge. But his subconscious hadn't, and it was filling the detail in, inside his head. The system had known nothing about the gouge, since it had faced the wall and not been captured in the imaging; therefore, the data to define it were absent from the optical input being generated for Lilly.

"Now it's caught in a direct conflict," Corrigan said. "It knows that you and I are seeing different things, violating its primary reality criterion. It can't resolve the issue by deleting what I see, and it can't correct what you see because it doesn't have the information to draw it. And either way, even if it could, that would violate its consistency rules."

Lilly shook her head helplessly, as if it were her problem. "So how will it handle it?" she asked.

Corrigan shrugged. "I have no idea. The system has

been evolving its own associative structures. That's what it was designed to do. Its internal complexity will be so great by now that neither I nor anyone else could tell you what it'll do. It's going to be interesting finding out." Lilly looked around uneasily, as if half expecting the house to cave in. Corrigan grinned cheerfully and took her arm. "Come on," he said. "Let's take a stroll around the house and see what else we can find."

They went out through the living room and into the den. It was getting dark. Corrigan switched on the light and gazed around at the desk, the terminal, shelves of books, ornaments, pictures and other hangings on the walls. Finally he went over to the bookshelves and began peering more closely at the titles. "Now, I can't remember exactly everything that was here," he said. "But it seems the kind of place that I might have stuck a reminder to myself. . . . Ah! Now, see this one, for example." He took down a thin, green-covered volume with the title *The Stories Behind the Flags*. "You see, I can't remember where this book came from at all. It could be something that Evelyn put there and didn't tell me about, or I forgot." He glanced at Lilly pointedly. "Or maybe I put it there for a reason, just before Oz went live, and the memory got suppressed along with everything else from those last few days. See my point?" He rippled through the pages idly with a thumb.

Lilly caught glimpses of the pages, replete with text and illustrations. "The pages are all there," she said, indicating with a hand. "Surely the people who scanned the house couldn't have gone through every one."

"No need," Corrigan said. "You just get the titles from a high-resolution scan of the room, and the system obtains the contents electronically from a library." He nodded toward the file cabinet in a corner. "I bet you'd find a lot wrong in there, though. Nobody's going to wade through that lot."

"Are you going to look?"

"Oh, we'll get to it. Meanwhile, what about this book? Is it the clue to the magic word?"

Lilly turned up her hands. "I don't know. How do we find out?"

"We experiment. . . . Maybe all you have to do is say the right words in the right place, like in a D and D game.

Maybe it's the title." He raised his voice and recited, " 'The Stories Behind the Flags.' " He waited a moment, then shrugged. "Maybe the name of a flag. How about, The Stars and Stripes? . . . Old Glory? . . . Irish Tricolor? Union Jack?" He looked back at Lilly. "You see. Nothing happens."

"Just like D and D games," she remarked.

"Maybe we have to type it into the system." He went over to the terminal, sat down and switched it on, and began entering any phrases and references to flags that came to mind.

"This could take until the next ice age," Lilly said bleakly as she began to get the idea.

"I told you, having to try and hit on the right thing from twelve years back doesn't help. If it was a connection that meant something a couple of days ago, the way it was supposed to, it would probably be obvious already."

He carried on resolutely. Lilly looked around the room, searching for anything that might suggest itself. She was about to say something when the headlights from a car turning into the driveway outside came in through the window.

Corrigan stopped what he was doing and got up to cross the room and peer out. A familiar tall, loose-limbed figure, yellow-haired in the glow from a nearby streetlamp, straightened up from behind a Ford parked next to Corrigan's Mercedes and headed with tense, agitated footsteps toward the front door of the house.

"Well, there's one lot of questions we won't have to worry about for very much longer," Corrigan said, letting the drape fall back. "Tom's here."

Chapter Thirty-eight

The bell started ringing when Corrigan was halfway to the door and carried on ringing until he opened it. Hatcher looked as if he had been in a private war. His hair was tousled, his face showing two days of yellow stubble, and his eyes, which in all the years they had worked together Corrigan had never seen other than mild and mockingly easy-lazy, mirroring the way Tom ambled through life, were red-rimmed and glazed. He was wearing a gray, hooded zipper jacket, torn on one side, over a stained khaki shirt and blue jeans.

He gestured back toward the driveway and said without preamble, "Can I move the car into the garage? I need to get it out of sight, off the street."

"Well . . . sure, Tom." Corrigan went past him to open the garage door, while Lilly watched from the doorway. Corrigan heard the door of Hatcher's car slam behind him, and the engine start. He fumbled with the keys and had to try several before he found the right one to open the door. Hatcher drove in past him and got out; Corrigan closed the garage door from the inside and led the way through a side door into the kitchen. Lilly joined them from the hallway a few seconds later.

"I was right, wasn't I? It happened to you too," Hatcher said, again wasting no words on preliminaries. "You couldn't remember which key opened the garage. It's been twelve years since you did it last, right?"

Corrigan waved a hand to indicate one of the chairs by the kitchen table. "Why don't you take a load off your feet before we get into this, Tom? You look beat. We've just made some fresh coffee."

"What does it matter—any of it? We're not really here. None of it's really here. Coffee? You act like . . ." Hatcher checked himself, then indicated the surroundings with a wave of his arm. "Just to be sure that we're talking the same language—we *do* both know what all this is, right?"

Corrigan nodded. "It's the simulation. We know that. And to save any more comparing of notes, yes, we both went through twelve years of it. And yesterday we woke up back at the beginning, all set to start over."

"Her too? You mean she's not a . . ." Hatcher threw up a hand in a way that said call them anything you want.

"This is Lilly Essell," Corrigan said, his tone making the point that bizarre circumstances didn't excuse bad manners. "Space Defense Command, Inglewood. Lilly's a scientist with OTSC—one of the surrogates recruited from outside. She was involved with DIVAC development. We met in the simworld the first time around."

Hatcher sighed, sank down onto the chair, and nodded wearily. "Excuse me, Lilly. . . . Yeah, man, could I use some coffee."

Lilly had already taken down an extra mug and was filling the three of them from the pot. "Thanks," Hatcher acknowledged as she set one of them down in front of him. Some of the fury that Corrigan had sensed when Tom came into the house was abating, but his movements were still tense. He picked up his mug and sipped from it, clasping it in both hands. "Having those freaks around for too long," he said by way of explanation. "That's what it does to you."

"It's been tough all around," Lilly said.

"This is the Tom Hatcher that we talked about," Corrigan told her. "Worked with me on software for years. Now he runs a big slice of the development work at Xylog."

"I've heard a few things about you, Tom," Lilly said.

"Well, wait until you hear my version before you make your mind up. You know how it is with these Irish guys." Hatcher's voice had dropped. The forced humor was an offering to placate.

"Hi," Lilly conceded with a nod.

Hatcher turned his head back to look up at Corrigan.

"I figured out how it must have happened. You remember how it was between you and Frank Tyron back then? There was a group who had him all set up as their man to run COSMOS as a way of cashing in on the work done at SDC. But you screwed that up by selling the company on Oz, and the war changed to which one of you would move into Jason's slot when he went back to Blawnox. You remember all that?"

"How was I supposed to forget?" Corrigan said.

Hatcher went on. "They had another group somewhere that we didn't know about—probably back in SDC—that they kept updated with all the research work that we did. These other guys worked it up to a full-world sim and added in a memory suppressor. You, me, and the others who were part of the regular schedule got wiped as soon as we were inside, and the Tyron campaign committee has been running a gimmick-tester for Madison Avenue ever since. That's how come all that money kept pouring in. And now somebody has decided to restart the whole thing. But this time there isn't going be a discontinuity at the change-over that needs to be camouflaged. The simulation has gotten good enough to merge in smoothly with reality. We weren't supposed to know anything about that, but this time the suppression screwed up."

Corrigan made a sign that there was no need for Hatcher to go on. "Okay, we pretty much figured it out the same way, Tom," he said. "I found myself coming together again after supposedly being messed up in the head by a project that was canceled years ago. After years of being a convalescent, I ended up working as a bartender." He looked across at Lilly. "Lilly was on the right track before I even suspected."

The news seemed to deflate Hatcher, as if something that he had been pinning a hope on had collapsed. "So you're not . . . you're not just in here as an observer right now?" he said. "You can't decouple and go stop this from the outside?"

Corrigan looked surprised. "How could I? We're both in the same situation. You just spelled it all out. . . ." His voice trailed away as he realized that Hatcher had been asking him again to double-check: Was Corrigan *really* a memory-suppressed surrogate? Or did he know more than he had let on? In short, had Corrigan been a party to the group that had sprung this?

Hatcher's manner became more subdued. "I had to ask," he said. Clearly this had been one of the reasons why he had contacted Corrigan.

"I understand," Corrigan said.

Lilly caught Corrigan's eye in a way that asked if any of this mattered. Weren't they missing the whole point that this was supposed to be all about? Corrigan got them back to it.

"On the phone earlier, you said we put in ejector buttons. What was that all about?" he said.

Hatcher took a long drink from his mug. "By the time we got into the serious tests, some funny things were going on. More strangers being brought in from outside that we hadn't expected. Installations and integrations that weren't scheduled. We couldn't get a straight answer out of anybody. . . ."

Corrigan could only shake his head. "I don't really remember." It was all mixed up in the confusion of half-memories from immediately after that time, twelve years ago.

"We didn't like it, Joe. And the more we talked it over, the more we agreed there was no way we were gonna go into the sim with all these guys we didn't know pressing buttons on the outside, without taking out the kind of insurance that we'd figured out for memsupped surrogates. You went into the simworld that night—the day we talked about it. Your memory must have been wiped back to take out that day, which is why you don't know anything about it. But I wasn't due to go in until a day later. So I remember us talking about it."

Lilly, who had been looking from one to the other as she tried to follow, raised a hand to hold everything there. "Wait a minute, let's see if I've got this straight. You're saying that sometime between the time that you two talked and the time Joe went into the simworld, he placed some kind of escape device in here that only he would recognize when the right time came. But he's not only forgotten what it was; he's even forgotten that he ever had the intention."

Hatcher made a face. "Well, I can't *know* for sure that he did. But from the way we talked about it, yep . . . I'd be pretty sure that he did."

Lilly still wasn't clear as to the problem. She shook her

head. "But I thought you said that you *both* set up one. Your memory wasn't wiped that day. So why do you need Joe, anyway? Don't you know what *your* escape button was?"

To her surprise, Hatcher set down the mug, showed both his empty hands, and shook his head helplessly. "There's nothing there that I can recall. Maybe I didn't get around to implementing it until the next day—because I knew I wouldn't be going inside until then. Then that day got wiped, just like the day before it did with Joe, so I ended up remembering saying that I was going to do something, but not what I actually did."

Lilly looked at him dubiously for a moment or two. "Then it doesn't sound as if it was very effective, does it?" she commented. "I thought that was the whole idea."

"We were thinking in terms of something that would only need to have some kind of significance after a matter of days," Corrigan said. "We never dreamed it would have to mean the same years later. Things get fuzzy over time. Who can remember what was and wasn't important twelve years ago?"

Hatcher shook his head, and all the pent-up feelings that had been simmering boiled up again. "You take it all so cool, Joe. They're in charge right now, goddammit! Doesn't it *mean* anything, what these people are doing out there?" His voice rose. "It might be only a few more days to them— that they think they'll be able to buy their way out of when it's over. But it'll be more *years* for us!"

"Tom, I do know that," Corrigan said, trying to calm him.

Hatcher didn't seem to hear. "Do you know what it means to me?" he asked, pointing at his own chest. "What those twelve years were for me in there? I didn't end up convalescing and meeting lots of people as a bartender. I figured out early on what was going on. Only, those . . . 'people' I was dealing with didn't know any better. They thought I really was crazy, and they weren't about to let me out."

"*What!*" Lilly gasped. "You mean, all that time? . . . You were shut up in an institution or something?"

"They called it a 'remedial care center.'"

Corrigan stared, horrified. Whatever the reasons in the

cases of the other surrogates, it explained why he had never bumped into Tom during those years in the simulated city. Surely, though, he thought to himself, a case like Hatcher's would have been monitored by a contact from outside, as had his own by Dr. Zehl.

"But aside from animations, there must have been outside controllers showing up too," he said. "You could tell them apart. You'd have been looking for it."

Hatcher nodded cynically. "Oh, sure, there were several of those—usually passing themselves off as 'supervisors' to the regular animations, or some such. But they could only ever see it from the angle that it was just a few days. They're probably the ones who told the animations to keep me off the streets—they didn't want to risk me meeting other surrogates and blowing the whole thing."

"One of them showed up at Xylog yesterday," Corrigan said. "I called his number and left a message saying we know the score and want out. But it'll be tomorrow before we hear anything back."

Hatcher sighed, closing his eyes for a moment. "You think they're really going to take any notice?" he said. "Come on, Joe, let's get real. They've got high stakes riding on this. You and I don't even come into it anymore. You're wasting your time."

Maybe. But at least Corrigan had been looking around constructively for the hope of a way out, Lilly thought. Perhaps if Hatcher had kept a cooler head in the previous run, he might not have ended up as an interesting test case for animation counselors to sharpen their notions of human psychology on.

"We're not *just* waiting for the guy from Washington to call back," she said. "Even since we got back here, we've been looking for the whatever-it-is that you say Joe set up somewhere. Did you? I mean, have you even *tried,* instead of saying it was all too long ago and you can't remember?"

Hatcher made a tired throwing-away motion in the air. "Ah, there's no way you'd even know where to start. The possibilities are endless. What am I supposed to do—go running all over the place like some kid chasing clues in a treasure hunt, because people like them won't talk to me? The hell I will." He waited for Corrigan or Lilly to disagree, and when they said nothing, waved a hand to indicate the house.

"Show me I'm wrong. How did you two make out? Find anything?"

Lilly shook her head and drew back with a sigh. "No. We didn't."

Corrigan reversed one of the other chairs and sat down on it straddle-legged. "Okay, then suppose you tell us what else you've been doing yesterday that didn't work either," he suggested. "At least we're not driving around looking like a survivor from the Burma Railway. What happened to get you into that mess?"

Although the question had to come sooner or later, Hatcher sat with his shoulders hunched, contemplating the mug between his hands for some time before replying. At last, instead of answering directly, he went back to the morning of yesterday.

"Suddenly, the whole crazy nightmare was over. I woke up at the start of a day I'd lived twelve years ago when the project was about to go live. It took me half a day in a daze to be sure that it hadn't all been some kind of way-out, unheard-of lucid dream."

"I had the same problem," Corrigan said. "In fact, it had me fooled until Lilly walked into my office a few hours ago—even after the last experience. Would you have believed it could get as real as this?"

Hatcher shook his head. "No way. This is scary."

"What put you onto it?"

Hatcher looked at Corrigan curiously for a second. "Did you talk to Barry at all since this flip-back thing happened—since yesterday?"

"Barry Neinst? No, I've had all kinds of things going on. What about him?"

"It isn't him. Not the real Barry that you and I knew. The one who's been walking around Xylog since yesterday is an animation."

Hatcher waited for Corrigan's reaction. It was not as strong as it might have been had it not been for Corrigan's own experiences with Pinder and Judy Klein. He just nodded and said, "I've seen it too."

Hatcher went on. "There were some things that Barry and I talked about twelve years ago that the Barry yesterday didn't know anything about. And in any case, after twelve years of dealing with animations, you can tell."

Corrigan nodded to say that Hatcher didn't have to go into that. They had been there too—they knew what he meant. "So what did you do?" he asked.

"The first thing? I just walked out. Screw it. I wasn't gonna be part of the game anymore. . . . Then I got in a car and went driving—out, away from the city. I wanted to see just how far they'd extended the realscape. And do you know something—you can't tell. It just goes on and on. Somewhere there's a join where it stops being a replication from the image banks and turns into a synthesis that the system will keep spinning for you for as far as you wanna go, but you can't tell where it is. It'll just keep painting highway. Stop at a Waffle House and go inside for a coffee, and it'll create an inside of a Waffle House—it knows how. And it'll put people in there who'll talk to you all day. Kind of strange—like some of those games you can play that keep generating landscapes that go on forever."

"Not forever, surely," Lilly objected. "What happens when you come to somewhere you know? I mean, suppose I decided to drive back to L.A.? I might get taken in by a lot of invention along the way, but not when I got there. Even if they mapped in a few blocks around Inglewood, there couldn't have been anything as comprehensive as what was done for Pittsburgh."

Hatcher was nodding in the slightly impatient way that said yes, anyone with a brain functioning on the positive side of imbecile level knew all that. It wasn't intentional, Corrigan told himself. Tom had spent too long surrounded by animations that he knew were animations, and by the sound of it, hating them. Tact was not a habit that could be regained instantly after years of dealing with elaborate mimes that had no feelings.

"Last night I had a ball just being out around the city again, even if it was all a fake," Hatcher told them. There was a strangely satisfied, yet at the same time malicious look in his eye as he spoke. Corrigan had never seen Tom quite like this. Here was something that they had never really stopped to consider in all their debating about the project and its possible consequences: a personality being radically altered in a space of what, in the outside world, had amounted to only a few days. He wondered what alter-

ations had taken place in himself—perhaps irreversibly—
that he was even now unaware of.

"Where did you go last night?" Corrigan asked uneasily.

Hatcher's expression broadened into a smile that Corrigan wasn't sure he liked—the smile of a chain-saw murderer
bragging about his exploits. "Here, there—what does it
matter?"

"What did you do?"

"I was getting even, man!" Hatcher's voice began rising
again, with an edge to it that said his patience was being
stretched. Maybe he'd had enough of interrogations in the
last few years. "I had a lot in my system that I needed to get
rid of. Smashing bottles can be very satisfying, even if it
wasn't them that got you mad, and they don't know they're
being smashed."

"Okay, okay." Corrigan put a hand up to his brow and
nodded, not really wanting to hear all the lurid details
spelled out. So what had Tom done? Started a fight? Broken
up a bar? Heaved bricks through a jeweler's window? A
lifetime's instincts tried to feel shocked, but they were over-
ridden by the intellectual awareness that in a simulation
such acts carried no more moral significance than shooting
monsters on the screen of a video game. In fact, now that
the worst was out, Corrigan found himself tempted to smile.

Hatcher looked across at Lilly. "Then, today, I asked
myself what you just asked—only, I wasn't about to go driving for days to get to L.A. or anywhere else to find out. So I
went out to the airport, walked up to the ticket desk, and
said I wanted to go to Vancouver."

Lilly was catching the changing mood on Corrigan's
face and did smile. "That's one way to give them a hard
time," she said. "How did they handle it?" But Corrigan
had stiffened at Hatcher's mention of the airport.

Hatcher snorted. He seemed to be enjoying reliving the
experience. "By getting flustered and irrational and stupid,"
he replied. "First they tried to say the flight was canceled.
Then, when I said okay, I'd take the next, they said the
airport there was closed—there had been a freak blizzard,
and the area was a national emergency." Corrigan recalled
the antics that he himself had forced the system into when
he put the call through to Ireland. Hatcher showed an up-

turned palm. "Would you believe, the turkey of a supervisor there tried to talk me into making it Japan instead? Who ever heard of a passenger showing up at an airport, who wants to go to Vancouver, being told maybe they ought to try Japan instead?"

"That was because it's in the bank," Corrigan said needlessly. The parts of Tokyo realscaped by Himomatsu had been merged into Oz as part of the project.

"So, since you're still here, what happened?" Lilly asked.

Hatcher sighed heavily and pushed himself back from the table. "Well, it got kinda noisy. First, airport security showed up, then the cops came muscling in . . . and I guess after all the crap I went through last time, the freaks just pushed me too far. But I'd probably gone there with trouble in mind anyhow." He reached inside his coat and drew out a handgun—a large one, .44 or .45.

"Oh, my God," Lilly breathed. It was what Corrigan had feared.

Hatcher held the weapon between his hands above the tabletop, staring at it for a few seconds as if savoring the memories that it evoked. Then he looked up at Corrigan with a challenging expression and shrugged nonchalantly. "I started blowing 'em away. There's probably something about it on the news if you turn it on."

Corrigan groaned—not at the news so much as from the realization that his letting-up of fears had been a delusion. Tom was still very much borderline—right on the edge.

Hatcher interpreted his frozen expression as censure and rose up from the chair. "What's the matter, Joe? Don't you understand?—*I've had it* with animation freaks! There was *no way* they were gonna shut me up inside anywhere again. . . . But it doesn't matter a shit anyway. They're just walking bundles of code. It doesn't mean a goddamn thing—any of it." He stood, waiting for a sign that they understood. But despite himself, just for that instant Corrigan was unable to return anything but a blank stare while his mind fumbled for the right thing to say. Lilly seemed to be affected the same way.

Hatcher looked at them and colored, angry now. He pointed back toward the front door, indicating the direction to the outside of the house but meaning the outside of the whole simulation. "Do you expect me to just walk around and carry on being a good guinea pig for those guys out there? I'm telling you, I'm getting out, and it won't be with any of their permission." He grinned crookedly as a new thought struck him, and turned the gun toward Corrigan. "I could get you outta here too, if you want, Joe—real quick."

Corrigan's reaction was reflexive. "Don't point that bloody thing at me. Look—"

"What's up, Joe? You're getting this confused with reality. All that happens is the impact function of the bullet transforms as a superposition into the physical subfile of your physical matrix and makes it nonviable, and you'll wake up in a cubicle. Why put up with any more of this shit?"

"Tom, you just let me handle it in my own way, okay?" Corrigan said tightly.

"We know how you feel, but why don't we just relax and—" Lilly began, but Hatcher thrust the gun back inside his coat and was already moving toward the door. There was a look in his eyes that hadn't showed earlier—final surrender when a last hope had failed to materialize.

"I came here because I thought you might be on an open wire out, Joe," he said. "But it seems you're just as trapped in here, and I sure as hell am not gonna sit around waiting for them to call me. Okay, you solve it your way, and I'll solve it mine. This isn't gonna get us anywhere. Sorry I messed up your evening. So could you just let me have my car?"

"Now don't do anything—" Corrigan began, but Hatcher cut him off with a laugh.

"I don't believe it. Joe. You still haven't gotten it into your head. . . . There isn't anything stupid that I *can* do. All those years must have got you really conditioned. Maybe I had it better after all." He crossed the kitchen and opened the door leading to the garage. "Now the car, Joe—please?"

They watched the Ford drive off with a squeal of tires, and only then did Corrigan notice for the first time that one side of its front fender and the wing were mangled. He went back inside with Lilly, and they ate an uninspired meal of bachelor-fare oddments from the refrigerator.

Afterward, they resumed poking around the house for possible clues to an escape switch, but the enthusiasm went out of it as they soon found that Hatcher had been right about one thing: with no idea what they were looking for, the possibilities were virtually unlimited, and so was the amount of time that finding it was likely to take. Finally they agreed that it would probably be smarter to await a response from Sylvine as a first option. They retired early, Lilly taking the guest room, and drove back to Xylog first thing the next morning.

That was when they learned that Hatcher had hit a truck head-on at what witnesses said must have been eighty miles per hour, shortly after leaving them the previous night. According to the accounts, his car had been accelerating as it crossed the central dividing line, and had made no attempt at evasion. One driver, still in a state of bewilderment, who had been following a short distance behind told the police, "It was like nothing you ever saw—like it was deliberate. There wasn't a piece left big enough that you could have made a planter out of. Nuthin'."

Shortly afterward, the police released a statement that the driver of the Ford had been tentatively identified as the "Greater Pitt Gunman," who had left a security guard and two city policemen dead, along with four others wounded, in the airport shooting earlier the previous day. Since then, there had been twenty-three further incidents of multiple shootings in public places, and reports were coming of other, similar happenings around the country.

Chapter Thirty-nine

Corrigan watched across his desk while detective Yeen from city police headquarters checked over the notes that he had made. "And you didn't talk to him at all yesterday? The last time that you did see him, did he seem to be acting normally?" Yeen's tone sounded dubious, as if he were giving Corrigan a chance for second thoughts.

"We had a meeting scheduled for yesterday morning, but Hatcher didn't show up," Corrigan said. "I got a message late in the day that he'd called, but I was in a hurry and didn't return it. That really is all I can tell you." And neither was he really interested, nor especially inclined to make any effort at pretending that he was. None of this was going to make any difference. Besides which, some of Hatcher's cynicism seemed to have rubbed off on him. There was something mildly degrading about the thought of acting out a charade to placate an internal construct of a computer. After seeing what this whole creation had driven Tom to, he was as ready as Tom had been to blow the whole thing sky-high from within. The problem was figuring out how, and that would take just a little more patience yet.

"The car was heading north on eight, which passes close to Fox Chapel," Yeen commented. "At least one person remembers seeing a brown Ford with a damaged front wing just a few streets from where you live."

Corrigan shrugged and held up his hands. "He might have stopped by the house before we got back. All I can say is that I didn't see him."

"We?"

"Lilly—Ms. Essell, who's sitting outside. She's a journalist from California, writing an article about the Oz project. We went back to talk about it in the evening. Yesterday was too hectic earlier."

"And she's still here this morning. Did she stay at the house?"

Corrigan sighed, wishing for an instant that he, too, could simply pull out a gun and dispatch the whole irritation. Already, he was understanding a lot better how Tom had felt. If he made up some other story and it didn't fit with Lilly's, there would be no end to this. He had other things to do.

"Yes," he replied testily. "In the guest room. She also happens to be an old friend."

The detective's eyebrows rose, but he didn't pursue the point. "So you can't really be of any more help?" he said.

Corrigan spread his hands in a suggestion of being tactful. "That *is* what I've been trying to say."

"I see." Yeen got up and put the notebook back inside his zippered document holder. "I appreciate the time, Mr. Corrigan. You will be available here if there are further questions?"

"Of course."

Corrigan walked around the desk and opened the door. Lilly was sitting outside in one of the visitor chairs opposite Judy's desk, where she had waited the previous evening. "Is there anywhere that I could have a few words with Ms. Essell?" Yeen asked Corrigan as they came out.

"There's a room just along the corridor that you could use if it's free," Corrigan said. "My secretary can show you the way. Judy, could you check the small conference room and take Mr. Yeen and Lilly there if it's free?"

Judy rose from her seat. "You've got some urgent messages," she said, handing Corrigan a couple of slips. "One from Endelmyer, one from Pinder. They both want you to call back straightaway." Corrigan nodded and took them.

"Would you mind answering a few questions, Ms. Essell?" Yeen asked Lilly, his tone not really leaving a lot in the way of options.

"Well . . . I guess not." Lilly met Corrigan's gaze as she got up, but Yeen had left them no opportunity for agreeing on details.

"I'll see you later," was all that Corrigan could say. Just like in the books. Somebody must have fed the system detective stories, he reflected as he watched the two of them follow Judy away around a corner.

A sandy-haired, wide-browed, bearded figure in a black, V-neck sweater with a white-stripe diagonal design approached from the other direction and caused him to turn. It was Barry Neinst. He looked solemn, but although it was he who had come to see Corrigan, he hesitated longer than would have been natural, letting Corrigan set the tone of what was appropriate by speaking or acting first. As had been the case with Judy, Corrigan could detect nothing from outward appearances that told him if he was talking to an animation or a surrogate. It was only their subtle differences in manner that set them apart. Corrigan waited curiously, deliberately refraining from offering any cue. Finally, the system capitulated, and Barry said:

"I don't know what to make of it—about Tom. It's just . . . too terrible. I mean, what do you say? . . ."

"What can you say?" Corrigan answered. "It's been a lousy morning. Life goes on. Tomorrow might be better." Barry's eyes widened into circles of confused surprise behind his spectacles. In some half-amused, cynical way, Corrigan enjoyed being no help at all, watching the system dither and flounder.

"I guess you're right," Barry said. In a matter of seconds the about-face was complete. Yet such shallowness had been there all the time in the animations that had been all around him since yesterday, Corrigan reminded himself. So adept was the human mind at the art of seeing what it expected to see. "There's nothing we can say that'll change anything, eh?" Barry went on. Already the system was trying out the new line, fishing for confirmation that it had got it right.

Corrigan obliged. "Not a thing." His eyes strayed down to the two slips of paper in his hand. The project— this unreal version of it, anyway—was no longer of any interest, and neither, therefore, were the concerns of unreal Pinders and unreal Endelmyers. He wondered what way of dealing with them would entail the least distraction from the things that did matter. Perhaps simply to ignore them.

"Let's just hope he hasn't started too much of a craze," Barry said.

Corrigan looked up, only half hearing. "Who?"

"Tom."

"What about him?"

"All the others."

"Other what?"

"Haven't you seen the news this morning?"

Corrigan's brow creased. "No, I haven't. What's happened?"

"Oh. Then you don't *know*!" Barry moistened his lips and moved a step closer. "Since it was on the news last night, more people have been driving their cars into oncoming traffic. It's as if a lot of people out there suddenly discovered a new way of solving their problems that they hadn't thought of before. When I was driving in, the count was up to fifteen. The whole city's going crazy. People are afraid to go out."

Corrigan stared at him in astonishment. First the shootings that had been breaking out since the incident at the airport. Now this. He thought back to the way Pinder and the others had behaved yesterday and the day before, the plasticity of Meechum, Borth, the CLC Board. . . . An instinct told Corrigan that there was some kind of pattern behind it, connecting them all. But before he could give the matter any further thought, the phone on Judy's desk rang to announce a voice call.

"Excuse me." Corrigan picked up the handset. "Yes?"

A man's voice said, "Is there a Ms. Klein there, please?"

"She's away from her desk at the moment, I'm afraid."

"Is there a Mr. Corrigan?"

"This is Joe Corrigan speaking."

"Good morning. My name is Ulsen. I work with Mr. Sylvine, at the Advisory Office of Advanced Technology in Washington. . . ."

"*Yes!* Good morning. Could you hold for a moment?" Corrigan covered the mouthpiece and made waving motions. "Sorry, Barry, but I have to take this inside right now. Can I catch you later?"

"Sure. But we need to go over the initialization checklist for tomorrow."

"It may have to be postponed with this other business. I'll let you know later this morning."

"Okay." Barry shrugged and turned to leave, just as Judy reappeared from the direction of the conference room.

"Judy, can you switch this through? I need to take it inside," Corrigan said as she came back to her desk. She nodded as she sat down, and tapped a couple of keys. Corrigan went into his office and picked up. "Hello? Mr. Ulsen?"

"Yes. You left a message yesterday for Mr. Sylvine to call you?"

"That's right."

"Well, he's out of town right now and not due back for some days. Can you tell me what it's about? Maybe I can help."

Corrigan thought quickly. Seventeen or eighteen hours had gone by since he had made the call from Main Reception, when he and Lilly returned to Xylog the evening before. In the world outside, that would be a little over five minutes. Sylvine had no doubt decoupled after the dinner the evening before that (an additional seven minutes earlier) to make his report, which was why he wasn't replying. Although "Ulsen" might not necessarily be playing an active role in the simulation, he was coupled into the system, since he was able to synchronize with Corrigan. But he would be a temporary liaison, there to provide a contact of sorts; he would be able to disconnect and talk to the outside.

Corrigan said curtly, "Look, whoever-you-really-are. No bullshit, okay? I know the score. The memory erasure of the first run didn't work. Get this whole thing terminated immediately. Do you understand?"

There was a long, creaking pause. "I'll have to consult—"

"Consult, nothing. There isn't anything to consult about. In case you aren't aware of it yet, one of the surrogates just checked himself out. The rest can follow. Whoever's behind this are facing enough lawsuits to paper CLC's Head Office with already. You tell them that it stops *now*! Out." Corrigan slammed down the phone and stood looking at it.

He was conscious of a feeling of anticlimax. So that was it? After all the talk, all that he had been able to do amounted to no more than issue a demand into a phone and hang up. And now, back to the interminable waiting. All of a sudden, Hatcher's uncompromising solution was beginning to look clean and decisive by comparison. Not prepared even to consider the demeaning passivity of waiting, he had gone straight over to the offensive. Probably he was causing consternation outside, right at this moment. Anything that Corrigan might do now would be merely a supporting action.

Then the sound of new voices came from outside the office door, which Corrigan had left open. He looked away from the desk and saw that Harry Morgen and Joan Sutton had arrived. Morgen was talking to Judy and pointing at a configuration on her screen that looked from a distance like Corrigan's call-log format. Sutton was standing behind him, gazing about at the surroundings as if she had never seen them before. Then Morgen, in the process of uttering something, brought his right hand up to touch his temple with a finger in an odd, flicking motion, vaguely suggestive of a lazy salute. Corrigan had seen that mannerism before somewhere.

Corrigan walked slowly across the office and stopped in the doorway, studying them. Neither they nor Judy had noticed him yet.

Then he remembered where he had seen that temple-touching mannerism before: Zehl! Dr. Zehl had had the same unconscious habit. And, therefore, Graham Sylvine—since Corrigan had already concluded that they were the same person. So Morgen had been the outside controller who had masqueraded as Zehl and Sylvine. That much made sense—Morgen was a firm Tyron follower. The only thing that didn't answer was if *this* Morgen was another animation re-created from system profiles, like Pinder and Barry Neinst, or a projection of the real person, coupled in. If he was real, then maybe Corrigan had his channel to the outside standing here, right in front of him.

Chapter Forty

Judy stopped what she had been saying as she saw Corrigan moving out from the doorway of his office. "Oh, here he is now." Morgen and Sutton turned toward him and exchanged perfunctory greetings. Corrigan watched their faces as they spoke. As with Barry Neinst, there was no way of telling from outward appearances.

"People over at Head Office are trying to get hold of you, Joe, but you haven't been getting back to them," Morgen said. "With the project about to go live, that seems strange. Is everything okay over here?"

Corrigan was conscious of their eyes searching his face like mapping radars, almost as if they were trying to divine the true person behind the surface imagery as much as he was of them. Considering the events since the previous evening, Morgen's remark seemed curiously insensitive. And Corrigan thought he knew why. Here was his opportunity.

"He was one of our key people," Corrigan said. "And now the city's making a fad out of it. It *does* alter the perspective of things a bit."

His vagueness was deliberate. Involuntarily, Joan Sutton glanced at Morgen with a bemused look, and he returned one that was just as mystified. *They didn't know!* And in that instant Corrigan knew that they were real-person surrogates. The way that Sutton had seemed awed by the surroundings should have told him sooner.

For had they been Morgen and Sutton animations— permanent denizens of the simulated world—they would have been present since yesterday, and hence aware of what had been dominating the news. But Morgen, as Sylvine, had left only twelve minutes ago, outside-time, which would have given him barely enough time to report from his last visit, agree on the next objectives, and reenter. The fact that he had reappeared so soon, as himself, and bringing Joan Sutton with him, suggested that something irregular had been detected by the controllers on the outside. That would fit with why they were checking on Corrigan's behavior.

He looked at them coldly, making no attempt to hide the rancor that he felt. "You don't know what's been going on, do you?"

Morgen tried to feign a puzzled look. "How—"

Corrigan cut him off with a disdainful wave. "Don't try any acting, Harry—it'll save us all a lot of breath." He nodded back toward the doorway of his office. "Let's go inside." He extended an arm. Morgen's face was apprehensive. Sutton shot him what looked to Corrigan like an accusing look, and he sensed that all was not smooth between them. They went through. "Hold all calls, Judy," Corrigan said, and followed.

Inside, he closed the door behind him and turned on them. "Now let me guess what's been happening outside. The trait-assimilation parameter settings in the first run were wrong—yes?—which caused the animations to go off on self-reinforcing patterns and create a screwed-up world in which the surrogates—" Corrigan indicated himself with a finger and interjected in a scathing voice, "such as *me!* . . . instead of providing the models, became misfits. Yes, *Doctor Zehl?*" He glared at them and found that his breathing was heavy. Morgen had paled. His skin looked clammy in the pale light of the office. The system was picking up his physiological responses and projecting them perfectly. Even Corrigan marveled.

He went on. "But even so, the results were so far beyond anything we'd ever imagined that somebody out there decided to run the whole thing again from the beginning with the parameters reset. But that's where you messed up. You see, the erasure of the first run didn't work the way it was supposed to. We still remember it—all twelve years of it."

They stared at him numbly. He continued. "But yesterday, Tom Hatcher decided he'd had enough and wasn't about to go around again. And do you know what he did? He got a gun and blew away a heap of computer-code cops and security guards out at the airport. By nighttime, it had become the rage all over the city. Later, Tom ran his car up to eighty and pointed it head-on into a truck, so he's out of it already, and probably giving everyone out there hell." Corrigan's face creased into a mocking smile. "And guess what—this morning there's screwballs doing the same thing all over Pittsburgh."

The expressions on the two faces in front of him were completely stunned, causing Corrigan's smile to widen derisively. "You see what it means?" he said to them. "Now the parameters are *over*compensated. The animations are slavishly copying whatever the surrogates do—if you'd looked hard enough around the dinner table, you might have seen it yourself when you were here a little while ago as Graham Sylvine. With surrogates acting rationally in the way everyone assumed they would, that might have been okay. Oz could have worked. But what the experiment never bargained for was any of them going off the rails the way Tom did. Now you're about to create another world full of lunatics, only this time psychopaths and suicides." Corrigan tossed out a hand in a dismissive gesture, and the smile vanished from his face. "So it's over, and a lot of heads are going to roll out there. Get it terminated."

"I did try and tell you," Sutton began, looking at Morgen. "I said that the—"

Morgen waved her aside in a way that said all that could wait until later. "It was the pressure from the F and F consortium," he told Corrigan. "They insisted on going straight to a full-world implementation, and they funded additional outside programming to do it. That was what they'd always wanted—a virtual world. They weren't interested in developing AI. We had to go along to get the backing."

Corrigan looked at him disdainfully. "What do you take me for? I've grown twelve years in the last three weeks. Come on—I want *out*!"

But Morgen persisted in the line that had been agreed upon in his excursion outside. "Look, Joe . . . I know that the way it's been done has been a bit underhanded. . . ."

"*Underhanded!* By Christ, I—"

"Hear me out, please. Look, I know you've had a raw deal. But that can all be straightened out. As you just said, this whole project, this process of yours, has worked out way, way better than anything anyone ever dreamed of. If—"

"Right! *You* just said it: this process of *mine*!"

"I understand what you're saying, Joe. But let's not allow the project to suffer just because you're feeling sore in the short term, right now." Morgen showed both palms hastily. "Don't get me wrong—I'm not saying you don't have good reason. Rerunning and knowing what we know now, it might actually get so close to reality that you can't tell the difference. That was the original success criterion, remember? And we're almost there already. After this we can do more realscaping and expand the territory. Maybe tie in a whole list of remote places." Morgen forced a jocular tone. "Hey, remember that time you wanted to visit Ireland, and Zehl had to pull rank?"

"Somebody seems to have it all figured out," Corrigan remarked sarcastically.

"See it through," Morgen urged. "You'll be more than compensated. It's already been agreed. We're only talking about another few days."

That was too much. *"For you!"* Corrigan exploded. "A few days for you! Don't you understand what I said a minute ago? Suppression of the first-run memories *didn't work.* For us, you're talking about years. I want this thing stopped now, and I want out. So get on with it."

Morgen shook his head, still unwilling to give up but at a loss for a continuation. "Is there a choice?" Sutton asked him. "From the sound of it, it's all about to go off into a different brand of craziness in the other direction anyway. It's time to hold, analyze the data we've got, and reevaluate."

Still, Morgen wavered. After a few seconds of waiting, unyielding, Corrigan pointed out, "You might as well. It can't work now, whatever you do. I'll just start tossing people out of the windows, and by lunchtime everyone'll be doing it. What use is that going to be to your precious backers? It's over. Accept it. Get us out."

Finally Morgen capitulated. "I can't make the decision. It has to go back to the people outside."

"Okay, but you don't have to decouple. Use one of the direct gate codes," Corrigan said. As a transient observer, Morgen would be able to signal the outside via a special calling number like the one that Corrigan had used to leave messages for "Sylvine." Probably he had recourse to other means, too.

"Better do it, Harry," Sutton murmured in a tone that said he might as well get it over with. Morgen hesitated, then drew a pocket communicator from his jacket and tapped in a numeric sequence to flag a precoded message that would be transmitted practically instantaneously. Hence he was able to get information out straightaway, which was the option that Corrigan had not had access to.

"You might as well tell them to reduce the time-acceleration down to unity, too, while you're at it," Corrigan suggested. "Communication would be a lot simpler. It won't make any difference now. This run isn't going anywhere."

While the time-rate differential existed, however, and allowing for even a couple of minutes' deliberation on the outside, there would be a considerable delay before any response became known. Joan Sutton was at boiling point, tight-mouthed and sending Morgen dagger looks. Corrigan guessed that she had opposed the decision to reset the simulation and been overruled. Corrigan decided it would be easiest to leave them to it. He had said all he had to say for the time being.

He moved back to the door and opened it to look out. Lilly was back sitting on her chair opposite Judy's desk. Yeen was standing nearby. He came across when Corrigan appeared.

"Er, Mr. Corrigan," he said. "There are one or two inconsistencies between your account and Ms. Essell's that we'll need to go over." Corrigan did his best to look surprised. "I must ask you to be available again later today."

"Very well," Corrigan said.

"If you do have reason to go elsewhere, you will leave details of how you can be reached?"

"Of course."

"Then that will be all for now. Thanks for your cooperation. I can find my own way out, if that's okay."

Corrigan smiled apologetically. "Sorry—company rules. Judy, would you take Mr. Yeen back down to Reception, please?" Judy got up and walked away with Yeen in the direction of the elevators. Corrigan shrugged at Lilly in a way that said none of it mattered. The sound of Joan Sutton's voice rising came through the doorway behind him. Corrigan half closed the door behind him and went over to Lilly.

"I think we might have cracked it," he said in reply to her inquiring look. His voice lowered. "Two of the outside crew showed up as observers while you were gone. I've told them the game's up. They're on the line back to base right now."

She gaped at him. "Cracked it—already? You mean we're getting out?"

"Right. There'll probably be a bit of a wait before anything happens, but they know it's blown. And thanks to Tom, we know how to wreck everything from the inside now, if they try to be obstinate. They don't have any choices."

Lilly was about to reply, but then she looked away toward his office door with a puzzled expression. Corrigan realized that it had suddenly gone curiously quiet inside. He went back, pushed the door open, and looked in. Morgen and Sutton had vanished.

Chapter Forty-one

Harry Morgen stood facing Frank Tyron in the Monitor & Control Center on the third floor of the Xylog Building. Sutton was with him. They had just come up from the gallery of interface couplers on the level below after breaking one of the cardinal rules for transient observers visiting the simulation: effecting entry and exit in such a way as to risk confronting the inhabitants with abnormal phenomena. Endelmyer had heard the news about Hatcher and was on his way over from CLC headquarters across the river with John Velucci from Corporate Legal. Rumors were flying around the building that the whole Oz simulation was about to self-destruct.

"It doesn't matter anymore," Morgen insisted. "Time is more important now. The longer Corrigan has to wait in there, the more likely it's going to get that he'll start doing something to sabotage the whole works. You have to believe me, Frank—he's mad as hell and he'll do it." Morgen pointed to the lanky, yellow-haired figure with a pallid, tired-looking face covered in unshaved growth, who was sitting by one of the consoles along the wall, a blanket drawn around his shoulders and clutching a mug of hot, black coffee. "He showed them how to do it. We overcompensated on the TAPs. Now half the animations are shooting each other and crossing over highways. It's an asylum in there."

Hatcher's chest heaved with laughter that was stifled by the thermometer in his mouth. The medic standing by him took it out and nodded that it was okay for him to drink the coffee now. He had flatly refused to be taken to the medical department for a rest and checkup as stipulated in the exiting procedure, and come straight up to the M & C floor instead. Nothing would make him miss what happened now, and that was final. Jason Pinder was hovering nearby, watching him anxiously, genuinely concerned.

"We're initializing real-time resynch now," a supervisor called from where he was standing behind two of the console operators. "T-by-tau is dropping at one per second. Should have reintegration in about three minutes." It meant that the simulation's accelerated time was being slowed to bring it back into synchronization with the real world.

Despite all these signs that it was over, Victor Borth was not ready to concede final defeat just yet. He turned from where he had been listening with his back toward Tyron and the others, and spread his hands appealingly. "This is crazy," he told them. "Somebody tell me I'm not hearing this. Are you people saying that two guys can screw up a whole project of this magnitude? I mean, what does it take to keep two guys sweet? All they've got to do is name it." He turned and walked toward the side of the room where Hatcher was sitting. "Hey, you. Tom, is it? What's the biggest thing you've ever dreamed of getting out of life? Cars? Boats? Broads? You could be a millionaire, know that? Everybody's got something. You could have some of the most powerful people anywhere on your side for the rest of your life—anything you wanna do. There has to be room for us to talk, right?" Hatcher shook his head, sighed, smiled wearily to himself, and looked away.

Of more concern to Tyron than Hatcher's future right now was the matter of his own. He was the one who had convinced the consortium of F & F's client-backers that a functioning pseudoworld was feasible; he had coordinated outside development of the advanced system that went past the original specification drawn up inside CLC; and at his instigation, Borth had organized the flow of funds to support it. If he delivered as promised, the wherewithal to smooth over all these embarrassments would be forthcoming. He'd have the leverage; he'd have the friends. If he failed to . . . No, they were all in it too far. There could be no backing down now.

He had authorized temporary resynchronization to permit direct communication with Corrigan from the outside. Now he decided that a more direct form of intervention was needed. He turned to the operators at the section monitoring operation of the COSMOS neural-coupling interfaces on the floor below. "Initialize another two units." Then, curtly, to Morgen, Sutton, and Borth, "We're going back in."

Borth looked taken aback. "All of us? You mean . . ."

Tyron smiled thinly at him. "Why not? You've been saying for a long time that you'll have to try this thing yourself someday. Well, now's your chance. Use your arguments on the guy who matters."

"T-tau one seventy-five and falling," the supervisor reported.

"Come on," Tyron said, striding across the floor in the direction of the way out to the main corridor. Borth followed, and after a moment of faltering Morgen and Sutton fell in behind. "And anyhow, we still have the final argument," Tyron tossed back at them over his shoulder as he reached the doors. "We've got the switch out here, and he doesn't."

They disappeared, and the doors closed behind them. Some of the operators exchanged curious looks. Others shrugged. Pinder leaned closer to Hatcher with a worried expression. "How do you feel?" he asked.

Hatcher stared dully across the room and considered the question. "I'm not sure," he said finally, looking up. "How is the victim of a successful suicide supposed to feel? . . . Not bad, considering, I guess."

Chapter Forty-two

For Corrigan this was the most unreal part since the beginning of the entire experience. The full-scale Oz project, culmination of everything he had been working toward for the past several years, was about to go live in the next couple of days. Technicians and managers assailed him constantly for decisions about last-minute details; Endelmyer, the president of the corporation, was demanding that his calls be returned. And none of it mattered. There was going to be some delay no matter how quickly events moved in the world outside. His only choice was to either make a dramatic exit as Hatcher had done, or wait it out.

Judy had been away from her desk seeing Yeen from the building, so Corrigan was spared having to improvise some other pretext for getting her away from her desk to cover for Morgen and Sutton's abrupt disappearance. One other detail that he did need to justify to keep things from getting difficult, however, was the continuing presence of Lilly. It seemed odd, at a time like this, to have to give consideration to satisfying the pseudocuriosity of a computer animation, but it was the easiest way of keeping things simple in the meantime for himself.

When Judy returned, Corrigan informed her that Lilly wanted to spend the rest of the morning going through her notes and listing any final questions before going back to California, and would be using the small conference room that Yeen had questioned her in. Lilly disappeared accordingly, and the routine calls and queries continued unabated until late morning. Then Judy announced that Mr. Ulsen was on the line from the Advisory Office of Advanced Technology, Washington. Corrigan told her to put the call through.

"Mr. Corrigan?"

"Yes."

"Ulsen again. How are things in there?" At least there were no attempts at pretense this time.

"Never mind the niceties," Corrigan growled. "Morgen and Sutton are back out, so you know the score. What's the situation?"

"Your request is understood and appreciated, Mr. Corrigan. A delegation is on its way back into the simulation to talk to you."

"That wasn't a request, dammit. And there isn't anything to talk about. Do you intend doing as I said, or do we start unhinging the whole works from the inside here?"

"Please understand that I am merely an intermediary. I have no personal authority in this. It's all gone way over my head."

"Then just get back out there and tell whoever is in charge to shut down the whole operation—now. That's all there is to it. End. Period. Do you get the message, Mr. Ulsen?"

"Yes, I understand perfectly. But I have been asked to remind you of the reality of the time-rate differential. Some finite time will be required however urgently matters are expedited out here, and that will translate into a delay that may seem unduly protracted."

"All you have to do is restore tee-tau to unity. Then we'd be able to talk direct and wouldn't need an intermediary. It's perfectly simple."

"That is already being done. But as I'm sure you appreciate, it will still necessitate a considerable delay at your end. All we're asking is for you to bear with us."

Only if the intention was to talk. But Corrigan had already said that there was nothing to talk about. He was just about to launch into another outburst of invective when he saw Pinder hovering in the doorway of the office. Pulled in two directions, he wavered suddenly. "Be quick about it, then," he muttered to Ulsen.

"Thank you for your understanding."

Corrigan put the phone down and looked up. Pinder

came in, closing the door. His expression was accusatory, yet at the same time questioning—unable to condone but reluctant to prejudge. Corrigan had been expecting it. Pinder had been involved when the police appeared with the news about Hatcher, and gone over the river to convey the tidings to Head Office. The calls from on high had begun soon afterward, and now he was back as an emissary to find out what in hell was going on.

Pinder opened. "I was prepared to overlook your indiscretion of yesterday, Joe, but this is going too far. Don't you realize, *the president of the company* has been *personally* trying to contact you since first thing this morning. And you don't seem to give a damn. What on earth's gotten into you? I told you the last time that you are not the technical director yet. Now I think I'm beginning to realize just how unsuited you'd be to that task. Now, are you going to at least cover while we get the project up and running, or do I put in Frank Tyron as acting coordinator, effective immediately?"

Corrigan stared at him indifferently, feeling like Archimedes having to put up with the babbling soldier from Rome while trying to ponder things that mattered. On the other hand, Archimedes had gotten himself killed. There could be no letup yet; the game had to continue. But he had learned how to deal with animations.

He forced an expression of shocked surprise. "Surely you're not referring to the project . . . not at a time like this, after the news about Tom?" He shook his head to say he knew that Pinder hadn't meant it—giving him the opportunity that any decent person would have to put it another way. "We're not imagining that tomorrow's schedule still stands?"

Pinder faltered while unseen circuits hastily recomputed weighting evaluation matrixes. His change of stance was as abrupt as yesterday's, or as Barry Neinst's a few hours earlier.

"Well, of course, I didn't exactly mean to imply that. Naturally we must observe a proper sense of priorities. . . . But there are certain interests with a considerable stake in the outcome, who don't share our dimension of, shall we say, 'personal involvement'—as I'm sure you appreciate. If the schedule is affected—as it has to be, of course—we still owe it to them to be kept informed."

"I'm working on it now," Corrigan lied. "But I don't have a full picture yet. Yeen should be getting in touch again at any time."

"Very well. But in that case please call Endelmyer back and inform him of that much."

Corrigan sighed beneath his breath, nodded, and entered the code into his desk unit. Anyway, it would be as easy to turn Endelmyer's animation around too, he reasoned. The features of Endelmyer's secretary appeared on the screen. "Hi, Celia. Joe Corrigan for himself," he said.

"Oh, at last. I'll put you straight through."

Then Judy's voice came from outside on another line. "Sorry to interrupt, but Harry Morgen and Joan Sutton are back with Frank Tyron, wanting to see you. Victor Borth is with them. They say it's urgent, and you know what it's about."

"All right!" Corrigan exclaimed with relish, and forgetting all else, sprung up from the desk and headed for the door.

"Joe? . . . Joe Corrigan, where are you?" Endelmyer's puzzled voice said from the screen.

"Hello? No, it's me," Corrigan heard Pinder splutter behind him as he went out. "Well, he is, but he's just gone. I don't know what's happened to him. . . ."

Whereas Morgen's approach had been conciliatory and placating, Tyron immediately launched into the offensive—possibly because Morgen had got nowhere; more likely to maintain a firm image of the heavyweight in front of Borth.

"What do you people think you're playing at?" he demanded. "Don't you realize that the information that's coming out of this is already priceless? You're sabotaging what could be the biggest breakthrough in the whole field in the last fifty years."

"Everything's on this now," Borth pitched in, pushing his way forward beside Tyron. "If it blows, Xylog folds—the whole works. If it flies, we've got the oyster. You have to see this one through now."

Corrigan, furious, pointed an arm in the general upward direction to indicate "out there." "That's all you can think about, even after what you forced Tom Hatcher into?"

"Unavoidable collateral," Tyron said. "It's a shame it has to happen, but there's some in every operation."

"*Unavoidable collateral!*" Corrigan exploded. "Is that what you call it? It's still all just—"

Tyron brushed it aside with a tired wave. "Look, he's okay. I just talked to him. If you want to be part of the Big League, you've gotta start thinking in big terms, Joey boy."

Judy, who had been listening bemusedly from her desk, gasped. "Tom, okay? But how could he be? I don't understand. . . ."

Tyron ignored her. Corrigan, however, was a person whose habits died hard. "Let's do this somewhere less public," he said. He looked back at the open door of his office, but Pinder was still talking at the screen in there. There was still the room where Lilly was ensconced. "Come on. This way." And before anyone could object, he began herding them away. "Don't worry about it, Judy," he threw back as they disappeared around the corner. "I'll explain it all later."

Lilly was sitting in a chair to one side of the room, apparently thinking to herself, when Corrigan came in followed by the others. Tyron halted when he saw her, a frown of puzzled recognition on his face. She seemed unsure of whether she had met him before or not.

"Yes, you know her, Frank," Corrigan said, reading the situation as Morgen came in last of all, closing the door. "This is Lillian Essell, one of the Air Force volunteers that you interviewed in California a month ago. Except for her it's been twelve years. I'm not sure if they've made that clear to you yet, out there—the memory suppression of the first run didn't work. It was a neat idea, but you messed up. We still remember everything."

But Tyron was already waving a hand impatiently and grimacing. "You don't understand. The rerun is showing some amazing things already. Just stay with it for a few more days. There's—"

Corrigan slammed a hand down on the table in the center of the room. "*Days for you!*" he stormed. "That's the whole point I'm trying to tell you, but you don't seem able to get it into your head. It's going to be years all over again for us!"

"Not years," Tyron argued. "The contradictions are

beginning to show now. It can't go much farther. You've *got* to push it to its limits. That's the only way we'll learn what we need to know to make it better."

"So that *you* can deliver what they want, while I'm the schmuck locked up inside it? What do you take me for? I might be Irish, but I'm not all Kerry green. The answer's no —no way. Forget it. It's over. We're getting out."

Tyron's expression changed to something approaching a leer. "Well, it's a pity you feel that way, Joey boy, because when the chips are down you don't really have that much of a choice. *We* can exit at any time. . . ." To prove it, Tyron vanished before their eyes and reappeared a moment later ten feet away, on the opposite side of the table. He pointed a finger at Corrigan. "But you depend on an external disconnect." He shrugged with a grin of emphasized unapology. "And we've got the switch out there. You don't."

Lilly stood up and broke in, "That's not true. What about Tom Hatcher? We can get out anytime."

Tyron shrugged again, evidently having already considered the point. "So go ahead and opt out," he told them. "That won't score very high with the people who own the show, will it? So the simulation loses a couple of surrogates. So what? There are still four dozen others. The show goes on, with you or without you."

"You talk as if you think it's yours," Corrigan said.

Tyron leered again, more broadly this time. "You quit now, and it will be," he answered.

Corrigan shook his head, bunching his mouth grimly, and threw out an arm. "Oh no, it isn't as simple as that, at all. Haven't you heard? You've created another crazy world out there. Ever since Hatcher showed them how, they've been wiping each other and themselves out all over Pittsburgh. What use do you think a simulation like that is going to be to anyone?"

Tyron made a show of being unperturbed. "We overcompensated on the assimilation parameters. So we set them back a little. It's no problem."

Corrigan's neck reddened. He was about to reply, when the door opened again and Pinder appeared. Pinder moved a pace into the room and stood looking around at the company perplexedly. "Will somebody tell me what the hell's going on around here?" he demanded. His eyes singled out

Corrigan, and he was about to say something further, when he noticed Lilly beside him, and her visitor's badge. "Who are you?" he asked her.

Pinder was an animation. He would know nothing of what was being discussed in the room. Corrigan knew more about what Lilly was doing there than any of the others. He gave the only answer that he could: "Her name's Lillian Essell. She's a journalist from California, doing a piece on the project. I told her she could use this room for the morning."

Pinder waited a couple of seconds to see how that explained anything, and when nothing more was forthcoming, shook his head, refusing to add another layer of complication to what there already was. "I'm sorry, Ms. Essell, but this is strictly an internal company matter. I must ask you to leave us, please."

Lilly looked questioningly at Corrigan. "My office is empty," he said. "Use that for now. You know where it is." He moved with her to see her to the door. She nodded, happy to let them get on with it. Pinder stood aside and held the door for her to leave. But just as he was about to close it behind her, he saw Ken Endelmyer and John Velucci approaching along the corridor. They halted just outside the room. Endelmyer looked at Pinder strangely. Pinder looked strangely at him.

"What are you doing here?" Endelmyer asked, looking puzzled. "I thought we left you outside. How did you get inside?"

"Inside what?" Pinder replied, just as puzzled. "I've just come across."

"Across what?"

"Across from HQ. You asked me to."

"*I* did? When?"

Pinder tried desperately not to look like a subordinate suddenly confronted by a superior who has taken leave of his senses. "Ten minutes ago. You wanted me to get over here and see what the problem was with Joe."

"No, *you* were already here," Endelmyer said, looking equally suspicious. "*We've* just come over from HQ—to join Frank and the others here. But we left you outside in the Monitoring Center."

"Outside?" Pinder queried.

"Outside Oz—outside the simulation," Endelmyer replied.

Pinder looked uneasily around the room in a silent plea for somebody to tell him that he wasn't the only one for whom this was getting insane. The others returned looks as devoid of expression as a fog bank.

Then Corrigan realized what had happened. Pinder, the animation, had just left an Endelmyer animation in HQ, across the river, and now had run into the *real* Endelmyer, who had entered the simulation as a surrogate; and since Pinder knew only the animation Endelmyer, he was presuming this one to be he. The real Endelmyer, on the other hand, had come over from HQ in the real world, and by the sound of things had talked to the real Pinder before being coupled in. Corrigan groaned inwardly. It could only get worse. Nothing was going to sort this out now.

Pinder looked back at Endelmyer. "Outside the simulation," he repeated. "That's very interesting. I'm not quite sure I follow, though, since the simulation isn't due to begin until tomorrow." His voice was polite and inoffensive, like a student not wanting to say that the professor was wrong when it was obvious. "Perhaps you could explain?"

"Tomorrow?" Endelmyer blinked, nonplussed. "It's been running for three weeks, Jason. What in God's name are you talking about?" He sent an uncertain look around the room in his turn, then moved in through the doorway to appeal to them all directly. "Is Jason not making sense, or is it me?"

Tyron hadn't quite seen it yet either. "I understand you, but not him," he said, but sounding distant as if fearing that he might be missing something. "Of course, it's been running for three weeks. We just came into it."

"You're all mad," Pinder declared flatly.

"What kind of talk is this?" Endelmyer demanded. "First Hatcher flips. Then Corrigan won't talk to anybody. Is there something we don't know about this process that affects . . ." His voice trailed away when he saw that Corrigan was staring past him, out into the corridor, with a look of open disbelief. Endelmyer turned to follow his gaze, and his jaw fell. Another Endelmyer and another Velucci were coming along the corridor from the elevators.

"Ah, there you are, Joe," Endelmyer called ahead, see-

ing him. "I figured that maybe you were having bigger problems over this Hatcher business than I realized, so John and
I decided to follow Jas—" He stopped in midword and came
to a dead halt as he saw who was with Corrigan, just inside
the doorway of the conference room. The Endelmyer and
the Velucci inside stared at the Endelmyer and the Velucci
outside. The ones outside stared back. All of them seized up.

Joan Sutton came out of her stupor first. "Frank, freeze
the animations," she said sharply.

At the far end of the room, Tyron fished out a communicator and hammered in an emergency code. "Control? Do
we have synchronization yet? Hello? Does anyone out there
read? This is critical. . . ." All attention in the room focused upon him. Perspiration showed on his forehead. His
eyes were wide with alarm behind his spectacles.

"Will somebody tell me what in Christ is going on
here?" Borth demanded darkly.

"Oh shit," Harry Morgen groaned as the truth slowly
dawned.

"Who are you talking to?" the animation Endelmyer
asked, moving in through the door and pointing at Tyron.
"I *demand* an explanation!"

That was enough to shock the other Endelmyer into
life. "*You* don't demand anything around here. *I* run this
company."

"Come in, control. Does anyone read? . . ."

In the middle of it all, Corrigan slipped out into the
corridor. He walked quickly back to his own office, past
Judy, who was talking with Betty, the sixth-floor receptionist, and straight in through his own door. Lilly was sitting in
a chair to one side of the desk, contemplating a figurine of
an Irish leprechaun that she had taken from the shelf above.
She looked up before Corrigan could say anything and
asked him, "Didn't you tell me that somebody gave this to
you and Evelyn as a wedding gift? But I saw it at the house,
too, last night. How do you come to have two of them?"

"Jesus, can you believe women? We've no time for
things like that right now. The whole . . ." Corrigan
stopped speaking abruptly and jerked his head around to
look at her as he realized what she was saying. "Are you
sure?"

"Yes. It was on a ledge in the den." That was right. On

the morning of his mysterious awakening, when he came into work and looked around his office, Corrigan himself had thought that it ought to be at the house. But he hadn't been sure because it had been twelve years ago. Then, with everything else going on, it had completely gone from his mind to check in the evening. He took the figurine from her and turned it over in his hands, staring at it.

"You said, something that would be meaningful when you looked for it—something that would become significant when the time came," Lilly said unnecessarily. "And it *was* there the last time, too. We saw it in the shop window. You told me you had one just like it at home. You said that it haunted you." Yes. And he had seen one when he was out by himself, in the bar, Corrigan remembered. The system had been prodding him, reminding him all the time that the leprechaun was there. Because that was what, sometime in that lost day that he had forgotten, Corrigan had told it to do.

"By God, Lilly, I think you might be a genius," Corrigan whispered. He walked quickly around the desk and sat down, still holding the figurine. From outside, the sounds came of voices rising in an angry clamor. What would he have expected himself to do with it? he asked himself frantically. What associations did he have with leprechauns? A word? A phrase? A code that would have a special meaning only to him?

And suddenly he smiled as he remembered his cousin Jeff giving it to him in the lounge of the Royal Marine Hotel in Dun Laoghaire, and himself and Evelyn talking to a somewhat cynical Marvin Minsky years ago. . . .

"I wonder," he muttered aloud. Working quickly, he activated his desk unit and keyed it into "System" mode. A command prompt appeared on the screen. Lilly came around to stand behind him and watch. He entered the word IRELAND.

Nothing happened.

He tried LEPRECHAUN.

A cry of alarm came from Judy outside.

"What are you doing?" Lilly murmured tensely by his ear.

"Shhh." He entered MICK.

The system responded with: "WHEN IRISH EYES ARE SMIL-
ING . . ."

Corrigan's face broke into a wide, triumphant grin. He
completed: YOU'VE PROBABLY JUST BEEN RIPPED OFF.

There was an instant's delay that seemed eternal. Corrigan stared at the screen, vaguely aware of Judy coming in
through the doorway, waving her arms wildly at something
behind her.

And then the screen changed to:

```
      CONGRATULATIONS!!!
YOU ARE NOW IN CONTROL OF THE SYSTEM PRI-
MARY COMMAND EXECUTIVE. ENTER:
''OUT/OUT'' FOR IMMEDIATE DECOUPLING
(EJECT)
''AB'' FOR GENERAL SYSTEM ABORT
''OV'' OVERRIDES ALL EXTERNAL COMMAND
FUNCTIONS UNTIL UNLOCKED
''DF'' LISTS OTHER DIRECTIVE FUNCTIONS
''VM'' SWITCHES TO VOICE MODE (COMMAND
EXEC ANSWERS TO ''ROGER'')
```

Lilly gasped, awed. "Joe, is this what I think it is?"

"Joe," Judy's voice came, strangled, fearful. "Out there
—Betty. Something's happened to her." Corrigan looked
past the doorway and saw that Betty was standing by Judy's
desk, inanimate like a mannequin, her mouth open and arm
raised in the middle of a gesture. Tyron had gotten through:
the controllers outside had deactivated the animations.
From outside the building there came the distant, muted
sounds of multiple vehicles crashing. Corrigan looked back
at Judy suddenly as the further implication registered.

"You're real!" he said in astonishment.

"What are you talking about? Of course I am," Judy
said. "Do something about Betty." She must have volun-
teered for the rerun and had her memory suppressed, just
like the others the first time. She didn't know anything
about the first run.

Farther back, Tyron, Endelmyer, Velucci, and Borth
were coming across the area of open floor beyond Judy's

desk, looking grim and purposeful, with Morgen and Sutton
following. Behind them, just before the corner to the corridor, another Endelmyer, another Velucci, and Pinder were
standing immobilized.

Corrigan hurriedly tapped OV into the pad, followed by
VM, and then said aloud, experimentally, "Roger, do you
read?"

"Loud and clear," a voice answered. It was in his head,
but he heard it in his ear.

"I'm in full exec access now?"

"You've got it."

Oh, boy. He was going to enjoy this. "Define operand
class: all current surrogates," he instructed. "Exceptions by
name: Corrigan, Essell, Tyron, Morgen, Sutton, Endelmyer,
Velucci, Borth."

"Specify operation?"

"There's nothing to worry about, Judy," Corrigan muttered. "I'll explain later." Then, louder; "Disconnect them,
Roger."

And Judy vanished—as, in that same instant, did all the
other bewildered surrogates all over Pittsburgh who had just
seen the world around them turn into statues.

Tyron strode into the room ahead of the others. "What
do you think you're doing?" he barked at Corrigan.

Corrigan ignored him. "Roger, put SPD generic on my
screen." A format appeared specifying the set of Surrogate
Physical Descriptors that the system used to manage the in-
teractions of each projected persona with its environment.
Speaking quickly, Corrigan directed, "Operand class by
name: Corrigan, Essell. Zero reaction coefficients of
M-sub-M, M-sub-P, and delete spatial conflict restrictions."

"Get away from that. . . . *What the?* . . ." Tyron
came around the desk and grabbed at Corrigan's shoulder
to pull him away from the screen, but his hand met no
resistance and went straight through. Corrigan had in effect
turned himself and Lilly into ghosts.

Tyron brought the communicator up to his mouth and
snapped, "Control, do you read?"

A harassed voice answered, "We seem to have problems. Nothing's responding out here. I don't know what to
tell you."

"You don't have control anymore," Corrigan said. "I do."

"That's impossible," Tyron declared. He stepped forward, moving through Corrigan's body, but struck his knee on the edge of the chair, causing him to curse. Corrigan smirked and waved a hand invitingly toward the touchpad. Tyron stabbed savagely at several keys and saw that it was ineffective. The others closed around the desk, all seemingly talking at once so that Corrigan was unable to understand what they were saying—not that he cared a great deal anyway.

"Roger, display Global Dynamics. Reset k-sub-g to twenty percent."

"Done."

The plant out on Judy's desk straightened itself up visibly. Papers that had been lying on the desk and in other places around the office and outside suddenly lifted and began blowing about in currents from the air-conditioner vents. Velucci, who had been walking around the edge of the room behind the others, seemed to unglue from the floor in midstep, went into a strange, floating leap that carried him toward the wall.

"Jesus Christ!" he yelled, losing his balance and falling in slow motion over a chair. The others felt giddy and strangely light on their feet. Sutton tried to sit down on the nearest chair, but everything about the movement felt wrong; she misjudged the distance, succeeding only in tipping the chair over, and she and it went down together. Corrigan had reduced the gravitational constant to a fifth of normal.

"What do you think you'll achieve by this?" Tyron snarled. "You'll pay—you realize that, don't you?"

"Just having a little fun, Frankie boy. What *you* don't realize yet is that it doesn't matter anymore—any of it," Corrigan said. He looked back at the screen. "Let's see, now . . . Roger, reset all mu-f to zero."

"Done." Which reduced to nothing all the coefficients of mechanical friction.

Velucci, who had been hauling himself back up with the help of a bookcase, went down again as his feet shot from under him, tilting the bookcase and burying himself under a torrent of volumes coming off the shelves. Sutton sprawled flat on her back as the floor she had been pushing herself up from turned into ice. Morgen felt the treacherousness beneath his feet and reached out instinctively to steady himself against the wall, but his hand skidded away and he fell over into Endelmyer, taking them both down in a heap on top of Sutton. Tyron managed to stay upright, but his spectacles slid off. Pictures fell from the walls as their fastenings came out. The drawers of a file cabinet standing in the corner slid slowly out and tipped the whole unit over on its front with a crash. More crashings and breaking sounds poured in through the doorway from all over the building. In her chair across the room, Lilly had started to laugh uncontrollably.

Tyron, unable to contain himself, his face contorted with rage, swung a fist at Corrigan's head. Corrigan laughed derisively as it passed harmlessly through; at the same time, the opposite reaction sent Tyron's legs off in the other direction, and he fell through Corrigan, over the chair, and became entangled with Velucci, who was floundering like a beached whale.

"Roger, rotate k-sub-g vector field ten degrees northward."

"Done."

So now gravity was no longer vertical, and all the surfaces that had been horizontal were, in effect, sloping. Everything on the desk slid to the edge and then over in a slow cataract to join the collection of anything loose—books, pens, folders, furnishings, wildly flailing and protesting CLC executives—accumulating against the far wall. The desk slid across behind them, followed by the chairs that Corrigan and Lilly had been sitting in. They could stand and watch from where they were, their bodies had no effective mass for gravity to operate on—vertical or otherwise.

"Continue rotating at ten degrees per minute, Roger," Corrigan said.

Tyron tried pulling himself up the tilted floor, but his hands slid futilely. "You'll regret it, Corrigan," he screeched as a tide of oddments from the room swept him back down again.

Corrigan shook his head. At last he grasped the meaning of the words that he had borrowed from Eric Shipley long ago but never really understood. "No," he said. "None of you control anything that's important to me anymore. I'm free. You'll get out of this, Frank, but you'll be trapped in your own slow-motion tumble dryer all your life. Have fun." Corrigan looked away. The desk unit and screen had gone with the desk, but it didn't matter. "Roger, operand class by name: surrogates Corrigan, Essell," he directed.

"Specify operation?"

"Out-out. It's time to go home."

And Corrigan was instantly in a reclining position, feeling stiff and cold, his head and neck restrained. He opened his eyes sluggishly and saw cables and pickup assemblies connected to banks of apparatus indistinct in the reduced lighting. Already his senses were overwhelmed by a level of clarity and detail that he had long forgotten was normal.

"Done," a synthetic voice from a speaker somewhere announced matter-of-factly.

Epilogue

The irony of it all was that in those first two days, it was the *animations* that had behaved rationally and commendably. In his TV interview, Corrigan had set the precedent that personal integrity was more important than dishonest gain, and in succession the system-generated analogs of Pinder, the CLC Board, then F & F and its clients, had followed him. It was only when the real people got involved that the old, familiar human formula had reasserted itself of rivalry, hostility, aggression, and mistrust. That was when Corrigan knew he could no longer be a part of it, and whatever happened from there on didn't matter.

He still had his wife, of course—their supposed splitting up as told to him in the simworld had been contrived simply to account for Evelyn's absence, since after her return to Boston nothing could have induced her to have anything further to do with the Oz project. But Corrigan could only think of her as a stranger from long ago.

He did go up to Boston to see her. And she found great changes in the person who, just a matter of a few weeks before, she had come to despise. The self-assuredness that had turned into arrogance, and the pride that had soured into conceit were no more; but neither were the blithe youth and roguishness that had captured her, with which they might have grown together. At the same time, she, to him, had become childlike. For with Corrigan, it had not been a matter of a few weeks. A chasm existed that no amount of sacrificial forbearance could hope to bridge. They mended the wounded feelings, confessed to some regrets, and promised that they would remain friends. Three days later, Evelyn filed the papers finalizing the arrangement.

By that time, the notices of impending lawsuits, corporate and private, were already flying between CLC, F & F, F & F's clients, various members of the funding consortium, and dozens of involved individuals from all of them. Corrigan was advised that he had a solid case for millions. There was deceit with malicious intent, conspiracy to defraud, violation of patent rights, criminal abuse and neglect, willful and malicious misinformation and withholding of information, violation of just about every employment act, violation of contract, breach of rights, technical assault and abduction; in addition, a case charging the entirety of his collateral domestic and marital problems would be indefensible. Corrigan listened as the words echoed around him: force and counterforce; strengths and weaknesses; attack and defense; strategy and counterstrategy . . . And somehow, in spite of all his earlier passions, none of it seemed worth the real cost anymore. In the end, he just walked away.

The green slopes rising up to the mountains behind Ballygarven were splashed with purple patches of heather. On the neck of water beyond the town, a fishing boat trailing a cloud of screeching gulls chugged its way out past the headland toward the open sea.

Wearing jeans, sturdy boots, and an Aran sweater, Corrigan arrived on foot at the Cobh Hotel at a little after noon, having spent the morning on his own, walking on the cliffs, looking at the ocean, feeling the wind, and thinking. Brendan Maguire was already there at the bar with a pint of stout, talking to Rooney and a couple of the locals. Dermot Leavey was with him.

"Ah, here's the American himself now," Rooney said as Corrigan joined them. "A pint, Joe, is it?"

"A well-earned one, I'll have you know. And enough of this 'American,' if you please. Can't a man take a break to see somewhere else for a while without it following him around for the rest of his life?"

"Here, this one's mine," Maguire said, producing a five-pound note as Corrigan reached toward his pocket.

"So did you have a good wander around this morning?" Dermot asked.

"I saw a lot, anyway."

"You'll be joining Brendan and his crowd up at the Rectory, I'm told," Rooney observed, holding a foaming glass under the tap.

"That's the way it looks," Corrigan said.

"Aren't we after telling you the last time you were here that you'd get tired of all that paranoia and dashing around soon enough?" Rooney said.

Corrigan held up a hand in a what-can-I-say? gesture. "Well, here I am. I guess I'm learning how to be a self-unmade man."

Rooney grinned as he set down the glass. "Oh, you remembered that, did you? Ah well, working up there with them professors and all only gets you halfway there, you understand. Next you have to go all the way and try your hand at tending a bar. You'd be astounded at some of the people you meet. It's the only form of true philosophy left."

"Is that a fact, now?" Corrigan smiled distantly to himself and left it at that.

"Ah, yes, talking about philosophers . . ." Maguire felt in the inside pocket of his jacket and pulled out several folded sheets of paper. "This came through over the fax from your friend Shipley in Pittsburgh. It looks good. He's interested, and his approach is just the kind of thing we could use. I've already got approval for another senior slot, so I can't see there'll be a problem."

"That's great. Let's hope it works out." Corrigan picked up his beer and closed his eyes while he treated himself to a long, steady swig. It was cool and refreshingly tart after his exertions. Working with Eric again would be good. He was glad that he had been able to do something to make amends for the way things had ended last time. In a strange kind of way, he really was getting a chance to live a part of his life over again.

"Oh yes, Joe, and there was an American in here asking for you while you were out," Rooney said.

"Oh, really?"

"A woman—quite a nice-looking one, too, if you want a professional's opinion."

Corrigan was suddenly all attention. "When?" he

asked, putting down his glass with a thump. "Where'd she go?"

"About ten, ten-thirty, I'd say. I've no idea where she went. Paddy might know something."

"He's got a different one after him every time," Dermot muttered, but Corrigan was already halfway out and didn't hear.

He found Paddy, the owner of the hotel, checking an order list at the front desk. "Rooney says you had somebody in looking for me this morning," Corrigan said.

Paddy looked up. "Joe. . . . Ah, yes. An American woman, it was. Didn't give a name." He turned to the pigeonholes on the wall behind. "She did leave something for you, though. . . . Here we are. I told her we expected you back for lunch, and she went off to look around the town." Paddy handed Corrigan a slip of paper. "Said she'd be back about now."

Corrigan unfolded it. Written neatly with an ink pen were the words:

> *I'm assuming this is real, but have gone to buy a leprechaun just in case. Back later.*
>
>   *L.*

Corrigan smiled, and at that moment Paddy's voice said, "In fact, if I'm not mistaken, here she is now."

Corrigan looked up, and through the double, paned-glass doors saw a figure in a white raincoat and tan skirt approaching the bottom of the steps. She was tall, with dark wavy hair, and walked elegantly. He went out through the doors as she approached, and waited for her at the top, smiling.

"I wondered when you'd show up," Corrigan said.

Lilly didn't ask what had made him so sure that she would. There was no need. In the way that it had always been between them, most of their conversation remained unvoiced.

That was why they had made no elaborate agreements and plans when she left Pittsburgh to return to California. He'd had a no-longer-viable marriage to disentangle himself from; she'd had the Air Force. Neither needed to ask or be told that they would pick up again where they had begun, when the time was right. It had been too obvious to need saying that the place would be here.

"How did things go with Evelyn?" Lilly asked him.

"She's fine. Do you remember I told you there was always that attraction there between her and Tom? Well, they got together, and it's working out okay. In fact, I talked on the phone to Tom yesterday."

"I'm glad," Lilly said.

"How about you?"

"No real problems. What happened at Xylog?"

Corrigan shrugged. "Everyone's fighting like mad dogs there. I just left them to it. They're welcome. Some things aren't worth making lawyers millionaires over."

Lilly nodded. "Somehow I can't see Tom feeling that way," she said.

"Oh, he's going for the throat—every ounce of blood he can squeeze. Then he says he and Evelyn are going off to see all of the real world and enjoy it. After that, who knows? I shouldn't think we'll lose touch."

Lilly turned and took in the scene of the town with the sea and the mountains. "It's pretty," she agreed. "So did you get fixed up with the project that the professor of yours from Trinity is running here?"

"It looks like it. And he got a fax this morning from Eric Shipley. They're both interested, so it looks as if Eric might be moving over with Thelma too."

Lilly turned back, they looked at each other for a moment, and she moved a step nearer. Corrigan slipped an arm around her shoulders and drew her close for just a second. Then he reached out with his other hand and pulled open one of the doors. "In fact, Brendan's inside now," he said. "Come on and start meeting some new friends. They're all real this time, I promise."

"You're sure?" Lilly checked dubiously.

"Oh, definitely. No computer on earth could simulate these people."

They went through into the hotel. With their unique experience of sharing a world that most people would never know had even existed, they were natural companions for life. That much didn't need saying. And there was no particular rush to figure out exactly what they intended doing with it. Here, time ran to suit itself.

ABOUT THE AUTHOR

JAMES P. HOGAN was born in London in 1941. He worked as an aeronautical engineer specializing in electronics and for several major computer firms before turning to writing full-time in 1979. Winner of the Prometheus Award, he has earned wide popularity and high praise for his novels with their blend of gripping storytelling, intriguing scientific concepts, and convincing speculation. Mr. Hogan currently makes his home in Florida.

BANTAM SPECTRA

CELEBRATES ITS TENTH ANNIVERSARY IN 1995!

With more HUGO and NEBULA AWARD winners
than any other science fiction and fantasy publisher

With more classic and cutting-edge fiction
coming every month

Bantam Spectra is proud to be the leading
publisher of fantasy and science fiction

KEVIN J. ANDERSON • ISAAC ASIMOV • IAIN M. BANKS • GREGORY BENFORD • BEN BOVA • RAY BRADBURY • MARION ZIMMER BRADLEY • DAVID BRIN • ARTHUR C. CLARKE • THOMAS DeHAVEN • STEPHEN R. DONALDSON • RAYMOND E. FEIST • JOHN M. FORD • MAGGIE FUREY • DAVID GERROLD • WILLIAM GIBSON • STEPHAN GRUNDY • ELIZABETH HAND • HARRY HARRISON • ROBIN HOBB • JAMES HOGAN • KATHARINE KERR • GENTRY LEE • URSULA K. LeGUIN • VONDA N. McINTYRE • LISA MASON • ANNE McCAFFREY • IAN McDONALD • DENNIS L. McKIERNAN • WALTER M. MILLER, JR. • DANIEL KEYS MORAN • LINDA NAGATA •JAMIL NASIR• KIM STANLEY ROBINSON • ROBERT SILVERBERG • DAN SIMMONS • MICHAEL A. STACKPOLE • NEAL STEPHENSON • BRUCE STERLING • TRICIA SULLIVAN • SHERI S.TEPPER • PAULA VOLSKY • MARGARET WEIS AND TRACY HICKMAN • ELISABETH VONARBURG • ANGUS WELLS • CONNIE WILLIS • DAVE WOLVERTON • TIMOTHY ZAHN • ROGER ZELAZNY AND ROBERT SHECKLEY

JOIN

STAR WARS®

on the INTERNET

Bantam Spectra invites you to visit the
Official STAR WARS® Web Site.

You'll find:

< Sneak previews of upcoming STAR WARS®
novels.
< Samples from audio editions of the novels.
< Bulletin boards that put you in touch with
other fans, with the authors behind the novels, and with the Bantam editors who bring
them to you.
< The latest word from behind the scenes of
the STAR WARS® universe.
< Quizzes, games, and contests available only
on-line.
< Links to other STAR WARS® licensees'
sites on the Internet.
< Look for STAR WARS® on the World Wide
Web at: http://www.bdd.com

SF 28 1/96

®, ™, and © 1995 Lucasfilm Ltd. All rights reserved.
Used under authorization.

Also from BANTAM SPECTRA

A MIND'S-EYE VIEW INTO THE FAST AND HARD-EDGED WORLD OF FUTURE TECHNOLOGY

VIRTUAL LIGHT WILLIAM GIBSON ___56606-7 $5.99/$7.99 in Canada

A tour-de-force of relentless suspense, daring insight and graphic intensity. A
provocative and unforgettable portrait of life on the edge of the twenty-first century.

SNOW CRASH NEAL STEPHENSON ___56261-4 $5.99/$6.99

A startlingly original mix of virtual reality, Sumerian myth, pizza delivery,
and everything in between. A cool, hip cybersensibility to redefine
the way we look at the world.

TERMINAL CAFÉ IAN McDONALD ___57261-X $5.99

A provocative new look at life-in-death. For when the dead can be resurrected,
what will happen to the living? A relentless tapestry of
potent imagery and imagination.

LETHE TRICIA SULLIVAN ___56858-2 $5.50/$6.99

A dark, compelling vision of a ravaged future. Two worlds—one struggling
to escape a tragic past, and one facing an uncertain rebirth—
discover a tragic secret which links them.

QUASAR JAMIL NASIR ___56886-8 $4.99/$6.50

A stunning examination of the future of neuroscience.
A psychiatric technician must journey to the depths of a psychotic's soul
to discover the truth about his world.

- -

Ask for these books at your local bookstore or use this page to order.

Please send me the books I have checked above. I am enclosing $____ (add $2.50 to
cover postage and handling). Send check or money order, no cash or C.O.D.'s, please.

Name _____

Address _____

City/State/Zip _____

Send order to: Bantam Books, Dept. SF 27, 2451 S. Wolf Rd., Des Plaines, IL 60018
Allow four to six weeks for delivery.
Prices and availability subject to change without notice.   SF 27 12/95